An Irish Christmas Feast

Also by John B. Keane

An Irish Christmas

Durango

The Contractors

The Ram of God

A High Meadow

The Bodhran Makers

A Christmas Surprise

Death Be Not Proud and Other Stories

Stories from a Kerry Fireside

Letters of a Country Postman

The Voice of an Angel and Other Christmas Stories

An Irish Christmas Feast

The Best of John B. Keane

John B. Keane

Carroll & Graf Publishers
New York

To John and Dors

With Much Love

An Irish Christmas Feast
The Best of John B. Keane

Carroll & Graf Publishers
An Imprint of Avalon Publishing Group Incorporated
161 William Street, 16th Floor
New York, NY 10038

First Carroll & Graf edition 2002

Library of Congress Cataloging-in-Publication Data is available.

ISBN: 0-7867-1054-3

Printed in the United States of America
Distributed by Publishers Group West

Contents

A Look Back 7
The Course of Time 10
Twelve Days' Grace 14
A Christmas Visitor 24
The Curriculum Vitae 35
The Miracle of Ballybradawn 40
The Scubblething 50
A Cock for Christmas 57
Groodles 61
The Great Christmas Raid at Ballybooley 69
The Magic Stoolin 78
The Order of MacMoolamawn 85
Cider 93
Many Years Ago 103
A Christmas Performance 106
Conscience Money 119
Spreading Joy and Jam at Christmas 135
The Voice of an Angel 138
A Tasmanian Backhander 149
Christmas Noses 160
High Fielding 162
A Christmas Diversion 169
The Woman Who Hated Christmas 178
Pail But Not Wan 187
The Good Corner Boy 189
Something Drastic 192
The Woman Who Passed Herself Out 202
The Best Christmas Dinner 216
The Long and the Short of It 228
Christmas Eruptions 242

A Last Christmas Gift 244
The Urging of Christmas 259
The Fourth Wise Man 262
A Christmas Come-uppance 271
Angels in Our Midst 278
The Resurrection 284
Dotie Tupper's Christmas 296
A Christmas Gander 304
The Hermit of Scartnabrock 309
Johnny Naile's Christmas 319
Mackson's Christmas 327
The Greatest Wake of All 335
The Seven-Year Trance 352
Awlingal Princess of Cunnackeenamadra 363
The Sacred Calf 377
Two Gentlemen of the Law 384
The Great William Street Showdown of 1964 389
The Word of a Wrenboy 392
A Christmas Surprise 401
A Christmas Disappearance 406
Oh! Oh! Antonio – You Left Us All Alonio! 410
Last Christmas Eve of the Twentieth Century 413

A Look Back

Don't talk back to me about poverty. I remember a time when there was nothing anywhere. Only the very few had more than enough to eat. Only half the population had barely enough. The rest were simply hungry and broke. One of the saddest memories of my youth was the national school. The teachers were, for the most part, caring but often caring with too much force. The sad part of school was the hunger of small boys who came from impoverished backgrounds. I remember when I was first elevated to the upper classes, fourth, fifth, sixth and seventh, I was approached by the smallest scholar on the upper floor.

'Keane!' he called listlessly, 'any chance you'd bring us a cut of bread and jam.'

This was during the morning break. Every so often I would bring him something to eat. He died from diphtheria in the late 1930s. He was a lovely soul. His emaciated face is still with me. He had a voice like a lark and a spirit that was pure and free but he was no match for poverty and indifference.

At the time there was a saying 'he's out of all books now' which meant that the *garsún* in question would have gone through all the classes in the national school, first book, second book, third book and so on. 'He's out of all books now,' the mother of an aspirant would say proudly to a prospective employer as she tendered him for the inspection of a grocer or a hardware merchant or a draper.

I knew another boy in that school at the top of Church Street in my native Listowel who confided in me once that he had never eaten an egg, not even at Easter. When I looked at him in astonishment he declared that he had eaten the half of an egg all right on occasion, and sometimes a quarter of an egg and sometimes the cap of an egg but a whole egg never. Other things I remember about this boy were: (1) He never wore shoes; (2) He never wore an overcoat; (3) He never wore underclothes; (4) He always wore a smile.

There was a crude joke circulating at the time about a poor widow who was sometimes given to grandiose actions. She had seven children. Each morning she would boil an egg and distribute it between the seven before they went to school. The egg, of course, would be soft boiled so that the yolk could be spread over the faces of the offspring in order to give the impression at school that there were eggs galore at home. The reason I recall these incidents is to highlight the degrading, debilitating poverty forced upon a long-suffering people and to show how infinitely better-off we are in the new millennium. I know there's still poverty at home but it's nothing like what it was. I know because I was there and I saw it. Outspoken people would ask in anger if this was what Irish patriots went out for. Other folk would ask was this what Pearse and Connolly died for. You will find many historians who will tell you that there were no real solutions to the horrific problems of the last millennium on its countdown to its last gasp.

Surely, the Holocaust need never have happened. The story, however, could have been worse and the megalomaniac Hitler might have succeeded. I wish I could say that the Holocaust was the final chapter in man's inhumanity to man. Alas more recently we have had the Serbian conflict and the barbarity of East Timor and there will be more because, as the old woman said when her husband threw her out into the cold of winter, that is the nature of the bashte.

The bashte in question is the raging animal inside us which has to be subdued every hour. If the dear and gentle reader finds me in a reflective mood he must make allowance for the fact that I haven't touched alcoholic drink for several days in a bid to improve my lot and answer my correspondence. Writing on an empty stomach is dehydrating so I propose presently to take up my glass and empty it before it's too late. There's a time to drink and a time to drive but never at the same time.

The simple truth at the end of the day is that the people of this country never had it so good but like all people in such a position they don't know when they're well off. They lose weight so that they can put it on again. I decided that I was not going to walk into the new millennium nor was I going to run or gallop or tiptoe. Instead, I was going to dive in and fervently hope that I surfaced in another world surrounded by friends who were my enemies and without that accursed pain in my back.

There's a man in this town who goes to bed in the early afternoon of Christmas Eve and does not rise until the following night. He does it, he once told me, because he doesn't want to be happy. He mistrusts happiness because it always fizzles out on him and leaves him sick and sorry. Now I'm a man who wishes to be happy and a man who wishes happiness on everybody and this, remember, is the very same man who has hurled wild abuse at innocent football referees merely doing their job. Towards the end of the last millennium I desisted from abusing referees because of age and reduced voice power.

In my probe into that part of the millennium through which I have lived I recall a confrontation I had with a teacher in my final year in the national school. Our catechism told us that the world was four thousand years old and when I questioned this with another boy we were told that we were guttersnipes. Then, not long after, in the secondary school there was a priest who was also a teacher. If you mentioned to him the name of Charles Darwin he would strike you with his walking stick and if he hadn't a walking stick he had an equally damaging fist.

Were there no solutions then to the evil procedures which governed us? I believe that the first place to look for a solution to injustice and inhumanity is deep within one's own heart or better still look to the Sermon on the Mount according to Matthew beginning with:

Happy are the poor in spirit:
Theirs is the kingdom of heaven

Happy are the peacemakers:
They shall be called sons of God

Happy are those who are persecuted in the cause of right:
Theirs is the kingdom of heaven.

As I look around me I don't despair. The good in us marginally outweighs the evil so there is hope for the future and here to cheer you up is a quote from St Paul's epistle to the Corinthians: 'Take a little wine for thy stomach's sake and for thy frequent infirmities' and as my late and great friend Roger O'Sullivan used to say, 'What profit it a man to gain the whole world and be wet in his shoes'. A sobering thought my friends, a sobering thought, but one that reminds us that we should look for the antidote of humour when we are threatened with evil.

THE COURSE OF TIME

Edgar Guff, if one was to believe the observations of his parish priest Canon Coodle, was the possessor of an enormous appetite for whiskey. His puce-coloured nose would also bear this out as would his bloodshot eyes and unsteady gait.

'He would drink whiskey,' the canon informed his housekeeper Hannie Hanlon, 'out of a senna saucepan.'

Hannie shook her head in disgust.

'Otherwise,' the canon continued, 'he's not a bad fellow at all and you could trust him in any enterprise that doesn't involve whiskey.'

The pair had adjourned to the presbytery kitchen after the evening meal and, as was their wont, would discuss minor parochial business until the evening confessions commenced in the parish church which stood impassively next door where it dwarfed every other building in the town square.

Hannie Hanlon had, a few moments before, completed the dusting of the four ornate confessionals. As she neatly folded her duster she heard the muted but unsteady footsteps approaching along the side aisle where she stood admiring the copper plaque which carried the name of Canon Cornelius Coodle and was affixed prominently to the central door of the canon's confessional. The canon's box, as it was called, was greatly favoured by penitents of both sexes and all ages and not merely because he was somewhat deaf but also because he was tolerant, discreet and sympathetic.

'Sure you couldn't shock the canon,' the more hardened sinners would assure themselves as they confidently made their way to his box.

Hannie did not have to look around to discover who the first arrival was. The creature's light footfall indicated that it could be none other than Edgar Guff who, despite his surname, rarely expressed himself in public. There was also the fact that he always arrived at the confessional well ahead of the prescribed time, often by as much as an hour on busy occasions such as Christmas and Easter. Seating himself on the innermost extremity of the long wooden stool, which led to the confessional, he nodded respectfully in the direction of the stern-faced housekeeper. She acknowledged the salute with a solemn nod, decidedly discouraging and not in the least bit conducive to further exchanges.

People of the parish would say that Edgar Guff was an exceptional listener and could hear most of what the penitents said especially when they were expected to raise their voices or provide clarification for transgressions at the confessor's behest. This was not often but when it occurred it was always interesting, not that Edgar would ever dream of betraying the confidences which his proximity to the confessional conferred on him.

Edgar was a professional sitter. That is to say, he was engaged by busy sinners such as lawyers, doctors and wealthy businessmen to hold places on their behalf next to the confessional. As soon as one of his clients arrived, always impatient and always in a hurry, he would hand over his seat near the confessional door and make his way to the far end of the wooden stool. For this service, he would be paid a half crown. From his lowly position at the end of the stool he would patiently wait as those who were seated nearer the confessional were shrived, thus allowing him to advance in the right direction. After a while he would find himself in the most prized position, right outside the confessional door. If his next client noted that Edgar was too far from the confessional the restless creature would exit to the town square and indulge in measured peregrinations until he judged that his sitter would be better placed.

During the busy seasons Edgar would spend nearly all of his waking hours on the stool. He was often asked by cronies if he was ever obliged to vacate his place due to a call of nature.

'Never!' he would answer firmly and then he would explain that he was always on the move so to speak in his earlier years when he was addicted to pints of stout. It was costing him too much in lost revenue so he changed over to whiskey which made hardly any demands because his bladder was never full.

When Hannie Hanlon returned to the presbytery kitchen she was asked by the canon if Edgar Guff had taken up his place.

'Just a few moments ago,' she answered.

'That gives me the best part of an hour,' the canon intoned happily as he settled himself comfortably in front of the gleaming Stanley. Later when the three curates arrived the canon was ready to lead his curates onward and outward against the forces of evil. From their confessionals they would keep the enemy at bay with forgiveness.

As the first penitents arrived, several at the same time, Edgar Guff, sitter-in-chief of the parish, fortified himself for the long hours ahead. He withdrew a voluminous handkerchief from his ample, inside pocket and gently blew on his purple proboscis after which he skilfully removed the cork from a noggin of whiskey, cleverly camouflaged by the handkerchief, and indulged in a modest swallow which instantly alerted him to his responsibilities.

Thereafter his clients began to arrive like clockwork. It was a boom time for sitters especially for Edward who had a large clientele, most of them generous if the occasion deserved it. Their contributions were nearly always doubled at Christmas so that Edward need not worry about the wherewithal required for the purchase of extra whiskey. He had already swallowed several half ones in the two public houses closest to the church and since these activities took place during intervals he wasn't in the least befuddled. To employ one of his own phrases he was just warming up and would be quite capable of swallowing the two noggins in his pockets before confessions ended for the night. He would, of course, feel a little groggy later but he would find his way home without difficulty and enjoy a good night's slumber before the noonday sittings of the morrow.

As the night wore on he started to grow drowsy, finding it difficult to keep his eyes open for long. The spirit of goodwill, luckily for him, was abroad and whenever he started to drop off he would be wakened by concerned penitents who sat near him. His clients came and went and not one neglected to pay his fee. He found his hands being opened wide on numerous occasions and almost always two half crowns were pressed against his palm.

Only once in that long night was he jolted into wakefulness and that was when Canon Coodle raised his mighty voice in anger in the nearby confessional. Edgar sat upright at once. It must be some sin of outrageous proportions if the canon raised his voice to a shout. Edgar Guff nor indeed any of the other penitents had ever heard anything like it before.

Edgar deduced from the trembling, plaintive utterances that the penitent in the box was female. She was in the process at long last, after years of neglect and suffering, of acquainting her parish priest with the behaviour of the perfidious wretch to whom she had been chained for more than forty years. Edgar had missed the earlier part of the poor woman's disclosures but he gasped as he had never gasped before when she made the ultimate accusation. This was that she had not been in receipt of a single kiss from her husband for twenty agonising years. It was this that prompted Canon Coodle to shout 'What!' at the top of his voice. When she repeated the charge in broken tones he thundered the word 'What!' a second time.

Drunk as he was, Edgar Guff's heart went out to the victim of this disastrous marriage. He longed to lay his hands on the throat of the monster who had treated her so abominably for so long. But no! He must never reveal what he had heard or allow what he had heard to influence any future actions of his in relation to this confession or any other. The secrecy of the confessional was sacred and it dawned on a drunken Edgar, not for the first time, that he was an officer of the Church. He would agree that he was not a very high-up officer, that he was below the rank of assistant-to-the-sacristan or even a common altar boy but he was a Church officer no matter what.

He sat fully attentive as he heard the movements in the confessional. The penitent's door opened and there Edgar Guff beheld the dowdy clothes and tear-stained face of his wife, his one and only who had not qualified for a solitary kiss in twenty years. He sat stunned as she shuffled along the aisle and then she was gone.

Suddenly he sprang into action and dashed into the night.

Outside she moved slowly and carefully, picking her steps in the darkness. Gently he forestalled her and placed an arm around her shoulder, his drunkenness totally dissipated by what he had heard. She turned to look into the face of the person who had come to her aid. Suddenly her sobs filled the night so that passers-by turned to stare. Overcome by grief he shepherded her into a laneway where he held her in his arms until her convulsive sobbing ended and she stood silent and limp, totally dependent on his support.

He took her hand and led her homeward. The days that followed were filled with silence and when she accepted silently his offer of a walk by the river on St Stephen's Day he knew that if he played his cards right there was a chance, just a chance mind you, that things might work out in the course of time.

Twelve Days' Grace

Agnes Mallowan shot the iron bolts into place in the back and front doors of the presbytery. Then she did the rounds of the house upstairs and downstairs, securing the windows in the curate's room but firmly resisting the temptation to inspect his belongings. She could have carried out the inspection with impunity if she so wished, she told herself, seeing that he was enjoying a short Christmas break at the other end of the diocese in his parents' home.

As was his wont the parish priest Father Canty would read in bed until she brought him his nightcap after which he would fall fast asleep until the seven o'clock bell sounded.

There had been no exchange of Christmas presents. As always he had handed her an extra week's pay but repeated his insistence that she was not to invest in a present on his behalf. From the beginning he had made it clear that there were to be no Christmas gifts.

'The best present you can give me,' he had warned, 'is to keep your money in your purse.'

Neither would he let her spoil him. 'Plain fare for me,' he would raise his hand aloft, 'and the plainer the better.'

The few luxuries he permitted himself were the nocturnal glass of punch and a glass of wine on Sundays with his dinner. He had partaken of wine earlier that day but only, he had reminded her, because it was Christmas. Sometimes she worried about his health. What concerned her most was the wheezing when he paused on the landing, having forgotten to take his time when ascending the stairs. She used every conceivable subterfuge lest he over-exert himself. Sometimes his irritability showed when he found the cob tackled and waiting preparatory to a sick call.

'Who tackled the cob?' he would ask pretending to be angrier than he really was. There would be no answer while she prepared him for the journey. There were times, he would reluctantly admit to himself, during epidemics as the calls came pouring in when he was grateful. Normally the chores of catching and tackling the cob would fall to the sacristan but such a post had been vacant for years.

'The parish just can't afford it,' he had explained only the year before to the bishop who had intimated in his usual roundabout way that the elderly parish priest ought to be taking things easier.

'I'm only seventy-three,' Father Canty had retorted mischievously, 'which makes me two years younger than my bishop.'

'True,' came the unruffled response, 'but I don't have to go on sick calls at all hours of the night and you do and that is why I am giving you a curate. You have been playing on my conscience a lot lately.'

'We can't afford a curate,' Father Canty responded testily.

'We'll manage,' the bishop had concluded blithely.

The curate, Father Scanlan, had proved himself to be a hardworking, likeable young man well able to generate income through football tournaments, card-drives, raffles and silver circles. The parishioners might protest about the cost but they quickly became involved in the new activities and were to wonder in the course of time how they had managed to retain their sanity for so long without such diversions. Unfortunately for him Agnes Mallowan saw the new addition as an interloper whose every act seemed calculated to usurp the authority of the ageing parish priest. She felt it her duty to protect her employer. The younger man sensed her hostility but was prepared for it and had been counselled by colleagues in the art of countering it.

'Play second fiddle to the parish priest,' he was advised, 'and she won't see you as a threat to him.'

In truth, the new curate presented a greater threat to the housekeeper. She knew this from the beginning. When Father Canty retired and retire he must, sooner rather than later, she would find herself unemployed. There would be no place for her in the Old Priests' Home where elderly parish priests spent their declining years. No lay people were employed on the staff which was made up exclusively of nuns. With care, however, and unremitting attention to Father Canty's welfare she would see to it that it would be many a year before he relinquished his pastorship. Please God they would sustain each other to the very end. It would not be her fault if his parochial duties were terminated prematurely.

Agnes heaved a great sigh of contentment as she poured the boiling water over the whiskey, lemon, sugar and cloves in the tall glass. The sugar began to melt instantly while the glistening lemon surfaced tantalisingly at the rim.

Agnes Mallowan inhaled the uprising steam and wondered, not for the first time, if she was placing her Confirmation pledge in jeopardy. Always she would reassure herself that there was no harm in steam and that the whiskey content therein was at such a minimum that it must surely be rendered ineffective before infiltrating the nostrils.

Just to be sure that her pledge remained intact she inhaled only once. She might have averted her head but then how would she identify the tiny foreign bodies such as flecks, specks and motes which needed to be extracted from his reverence's punch before she deemed it worthy for delivery not that he would notice for he always kept his eyes firmly closed as he swallowed.

He drank noisily.

'There is no satisfaction,' he would explain, 'unless I can hear myself drinking. It helps me relish the punch even more.'

From the moment he closed his eyes preparatory to the first swallow he would keep them closed, blindly extending the glass in her general direction, before drawing the coverlet under his chin. She always stood in close attendance while he drank and, upon receipt of the glass, would lower the wick in the shapely globe of the paraffin lamp before blowing out the flame. Then she would withdraw silently, closing the bedroom door behind her. Now, as she gently stirred the amber mixture with a slender spoon before embarking on the upstairs journey, the contentment departed her placid features and was replaced by a frown. It was a frown with which every parishioner in the remote, rambling parish was familiar. Agnes Mallowan was best avoided while the frown was in residence. Otherwise she was good-humoured and tractable. The frown deepened when the front door bell rang for the second time.

'Let them wait!' she spoke out loud and ascended the tarpaulin covered stairs. Gently she knocked on the bedroom door.

'Come!' the response was immediate.

She stood silently at the bedside while he closed the leather-bound copy of *Ivanhoe* without marking the page and placed it on the table near the bed. He liked to open the covers of his favourite novels at random and proceed from the beginning of the paragraph which presented itself.

'It was a quiet Christmas thank God,' he said as he accepted the punch. He swallowed without closing his eyes and she knew that he had heard the front door bell. He would ask about it. If only she had brought him the punch ten minutes earlier he would be fast asleep and the caller or callers could be fobbed off till morning.

Certain parishioners, especially the more isolated, had a habit of making mountains out of molehills as far as sick calls were concerned.

'Better go and see who's at the door Agnes,' he spoke resignedly, 'we don't want to be the cause of sending some poor soul to hell for the want of a priest.'

'Yes Father. At once Father,' she answered dutifully. She could truthfully say that never once had she questioned one of his commands in all of her twenty years as his housekeeper. He was a good man. Others had not been so good, other employers after her husband had expired prematurely and left her with four young children, all now safely emigrated to America and corresponding regularly. Her husband had not been a good man nor had her father. Her two brothers had been good men. She remembered them fondly. No need to pray for them. She knew for sure they went straight to heaven when they died. She prayed every night for her husband and her father. God knows they needed prayers if ever a pair needed them.

In the doorway she addressed herself to the two men who stood together sheepishly, one waiting for the other to open the negotiations.

'Where did ye get the rain?' she asked coldly, 'there's nothing but a bare mist outside.'

'That's the thick mist up the mountain missus,' the taller of the pair informed her.

She looked from one to the other without inviting them in. They wore tattered overcoats but no head-gear. The rain had plastered their scant grey hair to their heads.

'How did ye come?' Agnes Mallowan asked.

'We walked missus,' from the smaller man.

Agnes recognised him from the way he shuffled his feet. He indulged in the same motions when he stood outside the church on Sundays. From the age of fourteen onwards neither had entered the parish church. They came to church all right but only to stand with their backs to the outside walls while the mass was in progress. She would attest under oath that they never paid Christmas dues nor oats' money nor any church offerings so that their priest could keep body and soul together and feed and pay his housekeeper and curate. Now, more than likely, they would have somebody sick, so sick, or so they believed, that a priest was required. Her worst fears were realised when the taller asked if the curate was available.

'You know as well as I do that he's gone home for Christmas and won't be back until the day after tomorrow. In fact the whole parish knows it.'

'Well then,' from the smaller brother, 'himself will have to do. Our dada is dying and he needs a priest.'

'And who decided your dada was dying?'

'Doctor,' the taller responded smugly.

'And when did he have the doctor?' Agnes, a veteran of rustic interrogation, wasn't going to allow the parish priest out on such a night till she had confirmed that death was imminent.

'Two hours ago,' came the reply.

'And why didn't the doctor get in touch with us?' she asked.

''Cos,' said the other brother, 'him be gone to the other side of the mountain to deliver a baby and there's rumours of a man killed when his horse and cart capsized farther on. There's other calls too.'

'Ye can bide yeer time out in one of the sheds for a while then,' the housekeeper informed them, 'till 'tis a bit closer to morning. Father Canty needs a few hours' sleep.'

'Our dada won't last that long,' the taller brother placed a leg in the hallway. 'Him was gasping and us leaving,' the smaller added, pushing the taller man forward.

'Mind ye don't wet my hallway that I polished specially for Christmas,' Agnes Mallowan countered as she pushed the persistent pair to the outside.

'Call the priest before we call him!' The tone of the taller brother's voice was unmistakably threatening.

'Who is it Agnes?' Father Canty called from the upstairs landing.

'The Maldooney brothers looking for a priest Father.'

'The Maldooneys of Farrangarry is it?' Father Canty asked.

'None other.' Agnes threw a withering look at the unwelcome visitors.

'Ask them in for God's sake. I'll go tackle the cob.'

'Let one of these tackle him,' Agnes called back as she withdrew to allow them access to the kitchen where the parish priest joined them.

'No,' he spoke half to himself as he took stock of the dripping brothers, 'make them a pot of tea. I'll see to the cob. Light a lantern while you're at it Agnes.'

Obedient to a fault the cob, stout, firm and round, submitted itself to harness and backed itself docilely between the long slender shafts. Father Canty draped a partially filled oats' bag around the powerful crest and returned to the kitchen.

The brothers sat amazed as the housekeeper prepared the parish priest for his journey. They were even more amazed when, childlike, he submitted himself to her fussy ministrations which began with the removal of his slippers and their replacement with stout, strong boots and gaiters. She then removed the short coat which he had worn to the stable and placed a heavy woollen scarf around his neck and shoulders. This was followed by a heavy woollen cardigan and a heavier short coat and finally on top of all came a long leather coat which reached all the way down to his ankles. With mouths open the brothers watched in wonder as she placed a wide-rimmed black hat on his balding pate and, finally, handed him the small suitcase which contained the oils, missal and stole. All that remained to be done was the collecting of the sacred host from the tabernacle and here, they were surprised to note, the housekeeper had no role.

'You'll find dry sacks in there,' Father Canty indicated an outhouse. 'They'll cover your heads and shoulders.'

They were surprised when he opened the trap door for them. They would not have been dismayed if they had been called upon to walk behind. After three miles of moderately undulating ground they entered the side road which would take them to the Maldooney abode, three-quarters of the way up the mountain. It was a steep climb but not for a single moment did it tax the short-gaited cob. After the first mile when they left the presbytery there was no attempt at conversation. Despite repeated attempts to involve them Father Canty gave up. He found it difficult to stay awake without the stimulus of verbal conversation. He attempted a rosary but there were no responses forthcoming. Thereafter, he prayed silently to himself. He was not unduly worried. The cob had conveyed him safely in the past while he slept and could be depended upon to do so again. When eventually they reached the Maldooney abode some waiting neighbours came forward and took charge of the cob.

The old man lay propped on an ancient iron bed. His breathing was erratic but his eyes opened when he beheld the priest in the faint light of the three spluttering candles, precariously placed especially for the occasion on the mantelpiece, bedpost and windowsill.

'You'll hear my last confession Father?'

Father Canty was surprised. The voice was weak and spluttering like the candles but there seemed to be no doubt that he was strong enough to make himself understood.

Two elderly women, shawled and praying, vacated the room the moment the priest bent his head to hear the sins of the dying penitent. The old man went on and on sometimes incoherently but mostly articulate as he recited the sins of a lifetime. He was well prepared for the ultimate shriving. He did not spare himself as the nauseating recall of human folly poured forth. Then suddenly he stopped, gasped and fell into a deep sleep from which, all present were agreed, he would never wake.

The ritual over, Father Canty left the house and entered his transport but not before he turned the bottom and dry side of the trap cushion upward. There was no sign of the brothers. The neighbours could not explain it. One minute they were in the kitchen standing with their backs to the dying fire and the next they were nowhere to be seen.

Agnes was on her feet the moment she heard the hoof-beats at the rear of the presbytery. When she drew the bolt and went outside the animal was standing still. In the trap Father Canty was fast asleep, the rain dripping from his hat. Gently she awakened him and led him indoors. She seated him close to the fire where she had drawn the kitchen table.

'You're a life-saver Agnes,' he spoke with unconcealed fervency as he ravenously spooned the steaming giblet soup into his waiting mouth. She tip-toed from the kitchen and up the stairs. She lit the paraffin lamp and replaced the hot water bottle with another of more immediate vintage. As she silently descended the stairs she met him on his way up. He seemed to be overcome by drowsiness. She allowed a short interval to pass before knocking at the bedroom door.

'Come,' came the voice.

'You have it well-earned,' she assured him when he expressed doubt about his entitlement to the extra punch. She stood by while he swallowed and took the empty glass when it was extended to her. She quenched the lamp and closed the bedroom door behind her. Rarely did he snore but he snored now. The snores were long and profound. As she passed his bedroom door a short while later the snores were deep and even. She could not believe her ears when the irritating sound of the front door bell shattered the silence.

'What now?' she asked as she hurried down the stairs lest the continuous tinkling disturb her master's slumber.

'Who's out in God's name?' she called without drawing the bolt.

'It's us missus,' came the unmistakable voice of the taller Maldooney.

Slowly Agnes Mallowan drew the bolt and opened the door.

They stood huddled together as they had on the previous visit. Agnes Mallowan folded her arms and spread her legs across the width of the doorway to prevent access to the hallway. The brothers, dripping wet, looked at each other and then at the housekeeper.

'State your business,' she said coldly.

'We want the priest,' from the taller brother.

'Is it to pay him the Christmas dues you want him?' Agnes asked as the smaller of the pair snuffled and sniffled, sensing that there was to be no tea on this occasion.

'We want the priest for our father,' he explained between sniffles, 'he forgot a sin.'

'And you expect Father Canty to get out of his bed and go back up the mountain to Farrangarry because your dada forgot to tell him he wet the bed.'

'Oh now!' said the smaller brother, ''tis a deal worse than wetting the bed. No one will go to hell for wetting the bed but fornicating will get you there on the double.'

'Fornicating!' the housekeeper's curiosity got the better of her.

'And who was he fornicating with?' she asked.

'Never mind who,' from the taller brother. 'It's enough for you to know that he'll face the fires of hell on account of he deliberately failing to mention this particular one.'

Agnes found herself in a dilemma. If she called Father Canty the journey to Farrangarry and back could be the death of him. If she didn't call him and the man died with an unforgiven sin on his soul she would be guilty of sending a soul to hell. She came down in favour of her employer.

'I'm not calling him,' she said, and was about to close the door when the smaller man pushed her backwards into the hallway.

'You call him,' he shouted angrily.

Agnes stood her ground. Her mission in life was to protect her master. She decided on a change of tack.

'There's no fear of your dada,' she assured them.

'Without a priest he's bound for hell,' the taller brother pushed the smaller forward.

The housekeeper refused to be intimidated. Not an inch of ground did she yield.

'Didn't I tell ye there was no fear of him,' she drew herself upwards and refolded her arms, 'for don't it say in the Cathecism that hell is closed for the twelve days of Christmas and anyone who dies during that period goes direct to heaven.'

The brothers exchanged dubious glances.

''Tis there in black and white,' the housekeeper assured them.

The brothers turned their backs on her and consulted in whispers. After several moments they faced her secondly.

'You're sure?' the smaller asked.

'Why would I say it if it was a lie?' she countered.

'Why then,' the taller brother asked, 'did the priest come all the way up to the mountain if there was no hell?'

'Mohammed went to the mountain didn't he?' Agnes replied with a straight face, 'and there was no hell.'

Both brothers shuffled uneasily at this revelation. Comment proved to be beyond them. What she said was irrefutable. Also was she not well placed to be in the know about such matters. She was of the presbytery, therefore of the church and of the inner circle at that. The Catechism had always confounded the Maldooney brothers in their schooldays and this woman was confounding them now.

'Go on away home,' she said, 'and let yeer minds be at ease. If yeer dada is dead his soul is in heaven and if he's not dead it will be there soon.'

Slowly, sheepishly the brothers backed away from the door. Exhausted she shot the bolts and retired upstairs to the sleep of the just. On the Sunday after Christmas she was delighted to see the brothers in their customary positions outside the church as the holy mass proceeded solemnly within. Sidling up to the smaller of the pair she enquired in a whisper after his father.

'He's sitting up,' came the happy response.

'He's eating a bite,' the taller brother concurred.

'Well I declare,' Agnes Mallowan joined her hands together as though she were about to pray.

The smaller brother cleared his throat and permitted himself a toothless smile as he disclosed in reverential whispers, out of respect to his surroundings, that the quickly recovering parent intended presenting himself at Cassidy's wren-dance on the following Saturday night, a mere six days away. Agnes made a mental note to enquire from one of her many parochial informants about the general goings-on at Cassidy's wren-dance and about the antics of Maldooney senior in particular.

She admitted her source by the rear door of the presbytery one week later. Maldooney senior had excelled himself, displaying a variety of fancy steps that put younger terpsichoreans to shame. He crowned his display by dancing a hornpipe at the request of a buxom lady from the other end of the parish and astounded all and sundry by enticing her to the well-filled hay shed at the bottom of Cassidy's haggard where they sojourned rapturously till the dawn's early light reminded them that it was time to go their separate ways. They promised to meet again while the sons, for better or for worse, did nothing but stand idly by and never once opened their porter-stained mouths to any member of the opposite sex.

A Christmas Visitor

The unique set of circumstances which preceded the arrival of John J. Mulholland merchant tailor into the world deserve to be recorded, at least according to John J. Mulholland.

'I will,' he declared as we sat in Mikey Joe's Irish-American bar in the seaside resort of Ballybunion, 'offer up a novena of rosaries for your intentions provided you adorn futurity with my peculiar beginnings.'

John J. was never direct when he could be diffuse.

'My paternal grandfather,' he began before I could drain my glass and make good my escape, 'hated Christmas and if he could lay his hands on Santa Claus he would surely dismember him. He used to stuff his ears with cotton wool to shut out the sound of Christmas bells and usen't he disappear altogether on Christmas Eve, moving off with a day's provisions at first light and not returning until long after dark.'

'It's your face that attracts them,' a boozing companion had observed earlier in the day when a man I had never seen before shot from a shop door and seized me by both wrists. He was a powerfully built fellow but, alas, a victim of the most excruciating halitosis. He held me fast for several minutes while he recalled the treachery of the wife who had abandoned him without warning for an amorous greengrocer.

John J. Mulholland did not hold me by the wrists but his ample frame overflowed a bar stool between myself and the exit. He was pointing at his neck around which was a crimson weal which might well have been caused by a hangman's rope.

'It's not what you're thinking,' he smiled grimly, 'and if you are patient you shall discover how it came to be where it is.'

I indicated to Mikey Joe that I wanted another whiskey. If I was going to suffer I would do so in comfort. My nemesis had also brought his stool nearer, totally eliminating every means of escape. The whole business had begun with the aforementioned paternal grandfather, one Jacko Mulholland, a trousers' maker with a tooth for whiskey and a profound hatred of Christmas.

When our tale begins Jacko was a mere thirty years of age. Both parents had died young and from the age of sixteen onwards he was left to fend for himself. Neighbours would explain in their good-natured neighbourly way that a general resentment for all things tender and sentimental had set in shortly after the demise of his father and mother.

'Say nothing to him about Christmas,' they would advise strangers who had no way of knowing about his bereavement, 'and whatever you do, do not wish him the compliments of the season.'

As is the way with neighbours they were patient with him when he reacted viciously to the least mention of the Yuletide season. They told themselves that his grief would diminish with the passage of time and they would regularly trot out the old adages; time is a great healer and the years cure everything and so forth and so on but they were disappointed when, after fourteen of those very same years, he persisted in ignoring the arrival of Christmas.

His kitchen windowsills and his mantelpiece were bare. None of the accumulation of Christmas cards so evident in the houses of his neighbours were to be seen in the Mulholland home. When a card arrived from a friend or relative he immediately consigned it to flame in the Stanley number eight.

'How dare they!' he would mutter to himself before returning to the stitching of the rough and ready trousers in which he specialised. Sometimes he thought of Mary Moles who lived just down the street and who was still unattached although she need not be for she was a trim cut of a girl with pleasant features and a virtuous name. She could have been his. All he had to do was ask. It had been understood. Their names had been linked since he started to pay her court but she grew tired of his moods and his own attitude hardened the longer the rift between them lasted. She would not marry another and neither would he but they cherished each other no longer. Concerned neighbours shook their heads at the woeful waste of it all. The entire street felt the pain of it and the entire street prayed that it would come right in the end.

'They'll be too old soon,' one old woman said at which another and then many others nodded sagely and concurred. In time the situation came to be accepted and the affair became part of the history of the street.

At this stage in the proceedings John J. Mulholland excused himself on the grounds that he had to visit the toilet. I could have vacated the scene there and then but I was hooked as indeed was my genial friend Mikey Joe. We spoke in undertones lest our voices carry to the toilet. Mikey Joe confided that he had long believed, as I did, that the disfiguring weal around John J.'s neck was caused by a hangman's noose but now we both knew better and hoped to be enlightened as to the true origins of the unprepossessing blemish before we were much older.

When John J. returned he resumed his position on the stool, swallowed from his glass and cleared his throat. We presumed foolishly that the clearing was the prelude to the remaining disclosures but not a solitary word was forthcoming. It was as though he had suddenly taken a vow of silence. Mikey Joe was first to get the message.

'Finish that,' he indicated John J.'s almost empty glass. As soon as the refill was placed in his hand John J. cleared his throat a second time, sniffed the whiskey, frowned, pondered, approved and sipped. He proceeded with his tale.

Apparently his grandfather Jacko was not above taking a drink now and then in the privacy of his kitchen. He always drank alone. On the morning of Christmas Eve he betook himself to the woods which surrounded the town and did not return till dark. He took with him the usual provisions and spent the day observing coot and heron as well as mallard and diver. He would have fished had the season been open. He listened without appreciation to the wide variety of songbirds who poured forth their tiny hearts as though they knew of the great celebration that was at hand. When Jacko came to the river he sat on an oak stump and, not for the first time, considered the dismal solution the depths below offered. As always he dismissed the thought but he would have to admit that the temptation grew stronger as the years went by.

A shiver went through him when he imagined his lifeless body laid out on a slab in the local morgue where he had once seen the decaying remains of a boy who had accidentally drowned some years before.

'I haven't the courage.' He spoke the words out loud and no sooner had they departed his lips than a hunting stoat wriggled its way urgently upwards from a small declivity at his feet before disappearing into the undergrowth.

He rose quickly, his dreary reverie suspended yet again. Shortly afterwards dusk began to infiltrate the woodlands. The face of the river darkened. Overhead the stars began to twinkle. The moon brightened as the sun dipped beneath the tree-tops to the west. From the depths of the woods came the unmistakable sounds of rooting badgers, heedless now that the evening shadows were merging into one.

Jacko Mulholland gathered himself and followed the river bank towards the lights of the town. A bell rang sweetly, its sacred tones carrying far up the placid river. Jacko Mulholland thrust his fingers into his ears and stood stock still. He would wait until the infernal pealing came to an end.

As he left the wood and entered the town the dark in all its fullness had fallen. In the kitchen of his silent home he stoked the range fire which he had earlier packed carefully with wet turf sods as well as dry to ensure its survival until his return. He lit the paraffin lamp and looked at the calendar which hung nearby. He took a pencil from the windowsill and crossed out the offending date, 24 December 1922. A few days now and the whole fraud would be over, the entire shambles brushed aside to make way for the new year. He decided to postpone his supper till nearer bedtime. Anyway he had eaten his fill in the woodlands before the arrival of dusk. He added several small dry sods to the fire and sat in the ancient walnut rocking-chair which had been in use since his great-grandfather's time and which was the nearest thing to a family heirloom one would find if one searched every house in the street.

There was a long night ahead. It would be the longest in the fourteen years since the disaster if normal progression was anything to go by. He rocked for a while in the vain hope that slumber would come. He knew in advance that it would be a futile bid. He rose and added some larger sods to the fire. Then from the recesses of the cupboard he withdrew a bottle of whiskey. He had purchased it in a nearby village after a football game to which he had cycled in late November with carrier bag attached for no other purpose. He shook the bottle thoroughly before uncorking. He stood it on the deal table for several minutes while he went in search of a glass. There was one somewhere, only one. He knew it wasn't in the cupboard. The people of the street kept their glasses, few as they were, in sideboards. Those who were not possessed of sideboards wrapped them carefully in old newspapers and arranged them loosely in a cardboard box which was always kept for safety under the parental bed.

He found himself searching the sideboard in the small sitting-room attached to the kitchen. Eventually he found the upturned glass under a tea cosy. He could not recall how it came to be there. He returned to the rocking-chair and stretched a hand as far as the whiskey bottle. He poured the contents into the four-ounce glass until it was brimful. He sipped, spluttered and coughed. It was always like that, he recalled, with the first drop unless one was partial to whiskey diluted by water. In the street the menfolk never mixed spirits and water. When the whiskey was swallowed it was all right to swallow a mouthful of water after a decent interval but to mix it in the glass was regarded as far less edifying than the pure drop.

He placed the glass on the table next to the bottle and removed the mud-covered boots. He would clean them in the morning. Nobody could clean and polish boots like his late lamented mother. Nobody could untie lace knots like her. He used to call her his knot-ripper-in-chief. He recalled how his father had laughed loud and long when the title was first conferred. Ah those had been happy days!

The tears flowed down Jacko Mulholland's face, remembering his father and himself squatting on the workbench, his mother attentive and obedient to their wants. It was she who delivered the finished trousers when, for one reason or another, the customer failed to call. She never came back empty-handed. When she returned without the money she always brought the trousers home. She never extended credit. Sooner or later she would get her money. Alterations were child's play to her.

Jacko extended a hand for the bottle and refilled his glass. He could not bring himself to resurrect past Christmases. The memories were too painful. He found a block of cheddar in the cupboard and cut himself a slice. His thoughts turned to Mary Moles as they did at the same time every year. He wondered if he would be any happier if he had taken her for a wife. Too late now. He had seen the grey hairs on her head and the puckered face of her through his window as she passed up and down. Hers was a stately walk. She would have to be granted that. Never looking to left or right she moved with the grace of a swan. It was her natural gait. Everybody in the street would agree that she was one unflappable female, maybe a mite too steady and maybe a trifle too demure and maybe somewhat conservative but she was the kind of girl one could present anywhere. Certain people in other streets considered her dull but this assessment had to be based on ignorance. Her true worth was known only to her neighbours and they would swear in any court in the land that Mary Moles had a touch of class and they would also swear that class was what really mattered in the long run.

She lived with her father, a cantankerous old man, a martyr to lumbago and catarrh, who chided his only child day in day out. His wife, or so the neighbours maintained, had simply given up the ghost having been subjected to twenty years of withering criticism, all undeserved. The only respite she enjoyed was when she visited the church. Who could blame her if she spent as much time as possible in its hallowed precincts, kneeling and praying and savouring the blessed silence no end.

Jacko Mulholland surveyed the glowing fire. If it held together without collapsing it should last till bedtime. Next he surveyed the whiskey bottle and was pleased to see that more than half of its contents remained. There is nothing as consoling or sustaining to the half-drunken imbiber as the presence of a whiskey bottle more full than it is empty. It is as comforting as hidden battalions are to a field commander whose forces have been decimated by a succession of foolhardy charges. It is akin to the feelings of a man who, upon waking in the morning, expects to be confronted by rain and storm but instead finds the sun shining through his window.

Jacko Mulholland refilled his glass and swallowed copiously, gasping for breath as the amber liquid set fire to his innards. Then he began to sob as he recalled other days – his mother's voice in the morning as she prepared breakfast, her gentle singing of the ancient songs, her lilting of dance tunes, hornpipe, jig and reel, her dulcet call from the foot of the stairs; fishing with his father and the delight when one or the other hooked a trout, sitting in the lamplight late at night watching his father tying flies. The sobbing became uncontrollable. Nobody heard for such was the extent of the celebrations in the neighbouring houses that no external sound had the power to penetrate the old stone walls. It was the same in every other house on the street save that of old Mick Moles and his daughter Mary. They sat silently at either side of the hearth. Sometimes he would call upon God to relieve his aches and other times he would call on the Blessed Virgin but if they heard they failed to bring him relief so that he rounded on his daughter before going to bed, falsely accusing her of concocting watery tea and burning his toast.

Jacko Mulholland was now at that stage of drunkenness where the victim starts to natter to himself, grinding his teeth as he recalls all the injustices he has suffered since first entering the world. He turned his attention to the whiskey bottle and, blurred though his vision had become, he was sorry to note that more than two-thirds of its contents had been consumed. He mourned its passing with a series of deep sighs and tedious lamentations after which his head began to droop. Vainly he strove to restrain the slumber which seemed set to overpower him but he was a poor match for its stupefying subtlety. Soon he was snoring.

There are few snores with the depth and resonance of whiskey snores. They rebounded from the walls and filled the kitchen to overflowing. The only danger to the whiskey snorer is that, more often than not, his slumber is disrupted by one of his own creations. In this instance it was another sound which infiltrated Jacko Mulholland's malt-induced insensibility. At first he stirred irritably, grimaced and then groaned before opening bleary eyes. The first object to catch his eye was the mantelpiece clock. The hands indicated that he had slept for several hours. There was that annoying noise again. It sounded as if somebody was knocking at the front door but who could be knocking at twenty past one in the morning? He decided to ignore it.

From time to time over the years he would be roused from his slumbers early on the mornings of religious festivals and football matches by agricultural labourers who would have specially commissioned new pairs of trousers for such occasions. He never minded, provided payment was forthcoming, but this was different. Twenty minutes past one on the morning of Christmas was downright uncivil to say the least. He decided to ignore it, certain that the knocker would become discouraged after a while. He reached out his hand for the whiskey bottle. This time he dispensed with the glass and lifted the jowl to his lips. The whiskey bubbled and gurgled as he upended the bottle. Just at that moment the knocking started again. He lowered the bottle and placed it on the table. The knocking persisted. He had never been subjected to anything quite like it and yet it wasn't loud nor was it sharp and still it grated to such a degree that he was obliged to place a finger in either ear. Normally this would succeed in at least diminishing the sound but not in this instance for the harder he pressed his fingers into the well-waxed canals the more piercing the knocking became. Perplexed he withdrew his fingers. Reluctantly he moved towards the door. He did not open it at once. He peered through the curtains of the sitting-room window in the hope of catching a glimpse of the knocker. There was nothing to be seen.

He climbed the stairs and entered the front bedroom. He looked down on to the street but there was nothing. Indeed, from his vantage point which afforded an unrestricted view of the entire street, there wasn't a solitary soul to be seen. All the sounds of revelry had long since abated and nothing stirred. The roadway was still wet after a heavy shower which had fallen while Jacko slept. A blissful calm had followed. Then came another bout of the nerve-shattering knocking. Silently he opened the window and, leaning out, peered downward. There was nothing. He withdrew but no sooner had he closed the window than the knocking commenced once more. He rushed downstairs and opened the door. Standing before him was a small boy who could not have exceeded seven or eight years in age. The youngster was impeccably dressed, shining white shoes, a snow-white shirt and red vermilion necktie, a double-breasted navy blue suit and a cream-coloured felt hat which he lifted respectfully from his immaculately slicked head as soon as Jacko Mulholland opened the door. On the child's face was an angelic smile. He was about to speak when Jacko seized him round the throat with his right thumb and index finger.

'Are you a lorgadawn or what!' Jacko roared as he tightened the grip on the pale, slender throat so easily encircled by the powerful fingers, stronger than any in the street from constant stitching, knotting and threading. The boy wriggled in his grasp, unable to answer.

'Are you a lorgadawn!' Jacko shouted a second time.

All the boy could do was shake his head but even this proved difficult. The pressure from the long, thin fingers was overpowering. Coarse and calloused they cut into his neck. Then suddenly Jacko let go. The boy gingerly felt his throat where the fingers had lingered for so long.

'Who in God's name are you?' Jacko asked gruffly but with none of the fury which accompanied his first question.

'I'll tell you who I am if you promise to keep calm,' the boy replied.

'You have my promise,' came the assurance from Jacko.

'I am your grandson,' the boy informed him.

'My what?' Jacko roared.

'See,' said the boy, 'you're breaking your promise already. You promised you'd keep calm,' the boy replied.

'Is this some kind of joke boy?' Jacko asked fiercely and would have seized him again had not the visitor lifted his hand and announced solemnly that beyond any shadow of doubt he was indeed his grandson.

'But how can that be?' Jack asked. 'I am only thirty years of age and I was never married. In fact I was never with anyone but the one woman and I never put a hand above her knee.'

'The fact remains,' the boy was adamant, 'that I am your grandson John J. Mulholland.'

'I am also John J. Mulholland,' Jacko informed him, 'but they call me Jacko.'

'I should, of course, have said,' the visitor was apologetic now, 'that I will be your grandson in the course of time. Strictly speaking I am not your grandson right now. What you see before you is an unborn presence which will arrive into this world on a date yet to be decided.'

'Oh,' said Jacko Mulholland impressed by the boy's forthrightness, 'I see. I see. Would you like to step inside?'

'I cannot do that,' came the polite reply, 'but thank you all the same.'

Jacko suddenly knelt down and took the boy's hands gently in his.

'And to think,' he chided himself tearfully, 'I treated you so roughly and you my very own grandson, my flesh and blood.'

'Don't blame yourself,' young John J. Mulholland's tone held a wealth of tenderness, 'how could you know who I was until I told you?'

At this juncture he helped Jacko to his feet.

'There are certain conditions to be fulfilled,' he warned, 'before all this comes to pass.'

'I'll play my part.' Jacko spoke fervently, the tears coursing down his dishevelled face.

'Know one thing now for certain,' he said, 'and that is your grandfather won't be found wanting no matter what the score.'

'First you must marry,' young John J. insisted, 'and, which is more, if all the heavenly calculations are to be accurately realised, you will go to the altar with your bride in six months' time to the very day.'

'My bride!' Jacko asked. 'Who is she to be?'

'My grandmother, of course,' came the emphatic response.

'Yes. Yes,' Jacko entreated, 'but her name. Tell me her name.'

'Her name,' said young John J., 'is Mary Moles.'

'Yes. Yes,' Jacko promised slobberingly. 'I'll face her at first light and propose.'

'Now,' said young John J., 'I must leave you. I have a long journey and further delay could be fatal.'

'Will I see you again?' Jacko Mulholland asked plaintively.

'Of course you will,' came the positive response. 'You will teach me how to fish and how to tie flies like a true grandfather.'

'And,' Jacko paused before posing the next question, 'will I have much time with you?'

'Oh yes,' came the heart-lifting assurance, 'you will see me to the very threshold of manhood and when your job is done you will depart this worldly scene for the happier climes of heaven at the great age of eighty-four years. Now I must bid you farewell.'

So saying young John J. took his future grandfather's hand and kissed it gently. Then he was gone.

The street was empty but it was no longer desolate. Lights were coming on in the houses and there was the sound of a baby crying for its morning milk. There were other sounds, laughter and song snatches and the crowing of roosters and there were odours, the tantalising aroma of frying rashers, the age-old smell of turf and timber smoke and the salty tang of the distant sea in the rising breeze.

Like all lonely men Jacko Mulholland adored the morning. He regarded it as the fairest of all the day's times, unsullied and pure, ever adorning and gilding. A whistling milkman cycled past, his gallons rattling from either handle-bar.

'A happy Christmas to you Jacko,' he called and redoubled his pedalling.

'And the same to you Eddie,' Jacko Mulholland shouted in his wake.

Later, after he had shaved and breakfasted, Jacko closed the front door behind him. The earliest of the Christmas morning mass-goers were abroad, mostly elderly, fearful of being without a seat in the crowded church. Their reactions were mixed when Jacko, taciturn for fourteen years, extended the compliments of the season. Some responded instantly while others were so overcome by shock and surprise that words failed them.

'It's you is it?' Mary Moles valiantly strove to hide her surprise when she opened the door and saw him standing there. He followed her into the kitchen where her aged parent sat at the head of the table spooning porridge into a toothless mouth. Between spoonfuls he protested, in undertones, about the perfidy of humanity, indicting females in particular. His mouth opened wordlessly when he beheld Jacko Mulholland. It opened still wider when without warning of any kind Mary Moles found her upper body imprisoned in the arms of her one-time suitor. She protested not nor did she yield an inch of ground. Rather did she place her soft hands at the back of his neck and respond with all the vigour she could muster.

Six months later they were married and they lived happily ever after apart from a spirited row now and then which only served to enliven the relationship.

Thus ends John J. Mulholland's tale. It was told to him by his grandfather not long before the old man passed away at the ripe old age of eighty-four.

'As for me,' John J. eased himself from his stool and handed his empty glass to Mikey Joe, 'I don't remember having hand, act or part in the proceedings.'

He moved to the life-sized mirror near the doorway, examined his reflection carefully and at length. He gingerly traced the finger-thin red weal, the origins of which, according to John J. Mulholland, had baffled the world's leading dermatologists since he was first referred to them by the family doctor at the tender age of eight!

The Curriculum Vitae

Fred Spellacy would always remember the Christmas he spent as a pariah, not for the gloom and isolation it brought him nor for the abuse. He would remember it as a period of unprecedented decision-making which had improved his lot in the long term.

Fred Spellacy believed in Christmas. Man and boy it had fulfilled him and for this he was truly grateful. Of late his Christmases had been less happy but he would persevere with his belief, safe in the knowledge that Christmas would never really let him down.

'Auxiliary Postman Required'. The advertisement, not so prominently displayed on the window of the sub post office, captured Dolly Hallon's attention. Postmen are nice, Dolly thought, and they're kind and, more importantly, everybody respects them. In her mind's eye she saw her father with his postbag slung behind him, his postman's cap tilted rakishly at the side of his head, a smile on his face as he saluted all and sundry on his way down the street.

If ever a postmaster, sub or otherwise, belied his imperious title that man was Fred Spellacy. It could be fairly said that he was the very essence of deferentiality. He was also an abuse-absorber. When things went wrong his superiors made him into a scapegoat, his customers rounded on him, his wife upbraided him, his in-laws chided him. His assistant Miss Finnerty clocked reproachfully as though she were a hen whose egg-laying had been precipitately disrupted. She reserved all her clocking for Fred. She never clocked at Fred's wife but then nobody did.

'Yes child?' Fred Spellacy asked gently.

'It's the postman's job sir.'

Fred Spellacy nodded, noted the pale, ingenuous face, the threadbare clothes.

'What age are you?' he asked gently.

'Eleven,' came the reply, 'but it's not for me. It's for my father.'

'Oh!' said Fred Spellacy.

Dolly Hallon thought she detected a smile. Just in case, she forced one in return.

'What's his name, age and address child?'

'His name is Tom Hallon,' Dolly Hallon replied. 'His age is thirty-seven and his address is Hog Lane.'

Fred Spellacy scribbled the information onto a jotter which hung by a cord from the counter. He knew Tom Hallon well enough. Not a ne'er-do-well by any means, used to work in the mill before it closed. He recalled having heard somewhere that the Hallons were honest. Honest! Some people had no choice but to be honest while others didn't have the opportunity to be dishonest.

'Can he read and write?'

'Oh yes,' Dolly assured him. 'He reads the paper every day when Mister Draper next door is done with it. He can write too! He writes to his sister in America.'

'And Irish? Has he Irish?'

'Oh yes,' came the assured response from the eleven year old. 'He reads my school books. He has nothing else to do!'

'Well Miss Hallon here's what you must get your father to do. Get him to apply for the job and enclose a reference from someone in authority such as the parish priest or one of the teachers. I don't suppose he has a curriculum vitae!'

'What's that?' Dolly Hallon asked, her aspirations unexpectedly imperilled.

'The jobs he's had, his qualifications ...'

Fred Spellacy paused as he endeavoured to find words which might simplify the vacant position's requirements.

'Just get him to put down the things he's good at and don't delay. The position must be filled by noon tomorrow. Christmas is on top of us and the letters are mounting up.'

Dolly Hallon nodded her understanding and hurried homewards.

Fred Spellacy was weary. It was a weariness imposed, not by the demands of his job but by the demands of his wife and by the countless recommendations made to him on behalf of the applicants for the vacant position. Fred Spellacy's was a childless family but there was never a dull moment with Fred's wife Alannah always on the offensive and Fred the opposite.

Earlier that day he had unwittingly made a promise to one of the two local TDs that he would do all within his power for the fellow's nominee. Moments later the phone rang. It was the other TD. Fred had no choice but to make the same promise.

'Don't forget who put you there in the first place!' the latter had reminded him.

Worse was to follow. The reverend mother from the local convent had called, earnestly beseeching him not to forget her nominee, a genuine vessel of immaculacy who was, she assured him, the most devout Catholic in the parish. Hot on her heels came others of influence, shopkeepers, teachers and even a member of the civic guards, all pressed into service by desperate job-seekers who would resort to anything to secure the position. Even the pub next door, which had always been a *sanctum sanctorum*, was out of bounds. The proprietor, none more convivial or more generous, had poured him a double dollop of Power's Gold Label before entreating him to remember one of his regulars, a man of impeccable character, unparalleled integrity, unbelievable scholarship and, to crown all, one of the lads as well!

'Come in here!' There was no mistaking the irritation in his wife's voice. She pointed to a chair in the tiny kitchen.

'Sit down there boy!' She turned her back on him while she lit a cigarette. Contemptuously she exhaled, revelling in the dragonish jets issuing from both nostrils.

Fred sat with bent head, a submissive figure. He dared not even cross his legs. He did not dare to tell her that there were customers waiting, that the queue at the counter was lengthening. He knew that a single word could result in a blistering barrage.

'Melody O'Dea,' she opened, 'is one of my dearest friends.'

Her tone suggested that the meek man who sat facing her would grievously mutilate the woman in question given the slightest opportunity.

Again she drew upon the cigarette. A spasm of coughing followed. She looked at Fred as though he had brought it about.

'Her char's husband Mick hasn't worked for three years.'

Alannah Spellacy proceeded in a tone unused to interference, 'so you'll see to it that he gets the job!'

She rose, cigarette in mouth, and drew her coat about her.

'I'll go down now,' she announced triumphantly, 'and tell Melody the good news!'

When Tom Hallon reported for work at the sub post office at noon the following day Alannah Spellacy was so overcome with shock that she was unable to register a single protest. When Tom Hallon donned the postman's cap, at least a size too large, she disintegrated altogether and had to be helped upstairs, still speechless, by her husband

and Miss Finnerty. There she would remain throughout the Christmas, her voice fully restored and to be heard reverberating all over the house until she surprisingly changed her tune shortly after Christmas when it occurred to her that the meek were no longer meek and must needs be cossetted.

Alannah had come to the conclusion that she had pushed her husband as far as he would be pushed. Others would come to the same realisation in due course. Late in his days, but not too late, Fred Spellacy the puppet would be replaced by a resolute, more independent Fred.

Fred had agonised all through the previous night over the appointment. In the beginning he had formed the opinion that it would be in his best interest to appoint the applicant with the most powerful patron but unknown to him the seeds of revolt had been stirring in his subconscious for years. Dolly Hallon had merely been the catalyst.

Fred had grown weary of being told what to do and what not to do. The crisis had been reached shortly after Dolly had walked out the door of the post office.

That night, as he pondered the merits of the score or so applicants, he eventually settled on a shortlist of four. These were the nominees of the two TDs, his wife's nominee and the rank outsider, Tom Hallon, of Hog Lane.

He had once read that the ancient Persians never made a major judgement without a second trial. They judged first when they were drunk and they judged secondly when they were sober. As he left the post office Fred had already made up his mind. He by-passed his local and opted instead for the privacy of a secluded snug in a quiet pub which had seen better days. After his third whiskey and chaser of bottled stout he was assumed into that piquant if temporary state which only immoderate consumption of alcohol can induce.

From his inside pocket he withdrew Tom Hallon's curriculum vitae and read it for the second time. Written on a lined page neatly extracted from a school exercise book it was clearly the work of his daughter Dolly. The spelling was correct but the accomplishments were few. He had worked in the mill but nowhere else. He had lost his job through no fault of his own. Thus far it could have been the story of any unemployed man within a radius of three miles but then the similarities ended for it was revealed that Tom Hallon had successfully played the role of Santa Claus for as long as Dolly could remember. While the gifts he delivered were home-made and lacking in craftsmanship his arrival had brought happiness unbounded to the Hallon family and to the several other poverty-stricken families in Hog Lane.

'Surely,' Fred addressed himself in the privacy of the snug, 'if this man can play the role of Santa Claus then so can I. If he can bear gifts I can bear gifts.'

He rose and buttoned his coat. He pulled up his socks and finished his stout before proceeding unsteadily but resolutely towards the abode of Dolly Hallon in Hog Lane.

He had been prepared, although not fully, for the repercussions. The unsuccessful applicants, their families, friends and handlers, all made their dissatisfaction clear in the run-up to Christmas. They had cast doubts upon his integrity and ancestry in language so malevolent and scurrilous that he was beyond blushing by the time all had had their say.

One man had to be physically restrained and the wife of another had spat into his face. He might not have endured the sustained barrage at all but for one redeeming incident. It wanted but three days for Christmas. A long queue had formed at the post office counter, many of its participants hostile, the remainder impatient.

From upstairs came the woebegone cronawning of his obstructive spouse and when the cronawning ceased there came, down the stairs, shower after shower of the most bitter recriminations, sharper and more piercing than driving hail. He was very nearly at the end of his tether.

'Yes!' he asked of the beaming face which now stood at the head of the ever-lengthening queue. There was no request for stamps nor was there a parcel to be posted. Dolly Hallon just stood there, her pale face transformed by the most angelic and pleasing of smiles. She uttered not a single word but her gratitude beamed from her radiant countenance.

Fred Spellacy felt as though he had been included in the communion of saints. His cares vanished. His heart soared. Then, impassively, she winked at him. Fred Spellacy produced a handkerchief and loudly blew his nose.

THE MIRACLE OF BALLYBRADAWN

The village of Ballybradawn sits comfortably and compactly atop a twenty-foot-high plateau overlooking the Bradawn River. The Bradawn rises in the hills of North Cork but enters the Atlantic in North Kerry. The village with its one thousand souls lies half-way between sea and source.

In the early spring the salmon run upwards from the sea to the spawning beds, silent and silvery, shimmering and shapely. It is a most hazardous journey. Survivors are few. Man is the major enemy.

Our tale begins in the year of our Lord 1953, a climacteric span which saw the demise of Stalin, the flight of the Shah, the inauguration of Eisenhower and the conquest of Everest.

Not to be outdone, Ballybradawn was to witness its own breathtaking phenomenon shortly before Christmas of the year in question.

The spring and summer of the said year had been extremely disappointing seasons for local and visiting anglers. For some reason best known to themselves the dense schools of celebrated *salmo salar*, princes of the Atlantic, had failed to appear as had been their wont for generations. They had arrived all right but in pitifully small numbers. There was intense speculation as to what calamity might have befallen the missing fish and there was widespread belief that full compensation might be expected early during the following spring because that was the way with nature. She was known to be bountiful in the wake of insufficiency.

Indeed there were whispers from the middle of December onwards that spring fish had been sighted in the estuary. Experienced drift-net fishermen, not given to fishy tales, would bear witness to the fact that the fulsome visitors were present in considerable strength in the wide expanse where the Bradawn joined the sea.

Doubting Thomases might insist that these were spent fish on their way downwards from the spawning beds but proof to the contrary had been incontrovertible. When a spring fish plopped back into the water after a jump from its natural domain it did so with a resounding smack followed by a noisy splash which could be heard for long distances. The spent fish, on the other hand, subsided in a minor eddy on his return from a despairing leap. The resultant sound was nearly always indistinguishable from the natural noises of the river.

There were other signs to indicate the presence of spring fish. The seal population had quadrupled in the estuary and its salty precincts and, emboldened by the prospect of a fresh salmon diet, had made unprecedented incursions beyond the tidal reaches of the Bradawn where the terrified salmon sought refuge in the shallows beneath gravel banks and overhanging foliage. Here, alas, were otters who would have no misgivings about sinking sharp teeth into the living, succulent flesh of the unwary refugees from the estuary.

Further on would be poachers armed with gaffs, illegal nets, clowns' caps, cages, triple-hooked stroke-hauls, poisons, explosives and many other deadly devices and ruses, all aimed at terminating prematurely the brief life of *salmo salar.*

For most fish it was a one-way journey fraught with peril from beginning to end. Conservators would say that it was nothing short of a miracle that any salmon at all managed to spawn and that the species itself had survived for so long.

When word went abroad in the village of Ballybradawn that a number of spring salmon were showing in the river before their time there was great excitement among the poaching fraternity. From morn till night they would discuss ways and means of supplementing their Christmas fare with the delicious flesh of an illicitly taken salmon. Mouths watered all through their conversations as the many methods of cooking this prize product of the Bradawn River were recounted. Plans were made but none saw fruition because of the vigilance of the local water-keepers who patrolled the river day and night. All known poachers were trailed as they indulged in seemingly innocuous walks along the riverside. Towards the afternoon of Christmas Eve a man by the name of Ned Muddle chanced to be standing at one of the village's more prominent corners when he was approached by a friend who informed him about the premature arrivals. Ned expressed doubts about the veracity of his friend's information.

'It's true!' that worthy assured him.

'But how come?' Ned Muddle asked.

'Some say seals,' said his informant, 'while others maintain that it's merely an error of judgment on the part of the salmon.'

A lengthy silence ensued while Ned digested the theories put forward by his friend. Ned was greatly addicted to salmon and if presented with a plate of it would not question its origins or the way it was cooked or the manner in which it was served.

Salmon, alas, were expensive and when Ned fancied fish his longings, of necessity, would generally be catered for by either herring or mackerel. Ned Muddle moved to the other side of the corner. His friend followed suit. They rested their backs against the wall while the friend held forth about the numbers and quality of the salmon which had presented themselves before their time and pointed out too how early fish fetched phenomenal prices in the country's fish markets and even a solitary kill was an assurance of drinking money for days on end.

'Yes. Yes,' Ned announced with some impatience, 'but what's all this to me?'

'What's it to you?' his friend expostulated incredulously.

'Why man dear,' he went on in a more mollifying tone, 'I would have thought it applied more to you than to any man.'

'Why is that?' asked an increasingly puzzled Ned.

'Don't you see?' said his friend, now facing him directly as he drove home his point, 'you are a handyman, probably the best handyman in Ballybradawn and maybe, just maybe, the greatest handyman in the country.'

Ned frowned and then smiled as he wondered if he might indeed be such a handyman, might just about be the greatest handyman in the country, the world!

'All right!' he conceded gruffly, only barely managing to conceal his pleasure, 'so I'm a handyman but what's a handyman got to do with there being salmon in the river?'

'Only a skilled handyman could make a wire cage to trap these salmon. Any ordinary handyman just couldn't do it. He would have to be the best. He would have made wire cages before this. He would have trapped salmon before this!'

'Before he went to jail you mean,' Ned Muddle suggested with a wry laugh.

The villagers of Ballybradawn would remember, but not if they were asked, when Ned Muddle went to jail and for how long and why. It had happened ten years before. He had received a three-month sentence. He had been convicted of poaching or, to be more specific, of being found in possession of explosive substances on the river bank for the express purpose of blowing the souls, if any, of the river's inhabitants to Kingdom Come and their filleted bodies to the empty larders of Ned Muddle and his wanton fellow poachers.

There had been a fine-related option but neither Ned nor his henchmen were in a position to avail of it since they were not possessed of the requisite funds. Neither were their friends, neighbours or relations so that they had nowhere to turn except to their long-suffering in-laws who would be seen as the ultimate natural redress in such contingencies except, of course, by the in-laws themselves. The in-laws, alas for the convicted poachers, insisted that they had already pledged and paid far in excess of what might be reasonably expected of them. Ned and his accomplices served the full term.

The two friends moved away from the corner. They found themselves heading towards the cliffs which afforded a commanding view of the widest and deepest pool along the entire river. They stood with hands in pockets, their experienced eyes searching the still surface for tell-tale signs.

Minutes passed, then a quarter-hour but still they stood their ground. Then it happened! A gleaming salmon, unmistakably fresh, powered itself out of the pool's centre and disappeared, almost instantly, with a mighty splash which shattered the surface of the deep pool, dispensing wavelets and ripples to both banks.

The friends withdrew their hands from their pockets and exchanged knowing glances. Words would have been superfluous and since seasoned poachers are men of few words to begin with, they hastened back to their favourite corner without the exchange of as much as a solitary syllable on the way.

'I have the makings of a cage in my back shed. 'Tis there, ready and waiting for a man of genius like yourself!'

Ned Muddle was flattered. He was not a well-loved person in the community. He was nasty to his wife and children. He was mean and he was dishonest so that words of praise rarely came his way.

In addition to being shifty, cowardly and unreliable, he had not been inside the door of the parish church, or any other church for fifteen years, since his wedding in fact, a sacrament in which he reluctantly participated and in which he might not have collaborated at all had it not been for the insistence of his in-laws-to-be who simply intimated that they would blow his brains out with a double-barrelled gun if he did not present himself at the church at the appointed time.

Despite entreaties from the parish priest and numerous curates as well as visiting missioners and pious lay people Ned Muddle steadfastly refused to conform. His neighbours would cheerfully forgive him all his other transgressions but they balked at the irreligious.

'I'll do it,' Ned announced more to himself than to his friend whose name happened to be Fred. In less than two hours they assembled the cage. Fred stood back to survey the handiwork in which he had played no more than a token part.

''Tis a work of art,' he announced, 'the village of Ballybradawn can be proud of you. Sure there's no self-respecting salmon would ignore it.'

Ned Muddle permitted himself a rare smile. Cage-making was his true metier. Even his arch-enemies the waterkeepers would concede without begrudgery that he was the best. Fred lifted the cage and bore it indoors to the bedroom which he shared with his wife. There he lovingly laid it on the large double bed which dominated the room. All that was now required was to wait until nightfall before setting out for the river where they would obstruct its flow and the passage of its denizens by constructing a low stone-built rampart from one bank to the other, leaving a gap in the middle where a strong but narrow current would attract the upgoing salmon. In this gap they would place the illegal cage which was designed to admit foolhardy fish but not to allow them egress. Large flat stones would be laid along its bottom to add weight to the structure. Otherwise, because of its lightweight composition, it would shift easily with the force of the concentrated flow.

Ned was a taciturn fellow of few words at the best of times unless, of course, he was berating his wife and family. His friend Fred, fortunately for their enterprise, eschewed conversation too except when it was absolutely necessary. Fred's wife, alas, was the opposite, a most congenial creature who, if afforded the opportunity, would spend hours at a time conversing with friends and neighbours and, when neither was available, with total strangers willing to pass the time of day. She was a woman without malice and even Fred, who rarely paid heed to her harmless narratives, would be the first to concede that his wife was incapable of misrepresentation or character assassination.

As was her wont every evening after supper, she made her way to the parish church where others like her and a small number of elderly males attended evening devotions. On the way home the good woman could not resist the waylaying of a neighbour to whom she secretly conveyed all the details of her husband's forthcoming expedition with his friend Ned Muddle.

'I know,' Fred's wife entreated her companion, 'that you won't breathe a word to a living soul.'

'Did I ever!' came the sincere response while she hurried off as quickly as her legs would take her in order to disclose the news of the planned undertaking to every Tom, Dick and Harry who would listen. Most took little notice for the good reason that previous disclosures by this particular informant had always turned out to be fabrications. Others, however, notably the wives and sweethearts of the village's established poachers, listened well and informed their menfolk. The menfolk bided their time.

No man bides his time as well as a poacher. This is because poachers, due to the secrecy imposed by their calling, are professional timebiders but how exactly do they bide it, one might well ask! The answer is by not seeming to bide it but by committing themselves wholeheartedly to a diversion far removed from poaching such as cardplaying or dart-throwing or, in the case of younger, unmarried members of this close-knit fraternity, to the unremitting pursuit of unattached females.

As the evening dragged itself out Ned and Fred passed the time spying on the village resident water-keepers. There were but two. Others from outlying villages would be summoned whenever the district inspector felt it was necessary to do so. The water-keepers lived close together. The friends maintained their vigil and expressed no surprise when one keeper visited the house of the other with his wife a half-hour before midnight. Ten minutes later the four emerged together and made their way towards the parish church where the celebration of midnight mass would begin on the stroke of midnight and where, God willing, the hearts of men and women would expand with the goodness, the charity and the forgiveness that only Christmas can generate.

As soon as they had seen the water-keepers and their wives safely into the brightly lit bosom of the church Fred and Ned made haste to the bedroom of the latter's house where they collected the cage. Fred led the way. Ned followed with the cage. They avoided the village's main street and its attendant laneways. Occasionally as they passed isolated homes a dog would bark and as they neared the river a home-bound drunkard shouted a minor obscenity as a prelude to extending the season's greetings. These they returned and continued cautiously along their way. After a mere five minutes they found themselves on the bank of the river less than two hundred yards from the village. They were somewhat apprehensive after the setting of the trap since they observed from the river bank that the light from the nearest street lamps brightened the area where they had placed it. Then, unexpectedly, from the south-west there arrived upon the scene overhead a sizable cloud which obscured the moon and brought welcome darkness to the immediate scene. It would be followed by other clouds for the remainder of their stay so that, all in all, it would be a night of intermittent light, the kind of light beloved by poachers and others whose business runs contrary to the laws of the land.

The ideal situation, as far as Ned and Fred were concerned, would be long periods of darkness interspersed with short periods of moonlight. The pair sat on dry stones not daring to utter a word. Sometimes they would nudge each other in appreciation of the night's own distinctive sounds such as the distinct rooting of a badger or the far-off yelping of a vixen summoning a dog fox to earth. From the opposite bank came the unmistakable call of a wandering pheasant, husky yet vibrant. They listened without comment to the furtive comings and goings of the smaller inhabitants of the undergrowth and to all the other lispings, chirpings and stirrings common to the night. They listened, most of all, to the gentle background music of the running water, savouring its eddies, its softer shallows-music and leisurely, lapping wavelets. These last were almost inaudible but as distinctive, nevertheless, to the silent pair seated on dry stones as the frailer strains of a complex symphony to the alert conductor.

Gentle breezes fanned the coarse river grasses and rustled in the underbrush whilst overhead, when the clouds gave the nod, the stars twinkled and the bright moon shone. Never had Ned entertained such a sense of sublime security. His cares had melted away under the benign influence of the accumulated night sounds. The same could be said for his friend Fred over whose face was drawn a veil of gratification, rarely enjoyed by the human species. Truly they had become part of the night. Truly were they at one with the riverside scene.

There were times when they leaned forward eagerly in anticipation and times when they partially rose to their feet but it was no more than the river changing its tune as it did when the levels began to lower themselves and the lessening variations presented a different concert.

From the belfry of the parish church the midnight chimes rang pleasantly and clearly. Ned and his friend made the sign of the cross. As the final chime sounded they were both on their feet, ears strained, their faces taut.

'Did you hear a splash?' the whispered question came from Ned.

'I heard something,' his fellow poacher responded.

'Then,' said Ned Muddle, a note of confidence in his tone, 'we had better take a look!'

They waded through the shallow water and there, gleaming far brighter than any of the stars over their heads, imprisoned in the cage, was a freshly arrived salmon. It turned out to be a splendid cock fish unblemished as far as they could see and shining with a radiance that belongs only to creatures of the sea. Such lustre would inevitably be dulled by a long sojourn in the upper reaches of the river but now the sea silver flashed and glittered. For a moment the creature explored its new surrounds and finding no escape began to thresh and flail for all it was worth. All, alas, was to no avail. Once a salmon enters a properly designed cage its fate is sealed.

'He's ten pounds!' Ned Muddle exclaimed with delight.

'He's twelve if he's an ounce,' his companion insisted.

Without further argument they lifted the cage and between them brought it ashore. It was Ned who extracted the struggling fish by its gills and it was Ned who located a large stone with which he smote upon the creature's poll after he had laid it on the gravelled shore and restricted its movements by holding its tail in a vice-like grip. Hands on hips, a stance copied by his companion, he stood for a while admiring the symmetry of his capture. Apart from an occasional, barely perceptible spasm, there was no movement from the fish.

'Hurry,' Ned Muddle urged his partner, 'hurry because where there's one there's more.'

'We should go while the going is good,' Fred contradicted.

'No!' Ned was adamant. Then with a chuckle he added, 'we'll hide this fellow in the bushes and go looking for his missus.'

He had but barely spoken when a whistle blew close at hand. The sound was loud and shrill and shattered not only the silence of the night but the shocked poachers as well. They stood paralysed, rooted to the ground, unable to move. The next sound to intrude upon the quiet of the night was a shot. It exploded deafeningly from a bush nearby. It was followed by a second shot. It electrified the lifeless cage-maker and his acolyte. The latter was the first to take off. Like any hunted creature he ran up the riverside. Ned Muddle who was the very personification of cowardice ran down towards the town.

'Halt in the name of the law!' The stentorian tones came from the same bush as the shots. The command only served to spur the fleeing pair to greater efforts. They ran for their lives. Finding himself unwounded after a hundred paces Ned now directed himself to where the sound of human voices in melodic union emanated sweetly from the parish church. His eyes bulging with terror he puffed his way to the only sanctuary available to him. He knew not the moment when his life might be ended with a bullet in the back. It did not occur to him at the time that the water-keepers of the Bradawn River were not licensed to bear arms nor would the local civic guards resort to such murderous tactics. It would dawn on him at a later stage that the underworld of Ballybradawn, as he was to dub the local poachers, was responsible.

As he drew nearer the church the sound of five hundred voices raised in the *Adeste* urged him to greater effort. Breathlessly he entered the blessed refuge of light and sound. In the pulpit the parish priest, venerable and portly, conducted the singing with fervour and total commitment. He suddenly lowered his hands when he beheld the stricken, dishevelled figure of Ned Muddle, poacher, wife-beater, lout and drunkard. He knew Ned well, had known him for years as a godless wretch and sacrilegious scoundrel. The parish priest's mouth opened but no sound came forth. His vast choir, without direction, was silenced as every member of the surprised congregation followed his amazed stare. They beheld Ned, his perspiring face as contrite as ever had been the face of any sinner, great or small. There were members of the gathering who could not make up their minds whether to laugh or cry. They looked to their parish priest for delivery from their indecision.

'Mirabile dictu!' the parish priest intoned the words while his eyes filled with tears. Great was the rejoicing as the congregation echoed

the Latin phrase. Most were not sure of its meaning but Latin it was and as such was sacred.

After the mass, Ned Muddle went forth into the world in peace. Need it be added that he mended his ways and came to possess the grace of God, that he became a model parent and husband and that his neighbours flocked to him when they found themselves in need of counsel or solace. He ended his days a parochial sacristan which, after the position of junior curate, is the highest ecclesiastical office in the village of Ballybradawn.

The Scubblething

Martin Scubble and his wife Mary lived on the verge of the boglands. Their cottage was the last thatched habitation of its kind in that part of the world known as Tubberscubble. For generations the Scubbles had farmed the twenty acres of deep cutaway which was the total extent of their soggy holding.

Martin was the last of the Scubbles. He would say that he never missed not having children and Mary would say that she had a child.

'What is Martin,' she would ask, 'but an overgrown child that wouldn't be here nor there without me?'

Childless they might be but theirs was a house that was never without children because of the constant activity in the boglands throughout most of the year. There was never a day in the summer when tea-making time came around that some boy or girl from the town or surrounding countryside did not call for hot water which was always freely available from Mary Scubble. Happy groups of turf-footers, turf-turners and stoolin-makers of all ages would seat themselves on turf sods or heather clumps under the open sky and relish every mouthful of the simple fare.

'Whatever it is about the bogland air,' the elders would say, 'it has no equal for improving the appetite.'

'I could eat frost-nails after it,' another might be heard to say.

Then in the late winter and early spring the proprietors of the bogland's many turf reeks would arrive with their horses and rails or donkeys and rails to replenish depleted stocks in the sheds and gable-reeks adjoining their homes. Always when a thunderstorm suddenly intruded or when the rain proved too drenching there was shelter and scalding tea to be had under the thatched roof of the Scubble farmhouse.

Martin and Mary Scubble were generous to a fault. All comers were welcome to their humble abode. There was, thanks be to the good God revered by both, never a cross word between them, never that is except Christmas alone when the solace beneath the thatched roof was fractured and when their conformable personalities changed utterly. Mercifully the transformation was of brief duration but it had succeeded in attracting the interest of young folk far and wide. They would arrive, unfailingly, to the boglands shortly before darkness on the Sunday before Christmas and conceal themselves in the decrepit out-houses which surrounded the farmhouse.

The annual event was known to the young generation as the Scubblething. According to their elders it had taken place for over two score years and had begun shortly after Mary Scubble had established herself as the new mistress of the Scubble holding. Some insisted that it had survived because the Scubbles had nothing else to do but the older and more perceptive of the neighbours would argue otherwise. As the neighbours grew older they paid scant attention to the goings-on at Scubbles. For them the novelty had worn off and they had come to take the whole business for granted. Not so the young folk who would nod and wink at each other eagerly as the Sunday in question approached.

'See you at the Scubblething,' they would whisper with a laugh. Many had built meaningful relationships on a first meeting at the event and there were a considerable number who had eventually married as a result. Such was its drawing power that upwards of two score of youngsters would present themselves at the Scubble environs, unknown to the principals, shortly before the winter sun reclined in, and sank into, the western horizon.

In the early years no more than a handful would hide themselves from the ageing pair, taking great care to maintain the strictest of silences before the curtain went up on the annual drama. Then as the years went by and the Scubbles grew older and feebler there was hardly any need to sustain the earlier lulls which had been so essential if they were to avoid detection by Martin and Mary.

Now in later years, the older teenagers would arrive with packs of beer and containers of Vodka. Smoking too was rife and although there was a general tipsiness to the occasion there was enough control over the proceedings to ensure that detection was avoided. Indoors Martin and Mary would settle down for the night after they had partaken of supper. Then would they seat themselves at either side of the open hearth while the rising flames from the roaring turf fire filled the kitchen with flickering tongues of light and mysterious ever-changing shadows. It could fairly be called a cosy time. Outside the young folk would silently leave their hiding places and advance to the front door and windows where they would crouch together in comforting closeness, swigging happily but noiselessly from their many bottles. Inside the ritual continued with Martin bringing his palms together and sitting erect on his *súgán* chair the better to fire the opening salvos.

'Do you remember last year,' said he, 'when we had that woeful argument?'

Patiently he awaited his wife's reply and when there was none he spat noisily into the fire before framing his second question.

'Do you remember,' he asked in a louder and more aggressive tone, 'the battle we had this very Sunday in this very spot at this very time?'

Still no answer from Mary. He regarded her silence as the most provocative ever imposed by a female on a long-suffering spouse and he stamped his feet noisily, one after the other, the better to register his protest.

'Dammit!' he exclaimed bitterly, 'are you deaf or what! Will you have me talking to myself for the rest of the night?'

He looked at her, his face screwed up now with hatred. It seemed for a moment that he must seize her by the throat and put an end to her gross incitement. He rose from his chair, speechless with rage.

'I'll ask you this once,' he screeched, 'and I'll ask you no more. Do you or do you not remember our fracas last year when we argued whether it was a duck or a drake that scuttered on top of the bed when we left open the window?'

'I remember nothing of the kind,' she spat back with all the vehemence she could muster. 'I'll tell you what I remember though and it is this. It was no duck and it was no drake. What we were arguing about was whether it was a cock or a hen and ducks and drakes have nothing to do with it.'

'Damn you for a pernickety oul' woman,' Martin cried out. 'It was ducks and drakes.' He pounded the rickety kitchen table with both fists. 'I will go into any court in the land where I will swear on the Holy Book that it was ducks and drakes.'

'It costs nothing to swear,' Mary replied calmly, 'if you're a born perjurer to begin with and I'll tell you this you black-toothed oul' devil! You can swear till the book lights in your grimy paw but it won't change the fact that we were arguing about a cock and a hen.'

'Blasht you for a liar,' he shouted. 'If tables and chairs could talk and windows could give evidence you'd be transported for perjury and you'd never see hide nor light of this country again.'

Outside in the cold night air the young people hugged themselves and each other with glee. The exchanges had not lost any of their bitterness or rancour since the year before and it seemed that in spite of their great ages the Scubbles were more venomous than ever.

Inside, a short silence held sway while they recharged themselves for a renewal of the conflict. They would not mention that they had the very same argument as far back as they could remember. What mattered now was to reach the climax without obstruction and to maximise their hostility towards each other. On the resumption their voices reached fever pitch. Outside the young people began to worry lest the extreme vocal exertions affect the larynxes of the contestants and bring a premature end to the performances. It happened on one occasion several years previously. The recriminations had been at their height when Mary's voice suddenly turned hoarse leaving the field of battle solely to her husband and frustrating both the Scubbles and their listeners to such a degree that all would claim later it had been the most disappointing build-up to Christmas that any of those involved could remember.

It was as though the Scubbles had suddenly realised that such a calamity was once again in the offing for, by tacit agreement, both unexpectedly paused in their detractions and defamations and drew rein as it were so that their over-worked vocal chords might recuperate. The listeners sensed that the best was about to come and they readied themselves for the final act by finishing off their near-empty bottles and lighting fresh cigarettes.

Indoors there followed barrage after barrage of the most intense, most damaging free-for-alls.

'The devil's a darling,' Mary was to say to the delight of her numerous fans on the outside. 'Oh the devil's a sweet commodity entirely when compared to some that I know, some that isn't a spit away from where I sit.'

Altogether incensed by this monstrous comparison Martin held forth with unprecedented spite.

'Repeat that before my face,' he bawled with all his might, 'repeat it that's a bitch and a backbiter's and a beggarman's baggage. Repeat it you barefaced bouncer that never wore a slip or a knickers till she was twenty-five years of age. Repeat it you virago and I promise you that I'll be vexed no more for I'll baptise you proper with a two pound pot of raspberry jam and the full chamber pot that you forgot to empty for weeks, all down on the crown of your lousy head!'

Mary Scubble rose to her feet and folded her arms in a frightening pose. She threw back her grey head so that more authority might be added to her next bombardment.

'I'll do as I please,' she replied at the top of her voice, a voice that showed no sign whatsoever of weakening, 'and while I have two feet I won't be daunted by blackguards with jam pots for my seed and breed didn't take it from the Black and Tans not to mind taking it from you and we didn't take it from the Peelers you dirty dago that would begrudge his own mother the colouring of her tea. If you don't stop your ranting straightaway, you balding battle-axe, I'll snip off your withering tassel with a stainless steel scissors.'

'Will you listen to her,' Martin extended a hand as if he was calling upon the fire in the hearth to bear witness. 'Oh what a mangy maggoty mongrel she is,' his tone soared in derision. 'Oh there is no gander as vulgar, there's no magpie as raucous and there's no badger as grey or mottled and to think she calls herself Christian!'

'Listen to what's talking,' Mary responded quickly before he had time to strengthen his advantage, 'with his rotten poll and his withered head that didn't host a black hair in forty full years and wrinkles all over him like they'd be ploughed by horses. Consecration is the only thing now that'll save you, consecration by the bishop and by the four canons of the diocese and then to steep the wretch in a barrel of holy water for nine days and nine nights till the evil inside and outside is washed away and then to have the water turned into steam and fanned away to the ends of the world for fear he'd contaminate the whole of humanity.'

Suddenly Martin cut across his wife and it seemed that he must surely strike her but no! He resorted once more to the spoken word.

''Tis not in my breeding,' said he coldly and murderously, 'to spill female blood but yours will flow like water if you don't put a reins on that runaway tongue of yours, that black tongue that should be hauled out by the roots and ground into mince!'

Mary circled her husband like a cat contemplating a mouse.

'He's gone mental this time for sure,' she informed the tongs which she had taken into her hands. She swung the cumbersome instrument dervish-like around her head before smashing it into the fire. The bright structure collapsed about the hearth sending showers of sparks upwards and outwards. Martin withdrew towards the doorway in alarm, his hands covering his head.

'In the asylum you should be,' he thundered, finding himself safely out of reach of the deadly weapon which his unpredictable spouse now twirled around her midriff, 'but what asylum would take you with your name for mischief and agitation! 'Tis no one but myself would endure you and when I face St Peter he'll surely say to me: "Come in, come in Martin Scubble, my poor unfortunate man for 'tis you surely has your hell suffered down below!"'

'Houl', houl', you bothersome oul' fool,' his wife called back, 'houl', don't I catch your rotten tongue with the tongs and pull it from your festering oul' puss!'

'Shut up you harridan,' Martin shouted back but it was clear he was tiring as indeed was Mary for she had dropped the tongs and was now circling the kitchen with her head in her hands. Her next act was to place her withered hands on the table and to raise her head ceiling-wards before indulging herself in a fit of high-pitched, protracted pillalooing.

Martin sat himself wearily in a chair, his legs out-stretched, his hands hanging limply by his sides, his mouth open. He looked the very epitome of exhaustion and dejection.

Outside, in the crisp night air, the listeners covered their laughing mouths with their hands lest their mirth filter through to the aching, exhausted couple in the kitchen.

In the surrounding countryside greyhounds and collies, terriers and beagles, filled the night with dutiful responses to Mary's lamentations. No dog barked. Rather did they cry soulfully to the moon and stars with compassion and commiseration as though they understood the plight of the demented creature from whom the sounds originated. The wailing lasted for several minutes and gradually subsided until there was silence abroad and silence indoors.

The young listeners gathered around the front door of the Scubble abode. One of the older girls knocked gently thereon but failing to elicit a response, gently lifted the latch and entered into the half-light followed by her companions. They were not surprised to see Martin Scubble seated on a chair near the fire and they were less surprised to see Mary seated on his lap. Benign smiles wreathed both their ancient faces while Martin gently stroked the grey hair of his contented spouse.

'Happy Christmas,' the young folk called out in unison.

Mary and Martin sat as though in a reverie. The young folk re-arranged the fire and trooped out noiselessly. On the way home they would agree that it had been the best Scubblething ever, that there were times when it had been almost unbearably uproarious. There were some who sensed that it could be retained as an episode in their lives which would be beneficial in the long run, as a tale to be told or an experience to be savoured over and over. Others, the more sensitive, could see themselves cast in the roles of Martin and Mary in given circumstances.

All would faithfully relay the ups-and-downs of the purification ceremony which had come to be known as the Scubblething and all, no matter how insensitive or how heedless the majority might be, would conclude that maybe their own abodes could do with scubble-things in the runup to Christmas – their own safe, solid, seemingly happy and yet somehow lack-lustre habitations by comparison. Some would not wish such a thing for the world or so they would say. The more thoughtful believed, however, that if people burdened with the great ages of Martin and Mary needed the Scubblething on an annual basis then it would be logical to assume that everybody might need it, on some scale, especially those who insisted they didn't although not necessarily for the general delight and benefit of the young folk in the homes contiguous to Tubberscubble.

A Cock for Christmas

As well as being a Christmas tale the following is also a story of romance, love and no little debauchery from the bird world. As stories go it is as true as any and it happened in my native town some time between the disappearance of the swallowtail coat and the closure of the Lartigue Railway.

It so happened that two young ladies of the so-called Ascendancy classes arrived at the Arms Hotel one September morning and asked if they might see the manager. In carefully cultivated tones from a mixture of non-Celtic origins they informed him that they required the services of the porter. On being assured that he was available they gave instructions that he was to go at once to the local railway station.

There he would collect a crate which had come all the way from Paris. The crate contained two French doves, gentler than a summer dawn and whiter than the untrodden snow.

Duly, the porter returned to the hotel where he deposited the crate upon a reading table in the foyer.

The young misses of the long-since ousted Ascendancy were delighted and, assuming that the birds must surely be starving procured, again with the aid of the porter, the appropriate birdseed.

The doves, however, refused to dine so it was decided that they should be taken from the crate and examined. Great care was taken since it was widely accepted even then that birds had a preference for the outdoors over the indoors and would frequently take to the skies when opportunity presented itself.

Tenderly they were extracted from the crate and there was great exultation when it was discovered that they were hale and hearty and none the worse for their long journey.

The young misses had planned to take the birds to their suburban home and then, after they had familiarised themselves with the new surrounds, they would be released. It was expected that they would take speedily to their fresh environs and, in the course of time, assume the nationality of their new country. So much for the best laid schemes of doves and damsels!

In the foyer the doves were much admired but unfortunately were being passed rapidly from one pair of inexperienced hands to another so that, eventually, the inevitable happened. A *garsún* accidentally mishandled the cock of the pair. Did I say they were cock and hen? The cock grasped his chance and flew out of the open door.

There was consternation. A well-known fainter in the company promptly collapsed so that a young lady who held the second dove in her hands lost her concentration. She had also attempted to obstruct the escape of the cock and in so doing gave the French hen the opportunity she had been waiting for. With a gentle fluttering of wings she followed her companion into the sunlight which had begun to brighten the scene outside.

In a flash the crowd in the foyer had emptied itself into the square. There was no sign of the doves. Spotters were dispatched to various parts of the town and to the nearby wood of Gurtenard which was a favourite haunt of local pigeons. Although the search went on all afternoon there was no sign of the missing pair. In their absence life was obliged to go on regardless. The afternoon drifted by and when evening arrived all hope was abandoned.

After all they were innocent strangers with no knowledge of local hawks. How then could they be expected to survive!

However, an observant corner-boy whose wont it was to gaze at the sky all day spotted them on the roof of the hotel, their gleaming whiteness contrasting sublimely with the dark grey slates.

Vainly did the hotel owner, the porter, the two Ascendancy misses and numerous other well-wishers seek to lure them down from their perches. Then one Dinny Cronin appeared on the scene for the first time. Dinny was a local pigeon-fancier and was possessed of a few magnificent specimens. Indeed in those pollution-free days the sky over the dreaming town frequently played host to large flocks of pigeons. The back-yards boasted many pigeon coops and in the mornings the townspeople were frequently serenaded by soft chortlings and other manifestations of pigeonly affection.

Dinny Cronin took stock of the situation for several minutes and eventually came up with the solution.

'At home,' said he, 'I have one of the handsomest cock birds ever seen in this neck of the woods.'

On hearing that the visitors were French, Dinny was taken aback but not for long.

'My bird might have no French,' said he, 'but he has the looks and he has the carriage.'

With everybody's approval he went home for the cock and returned in jig time with the pride of his flock in his coat pocket. As cocks went he was a strapping fellow, a biller and a cooer, forceful yet demure, a winner and a wooer and a charmer of pigeons from Listowel to Knockanure. Upon beholding the French arrivals he flew upwards till he was out of sight and then tumbled crazily downwards scorning all danger in the service of courtship.

After several such amorous sallies, all calculated to win the heart of the female Frenchie, he alighted on the roof. There followed some intimate bird patter, indistinguishable to all but themselves. It was apparent that there was no language barrier.

'They speak the language of love,' said Dinny Cronin, 'and that's the same in every land under the sun.' After the tender, verbal formalities Dinny's cock bird flew off and circled the nearby Catholic church three times. The Frenchies followed suit leaving the onlookers to believe that they subscribed to the same persuasion as Dinny's cock bird.

Then the trio disappeared into the fading light and were forgotten for the moment. However, when a week went by without a sign of the vanished ménage there was widespread alarm.

In the ancient town business went on as usual but around the pigeon coops there was little billing and less cooing. Dinny Cronin's bird was sorely missed. Dinny himself was heartbroken for the missing cock was the pride of his flock.

Then a letter arrived from Paris for the young misses who had ordered the doves in the first place. The letter stated that the pair of doves had arrived back in the French capital accompanied by a dark stranger, a rude fellow with country manners but much admired by members of the opposite sex. There was widespread mourning for it was taken for granted that the Cronin cock would never leave the romantic capital of the known world and who could blame him!

Slowly but surely Christmas drew near with an abundance of freshly revealed humanity and goodwill. Dinny was disconsolate. It looked as if he would never see his pride and joy again. He sat towards the evening of Christmas Eve by the kitchen window pondering the joys of the past and the emptiness of the future.

Then his heart soared. He sat upright when he head the familiar chortle that had melted the hearts of a hundred doves. It was weak and it was hoarse but it was unmistakable. It was his missing cock bird. Dinny jumped to his feet and opened the kitchen window. There on the sill lay his friend, worn and exhausted after his journey from France and from countless other engagements too delicate to disclose and too numerous to mention.

He was received with joy and tears.

'My poor oul' cratur,' said Dinny, 'them Frenchies went near being the death of you.'

'Hush!' said his wife, 'mustn't youth have its fling.' Thereafter there was joy in the pigeon coops of Listowel and Dinny Cronin's prize cock wandered afar no more.

Groodles

The decision to hold the Tubbernablaw wren-dance earlier than usual was brought about by a number of factors, the chief of which was an ominous forecast in *Old Moore's Almanac* concerning dire events in early January. First would come a blizzard so dense and driving that foolhardy travellers would not be able to see their own outstretched palms out of doors. This, according to *Old Moore,* would be followed in short order by a veritable deluge of rain and in the wake of these calamitous events there would come a frost so sharp that it would freeze the bark off the trees.

'I see nothing for it,' Billy Bonner the king of the Tubbernablaw wrenboys informed his wife on the night after St Stephen's Day, 'but to hold the dance tomorrow night. Otherwise we might have to wait until the spring and whoever heard of a wrenboys' dance in the springtime!'

The second factor to influence the decision was a sermon delivered by the parish priest in the nearby town on the Sunday before Christmas. He had begun as usual by admonishing wrenboys young and old and, as the sermon proceeded, whipped himself up into a frenzy while he denounced the debauchery and the drunkenness which were part and parcel of such orgies.

'If it comes to my attention,' said he, 'that a single wren-dance takes place in the New Year then woe betide the instigators. There can be no luck in a parish that allows these monstrous activities to take place. Therefore let it be known,' he concluded with upraised hands and tone hoarse with fury, 'that I shall come a-calling if word comes to my ear that the laws of church and state are being flouted.'

'If,' Billy Bonner addressed his wife who lay beside him in the bed, 'we hold no dance in the New Year we will be flouting no laws, whatever the blazes flouting is.' Beside him his wife murmured agreement. 'I therefore propose,' he declared solemnly as though he were addressing an assembly of wrenboys, 'that we go ahead with our dance tomorrow night and have done with it.'

'I second that,' his wife agreed with matching solemnity and with that she placed her arms round his neck and enquired if there was any law of church or state which might proscribe the unmentionable activities which her proximity suggested.

'Not that I know of,' Billy replied as he took her in his arms and implanted a gentle kiss on her receptive lips.

Early next morning the king of the Tubbernablaw wrenboys mounted his ancient bicycle and went westwards into his dominions in order to notify the wren-boys and wren-girls of his decision to advance the date of the wren-dance. The decree was widely applauded and in every abode to which he called he was graciously received as befitted a man of such stature. While ordinary mortals might be offered stout or beer or even whiskey out of Christmas stocks Billy was obliged to walk home leaning on his bicycle for support after the vast quantities of brandy which had been thrust upon him. Others, less valuable in the community and to the business in hand, would travel far and wide in his stead, spreading the news of the royal pronouncement. There was no dissenting voice. Billy arrived back at his home in Tubbernablaw shortly after noon. He slept for several hours before his wife deemed it prudent to rouse him from where they had cavorted so wantonly the night before. Two trusted deputies had already tackled the black mare to the common cart. All three set out earnestly for the town where they would purchase the wines, whiskeys, cordials, minerals and the indispensable two half-tierces of stout which should see them safely through the festivities which would end at the breaking of day on the following morning.

Maggie Bonner had already visited the town with the wives of the two viceroys. Cooked gammons, *crubíns*, dozens of shop loaves freshly baked, Yorkshire relish, sweet cakes and barm bracks had all been safely deposited in the vast kitchen of the Bonner farmhouse and presently the preparations for the most important element of the entire proceedings would be complete. A huge cauldron rested atop the great table. Inside sat four hocks of prime beef and a stone of freshly peeled potatoes. The three females chopped great bundles of carrots and parsnips preparatory to adding them to the cauldron's contents. A stone of onions, hard and mature and of uniform golf-ball size were peeled and quartered and then added. The Bonner soup was always the *pièce de résistance* of the wren-dance and was praised far and wide for its richness and sobering effects. When all the groodles had been added the three women lifted the cauldron between them and bore it to a great fire which burned brightly beneath an iron grid specially designed and wrought by the local smith. The soup would be allowed to boil and simmer for the duration of the wren-dance until all the constituents had disintegrated and become part of the mouth-watering mixture.

'The groodles is what does it,' Billy would proclaim to his cronies as they savoured the first delicious mouthfuls of the much-lauded soup.

'Groodles,' he would go on in his homely way, 'especially parsnips, is the backbone of all soups. As faith without good works is dead so also soup without groodles is dead.'

By eight o'clock in the evening all the guests had arrived. They were carefully vetted by Billy from his vantage point in the doorway of his house and by the great grey tomcat which sat astride the warm chimney on the thatched roof of the rambling farmhouse.

There were fiddlers and melodeon players, saw and *bodhrán* players, didlers and concertina players, comb players and bones' tippers. There were, in fact, all kinds of traditional musicians and exponents of horn-pipe, jig and reel.

In the early part of the night unwanted gate-crashers and known trouble-makers were ejected without ceremony by the king and his faithful subjects. During these minor skirmishes which were quickly quelled several black eyes were sustained and one of the invaders' noses was broken but otherwise the wren-dance was a most harmonious occasion which was enjoyed by all who attended.

Even the intelligence officer for the local Catholic Church, also the part-time parish clerk, in his verbal report to the parish priest spent several minutes describing the character and natural consistency of the soup.

'You would want to brief the housekeeper in that respect,' the parish priest interjected jokingly. Only the clerk knew how serious he was. The parish clerk's report also included an account of the drinking and philandering although truth to tell there was little of the latter and an expected excess of the former. There had been several proposals of marriage but since these came chiefly from octo- and nonagenarians as well as several drunken gentlemen who forgot that they were already married, no great notice was taken. Matters proceeded happily until midnight when the Rosary was said. Not a solitary titter was heard while the holy recital was in progress.

With regard to the serving of the food there was no formal procedure. Buffet rules were loosely applied but there was no evidence of the hogging one associates with such activities at higher levels.

Meanwhile on the outside the contents of the huge cauldron gurgled and spluttered propitiously. From time to time the king of the wrenboys and his queen, the gracious Maggie, inspected the interior and intimated to interested parties that all was going according to expectations.

Now all this happened at a time when motor-cars first began to make their appearance all over the countryside so that the wives of the inexperienced drivers entertained genuine worries about the fitness of their partners to handle the highly deceptive vehicles when under the influence. To counteract the effects of the night's drinking Billy Bonner hit upon the idea of the soup. This was the third year of the innovation. It had proved highly successful. There had been no accidents and no injuries and if drivers ended up in dykes and ditches no great harm was done to the cars' occupants. In part this would have been due to the shallowness of the roadside hazards but it was generally accepted that it was largely due to the reviving concoction so carefully prepared by the wives of the wrenboys.

It was widely believed also that Billy added a secret ingredient to the cauldron during the latter stages of the boiling but whether this was true or not was never really determined. There was, however, on this particular occasion an unexpected addition to the concoction. It was a most fortuitous supplementation and it came about in a most unusual manner.

The top of the cauldron was covered with two flat slabs of bog-deal. These would be removed from time to time to facilitate stirring with a specially rinsed, long-handled coarse brush which Billy and Maggie Bonner used with an expertise that made no concession to the clotting or cloying which is so detrimental to the consistency of all such mixtures.

Now it so happened that the large grey cat which spent most of its time stretching itself and licking its whiskers in the vicinity of the rooftop chimney was possessed of that curious streak which is part and parcel of the feline make-up. As cats go, the grey tom was a respected figure in the countryside. In his younger days he was known to roam far and wide in search of diversion, sometimes disappearing for days at a time. Now well advanced in years he had become more of an ogler than an adventurer and contented himself by maintaining his rooftop vigil during the day and, the occasional romantic saunter apart, hugging the kitchen hearth by night. He found as many tom-cats do when the years mount up that dabbling suits their age and temperament far better than the full-time fornicating in which young toms wantonly indulge.

From early morning on the eventful day he knew that something was afoot. In his younger days he would have made non-stop forays to the kitchen, making a general nuisance of himself and as a result testing the patience of his mistress and her co-workers. Nowadays nothing short of a cat invasion would lure him from the cosy precincts of the chimney when squatted in one of his reveries. Towards evening he betook himself leisurely downwards and did the rounds of his domain. Elderly cats never indulge in the exaggerated slinking or the fancy oscillations to which younger cats are addicted. They tend to slouch and sit. They start to take things for granted and this is always a mistake.

For all his years the grey tom leapt without difficulty on to the bogdeal slabs which covered the cauldron. The contents had not yet begun to simmer but an appetising odour issued upwards nevertheless. He peered between the bogdeal slabs but only darkness greeted his gaze. He sniffed appreciatively and would have sat for a while had not a female flung a wet dish-cloth in his direction advising him at the same time that he should make himself scarce if he knew what was good for him. Unhurriedly he leaped downward and made his way to an outhouse where there was always the outside chance of an encounter with an unwary mouse. The outhouse was empty so he sat for a while preening himself in the shadows. He recalled past encounters with pretty pussies beyond the bounds of Tubbernablaw and nearer home as the passing years confined him. Darkness fell while he sat immobile. With the darkness came a hard frost which decided him on his next move. He would discreetly explore the kitchen and partake of some supper before returning to lie in the lee of the chimney for an hour or two.

Indoors the festivities were at their height. The younger members of The Tubbernablaw Wrenboys' Band circulated on a regular basis with freshly filled buckets of stout drawn from the second half-tierce which had just been broached.

Pannies, mugs and cups as well as glasses, canisters, jam-pots and ewers were pressed into service. Even the grey tomcat was drawn into the revelry. He mewed for more after he had lapped up a partially-filled saucer of stout. He took his time over the second saucer, purring with uncharacteristic abandon as the drink began to take hold. Finishing the saucer he staggered out into the moonlit night. Stars twinkled in every corner of the heavens and a full moon shed its pale light on the cobbled yard where simmered the life-saving soup on its iron grid. The tomcat leaped and landed on the smaller of the bogdeal slabs. He was assailed by giddiness for a moment or two but recovered almost at once and sat himself on the larger of the slabs. He savoured the tantalising odour and held his head over the space between the slabs from where the odour emanated. Finding the larger slab a trifle too hot he removed himself to the smaller and arched himself drunkenly before composing himself catlike for a short sojourn away from the hustle and bustle of the kitchen. For the second time that day he lapsed into a reverie which saw him in his heyday seducing shecats at every hand's turn and devouring fish and fresh liver between bouts of concupiscence. It could truthfully be claimed that there wasn't a happier tomcat in the whole of Tubbernablaw that night.

Then the hand of chance imposed itself on the blissful scene. The sleeping tom felt neither its fingers or its shadow. He slept, impervious to the comings and goings near the house. He did not see the pair of drunken youths who had entered the moon-drenched haggard for no other purpose than to ease the strain on their over-pressed bladders.

When the business was complete they yelled loudly in unison at the unimpressionable moon and, finding that no response was forthcoming from that quarter, looked around for some other form of diversion. It was then they beheld the sleeping cat.

'Look,' said the drunker of the pair, 'at the neck of that cat, sleeping on top of the soup.'

'Let him be,' said the other, 'what harm is he doing?'

'Suppose,' said his companion in an outraged tone, 'that he piddles into the soup or maybe even worse!'

The pair tiptoed noiselessly until they reached the turf rick which dominated the far end of the haggard. Here they located two small black turf sods and, taking aim, dispatched both in the direction of the slumbering tom. The chance of either reaching the target, in any reckoning, must surely attract odds of thirty-three to one. The first of the small but rock-hard missiles veered left and landed harmlessly on the farmyard dung-heap. The second sped unerringly towards the victim as it raised its head, instinctively alerted by a sixth sense. It was, alas, too late. The sod landed on the crown of its head and laid it senseless. It slumped and then slid between the bogdeal slabs. It subsided without a miaow into the simmering soup.

The buck who pelted the fatal sod turned at once and rejoined the revels in the kitchen. He salved his conscience by making the sign of the cross and spitting over his left shoulder. Wisely, he and his friend decided to keep the story of the tomcat's demise to themselves. Why waste a perfectly good barrel of soup, give or take a cat!

Such were the philosophies that were in the air at that time and in that place. A cat could be replaced in due course but a cauldron of soup, in the circumstances, could not. In the kitchen the revelry went on unabated until dawn. Then at eight forty-five in the morning Billy Bonner stood on a chair and announced that it was time to bring the proceedings to a close. The announcement was made seven hours and fourteen minutes after the demise of the family cat. At first there were some minor protestations but common sense soon prevailed especially when the head of the house reminded his listeners that the soup was ready and would be served forthwith, that it would be served under the wide and starry sky and that those who were interested should proceed without delay into the night bringing with them whatever vessels were at hand. There was an immediate exit. Mugs, cups and canisters were waved aloft as the delighted revellers cheered with all their might in anticipation of the incomparable composition which awaited them.

There were gasps and cheers and screams and diverse exclamations of delight as cup after mug after canister of soup was consumed. The steam from hundreds of mouths, nostrils and receptacles ascended the frosty air while from the cauldron itself there issued a perpendicular column which disappeared into the heavens overhead and tempted the moon herself to indulge in an unprecedented descent from her starry climes.

Standing to one side in the shadows were the youths who had so unceremoniously dispatched the cat to the hereafter. They hugged their sides with glee as they eagerly awaited the convulsions and upheavals which they felt must inevitably assail the soup drinkers of Tubbernablaw and its hinterland. They waited but all that transpired, as the time passed and the morning brightened, was a clamorous demand from all present for more soup. As things turned out there was plenty for everybody.

When the cauldron was drained of its last drop Billy Bonner and a retainer spilled out the bare bones that remained on to the frozen ground. The cat-killers edged forward but before they could draw a solitary person's attention to the fact that they had all partaken of cat soup and that the evidence was there to prove it the three household dogs, a red setter, a suspect Collie and a retired coursing greyhound had fled the scene with mouthfuls of bones ranging from the head of the grey tomcat to the denuded hock bones of bullock and heifer. They would return almost at once to recover the few lesser bones that remained and add them to the others secreted where none but themselves would find them.

Search as they might, the disgruntled cat-killers failed to find a trace of their victim.

Nothing remained, not an eye nor a tooth nor a single, solitary cat's whisker nor any evidence whatsoever of any one of the nine lives which are the God-given right of all cats great and small.

The Great Christmas Raid at Ballybooley

It all happened back in 1920 when those heinous wretches known as the Black and Tans were hell-bent on maiming, murdering and all forms of diabolical destruction and showing themselves to be true credits to the calabooses from which they had been released in order to serve their country and shoot innocent Irish people.

No day passed without some skirmish or other between the dreaded invaders and the brave boys of the North Kerry Flying Column. The more notable of these encounters are suitably remembered in song and story but none more so than the great Christmas raid at Ballybooley. True, this singular event has its controversial side but in this respect it must be said that no two accounts of any battle are similar in every detail.

The year in question produced one of the driest summers ever recorded. The hills, in fact, turned brown. On the turf banks the sods dried of their own accord which was a blessing indeed to youthful turf-turners and stoolin-makers who were free to spend the long summer days by river and stream or lazing in carefree groups in woodland and meadow.

Nobody, however, can put forward the claim that Mother Nature spreads her output indiscriminately and as though to prove this point beyond doubt she presented the North Kerry countryside with a succeeding Christmas of unprecedented bitterness and savagery.

Hail, rain and snow were commonplace whilst, in between, Jack Frost worked overtime. The tinder-dry turf of the summer made no battle in the gusty hearths of cottage and farmhouse and people were wont to say, not for the first time, that if there was anything worse than turf that was too wet then surely it was turf that was too dry. Many of the roadside reeks were consumed before Christmas. Rusty saws and axes were resurrected for the felling of timber. Fuel theft grew rife as the winter wore on.

In all the bogland area perhaps the most practised lifter of the unguarded sod was a man by the name of Micky Dooley. He was well known to all and sundry as a professional turf thief. All through November and December when the moon shone fitfully, if at all, he would betake himself with ass and rail to a convenient bog, there to ply his shifty trade.

Under cover of darkness he would fill his rail from ill-made reeks whose appearances would not be affected by the disappearance of an ass-rail of turf. It was different with well-made reeks. A solitary sod out of place and the owner was immediately alerted.

A well-made reek was a match for anything be it thunder, gale or turf thief. Each sod was so close to the next and each corner so smoothed and well constructed that even the absence of a single cadhrawn would be easily detected. Consequently turf thieves shied away from well-made structures and concentrated on the badly-made, misshapen ones. It was to these latter on the dark and stormy nights around Christmas that Micky Dooley directed his ass and cart. His target, of course, would have been thoroughly reconnoitred beforehand. One might see him sauntering casually in the distance, his head averted from roadside reeks, his gaze fixed steadfastly in front of him as though reek-rape was the farthest thought from his mind. Yet without once inclining his head or slowing his gait he absorbed every detail of his night-time objective.

His attention might seem to be fixed on a flock of wheeling plover in the skies overhead or rapt in admiration at a particular rampart of cloud but all the while he stored detail after vital detail for future reference.

He would have to discover in the little time available to him if there was room for donkey and cart at the bogland side of the reek or if the reek had already been gutted by storm and above all to determine the quality of the turf. It was essential that it resemble in texture, size and shape the inadequate supply he had harvested for his own use in case a suspicious reek owner decided to investigate.

When his rail was filled he would skilfully rearrange the area which he had plundered so that it was always next to impossible to detect the loss. This was an art in itself. His efforts were always constricted by the absence of light. As a result he worked like a man demented whenever a ray of moonlight filtered through the flying clouds. Moonlight is the natural enemy of the night-raider but he needs a little now and then to be going on with.

Largely, however, Micky worked by the feel, waiting for a token of moonlight to add the finishing touches. He never took more than one rail from any reek and this was the real secret of his success. Suspect he might be but there was no proof and so long as he confined his looting to reasonable quantities his thieving excursions were taken for granted.

Those whose reeks escaped molestation were fond of saying it was a poor bog indeed that couldn't support a solitary turf thief.

Then came a fearful night shortly before Christmas. The north-eastern gales bore down the sky furiously whipping and flailing the already tormented countryside. Sitting by his fire Micky decided that it was an excellent night for an enterprising fellow like himself. Reluctant though he was to forsake his warm hearth the night was heaven-sent for his purpose.

Nobody in his right mind, a turf-thief apart, would venture abroad under such conditions and who was to say but the weather might take a dramatic turn for the better and so curtail his outdoor activities when they might most be needed. He resolved to venture forth.

He tackled the unwilling donkey to the ancient cart, assembled the rail thereon and, to ensure silence, liberally plastered the axle screw-nuts with car grease. He bound himself thoroughly against the elements and set forth on his journey.

A worse night he had never experienced. Within minutes his gloved hands were freezing, the fingers stripped of circulation. He closed his eyes against the storm and blindly followed the donkey. He would have turned back after the first quarter mile but he reminded himself sensibly that after a storm comes a calm and since his turf stocks were almost exhausted he simply had to make the most of his opportunity.

Slowly, patiently, man and beast battled against the savage blasts until both were on the threshold of exhaustion. At length they arrived at the bog lane where the several remaining reeks stood awaiting the inevitable. As they reached the first of these, one which he had rifled a bare fortnight before, the donkey stopped dead and despite all Micky's urgings refused to proceed against the gale-force wind. Micky knew that the poor animal had reached the end of its tether. There was nothing for it but to turn round and proceed homewards. At least they would have the wind behind them. He backed the donkey into the lee of the reek. There it would regain its wind for the return journey. As he waited, in the bitter cold, the combination of temptation and habit proved too much for Micky Dooley.

'All I'll take is a few sods,' he told himself, 'for since I have raided this reek before, to take any more would be folly.'

Alas his rapacious instincts prevailed and in no time at all he had the rail filled and clamped.

The days passed with no abatement in the weather. Soon the rightful owner of the turf put in an appearance with a horse and cart and proceeded to fill his rail. The first thing he noticed, upon his arrival, was a sizable declivity at the reek's rear. A grim smile appeared on his weather-beaten face. This merely proved to be the prelude to the heartiest of laughs and, this in turn was followed by a gleeful shout and a rubbing together of the palms of the hands.

For several moments he cavorted delightedly around the roadway. For long he had suspected Micky Dooley. He estimated that over the years the turf thief had relieved him of twenty ass-rails at the very least. When, a few weeks before, he visited the reek his suspicions had been aroused upon beholding a small mound of fresh donkey dung close by the reek. A sure sign, this, that a donkey had dallied there.

Carefully he had inspected the reek but could find no sign of interference. This did not surprise him in the least as it was not Micky Dooley's wont to leave evidence of his visits.

The proprietor of the reek was forced to concede that Micky was without peer in the art of restructuring turf reeks. He would have dearly loved to lay hands on him there and then if for no other purpose than to strangle him.

As he filled his rail he considered ways and means of snaring the thief. Suddenly an inspired albeit murderous notion struck him. Frequently he played host to men on the run and sometimes they concealed their guns and ammunition on his property. That night he revisited his reek, his pockets filled with live ammunition. With the utmost care he inserted a score of bullets in the softer of those sods which occupied the weakest corner of the reek. Now a fortnight later he congratulated himself on his foresight. He had gambled that the thief would pay a second visit because of the severity of the weather and he had won. That night in bed he conveyed the tidings to his wife.

'I have prepared,' he said, 'a terrific Christmas gift for Micky Dooley. It's a gift he'll never forget till the day he dies and I have to say that no man deserves it more.'

He then told her about the live ammunition embedded in the sods.

'Oh sweet Mary Immaculate,' his wife cried out clutching her rosary beads, 'suppose someone is struck by a bullet.'

'I don't care,' said her husband, 'if the hoor is blown to Kingdom Come. He'll never steal another sod from me one way or the other.'

Chuckling to himself he turned over on his side and slept the sleep of the just. His wife prayed into the small hours faithfully accompanied by the sonorous snores of her husband. She beseeched every saint with every prayer in her repertoire that no harm would befall the household of Micky Dooley.

Less than a week later, on Christmas Eve to be exact, Micky was seated in front of a roaring fire with his wife and children and a neighbour who had called to exchange titbits of gossip in return for basking cold shins before the glowing sods. Outside the wind howled and hissed whilst hordes of unruly hailstones hopped and danced on road and roof.

'God bless us,' said the female neighbour, by name Maggie Mulloy, 'isn't a good fire the finest thing of all.'

'True for you Maggie,' her host responded. 'I wouldn't swap a good fire for a bottle of whiskey.'

There they sat, happily contemplating the leaping flames, savouring the warmth and comfort of the hearthside. A happier scene could not be imagined. A black buck cat, fat and sleek, sat at his master's feet while the children intoned their rhymes in a drowsy hum that added to the somnolent atmosphere of the fireside scene.

'Thanks be to God for a turf fire,' Maggie Mulloy said under her breath and then in a louder tone, 'and thanks to them that has the heart and the nature to share that same.'

Micky accepted the compliment as befitted such a magnanimous benefactor.

'Tut-tut,' he said dismissively, 'tut-tut.'

The cat purred, the women nodded and Micky reached forward a foot to restore a wayward sod which had fallen too far from the fire. The sparks shot upwards in a bright display which boasted every conceivable shade of red. Then suddenly all hell broke loose. The first bullet smashed into the paraffin lamp which hung by a chain from a central rafter between two flitches of yellowing bacon. There followed immediately a minor explosion after which the light went out.

The second bullet smashed into the dresser and shook it to its foundations as well as sending saucers, cups and ware of all sorts flying about the kitchen. The third bullet went straight between the two eyes of the cat. Without as much as a mew he stiffened and expired where he lay, a taunting parody of the nine lives supposed to be his right.

For several seconds after the first shot Micky Dooley remained rooted to his chair, unable to move. His mouth opened and closed but no sound emanated therefrom. He was shocked to his very core. A bullet whistling past his ear brought a sudden end to his inactivity. Ignoring the cries of the women and children he bolted for the bedroom where he barricaded the door behind him and dived straightaway under the bed.

He shut out the appalling din in the kitchen by the simple expedient of thrusting a finger into either ear. His heart raced so violently that he feared for its continued beating. No heart, he felt, could continue at such a pace without coming to a sudden and untimely halt. Trembling, he invoked the aid of his dead mother after which he loudly beseeched the Sacred Heart to succour him in his final agony.

In the kitchen there was absolute bedlam. The screams were deafening. Neighbours, near and far, were brought to their doors by the mixture of shots and cries of human torment.

''Tis the Black and Tans,' one terrified listener called out. 'There's a battle on in Ballybooley.'

His cry was quickly taken up and in jig time every door and window in the district was barricaded. Lights were doused and Rosaries recited. Holy water was sprinkled here, there and everywhere.

Meanwhile back at the Dooley kitchen three more bullets went off. The first of these passed through the window. The other two ricocheted up the chimney and spent themselves harmlessly on the night air. Mercifully none of the kitchen's occupants was injured. A sustained silence ensued but a longer period was to pass before Micky Dooley opened the bedroom door. At that precise moment the last bullet exploded from the fire and pierced the upper of his left boot. It lodged in his instep. He fell to the floor, a cry of anguish on his lips.

'They got me,' he screamed.

His wife and children knelt by his side while Maggie Mulloy breathed an Act of Contrition into his ear. After a while, when it was clear that the shooting had ended, they lifted him onto a chair where he sat with the injured leg resting on another chair. Maggie, who lived less than a stone's throw away, had gone and returned in a thrice with a noggin of whiskey. Micky disposed of it without assistance. The eldest of the children was dispatched to a neighbour's house with the curt instructions that a doctor and priest were to be contacted at once.

Outside the wind had abated and soon neighbours from every house within a two-mile radius converged upon the house. The same question formed on the lips of every last one of them. What had happened?

'We were ambushed,' Micky Dooley explained.

'But why?' the communal question came.

The wounded man shook his head knowingly and brought a silencing finger to his lips indicating that there was more involved here than met the eye.

'We were ambushed,' he exclaimed to every newcomer.

'By whom?' the question came automatically on the heels of the others.

'Tans,' was Micky's immediate response. He kept repeating the word embellishing it every so often with choice adjectives. Eventually and inevitably the man who had planted the bullets arrived upon the scene. Tentatively he thrust his head inside the door.

'Black and Tans,' Micky disembarrassed him before he had a chance to apologise and spoil the entire proceedings. The bullet-planter nodded vigorously, relieved beyond measure that no one had been killed. As it was, if the truth were to become known, the least for which he would be held accountable would be attempted murder.

'Tans it was,' he confirmed. 'Didn't I see them with my own two eyes and they making off down the road.'

Micky Dooley bent his head in gratitude and relief. It was only then that he noticed the dead cat. He lifted the stiffening form to his lips and kissed it on top of the head which was a change indeed for the only other part of the creature's anatomy with which he had any previous contact was its posterior whenever he applied one of his hobnailed boots to that sensitive area for no reason whatsoever.

'My poor cat,' he called out while his eyes calefacted huge tears to suit the occasion. One by one the neighbours departed, arguing heatedly as to why such a savage attack had been made on a household which had no apparent connection with the Freedom Fighters.

They came to the only conclusions possible. The Tans had been seen by a reliable witness. They were, therefore, responsible for the attack. They would not have carried out the attack unless Micky Dooley was a dispatch carrier or was in the habit of secretly harbouring the men on the run.

Apart from Micky only one man knew the truth and that man's lips were sealed. It was that or subject himself to the possibility of a stiff prison sentence. There was no point in taking such a gamble. One thing was certain. Micky Dooley would never interfere with one of his reeks again. Others yes but not his. That had been the primary point of the exercise.

Time passed and word of the raid spread. The account was handsomely embroidered with the passage of the years so that, in the end, it transpired that Micky had single-handed, armed only with a double-barrelled shotgun, routed a score of Black and Tans killing none but wounding several while he himself would be a martyr to a pronounced limp for the remainder of his life. His neighbour Maggie Mulloy came to be revered throughout the countryside. Had she not fought by her neighbour's side? None begrudged her the paltry state pension and service medals which a grateful government had conferred on all those who had participated in the Fight for Freedom.

Micky Dooley fared better. Because of his limp he was awarded, in addition to his service pension, a handsome disability allowance which left him secure for the remainder of his days.

Maggie Mulloy eventually came to believe her own story. Without doubt, on a gusty winter's night under a fitful moon, shadows may be easily transformed into human shapes. No great effort is afterwards required to deck them in uniforms. Far from abandoning his old ways Micky Dooley redoubled his raids upon vulnerable turf ricks. Now he stole with impunity. Wasn't it his right he told himself. Didn't he single-handed defeat a company of Black and Tans! By God if he wasn't entitled to a few sods of somebody else's turf who was! Wasn't he one of the two surviving heroes of the Battle of Ballybooley. The bullet-planter would never mention the Christmas gift again, not even to this wife.

From time to time strangers visited Mickey Dooley's house to inspect the holes left by the bullets and to view the almost fatal wound upon his instep. Veneration was also paid to the memory of the cat whose life was ended so tragically in the service of its master. As Micky Dooley used to say when reminded of the creature's demise: 'Greater love no cat hath than the cat who lays down his life for his friends.'

The Magic Stoolin

I was tempted for a while to call this story *A Christmas Barrel.* Everybody, I told myself, has heard of *A Christmas Carol* so why not *A Christmas Barrel.* My wife thought the title too stereotyped when I submitted it for her approval. It was then I thought of *The Magic Stoolin* and, if you care to continue, you will see why.

Times were never worse in the bogland of Booleenablawha. On the run-up to Christmas the county council had reluctantly suspended all roadwork and there was no likelihood it would resume before spring.

Of all the seven families surviving on the bog road, Jack Tobin's was the hardest hit. The others had grown-up sons and daughters working in England and America but the eldest of Jack's *cúram* was only ten and the youngest still in swaddling clothes.

There was some consolation to be drawn from the fact that there would be plenty to eat over the twelve days of Christmas. Jack had seen to that. He had disposed of ten stoolins of dry turf in the nearby town. Each stoolin was the equivalent of a clamped horse rail and each had fetched a pound in the market place. Twelve stoolins remained in the bog, impervious, because of their perfectly tapering design and solid structure, to the rain, sleet and hail which would bombard them until the advent of May.

Jack might have disposed of three or four more and thus provided himself with the wherewithal for Christmas drink but this would mean sparser fires providing the winter wind with the openings it needed to freeze the toes and chill the blood. With Jack and his wife Monnie the children always came first.

'If we pinch and pare,' Monnie had whispered as they lay on the feather bed two weeks before Christmas, 'we might rise to a dozen of stout and a half-bottle of whiskey and maybe a few minerals for the children. There's three bottles of cheap sherry left after the wake and that will do the women.'

Jack's father had expired the previous summer from nothing worse than simple senility and the subsequent wake had made massive inroads into their insubstantial savings. The couple's concern with the drink stocks did not stem in any way from their own desires for intoxicating liquor although Jack could never be charged with missing a Sunday night at the crossroads pub. Monnie would truthfully declare that drink never troubled her. The problem arose because of an age-old custom whereby each of the seven houses in Booleenablawha hosted in turn, over the Yuletide period, a modest reception for the other six.

It wasn't that the hostesses vied with each other or that drinking was excessive but it had never been known, even in the blackest of black times, that a household had run out of drink. No other hostings, apart from wakes, weddings and wren-dances, could possibly be countenanced in the hard-pressed community at any other time of year.

If the neighbours but knew of Jack's position they would have cheerfully brought a sufficiency of drink with them but this was the last thing Jack and Monnie wanted. Jack also knew that he might borrow a pound or two from a friend or that he might secure credit at the crossroads where he was known but this wasn't his way either.

The pucker would remain unsolved until the week before Christmas. The morning rain had cleared and a fresh breeze rustled in the roadside alders. Jack Tobin went among his stoolins carefully selecting the drier, darker sods for his Christmas fires. A past master in the high art of stoolin rearrangment, Jack's turf castles, as his children called them, would not disintegrate under the buffeting winds and driving rains.

As he slowly filled his ass-cart he was surprised to see the heavily laden lorry making its way over the narrow, bumpy bog-way. Jack waved at the driver and the driver waved back. Then the lorry passed by, its precious cargo of wooden porter casks swaying dangerously because of the uneven contours of the quaking road.

The man who had waved at him, Jack felt, would be a relief driver hired temporarily for the busy Christmas period who would be unfamiliar with the terrain. Otherwise he would not have departed from the main road and chosen a shorter but far more hazardous itinerary. Then it happened! There was, a hundred yards further down the road, a hump-back bridge, covered with ivy and ancient as the road itself. A cannier driver would have slowed down. As the lorry passed over, its body was suspended for a brief while when the cab dipped on the downward side. As the airborne back wheels struck the roadway a barrel leaped upward and outward and fell onto the soft margin, rolling backwards until its progress was arrested by a sally clump. Jack Tobin immediately abandoned his labours and ran towards the roadway, furiously waving and calling out at the top of his voice in a vain effort to attract the driver's attention. Then the lorry was gone. Jack Tobin found himself confronted with an untapped half-tierce of approved porter.

A half-tierce, as every wrenboy knows, contains one hundred and twenty-eight pints of dun-dark, drinkable, delight-inducing porter, porter so profuse that the drinking folk of Booleenablawha would be hard put to consume it in the round of a single night. Jack Tobin stood without moving for several minutes. There was much to be resolved. Meanwhile he would roll the barrel deeper into the sally clump lest it attract the attention of passing vagabonds and heaven knows what fate.

That night as they sat by the dying fire, with the children sound asleep in their beds, Jack informed his wife for the first time of the day's happenings and the location of the sally-girt windfall.

Monnie Tobin lifted the tongs and discovered a number of small bright coals hidden in the ashes.

After she had rearranged the fire she pointed the tongs at her spouse in order to lend emphasis to her assessment of the situation.

'First thing in the morning of Christmas Eve,' she said, 'you will cycle to town and take yourself into McFee's the wholesalers. Find out if they're missing a half-tierce of porter. If they are, the barrel will be returned. If not, we'll see.'

They spoke long into the night concerning the state of the family finances but despite all her economic wizardry, all her penny-pinching and self-sacrifice, there was no obvious way the situation could be improved.

Despite the most assiduous of searches the clerical staff at McFee's could find no record of a missing barrel. No complaint had been filed by a shortchanged customer and the stock in their storehouse tallied accurately with the advice notes.

'Why?' asked the firm's chargehand with a laugh, 'is it how you found a barrel?'

'No,' came the instant reply. 'It's just that there was a rumour going the rounds.'

Later, as night was falling on the boglands of Booleenablawha, Jack and Monnie Tobin announced to the children that they were taking a stroll. When they returned there would be a distribution of lemonade and biscuits to celebrate Christmas.

Out of doors a crisp breeze blew steadily from the south-west. Overhead a full moon shed its pale light on the rustling boglands. Now and then passing clouds obscured its rays. It proved to be an ideal night for what Jack and Monnie had in mind.

At the sally clump where lay hidden the prized half-tierce they paused and awaited one of the night's darker spells. Even then they maintained a vigil for several moments. Then when the darkness was at its most impenetrable Jack rolled the barrel from its place of concealment and, aided by his partner, pushed it slowly to where a narrow passage led on to the turf-bank where stood the twelve unassailable stoolins.

Inside the wooden cask the porter chuckled and gurgled tantalisingly. After a few moments the interior noises stopped. Jack Tobin rightly surmised that the rolling movements had brought a head to the barrel's contents. His mouth watered at the prospect of savouring the first mouthful of the cherished brew.

He had not come unprepared. In his pocket was a brass tap, a relict from numerous wakes. Earlier he had deposited a hastily hewed wooden mallet at the blind side of a specially chosen stoolin. The mallet would serve nicely to drive the tap home when the barrel was in place. Jack had the additional foresight to bring along a brace and bit together with a tapering wooden spike which would be used to plug the bung-hole made by the former in order to facilitate an expeditious flow from the tap.

Jack's special skills and foresight with regard to regulating the condition and the drawing of porter came from long experience. In addition to the annual wren-dances which flourished throughout the region there were countless wakes where several porter barrels might be on flow at the same time. Consequently there were few houses in the countryside without some sort of porter tap and a brace and bit.

As in all trades there were the highly skilled and the botchers. With so much hinging on a successful outcome it would have been unthinkable to entrust the tapping of a full barrel containing such an irreplaceable commodity to an incompetent! Only the practised and the proven were elected to take charge of such a momentous undertaking. Jack Tobin was one of these.

On their arrival at the stoolin he quickly removed two-thirds of the upper body. Then with a mighty effort he lifted the half-tierce and laid it horizontally on the carefully structured base. Without hurry he bedded it firmly, but lovingly, so that it would lie still during the tapping. One, two, three rapid, accurate, beautifully timed strokes and the tap was firmly embedded in the barrel.

Without undue haste Jack Tobin remade the stoolin all around the recumbent cask. The demands of this difficult task brought out the artist in him. True, he was aided by a full moon but it is the touch as much as the perception that makes the difference between a great stoolin-maker and an indifferent one.

Smearing a liberal handful of turf mould over the exposed tap he extracted a tin pannikin from his coat pocket. Now would come the acid test. Those in the countryside who were partial to porter, and they were many, would quite rightly aver that every content of every barrel tasted differently. Some were too highly conditioned and some were too flat. Some carried a bitter tang whilst, worst of all, others were casky and decidedly unpalatable. Casky barrels were rare and were always replaced by the brewing house. Unfortunately, because of the nature of its acquisition, no such redress would be available to Jack Tobin if the lost barrel was tainted.

He looked upward first at his heavenly ally, still free of cloud and undisputed queen of the heavens. What if the barrel was filled with water or with cleansing fluid! Holding the pannikin under the spout he turned on the tap. A powerful jet of sweetly smelling porter foam knocked the pannikin from his hand. Quickly he turned off the tap and reclaimed the pannikin.

At his second attempt he only partially turned on the tap. The diminished outflow, still powerful, smote merrily against the bottom of the pannikin so that Jack was obliged to slant the shallow vessel in order to avoid a spillage. When the pannikin was filled he allowed it to rest atop the stoolin so that the froth might subside and the porter proper accumulate beneath. When he judged the time to be ripe he handed the pannikin to his wife. First she tasted and then, delighted by the first impressions, swallowed heartily, declaring when the pannikin was drained that she had never tasted the likes in all her days.

'It's like cream,' she announced, wiping her lips, 'only nicer.'

After several pannikins each they recovered their possessions and, hand in hand, returned homewards, their happy way benignly lighted by the liberal moon.

'Did you ever taste the likes of it?' Monnie Tobin asked as they neared home.

'Never!' Jack assented as he squeezed her hand and placed a frothy kiss on her upturned lips, frothy too. That night, full of porter-induced, seasonal mansuetude, Jack and Monnie Tobin sang the gentle songs of their youth for their delighted children.

Time passed until all that remained of the twelve days of Christmas were two. It was the night the Tobins played host to their neighbours all. Never was there such a night. Every half-hour or so Jack Tobin would disappear, through his back door, bearing two small milking buckets. In a matter of minutes he would be back again with two buckets brimful of the most nourishing, the most savoury, the most flavoursome porter ever consumed in that part of the world, or so the neighbours said.

Naturally they questioned its origin when it loosened their tongues. Jack informed them that it had come from the city of Limerick through the good offices of a calf jobber who was partially indebted to him for having extended credit to him earlier in the year.

And how had he transported it was the next question tabled? Oh by milk churn of course and had not Jack carefully transferred it from the jobber's churn to his own where it had, slowly but surely, acquired the immaculate condition which set it apart from the less exhilarating porter of former years! More evidence, however, was required by the discerning elders of Booleenablawha and, indeed, more evidence was forthcoming.

'And pray!' asked Jack's immediate neighbour, a man with an insatiable appetite for information, regardless of its veracity, 'could you tell us the name of the tavern where this porter was purchased?'

The question caught Jack unawares. There was also the lamentable fact that he did not know the name of a solitary tavern in the city of Limerick for the good reason that he had never been there.

'The name of the tavern you say!' He pretended to ponder.

It was his wife who came to his aid.

'The name of the tavern,' said Monnie Tobin, without batting an eyelid, 'is the Magic Stoolin.'

'The Magic Stoolin!' the neighbour repeated, 'sure don't I know well where it is.'

The last thing the poor fellow wanted to profess was ignorance of this well-known watering place which was surely known to man, woman and child in the city of Limerick and other places besides.

As it turned out the Magic Stoolin was known to several other accomplished liars in the gathering who had never been to Limerick either and also to their womenfolk who were in the habit of supporting them, without question, in all manner of spurious claims and submissions over the years.

From such unfailing corroborations are lasting marriages nurtured, are peace and probity maintained within the family and are Christmases revered and relished in the simple homesteads of Booleenablawha.

THE ORDER OF MACMOOLAMAWN

The wren, the wren, the king of all birds
On St Stephen's Day he was caught in the furze
Although he was little his family was great
Rise up landlady and give us a treat.

For those who found Christmas Day a trifle stifling St Stephen's Day or Boxing Day came as a boon to the residents of the town. There were some who simply called it Wrenboys' Day for the very good reason that from morning onwards until the public houses closed that night the wre-boys of the rustic hinterland converged on the streets and square. They came singly, in pairs, in small groups and great bands, bringing with them their songs and dances immemorial to gladden the heart and disperse the post-Christmas queasiness. They came in traditional costume of calico with tinsel-bedecked, peaked caps and a wide range of musical instruments, most notable of which was the goat-skin *bodhrán*.

They played, sang and danced their merry way by highway and byway until their cashiers and captains decided that sufficient monies had been gathered to cover the cost of the annual wren-dance which would be held in early January.

Those wrenboys and, indeed, wrengirls who chose to travel singly and in pairs retained the spoils for their own uses and benefits. Some used them to discharge outstanding debts while more availed of the windfalls to buy boots or shoes for themselves and their offspring. The remainder which represented the majority drank their fill without let-up until the proceeds had vanished. None, not even the virtuous, pointed the finger of denunciation at the profligates who might have spent their earnings more profitably for, in that place and in that time, life was often tedious and diversions few.

Our tale concerns two elderly wrenboys who were martyrs to the annual squandermania aforementioned. The years, as is the wont of years, had taken their toll on the pair and although the vigour had departed their steps they resolutely refused to submit themselves to infirmity. Both have now passed on to that happy clime where the gentle drumming of goat-skin *bodhrán*s forever assails the ear and wren-dances are celebrated on a non-stop basis. This would be their concept of heaven and why not! Hath not the Lord said 'In my father's house there are many mansions'. Then it must be remembered that life itself isn't exactly a wren-dance so that men may dream of the everlasting one.

Anyway, there they were, our intrepid friends away, away back in 1939 as drunk as two brewery rats on the very evening of Christmas Day. All around them the other illicit public house patrons spoke in rich whispers about the vagaries of life and the ultimate futility of excessive thrift, about wren-dances past and wren-dances to come and, in between, about brotherly love. They toasted friendship and loyalty and they clinked their glasses gently, vowing that they would surely meet again in the same venue at the same time on every succeeding year until they were called to another place. All they craved was that it be half as good as the present one.

Outside on the streets the forces of law and order paused in their perambulations outside the frontages of suspect public houses and listened intently or pretended to listen intently and then, satisfying themselves that no intoxicating drink was being served within, proceeded on their majestic way without the batting of an eyelid or the breaking of a step.

In those days there was in every town and village a public house or even two which would always remain open on Christmas Day. The publicans in question, otherwise above reproach, would proffer the excuse that they could not bear to see so many downcast souls suffering from untreated hangovers wandering the streets and laneways without hope of recovery. Out of the goodness of their hearts and nothing more these soft-centred public house proprietors would discreetly admit the needy and the suffering provided they were versed in the secret knock and had the price of the drink.

Our two elderly friends sat quietly in the darkest corner of the bar drinking their half-pints of stout and occasional nips of whiskey. In low tones they plotted the following day's itinerary. If their wren-day peregrinations were to be successful it was imperative that the route they would eventually settle on should be kept secret; hence their isolation and their inaudible murmurings. To be first on the scene was imperative if they were to extract the maximum dues which might quite easily amount to a shilling or even more whereas late arrivals might expect only pence and half-pence and sometimes nothing at all in houses where numerous bands of wrenboys would have already called. All the loose change, so carefully saved for the occasion, would have been expended. Timing, therefore, was of the utmost importance, timing and pacing, the latter meaning that only a limited amount of strong drink should be consumed so that drunkenness be kept at bay at least until the wrenboy itinerary had been completed. Then they would be free to relax in any pub of their choosing for as long as they wished.

For the final time they went over the carefully laid plans. They proposed to start in the morning, a full hour before first light, to daub their faces, one with black boot polish and the other, for contrast, with brown, then to don their calico suits and caps and finally to shoulder the embroidered green sashes which placed them a cut above the orthodox and the pedestrian. Each would carry an extra pair of shoes or boots strung around the waist to ensure dry and comfortable travel over the twenty miles of town and countryside which they had made their own over two generations. There would be no intoxicating drink until the first half of the journey had been completed but they would breakfast well. They would wrap their instruments in strips of discarded table coverings made from moisture-resisting oil-cloth. The *bodhrán* and the concertina need not be utilised, in the event of rain storms, until they found themselves indoors or sheltered by the tall houses of the town. If the weather remained fine they would lighten their journey with lively march tunes. The *bodhrán* and concertina, always an agreeable and harmonious combination, carried afar to the more isolated homes of the countryside so that the inhabitants thereof would have no trouble identifying the approaching wrenboys and have the appropriate contribution ready. Their plans finalised they sat back on their seats and, being somewhat incapacitated by the mixture of exhaustion, age and liquor, dozed fitfully until a kind neighbour alerted them before closing time and volunteered a lift home in his horse and rail. Both had earlier agreed to spend the night at the abode of the bachelor member of the duo to facilitate early travel. It would not have been the first time that the pair had spent the night together. On special occasions when the intake of drink far exceeded moderation the married member wisely decided to avoid a confrontation with his querulous spouse. Also there was the fact that the same spouse always exercised a poorly concealed antipathy towards her husband's best friend on the rare occasions when he chose to call to the house on some business or other. Hence her husband's willingness to accept his friend's offer to spend the night. The long hours passed blissfully and from time to time the friends would arise from their comfortable feather beds and sup from the fine stock of beer, wine and spirits which the carefree bachelor had the foresight to install under his own bed and the bed of his friend.

When one would awake at whatever the hour he made sure not to neglect his companion. There would be a tap on the shoulder and a bottle pressed to the lips of the party abed. Before returning to a trouble-free sleep they would sing and reminisce for short periods and then signify with deep, satisfying snores that nature was taking its course.

Then after a particularly long period of sleep both woke at the same time.

'Is that a thrush I hear or is it a blackbird?' the bachelor asked.

'It would seem to me like a blackbird,' came the drowsy response and with that both arose. Only then did they draw the curtains and peer into the darkness of the winter morning. Sure enough, birds everywhere were tuning up for the morning chorus as the darkness began to lighten. Opening the back door of the tiny abode the bachelor cast the waters of the night into a rivulet which flowed cheerily by. Afterwards he peered at the mantelpiece clock in the kitchen and was pleased to see that it still wanted twenty minutes for nine o'clock. He blew on his hands and lighted the bogdeal fire which had been specially set before his excursion to the town on Christmas Day. He applied a lighted match and at once there was a flame of many colours. Swinging the crane around he positioned the bottom of the black kettle above the leaping blaze. Both proceeded with the setting of the table and in this respect their needs were few. In those days side plates were often regarded as the emblems of upstarts and the large tea mugs were never designed to sit comfortably in a saucer. Egg stands were placed at either side of the table in readiness for the two brace of boiled duck eggs which had been lowered in a ladling spoon into the churning bowels of the kettle from the very moment that the first jets of steam came whistling from its spout. Ravenously and speedily they devoured the four boiled duck eggs and with them several mugs of strong tea as well as their fill of bread, butter and jam. It was, after all, Christmas and they were well entitled to jam in addition to the butter. Sated with this sustaining fare they drew on their calico suits and caps. Each placed the traditional sash around the shoulder of the other and applied the facial polish, brown and black. Then they sat for a while humming and didling to themselves as they sorted out their respective repertoires. Then came the first notes of the day and sweet they were, sweet as wild honey the bachelor *bodhrán* player was quick to admit. 'I declare to God,' said he, 'but that oul' doodle box grows sweeter by the year.' The rehearsal ended, they sloped out into the mild morning. From every bower and bush, bare and all that they were, came the songs and chirpings of a hundred birds. The pair would be cheered along their way by the contributions of thousands more, all eager and willing to extol the benevolent morning.

'We are indeed blessed with the day,' said the bachelor.

'God be praised,' said his friend.

'It could be teeming rain!'

'Or riddled with hail.'

'Or that awful sleet. How would you like that?'

'I wouldn't like it at all,' came the reply. With that the *bodhrán* player struck his drum in thanksgiving and for good measure the concertina launched into a series of rousing marches which would carry them as far as the town's outskirts. No happier pair ever trod the wintry road. No musicians ever revelled more in their vibrant renderings. No marchers ever tripped so lightly despite their ponderous years and no hearts ever beat so hopefully for by all the laws there were good times ahead and better times to follow.

'We're the first thank God,' said one to the other when he saw that no other wrenboy or band of wrenboys had preceded them to the rich, early pickings of suburbia. They decided to serenade the occupants of the imposing edifices at either side of the roadway with tunes of a romantic nature. Having provided a pleasing if short succession of same they waited for the doors to open. They looked upward as they had done for so many years expecting the bedroom windows to be opened and the coins to come cascading down. They were truly perplexed when nothing happened.

'Better knock 'em up and get 'em out of it.' The *bodhrán* player smote upon his goat-skin drum with clenched fist until the instrument trembled and boomed. The sound would carry through the empty streets and laneways from one end of the town to the other. As he advertised their presence his friend approached the first house and knocked lightly upon the door. It was an imposing residence with that kind of ornamental door which frowns upon loud knocking. After a short while a small, bespectacled boy answered. His mother, clad in dressing-gown and slippers, stood behind him, a confused look upon her kind face. The wrenboys knew her from other years. Always she was worth a shilling or a sixpence depending upon her mood.

'I'm sorry,' she explained, 'but we finished with all that yesterday.' Well used to rebuff, the pair moved on to the door of the next house only to be told the same story. Mystified they moved on to the next, now fearing the worst. The priest must have been at it again, turning the people of town and country against wrenboys! Baffled as to why the clergy should have undergone such an unexpected change of heart they decided nevertheless to proceed as planned. They were quickly brought down to earth when the crotchety old pensioner who responded to the irritating doorbell in the next house asked them if they knew the day they had.

Only then did it dawn on the luckless pair that they were a day late. To make doubly sure they asked the old man for a look at the newspaper which he held behind his back.

There it was, as plain as the ribs of the dangling concertina, 27 December 1939. So they were a day late. Little as it was in the calendar of the year it might as well have been six months. St Stephen's Day, the day of the wren, the day for which they had planned since the same day the year before, had slipped silently by while they drank and slept their fill in the curtained room of the tiny cottage.

'It's a pity we didn't think of drawing the curtains,' said the *bodhrán* player as he smote his instrument with bent head.

'If only we had taken a look at the clock now and then!' his friend moaned as he extracted a long, mournful note from his concertina. They stood silently side by side looking down at the roadway and tiring of looking down looked upward despairingly at the grey skies still devoid of rain.

'What possessed us at all!' the *bodhrán* player asked.

'What possessed us but drink!' came the instant answer. As they stood dejectedly not knowing which way to turn the housewives and children of the suburb where they found themselves stood in their doorways and gateways. None smiled at the plight of the elderly pair and there was no laughter, no titter and no guffaw to further confuse the latter-day wrenboys. Rather were their concerned faces tinged with sadness. They were reminded of the errors of age, of fathers and grandfathers once dearly loved but now, alas, gone forever from the scene, gone maybe but recalled for a while by the presence of the ancient pair who had arrived too late. After several uneasy moments the drooping, downcast musicians in their snow-white apparel and peaked caps decided to call it a day but then an odd thing happened. A postman with a bag of New Year cards slung around his neck came cycling past. The reason he had the bag slung around his neck instead of his shoulders was because he had a satchel, with a half dozen of stout inside, slung across his back. Upon beholding the strange pair on the roadway he dismounted.

'Attention!' he called sharply. Immediately the wrenboys sprung to attention. They were, in a sense, uniformed men and was not the man who had barked the order also in uniform. Uniform is as uniform does and those who are bound must obey!

Furthermore, was not this man's uniform provided by the state and was not the state the highest authority. They stood, therefore, awaiting further orders and never, it must be truthfully said, did two out of place, out of time wrenboys need orders so badly.

The postman, wheeling his bicycle at his side, circled the elderly pair as though he were inspecting a guard of honour. He noted the stubble on the jaws and shook his head sadly at such a lapse in standards. He noted the stale odour of intoxicating liquor and the untied flies and the rakish tilt of the caps and the mud on the shoes and all the other things that an old campaigner bemoans as he conducts his tour of inspection.

'At ease!' The order was given in a lighthearted manner and, explicitly, there came across the message that he was, difficult as it might be to believe, once a wrenboy himself. Who was to say, in fact, that he had not arrived late on the scene on some far-off occasion! He made a final circle around the now relaxed wrenboys, hummed and hawed a few times and asked who was the cashier.

The *bodhrán* player indicated that he filled such a post. Without a word the postman swept the cap from the *bodhrán* player's head and, allowing his bike to fall to the ground, thrust a hand into his trousers' pocket, located a sixpenny piece and dropped it into the cap. Then he moved among the many women who had gathered to agonise over the plight of the oldsters. Pence, threepenny pieces, sixpenny pieces and even a shilling were willingly contributed before the postman ran out of subscribers.

'Now,' said he as he handed back the jingling cap to its rightful owner, 'you will strike up a tune and you will march proudly with heads held high right into the very heart of the town and remember that a good wrenboy, like a good man, is never late.'

The tune, a rousing one, was forthcoming at once. The wrenboys drew themselves up to their full heights.

'By the left quick march,' came the curt command from the postman. Sprightly and in step the wrenboys marched off in tune with the music.

'Remember,' the postman called after them, 'once a wrenboy always a wrenboy according to the order of MacMoolamawn.'

'The order of MacMoolamawn!' they echoed the name, not knowing that MacMoolamawn was the first wrenboy of all the wrenboys. The postman mounted his bicycle and cycled outward with his bag of letters and satchel of stout.

Cider

I forget my exact age during the Christmas in question but I must have been at least seventeen for, dare I say it gentle reader, I was greatly addicted to cider and foolishly believed that I could drink any amount of it. Addicted though I was I drank it but rarely and always discreetly. My father had his suspicions but he never caught me in the act and always I made sure to steal into bed when I was intoxicated. With companions of my own age I would indulge in secret sessions on certain feast days and holy days about five times a year in all and once at Christmas. That would have been the Christmas I saw and heard the banshee.

The banshee was heard only when a person with an O or a Mac in the surname passed away. Originally my family were O'Kanes and none was surer than myself that this plaintive and panic-inducing apparition would not be duped by the minor deviation in name.

I had heard the banshee in the past. We would be sitting by the fire late at night, my mother darning socks, my father reading the newspaper of the day and we, the children, readying ourselves for bed.

'Hush!' my mother would suddenly raise a hand for absolute silence. In moments the requisite hush would have descended and then, fully alerted, we would wait for the inevitable with looks of alarm on our faces. From afar would come the supernatural wailing, spine-chilling and pitiful, not belonging to this world. My mother would make the sign of the cross while we all followed suit except my father.

'Another poor soul on its way to the great beyond,' my mother would whisper.

'Another sex-starved greyhound,' my father would announce with a good-humoured shake of his head.

Time rolled on and the family grew. One month I would be five feet six and by the end of the following month I would be five feet seven. It was growing time. By the time Christmas arrived I was five feet ten inches and rapidly heading for six feet.

It had been agreed that my father, my mother and the girls would assemble in the kitchen at eleven-thirty so that all would be in time for midnight mass at the church of St Mary's. Earlier we had partaken of lemonade and biscuits in honour of the season. After the turkey had been trussed and stuffed in readiness for Christmas Day my father was declared exempt from further involvement in the household chores. He headed at once for the neighbourhood pub where most of his cronies would already have ensconced themselves. For days before I had strenuously argued that I had grown too old to be a part of the familistic excursion to the church reminding my parents of my great age and height and pointing out that all my friends had received permission to attend mass on their own or with their chosen companions.

My sisters took my part but my father was adamant saying it had come to his ears that the teenagers of the parish were more interested in cider and porter than in the pursuance of their Christmas duties. In the end he relented but only when my mother forcibly reminded him that he had been young himself.

'Very well so,' I remember his words well as he clasped his hands behind his back, 'but if it comes to my attention that you place the consumption of cider before the fulfilment of your religious duties I will confine you to your room for twenty-four hours, without recourse to appeal, and in addition I will kick your posterior so hard that your front teeth will fall out as a result.'

'Cider!' I spat out the word disdainfully as though it were the last thought in my head.

Two hours before midnight I slipped out of the house by the back door and joined my friends in Moorey's public house. The only light in the tiny bar was from a flickering candle. The limbs of the law were abroad on public house duty and Moorey spoke in whispers.

'Happy Christmas!' he said and handed me a pint of cider on the house.

Moorey was old as the hills, grey as a slate, ribald, randy and irreligious but he was a generous soul and no other publican in town would serve us for fear of reprisals from parents and the custodians of the peace. Despite this my mother and the other matrons of the street liked him. They had known his late wife. He had apparently loved her dearly and had always shown it in his treatment of her while she was alive. He had not remarried although she had been dead for thirty years. Every Sunday he would place fresh flowers on her grave. Like ourselves he was addicted to cider with the difference that he would lace his pints with dollops of whiskey and yet we never saw him drunk. Sometimes there would be the barest suggestion of a lurch but nothing remotely resembling the phenomenal staggers executed by seemingly indestructible drunkards when the pubs were closed for the night.

While we sat quietly drinking pint after pint of cider we spoke for the most part about girls, sometimes maliciously and sometimes boastfully which is the way of youth.

As the midnight hour drew near we could hear the hurrying footsteps outside the window as young and old made their way to midnight mass. As if by common consent there was no conversation, no laughter, none of the raucous cries one associates with crowds or noisy clatter of boots and shoes. Such was the love and respect for the celebratory season that unnecessary noises were regarded in the same light as profanities.

At ten minutes to twelve Moorey announced that it was time to go. At such an hour, on any other night of the year, the session would only be starting but as Moorey explained gently: 'Because of the night that's in it boys I think it's time to douse the candle.'

We finished our pints in the pitch dark promising to meet again on St Stephen's night. In turn we shook hands with Moorey and extended to him the compliments of season. Outside on the street only the stragglers remained.

We had earlier decided against mass for a number of reasons; if our parents saw us they would immediately recognise our state of intoxication. Then there was the possibility that one or more of us would be nauseated by the heat of the church and the burning incense, which could well bring on a fit of vomiting. Then there was the most important factor of all and that was the likelihood that one or more of us would be obliged to lessen the strain on brimming bladders and to do this it would be necessary to stand up in the full view of the congregation and make one's way to the end of one's pew and thence up the long aisle under the suspicious stares of friends, neighbours, parents and strangers. Many would smirk knowingly, aware of our plight and destination, which would of necessity be the convenient back wall of the holy sanctuary which was attached to the rear of the church. Our parents, of course, would be infuriated, knowing full well that we would have to be truly cider-smitten to run such a gauntlet!

We went our separate ways with none of the boisterous farewells in which we would indulge on less devotional occasions. At home the kitchen was strangely silent. On the mantelpiece the clock, unheard throughout the day, was having its full say at last. A burned-out turf sod crumbled softly into the overflowing ash-pan of the Stanley Number 8.

I suddenly felt a profound longing for the girls and for my parents. Supposing they never came back! I dismissed the terrible thought and counted the twelve intrusions which introduced the midnight hour. The final chime extended itself to the ultimate limits where silence lay waiting to receive its spirit. Then, from the rear of the house, came a long, low, wailing sound which made the hairs stand to attention on that area of the head nearest to my forehead. I had known these hairs all my life and I can swear that they never behaved in such a fashion before. While I waited for them to resume their normal stance there came, stealing through the partly opened back door of the kitchen, the same wailing sound. My hairs remained alert while my heart raced and my whole frame shivered. Suddenly I grew less tense. This new state was no doubt induced by a mixture of cider and youthful bravado!

The wailing started again, this time more protracted and pitiful, as though the soul of the voice box from which it originated had been recently drowned in the unfathomable depths of black despair.

Again my heart raced and the hairs already standing were joined by their brethren from every quarter of the head. Such was their consistency that they would have served as a bed of nails for a novice fakir. Only the wailing of the banshee could stiffen human hairs to such a degree.

Then, for the first time in my entire life, my knees knocked and I was obliged to place my hands on the table for support. There came almost immediately a sustained high-pitched pillalooing of such intensity that I was obliged to stuff my fingers in my ears lest my hearing be permanently damaged. It was as though the ghostly proprietress of such unearthly vocal organs was endeavouring to reach notes never attained before. Their pitch seemed to far exceed the range of the most accomplished soprano and then, unexpectedly, came a collapsing and a crumbling followed by a mixture of base trebles and last of all by the most musical grunts and groans imaginable as though the banshee in question was about to give birth.

Emboldened by the cider I cautiously made my way into our back yard. The sickle moon shone fitfully, its pale glow frequently impaired by heedless clouds. Slowly I advanced towards the back door of the out-house where the winter's supply of turf was stored.

I had frequently heard of the silence of the grave when older folk spoke reverently of the dead and such indeed was the silence of the out-house at that point in time on that unforgettable night. I was not prepared for what happened next. I was standing close to the rickety door straining my ears for tell-tale sounds when I head the uneven breathing of some creature in the immediate vicinity of the door's exterior. On second thoughts, panting might be a more apt word. Then came a horrifying caterwauling as terrifying as it was unexpected. It exploded right into my ear which was pressed against the door. I was paralysed, my feet like hundred-weights of lead, my heart thumping as though, at any minute, it would burst through the walls of my chest. I would have taken off that instant but my legs refused to budge. I was tied down by my own terror. I prayed silently to the Blessed Virgin.

'Mother of the Sacred Jesus,' I whispered imploringly, 'come to my aid this night.'

Suddenly my natural courage, scant as it was, surfaced and with a mighty roar I opened the door. The creature tumbled in on top of me and we both fell in a heap astride the turf sods scattered around the floor. She persisted with her lamentations as she lay on the ground writhing and kicking out in torment.

It was as much as I could do to get to my feet. When I did I fell a second time on top of the black-shawled creature from the spirit world. I had accidentally stood on a turf sod which spun beneath my foot, capsizing me. This time I rolled over on my side in a desperate effort to escape the clutches of the hideous creature with the overpowering smell.

At that moment a wayward moon shaft entered the out-house through its only window and highlighted the features of the awful apparition which would surely tear my eyes out if she could but lay her filthy talons on me.

The moon shaft rested for a moment on the bloodshot eyes before drifting downwards to the almost toothless mouth, redeemed from emptiness by the presence of a solitary black fang from which venom dripped as she tried in vain to smite me.

In anguish I cried out to the heavens for help and the heavens in their mercy answered. I dived through the out-house window and into the back yard where my head struck a stone so that I was rendered half unconscious.

Fuming and screaming and uttering unmentionable maledictions she towered over me. A number of small bones materialised in her grimy paws. These she flung at me with all her might but most whizzed harmlessly by. One struck me just above the eye. There was no doubt about its origin. It was a human finger bone as were the others which lay scattered about the back yard.

I managed to crawl away from her towards the door of the kitchen. Curiously she made no attempt to follow me. On all fours, like a wounded animal, I made for the sanctuary of the kitchen.

I bolted the door behind me and ran up the stairs to bed where I pulled the clothes over my head without disrobing. I lay there shaking and moaning, beseeching the Blessed Mother of God to succour and comfort me.

After a while I slunk from the bed to the window which commanded a full view of the back yard and out-house. The moon had just unloaded a cargo of ghastly light. There was no sign of the banshee.

Making the Sign of the Cross I returned to my bed and promptly fell asleep. No doubt the shock of the night's happenings played a part in my sudden collapse into deep slumber. The next sound I heard was my mother's voice calling me in the half light of the morning.

'Hurry!' she was saying, 'and you'll just be on time for ten o'clock mass.'

I lay on my bed fervently wishing that I had not consumed so much of Moorey's cider. It was only then that the awful happenings of the night came flooding back. I hurried downstairs. My father sat at the head of the table smoking his pipe. He threw me a withering look before the commencement of his interrogation.

Before he had time to pose a single question I blurted out my story. Horrified, my poor mother clutched her bosom and flopped into the chair which my father had instantly provided lest she fall on the floor. As I revealed the full details of my horrific encounter my mother's face grew paler and paler. My father puffed upon his pipe at a furious rate. There was a cloud of blue smoke underhanging the ceiling by the time I finished.

'The banshee you say!' My father emptied the bowl of his pipe into the ash-pan of the Stanley.

'Without question,' I replied as we both waited for my mother to stop shaking her head. The shaking was accompanied by the most holy of spiritual aspirations, all directed upwards in thanksgiving for my salvation.

My father sighed deeply which meant that he was also thinking deeply. Without another word he filled his pipe while I waited for his verdict. There was none forthcoming. Instead he rose without a word and went into the back yard where he spent a considerable time. When he returned his hands were clasped behind his back.

'You say,' he opened, 'that the bones she flung at you were finger bones!'

'Yes,' came my ready answer.

'Human fingers?'

'Yes.'

He took his right hand from behind his back and threw a fistful of small bones on the table.

'These,' he announced solemnly, 'are the very bones which lay scattered around the yard just now. Will you confirm that these are the bones which were flung at you last night by the banshee?'

'There's no doubt in my mind,' I replied.

Guardedly I fingered the bones which still retained some tissue and a residue of meat. It was clear that they had been well and truly gnawed.

'And you say they are human?' My father was now at his most inquisitorial. All the family knew that he secretly fancied himself as a prosecutor. He was always at the head and tail of every domestic investigation, strutting around the kitchen with his hands clasped behind his back, taking them apart occasionally and joining them together at the uppermost point of his paunch as he listened to evidence and submissions.

Sometimes he would close his eyes as he questioned a hostile witness. Other times he would stand silently for long periods, his eyes firmly fixed upon the defendant who was generally myself. This tactic nearly always worked with the girls who would readily confess to anything, just to be free of his accusing eye. I must say that the entire household enjoyed such trials at the end of which everybody, except yours truly, was acquitted and exonerated. When convicted I would be confined to my bedroom for periods of one hour to a maximum of four although the possibility of a twenty-four-hour sentence was always on the cards.

'My Lord!' he unexpectedly addressed himself to my mother who had sufficiently recovered her composure to acknowledge the surprise judicial appointment, 'these bones you see before you which the defendant claims are human finger bones are nothing of the sort. They are, in fact, bones from a pig's foot or *crubín* which is the local term affectionately applied to this particular extension of the pig's anatomy.'

My mother rose to examine the evidence, nodded her head in agreement and resumed her seat.

'Not only is the defendant a pathological liar,' my father was continuing, 'but he is a deceitful scoundrel as well.'

'Please proceed!' was all my mother said.

My father cleared his throat.

'You are aware,' said he, 'of the existence of a woman known as Madgeen Buggerworth?'

'Yes!' I replied with a laugh.

'You will respect the court sir!' my father cautioned, 'or you'll be fined for contempt.'

I bent my head submissively and tried to look contrite. This wasn't easy, for the very mention of Madgeen Buggerworth's name was enough to make anyone laugh. She was a local beggar-woman and it was frequently said of her that she never drew a sober breath. On reflection it would be true to say that I had never seen her sober.

Madgeen was a powerful virago of a woman. Her husband had died after siring the final member of her thirteen-strong family and the family, the moment they were fledged, took off for foreign parts and were never seen again and small blame to them because she was never done with scolding and beating them.

Her favourite pose was when she spread her legs apart in the middle of the roadway and threw off the black shawl which truly covered multitudes. Up then would go the front of her skirts so that her bare midriff was exposed to the world. Then would come the drunken boast as she touched her navel with the index finger of her right hand: 'There now,' she would call out at the top of her voice for all to hear, 'there now is a belly that never reared a bastard!'

She would rant and rave, skirts aloft until the civic guards came on the scene and ushered her homewards. Other times she was to be seen lying in one of the town's laneways with her back to a wall, fast asleep, snoring in drunken abandon. Given enough drink she could sleep anywhere, regardless of wind or rain. She was to be seen too late at night staggering from one doorway to another singing at the top of her voice, if singing it could be called.

'If it please the court I would request that your worship and the defendant follow me to the out-house where I shall provide incontrovertible evidence that this man,' my father pointed a finger in my direction, 'was so bereft of sense from the consumption of cider that he confused our friend Madgeen Buggerworth with the banshee.'

He led the way into the back yard and on to the out-house where we were greeted by deep snoring punctuated now and then by outbreaks of spluttering and wheezing. There on the ground, partly covered by turf sods, lay Madgeen Buggerworth. By her side there lay an uneaten *crubín*.

'We'll let her sleep for the present,' my father announced, 'later,' again he pointed in my direction, 'when she wakes you will serve her with dinner and afterwards you will take her home.'

I hoped that this would be his last word on the matter but there was more to follow.

'Let us return to the kitchen,' he said solemnly, 'where your sentence will be handed down. Meanwhile I suggest you pray for mercy.'

So saying he preceded us into the kitchen where he announced that he was relieving my mother of all judicial responsibilities on the grounds that she would be incapable because of her known affection for the defendant of meting out a just sentence.

I stood with my back to the Stanley awaiting the pleasure of the court. My father stood at the doorway, hands clasped behind back. My mother sat in a neutral corner.

'I find you guilty of drunkenness in the first degree,' he said, 'and I hereby sentence you to twenty-four hours' solitary confinement in your room.'

I stood aghast! It was the toughest sentence he had ever handed down. I would have to admit that I expected no less. He was clearing his throat again.

'There are, however,' he proceeded solemnly, 'mitigating circumstances. This day as you know is the birthday of a great and good man who was once wrongly convicted and subsequently crucified. As a small measure of atonement for that woeful miscarriage of justice I hereby suspend the sentence imposed upon you. You are, therefore, entitled to walk from this court a free man.'

On my way home from mass I met him walking down the street against me. It had turned unexpectedly into the mildest of days.

'Let's have a stroll before dinner,' he suggested.

We took the pathway to the river which was in modest flood. He spoke about other Christmases, of his father and grandfather and of great wobbling geese especially stall fed for the Christmas dinner, of whiskey drinking, great-uncles and carol singing and the innocent pranks of his youth. We walked through the oak wood, marvelling at the splendid contributions of the songbirds despite the greyness of the day and the leafless trees and hedgerows.

We reentered the town at the end farthest from where we left it and proceeded down the long thoroughfare known as Church Street. We turned off into a laneway and found ourselves at the rear door of Moorey's premises. I was astonished to discover that my father was familiar with the sesame of admission, two knocks and a pause, two knocks a pause and finally three knocks. The door opened after a short wait and Moorey stood there, surprise showing on his face.

'Long time no see, Master!' he said with a smile.

Inside we sat on stools at the bar counter.

'Do you think this man has graduated from cider Moorey?' my father asked.

Moorey considered the question carefully before answering. Then after a while he said: 'Just about.'

'Then,' said my father as he laid a hand on my shoulder, 'we'll have two pints of stout to sharpen the appetite.'

Many Years Ago

Many years ago, in our street, there lived an old woman who had but one son whose name was Jack. Jack's father had died when Jack was no more than a *garsún* but Jack's mother went out to work to support her son and herself.

As Jack grew older she still went out and worked for the good reason that Jack did not like work. The people in the street used to say that Jack was only good for three things. He was good for eating, he was good for smoking and he was good for drinking. Now to give him his due he never beat his mother or abused her verbally. All he did was to skedaddle to England when she was too old to go out to work. Years passed but she never had a line from her only son. Every Christmas she would stand inside her window waiting for a card or a letter. She waited in vain.

When Christmas came to our street it came with a loud laugh and an expansive humour that healed old wounds and lifted the hearts of young and old. If the Christmas that came to our street were a person he would be something like this: he would be in his sixties but glowing with rude health. His face would be flushed and chubby with sideburns down to the rims of his jaws. He would be wearing gaiters and a bright tweed suit and he would be mildly intoxicated. His pockets would be filled with silver coins for small boys and girls and for the older folk he would have a party at which he would preside with his waist-coated paunch extending benignly and his posterior benefiting from the glow of a roaring log fire.

There would be scalding punch for everybody and there would be roast geese and ducks, their beautiful golden symmetries exposed in large dishes and tantalising gobs of potato-stuffing oozing and bursting from their rear-end stitches. There would be singing and storytelling and laughter and perhaps a tear here and there when absent friends were toasted. There would be gifts for everybody and there would be great good will as neighbours embraced, promising to cherish each other truly till another twelve months had passed.

However, Christmas is an occasion and not a person. A person can do things, change things, create things but all our occasions are only what we want them to be. For this reason Jack's mother waited, Christmas after Christmas, for word of her wandering boy. To other houses would come stout registered envelopes from distant loved ones who remembered. There would be bristling, crumply envelopes from America with noble rectangular cheques and crisp, clean dollars to delight the eye and comfort the soul. There would be parcels and packages of all shapes and sizes so that every house became a warehouse until the great day came when all goods would be distributed.

Now it happened that in our street there was a postman who knew a lot more about its residents than they knew about themselves. When Christmas came he was weighted with bags of letters and parcels. People awaited his arrival the way children awaited a bishop on confirmation day. He was not averse to indulging in a drop of the comforts wherever such comforts were tendered but comforts or no the man was always sensitive to the needs of others. In his heart resided the spirit of Christmas. Whenever he came to the house where the old woman lived he would crawl on all fours past the windows. He just didn't have the heart to go by and be seen by her. He hated to disappoint people, particularly old people. For the whole week before Christmas she would take up her position behind the faded curtains, waiting for the letter which never came.

Finally the postman could bear it no longer. On Christmas Eve he delivered to our house a mixed bunch of cards and letters. Some were from England. He requested one of these envelopes when its contents were removed. He rewrote the name and address and also he wrote a short note which he signed 'your loving son Jack'. Then from his pocket he extracted a ten-shilling note, a considerable sum in those far-off days. He placed the note in the envelope. There was no fear the old woman would notice the handwriting because if Jack was good at some things, as I have already mentioned, he was not good at other things and one of these was writing. In fact, Jack could not write his own name. When the postman came to the old woman's door he knocked loudly. When she appeared he put on his best official voice and said: 'Sign for this if you please Missus.'

The old woman signed and opened the envelope. The tears appeared in her eyes and she cried out loud:

'I declare to God but Jack is a scholar.'

'True for you,' said the postman, 'and I dare say he couldn't get in touch with you until he learned to write.'

'I always knew there was good in him,' she said. 'I always knew it.'

'There's good in everyone Missus,' said the postman as he moved on to the next house.

The street was not slow in getting the message and in the next and last post there were many parcels for the old woman. It was probably the best Christmas the street ever had.

A Christmas Performance

Hector Fitzpitter, player-manager-author, sat on his trunk. It was his only possession apart from his hat, suit, shirt and the shoes in which he stood. He had been sitting in the same position for an hour and a half. Occasionally he made a slight concession to ache and cramp by gently lifting and relocating his numb buttocks slightly because the shiny, well-worn seat of his trousers was beginning to fray and might not survive a more energetic adjustment. The last of his coins had been expended earlier in the day on a cup of tea and a cheese sandwich.

'You don't have enough for ham,' the restaurant owner had cautioned after he had calculated the pennies, halfpennies and solitary sixpenny piece which Hector had extravagantly spread across the counter top.

'What have I enough for then?' he had asked petulantly.

'Cheese sandwich,' came the disinterested reply, 'and even then you're short.'

Hector pretended he hadn't heard, secretly hoping that the sandwich and tea would be forthcoming without further reference to financial discrepancy. The chest on which he sat contained his costumes, tattered and torn and sadly reduced to three in number, Iago, Falstaff and Tontagio, in *The Bearded Monster of Tontagio,* the eponymous role for which he was best known and indeed revered in smaller towns and villages. It was a fearsome part which left unsophisticated audiences cowering and abject as he ranted and raved all over the stage, directing his more savage outbursts towards the meeker-looking members of the audience who faithfully responded with screams and fainting fits.

He had written the play himself. Once, in his hey-day, he had fallen through a trapdoor. He had broken a leg and had penned the piece during the subsequent six weeks of hospitalisation and convalescence.

'Would,' said a particularly scurrilous provincial critic, 'that he had broken his hand instead of his leg and spared us this infantile gibberish!'

Another called him the clown prince of balderdash and compared him with the village idiot on one of his worse days. The cruelest came from an amateur actor who wrote a weekly theatre column and who lambasted all visiting plays and players with unrefined vitriol and without exception, reserving his more generous encomiums for the annual offering of the local amateur drama group of which he was a member.

Said he, 'Not satisfied with the immortal roles created by Shakespeare, Sheridan, O'Neill, et cetera, Fitzpitter dives deep into his psyche and surfaces covered in his own crud.'

Another wrote that Herbert Fitzpitter should be hung, drawn and quartered, 'hung,' he suggested, 'for directing the play, drawn for taking the leading role and quartered for writing the damned thing!'

Hector Fitzpitter revelled in such notices, attributing the lack of appreciation to ignorance and jealousy. Now, virtually at the end of his career, his unpaid company scattered to the four winds and his pockets empty, he would surely have wept had it not been for the fact that he had never shed a genuine tear since he first embarked on an acting career at the tender age of seventeen, all of fifty years before his present predicament. A lesser man would have despaired and thrown himself at the mercy of the county.

For Hector his present plight was merely a temporary reversal, a minor stumbling-block on the long road to the recognition which surely lay around the corner. Meanwhile there was the question of board and lodgings. His leading lady and his several underlings knew how to look after themselves. They would regroup instinctively, aided by the theatre grapevine, at a specific venue during the first days of spring. All save he were now gone to ground in their own homes or other safe havens for the Christmas which was almost upon them. The spiritual balm of the season would quickly heal the trauma which they had all endured when *The Bearded Monster of Tontagio* closed prematurely. The proprietor of the theatre had confiscated the slender takings of the three nights before it folded, pointing out to Hector that the paltry amount would hardly pay for the electricity not to mention himself, the caretaker, the box-office staff, the cleaners and the general upkeep.

Wearily, Hector rose to his feet. He shivered as the north-eastern gusts reminded him that he should not have pawned his overcoat. Cutting as the gusts were they were not as damaging as the review of a local amateur.

'The audience,' wrote he, 'few as they were from front seat to back, were soon drenched by the spume and spittle which accompanied the uncontrolled rantings of Mr Hector Fitzpitter.'

There had been more but Hector had not read on. Attacking an actor over the incidental discharge of a minute particle of saliva was akin to criticising a person for having a hump or a stammer. It just wasn't done. He walked slowly down the street, dragging the cumbersome trunk behind him. Time was when he would have effortlessly borne it on his shoulder.

Hector was possessed of a large and ungainly frame. The excess flesh which once rippled on his torso now shuddered and trembled like a blancmange at the least exertion. He presented a formidable figure to those who encountered him for the first time. Younger actors feared him not at all.

'Blubber!' they would reply contemptuously when asked if the outsize player-manager-author might not be a dangerous adversary in a confrontation. Elaborating, they would explain that he was never less than a dangerous antagonist on the stage and finding himself with a naked sword in his hand was quite capable of slashing at anything that got in his way. Similarly when fisticuffs were demanded during a violent scene he was apparently the equivalent of a Jack Johnson and often knocked down younger opponents as though they were made of straw.

'But,' they would be quick to explain, 'in real life he is a cowardly wretch who wouldn't fight to save his life.'

'In fact,' one of Hector's closest friends informed a curious reporter, 'while the fellow would not hesitate for a moment to save a damsel in distress on the stage he would run a mile if called upon to do so in public.'

After several hundred yards of trudging he found himself at the front door of the lodgings which he had vacated that morning, having met half of his obligations before saying farewell and promising to pay the other half when funds came to hand as he put it to Mrs Melrick the accommodating landlady who tired easily of his many long-winded apologies.

She was anything but receptive to his second proposal of the day, board and lodgings until his ship came in. Rather curtly she pointed out that all of her lodgers without exception would be returning to their various homes for Christmas and since she expected to find herself with an empty house throughout Christmas Eve, Christmas Day and the three days following, she had decided to stay with her son and daughter-in-law in a nearby town for the period of the closure.

'I'm doing it for my son and grandson,' she explained to Hector, despondent of face, his jaws resting on intertwined hands atop his now vertical trunk. His thoughts were elsewhere, his attention diverted to the unlikely prospect of alternative accommodation. The thought of sleeping out was an appalling one. He had resorted to it on occasion in his younger days and then only in summer time. At his present age and in winter time it would have been suicidal. His ears pricked suddenly when she referred to her daughter-in-law directly for the first time.

'Bitch!' she was saying.

Her remarks were not addressed altogether to Hector. Ruefully she recalled, for her own benefit, the inexplicable antics and tantrums of her son's wife. From what he heard it was not difficult to gather that there was bad blood between mother-in-law and daughter-in-law.

'It beats me,' Hector cut across her ill-concealed disgruntlement, 'how you've endured it for so long.'

'God alone knows that,' she replied vigorously, roused to full articulation by the obviously sincere commiseration from this unexpected quarter.

'You know about her?' Mrs Melrick asked.

'Who doesn't!' came the ready reply.

'She's something isn't she?'

Hector thought for a moment before responding.

'She's might pull the wool over my son's eyes,' the landlady warmed to her task, 'but she won't pull it over mine!'

'She's not worth it.' Hector shook his head secondly. A great sorrow clouded his face.

'She's not fit to polish your shoes,' he continued as Mrs Melrick opened the door wide so that he might follow her, trunk and all, into the kitchen. Over the tea which followed they spoke at length about the wickedness and countless misdeeds of her son's wife. To add criminality to her natural sinfulness there was confirmation also that the awful creature was pregnant again.

'What next!' Hector asked as he lifted his eyes to heaven. He was enjoying the role no end. What a pity that playwrights, royalty-hungry, so-called moderns, could not write such parts! The exchanges between the pair lasted until the first of the boarders arrived for the evening meal.

'See out there.' Mrs Melrick pointed out the kitchen window to a tiny annex, erected by her late husband for their only son as a facility for his studies.

'You can stay there until my return,' his benefactress informed him. 'There's a divan and I'll leave in a few blankets. You can eat here tonight and tomorrow night but after I've left you must fend for yourself. You must not come near the house.'

There had been other conditions but, by and large, Hector felt that he had not been mistreated. The following day he would enquire as to the whereabouts of the local presbytery. He had always found, so long as one didn't overdo it, that Presbyterians were a most reliable source of food and small amounts of cash and, surely if they had been supportive in the past on everyday occasions, was it not likely that they would be even more charitable at Christmas!

Father Alphonsus Murphy had once seen Hector Fitzpitter on the stage. He had been holidaying at the time in a nearby seaside resort and finding himself with nothing better to do, forked out a florin he could ill afford to see the great man's version of Iago. He had intended after the holiday to repair to the diocesan retreat house for a few days' meditation and a subsequent revelation of his transgressions, minor and all that they were, but decided against it after he had endured two and three-quarter hours in the stuffy marquee which Hector Fitzpitter had rented for the season

'I felt,' he confided to one of his curates some time later, 'that my experience in that marquee was sufficient atonement for anything I might have done since my last visit to the retreat house.'

'Allow me to introduce myself,' Hector Fitzpitter opened rather grandly.

'No need. No need!' Father Murphy put him at his ease.

'Perhaps you've seen me on the stage Father?'

Father Murphy decided to ignore the question. Instead he asked if he might be of some assistance to his urbane visitor.

'You can indeed Father,' came the deferential reply.

After providing a résumé of his recent misfortunes in a style not unfamiliar to his listener, Hector asked if it might be possible to borrow a modest sum of money, to be repaid in full without fail as soon as the touring season commenced in the forthcoming spring.

'We are not in the business of lending,' Father Murphy reminded him, 'but if you are not averse to a day's work I can provide same and pay you when the job is done.'

'Work!' Hector recoiled instinctively as images of shovel and pick-axes assailed him.

'Don't be alarmed.' Father Murphy had experienced countless reactions of a similar nature. 'Your qualifications for the sort of work I have in mind are impeccable. In fact, I know of nobody off-hand who could do a better job.'

'You want me to read the lesson.' Hector's face beamed as he saw himself addressing a record audience and, more importantly, a captive audience. Father Murphy scowled uncharacteristically at the awful prospect.

'I merely want you,' he said icily, 'to play the role of Santa Claus tomorrow night. I will supply you with hat, beard and coat. After you've eaten I will take you, in advance, to the laneway where you will be delivering gifts to the underprivileged children of the parish.'

Hector smiled. The prospect appealed to him.

'And I will be paid?'

'Yes,' Father Murphy assured him. 'You will be paid the moment you finish your rounds. Now you may go around the back and tell the housekeeper that I said you were to be fed. I'll expect you to present yourself here tomorrow night at eight o'clock.'

Later, as they drove slowly up the laneway which ended in the open countryside, Father Murphy handed him a pencil and some paper with instructions to write down the name of the owner of each house so that there would be no instances of wrong delivery. Each parcel of gifts would bear the name of the recipient on the outside. By the simple expedient of requesting the house-owner's name the parcels would find their way into the right hands.

'Let me warn you,' Father Murphy's voice assumed a cautionary tone, 'in the very last house you are likely to meet with trouble so you would be best advised not to enter. When your knock is answered you will hand over the gifts to whatever person opens the door. Then, if you have any sense, you will make yourself scarce!'

'You're not trying to tell me that my life will be in danger Father?'

'Not your life,' Father Murphy forced a laugh, 'but the fact is that the parish's biggest bully and its most foul-mouthed drunkard, one Jack Scalp, lives in that house and if he happens to be at home when you call he will most certainly attempt to assault you. By not entering the house you will be in no danger whatsoever. Just turn and leave when your job is done and here,' said Father Murphy, 'is a half-crown. It's Christmas time and you could do with a drink, I dare say, only don't let me see you with a sign of drink on you tomorrow night or I'll clear you from the door!'

Hector sat upright in the car, a look of affront on his face.

'My dear Father Murphy,' said he, 'I have never drunk before a performance and I don't propose to start now.'

That night Hector slept soundly. He spent most of the following day walking up and down the laneway rehearsing his lines and his movements. He would have been happier with a dress rehearsal but given the circumstances he realised it would be out of the question. During his travels he kept an eye out for Jack Scalp. He had already developed a mental picture of the scoundrel and felt that he would instantly recognise him should their paths cross. He had made up his mind to ignore Father Murphy's warning and was determined to force his way into the kitchen if necessary. If needs be he would exercise his acting skills to their fullest. They had saved him in the past and, with simple presence of mind, would do so again. He drank not at all on Christmas Eve, resolving to splurge on a bellyful of booze as soon as he received his wages. He ate sparingly from the few provisions which Mrs Melrick had left out for him on the wickerwork table in the annex. He made a final inspection of the laneway before calling to the presbytery where Father Murphy awaited him.

'It's a pretty large bag as you can see,' the cleric advised him, 'and there are thirteen households in all. Tarry awhile in the kitchen of each before passing on to the next and take special care at the thirteenth for it is there, as I have told you, that Jack Scalp resides.'

'I'll take care,' Hector promised. If Father Murphy had noticed the contemptuous note in his voice he kept it to himself.

'I will drive you as far as the entrance to the laneway,' he told Hector. He stood by fingering his chin while his protégé fitted the false off-white beard. An elastic band held it firmly in place. Next came the boots which were a size too large but better too large than too small he thought. Then came the hat and finally the long red coat which reached down to his toes.

'Is there a life-size mirror?'

''Fraid not,' Father told him, 'we don't indulge in such vanities in this presbytery but you can take it from me that you look the part.'

Father Murphy wondered if he should inform him of the incident which had occurred on the previous Christmas Eve but decided against it. He had already told him to be on his guard. Anyway no great damage had been done, just a bloody nose and that had stopped bleeding after a few moments. The elderly member of the St Vincent de Paul Society who had filled the role at the time had been drinking all afternoon and when he had pushed Mrs Scalp aside in order to confront her husband he realised that he had bitten off more than he could chew. A string of expletives directed towards him had the effect of momentarily paralysing him. He immediately dropped his bag and made for the door. In vain did Mrs Scalp try to restrain her drunken husband. He knocked her to the floor and landed a solid punch on the somewhat outsize, puce-coloured proboscis of Father Christmas. The blow might have been followed by another but Jack Scalp tripped across a beer crate and fell in a heap on the floor. His intended victim emitted a cry of relief and never drew breath until he arrived at the presbytery, his artificial beard well and truly bloodied. He collapsed onto a chair, gasping for whiskey. His account of the incident differed greatly from the actual facts. He had, according to himself, fought a heroic fight and was forced to retreat lest he do further damage and maybe even be the cause of widowing poor Mrs Scalp who was fully exonerated for not taking sides.

Hector was rapturously received by the parents and children in the first house he entered. Whiskey and wine were pressed upon him so that he found himself unable to resist. It was the same at all the other homes. His best efforts to refuse the liquor which was so generously pressed upon him were to no avail. Glass after glass of whiskey found its way to his palate and later to his brain. He was, as he would say later, almost suffocated with alcohol.

'You're a big, brave man,' one poor woman had said to him, 'what's a little drop of drink to you?'

He was never possessed of the mettle to refuse drink when kindly souls insisted he partake. In one house a selection of sandwiches awaited him and in another a plate of crackers and cheddar. 'The poor are so open-hearted,' he would say later to Father Murphy, 'they would give you their hearts.'

Father Murphy concurred. He had more than adequate proof of the veracity of Hector Fitzpitter's conclusions.

Children sat on Hector's lap and plied him with dainties. A few days hence and the cupboards would be bare once more all along the little laneway but here was Christmas and it was a time for giving and no better man to receive than this outstanding representation of Santa Claus, undoubtedly the most colourful ever to visit the laneway. Hector was quite overcome in the face of such bounty, such cordiality, such love! In some of the houses there were sessions of hymn-singing and in others storytelling. Hector Fitzpitter never played so many roles in so short a time.

It was well on the road to midnight when he reached the last house. Drunk as he was he had not forgotten Father Murphy's warning. He drew himself up to his full height. He had played a bear once in *A Winter's Tale* and for a moment was tempted to roar like one. He resisted the urge and gently knocked at the door. None came to answer. He listened for a while but could hear nothing. He knelt and placed an ear against the keyhole. After a short spell there came the most unpropitious sounds. No actor, he told himself, could create such heart-rending whimperings. Faint and childlike, they seemed to emanate from the very depths of human despair. Hardened as he was Hector Fitzpitter found himself physically bereft of strength so moved was he by the broken whinings, eerie and awesome. They succeeded in transmitting a devastating anguish to his heart, an anguish that he had never before experienced. The salt tears coursed down his face and into his adopted beard as he silently rose to his feet determined to put an end to the pitiful ejaculations which so provoked his newly found humanity.

He knocked loudly upon the door and, upon receiving no response knocked as loudly as his clenched fists would allow. It was opened by a child, a tear-stained, grimy, undernourished little girl who looked at him with wonder-filled eyes. Behind her stood an equally famished little boy and then, suddenly, there were four more boys and girls, so obviously neglected and deprived, so stunted and wan of face that they looked as if they were all the same age.

'It's Santa Claus,' one whispered. Then in subdued confirmation all mentioned the name revered by children everywhere.

Cautiously Hector made his way into the kitchen. There was little light save that shed by a paraffin lamp with its wick turned down almost fully. There was no trace of a fire although the night was cold. There was no sign of the mother. The father, Jack Scalp, sat in a corner, his legs stretched in front of him, empty beer bottles all around and a partly filled noggin of whiskey clutched in one of his grimy hands. He snored fitfully. The little girl who had opened the door pressed a finger to her lips entreating silence from the visitor.

'Where is your mother?' Hector asked in a whisper.

'He put her out.' Every one of the six pointed a finger at their sleeping father.

'Why?' Hector asked.

'No why,' the girl who had opened the door replied.

'He does it all the time,' another whispered.

'If he wakes he'll beat us again,' said another still.

'For no reason of course?' Hector suggested. A chorus of affirmative whispers greeted his question.

'I have presents for everybody,' he informed the delighted children. How their faces transformed at the news.

'How little it takes,' Hector told himself between sobs and sighs, 'to please a child!'

He looked from one to the other of the angelic faces and was appalled by the bruises and bloodstains thereon. Hector Fitzpitter would never have the slightest compunction about kicking a fellow-thespian in the rear or socking him one to the jaw but to molest a child in such a fashion smacked of base cowardice and naked savagery.

'Your deliverance is at hand,' he announced solemnly to the children, now making not the least effort to lower his tone. He gathered them round him, quite overcome by the angelic radiance of their faces.

'I want you,' Hector informed them as he allowed his hands to linger on each individual head and face, 'to go and find your mother. I want you to bring her here no matter how she protests. Tell her that it was I, Santa Claus, who sent you. Go now.'

In a flash the children departed.

'Now my fine fellow,' Hector addressed the snorting drunkard in the corner, 'let us determine the quality of thy kidney. Awake fellow!' he bawled, 'awake to meet thy just deserts for as sure as there are stars in the heavens outside justice will be done in this house. Awake lout!' he roared at the top of his voice.

Blearily, angrily, torrents of the vilest curses exploding from his beer-stained mouth, Jack Scalp struggled to his feet. Upon beholding Santa Claus and nobody else he squeezed upon his whiskey noggin and would have smashed it against Hector's head had not the actor seized the hand that would smite him and brought its owner to his knees. Possessed of hitherto untapped strength Hector seized Jack Scalp by the throat and lifted him to his feet.

'My strength is as the strength of ten,' he roared quoting Tennyson, 'because my heart is pure.'

For the first time in his life Jack Scalp started to experience real fear. That he was in the presence of a madman he had absolutely no doubt. Hector flung him violently into the corner he had just vacated and stomped around the kitchen like one berserk. Suddenly he stopped.

'Do you know me?' he asked the cowering figure, askew in his corner.

Fearfully Jack shook head. He would have taken flight but that he was paralysed with fear.

'I,' said Hector, 'am the Bearded Monster of Tontagio. I have killed seventeen men in my time and maimed a hundred others. Make your peace with God while you may, you scurvy wretch, lest I send you to your maker this instant.'

So saying, Hector entered fully into the role he had created and played a thousand times. He stalked round the kitchen, striking further terror into his victim with maniacal roars of laughter.

'Rise!' he commanded. Jack Scalp staggered to his feet, drooling now, certain that his demise was at hand. From an inside pocket in the great red coat Hector withdrew Mrs Melrick's turf-shed hatchet and flung it at the cowering creature in the corner, making sure that he barely missed his head. Then seizing him by the throat he spread-eagled him across the kitchen table and choked him to within a breath of suffocation until the table collapsed beneath the squirming, wriggling child-beater.

Hector lifted him to his feet and slapped his face several times before seizing him by the throat yet again. Red froth bubbled from the monster's mouth as he applied the pressure to his victim's throat. Hector had bitten his tongue, just enough to assure that his spittle would be suitably coloured. Once again he flung the drooling drunkard to one side before presenting another terrifying facet of the monster's make-up. He started to smite upon his chest as though he were a gorilla. The grunting and screeching, the hysterical jabbering and high-pitched screaming which accompanied these most recent gestures were diabolical in the extreme. Jack Scalp fainted.

'Awake villain!' Hector Fitzpitter roared, 'awake to thy fate!'

With that he poured the remains of the abandoned whiskey noggin over the prostrate drunkard's face. Stuttering and begging forgiveness Jack Scalp crawled cravenly around the kitchen, sometimes seizing the trouser legs of his tormentor as he begged for mercy.

'I am tempted to kill you,' Hector spoke in what he believed were spine-chilling tones, the same tones that had sent faint-hearted rustics scampering for the exits before the enactment of another gruesome murder on the stage.

'Spare me. Spare me!' Jack screamed. 'Spare me and I will change my ways.'

'On your knees then.' Hector stood by with hands behind his back.

'Say after me,' he commanded, 'I will never from this moment forth molest my wife or children again.'

He waited as Jack Scalp repeated the words.

'I will never,' Hector continued, 'to the day I die, taste an intoxicating drink. I will be a model husband and father and I will devote the remainder of my life to the welfare of my children.'

'If you fail to honour your promises on this most sacred of nights I, the Monster of Tantagio, will return,' Hector's ominous tones were terrifying in the extreme, 'and I will split you right down the middle with this hatchet I hold in my hand.'

Silently Hector lifted his empty sack and disappeared into the night. There was no applause, no standing ovation, no cries of author! Yet Hector knew in his heart of hearts that he had given the finest performance of his career. Actors are never fully satisfied, no more than playwrights are after a play has been performed, but Hector had accomplished what all actors aspire to and few achieve. He had given the perfect performance. It mattered not that there was no audience and that there were no critics. He had fulfilled his lifelong dream and developments thereafter would prove him right. Early on the morning of Christmas Day, Jack Scalp presented himself to Father Murphy and took a lifetime pledge against intoxicating drink. It was a pledge he would keep. Never again would he spit at, shout at or molest in any way whatsoever his long-suffering wife and family. He turned into a model father and became one of the parish's most respected figures. Hector Fitzpitter's acting improved. He benefited greatly from his performance at the abode of Jack Scalp. During the following summer a new version of his masterpiece was warmly received by audiences and critics alike.

Conscience Money

The twins Mickelow, Patcheen and Pius, were lookalikes, proportionately built, robust and round and standing at five feet two inches in their stockinged feet.

'They don't chase work,' their parish priest Canon Mulgrave confided to a new curate, 'but they won't avoid it either so that you couldn't very well call them ne'er do wells.'

'Would you call them easy-going then?' the curate had suggested respectfully.

'Yes,' the canon conceded after some consideration, 'easy-going would be a fair characterisation.'

For the most part the twins worked for local farmers on a temporary basis. They were paid at the going rate at the end of each day. These modest but undisclosed earnings were supplemented by the weekly dole which the state provided all the year round.

By parochial standards the twins Mickelow would be classified as comfortable. They also had a cow. She provided milk and, as a consequence, sufficient butter for their needs.

The cow grazed throughout most of the spring, summer and autumn in the one-acre haggard at the rear of the house. In the winter she was transferred to the Long Acre except in the direst circumstances when the weather became unbearable, when she would be temporarily housed with a limited supply of fodder. On the Long Acre which in this instance extended to the nearest crossroads at either side of the house her search for grass would be supervised by one of the brothers. There was always the danger that in her eagerness to locate choice pickings she would over-reach herself and end up in one of the roadside dykes, very often filled with water during the months of January and February. Sometimes in areas of high risk she would be tethered as she sought sustenance beneath the bare hedgerows which sheltered the grassy margins of the narrow roadway.

In many ways the twins enjoyed an idyllic existence untroubled by strife or want. A small garden, sheltered from the prevailing wind by a narrow stand of Sitkas, provided potatoes and the more common vegetables such as turnip and cabbage. A latticed hen-coop overhung the wall above the front door in the kitchen and a sturdy hen-house of the lean-to variety rested against the rear of the house next to the back door. It had successfully resisted countless incursions from fox and otter since its erection. There were surplus eggs throughout most of the year and these could be exchanged for provisions when the itinerant egg buyer made his weekly call. Gentle and mild-mannered, the twins seldom or ever entertained conflicting opinions. Among strangers they were deferential and meek unless drawn into conversation. Even among those they knew they would be the last to initiate any form of communication.

Fuel for their fires was to be found in abundance in the adjacent bogland where they enjoyed turbary rights for generations. The quality was excellent and a small extra rick was held over until the week before Christmas when it would be disposed of to a local buyer who sold lorry loads to customers in the nearest town.

On Friday nights and Sunday nights they would unfailingly make their companionable way to the crossroads public house which was situated a little over a mile from their thatched abode. Arriving at nine they would depart at twelve. Four pints of stout was their nightly intake. Neither smoked or gambled. Neither paid court to females or fornicated in any way and neither visited the nearest town which nestled comfortably at the centre of a large fertile valley fifteen miles distant over dirt roads and tar roads. As a result they were never short of the wherewithal to indulge their crossroads excursions provided, they often reminded each other, that they stayed within the constraints agreed by themselves. These self-imposed limitations ordained that they attach themselves to no company other than their own. However if a drink chanced to come their way from some drunken or other well-meaning benefactor they allowed themselves the liberty to accept so long as it was clearly understood that nothing was to be expected in return.

There were always bountiful times in the height of summer when Yanks and English exiles came home on holiday. Then the drink would flow freely and there would be morning hangovers but nothing else and by this was meant, as far as the twins Mickelow were concerned, that there had been no extra financial outlay.

Those who came from England in particular spent heedlessly until all their hard-earned money was gone and they were obliged to return to the construction sites where abundant overtime had helped to finance the holiday in the first place. Full credit to them, they never mourned after their vanished earnings nor did they expect anything in return for their profligacy. They seem resigned, even content in themselves that their pockets were empty.

The twins had often been tempted to call a drink for their one-time benefactors, now possessed of nothing save a return ticket, but after weighing the merits and demerits thought better of it and resigned themselves to the prevailing attitude that such misplaced kindness might only result in a demeaning postponement of the exile's departure.

There had, in fact, been at least one occasion when the exile had remained behind as a result of not one but several acts of misplaced charity. After a week he became a travesty of the carefree holiday-maker who had breezed in the door a few short weeks before. Eventually for his own good he was frozen out and, all too long after his allotted time, departed the scene an abject and pathetic reject, the victim of ill-considered philanthropy.

'Never go against the tide boy,' Pius Mickelow had warned his brother Patcheen at the time. From the opposite side of the hearth Patcheen had nodded emphatically in total agreement.

Then came a particularly bitter winter of ice and snow and great sweeping gales, a winter that imposed a heavier than usual levy on the vulnerable and the elderly. The twins would remind each other that such winters were to be expected from time to time, winters that gave no quarter and for some winters against which there was no defence.

Several old folk would pass on before the snows melted on the more elevated hilltops. Among these was a neighbour of the Mickelows, an eighty-five-year-old cottier and widower, one Daniel Doody, who had been nursed throughout the final weeks of his illness by his forty-five-year-old daughter who had given up her position as a domestic in the distant city of Cork and come home to attend to her ailing parent.

He bore his suffering bravely and all were agreed that his only offspring Kitty was truly a ministering angel if ever there was one.

Night and day she cared for him, luring him to upright positions on what would eventually be his death-bed with tit-bits and delicacies which had been prepared with love and devotion.

When, eventually, he expired, holding her hand, the hearts of the entire countryside went out to her but none more so than those of the twins Mickelow who had kept themselves discreetly at hand at all times when the old man strove to hang on forever to that which had been no more than a brief loan in the first place.

Patcheen Mickelow, in particular, was frequently moved beyond words as Kitty Doody tiptoed quietly to and fro uncomplainingly. Never once did she make mention of her position in the city of Cork or of her lifestyle there. Rumour had it that she had once been friendly with a soldier but that he had left her for another after several fruitless years of courtship. Others had it that she had been a cook in a convent before leaving to take up a housekeeping post with an elderly schoolmaster. Still more maintained that she had worked as a drudge in an establishment of disrepute. There were other more fanciful tales but, as with all such idle speculation, another topic would displace it in no time at all.

Shortly after the moment of expiry on the fateful night Kitty Doody, her blue eyes filled with anguish, looked helplessly at the Mickelow twins who had been in close attendance all night. She had summoned them that evening in the realisation that the old man was nearing his end. He had been anointed the day before by Canon Mulgrave. The elderly cleric had advised Kitty that she should be prepared for the worst and in consolatory tones assured her that her father would surely see heaven. A last feeble cry followed by a low choking sound heralded his passing.

'I'll go for the priest,' Patcheen Mickelow had announced with fitting solemnity.

'And I'll go for the neighbours,' Pius had volunteered.

During the wake which followed, in the absence of relatives, the twins Mickelow acted as chief stewards and masters of ceremonies. It was they who distributed the wine, whiskey and stout and it was they who polished and shone the holders for the death candles. It was they who replenished the traditional saucers of snuff on mantelpiece, table and cranny all though the long night and morning.

During the wake Pius drank his fill but never allowed himself to cross the threshold of drunkenness. For his part Patcheen allowed not a tint of liquor to pass his lips.

Afterwards when the whole business was at an end Patcheen would partake of a drink or two but for the duration of the wake proper and while it was in progress he resolved that he would be the most responsible man at that wake. Of the twins he was by far the more resolute. It was he who decided that the town should be out of bounds after Pius was struck on the jaw one night many years before with a dustered fist for no reason whatsoever. The blackguards he encountered in the gents toilet had never seen him before nor had he seen them. Patcheen quite properly deduced that the only reasons why his twin was felled were his small stature and inoffensive manner. His pockets had not been rifled and he had not spoken a word.

'He is the sort,' Patcheen confided to the publican in whose premises the assault had taken place, 'who draws trouble on himself because of the way God made him.' He counted himself lucky to have escaped similar treatment himself at the hands of the many drunken blackguards who pack-hunted in large towns after dark.

Pius agreed instantly when Patcheen suggested that they stick thereafter to familiar haunts where they were known and respected.

After the burial of Daniel Doody the Mickelows decided that they would not present themselves at the Doody household until such time as they were invited. Fine, they felt, to have made themselves available during the latter stages of the old man's illness but it would not be altogether appropriate to do so now without good reason.

Spring would be well advanced with the wild daffodils withdrawn and brown before such an invitation would be extended. In between they occasionally met Kitty on the roadway and they nodded respectfully towards each other after mass on Sundays. Sometimes there would be words but these, for the most part, would be confined to views about the weather although Patcheen suspected that a more protracted exchange might not be unwelcome as far as Kitty Doody was concerned. For all that he played his cards in the conventional way and felt himself well rewarded when the invitation came on the final day of April. Pius was mightily pleased in his own way although the twins knew full well that the reason behind the summons was most likely related to the cutting and harvesting of the turf supply for the winter ahead.

For some years before his death as infirmity rendered him less active they had been hired by the late Daniel Doody to cut, foot and draw home the dry crop in their ancient but still serviceable ass-rail.

The drawing home was usually accomplished in less than a week and at the end of that time Daniel Doody's turf shed would be full to the rafters.

When they arrived at the Doody house they were made welcome at the doorway by the sole occupant, the beaming Kitty, who took note of their sheepishness by seating them near the hearth and handing each a freshly opened bottle of stout.

The Mickelows were pleased to learn that it was fresh and in prime condition. They would have been just as pleased to accept stout left over from the wake but this, they would be at pains to explain, was not Kitty's way at all.

She sat herself by the large, wooden table while the visitors drew on their bottles. They spoke about many matters. Every subject, in fact, was up for discussion save the one which brought them. That would be aired in its own time. It would have been a blatant breach of good manners to bring it up prematurely.

When a second bottle of stout and all the conventional topics had been exhausted Kitty Doody spoke for the first time about turf.

'I was wondering,' she said as her sad blue eyes swept the kitchen and finally the hearth-place where the twins were seated, 'what I should do about the winter's firing?'

'Turf is it you're worried about?' It was Patcheen who spoke on behalf of the pair.

'Turf it is,' Kitty confirmed.

'Let turf be the least of your worries,' Patcheen assured her.

'The very least of your worries,' his brother Pius added lest there be the slightest doubt about it.

'Her turf will be cut won't it boy?' Patcheen turned to Pius knowing full well what the answer would be. They had discussed the subject often enough across the winter nights.

'Let someone else try to cut it,' Pius had whispered to himself with uncharacteristic ferocity. Now the words gushed forth like a torrent as he pledged his commitment.

'We will first clean the turf-bank of scraws,' he said, 'and then we will cut it and foot it and refoot it and then we will make it up into donkey stoolins and then come September when it will be well seasoned we will fill your shed to the rafters.'

'That is exactly what we will do,' Patcheen concurred proudly. He was about to add further reassurances of his own but Pius had not yet finished.

'We will not be charging you a brown penny,' he rushed out the words lest he suddenly dry up, 'for we would be poor neighbours if we did not help a lady in a pucker.'

'Oh we can't have that,' Kitty tried not to sound half-hearted, 'we can't have that at all. The labourer is worthy of his hire.'

'Not these labourers!' Patcheen cut across, 'these labourers is doing it out of the goodness of their hearts so there will be no more talk about hire.'

Relieved that her predicament had been shouldered by such a doughty pair she rose from the table and wiped a tear from her eyes with a corner of her apron. Her visitors had the good grace to turn their heads and used the opportunity to carefully examine the glinting soot which adorned the back wall of the chimney.

'If ye will come to the table now,' Kitty suggested without the least sign of stress or worry in her voice, 'I will grease the griddle and we'll have fresh pancakes for supper.'

After that April visit the twins called regularly across the summer to render a progress report on their turf-cutting activities. Always there would be fresh pancakes and then one glorious day in the middle of June she made her way to the bog in order to see for herself the advances being made and to invite her champions home for supper.

The sun shone from a cloudless sky and from every quarter of the boglands the larks sang loudly especially when the sun departed the centre of the heavens and moved slowly down the sky.

'On such a day as this,' Patcheen Mickelow spoke with awe in his tone, 'God do give his voice to the larks and then the larks do tell us about God.'

'Oh well spoke brother, well spoke!' Pius made the sign of the cross reverentially and turned to Kitty whose sparkling blue eyes radiated appreciation of the heavenly sentiments expressed by Patcheen.

'Was it not well spoke Kitty?' Pius asked and then he fell silent as he awaited Kitty's reaction.

'It was well spoke,' Kitty agreed, 'in fact it could not be better spoke if it was spoke about forever.'

Pius marvelled at the wisdom of her answer. For some time he had the feeling that the pair had a special relationship, nothing that he could put his finger on except that he knew it to be there.

'It's there,' he said to himself, 'as sure as there's frogs in the bogpools and hares in the heather.'

'Oh you may say it was well spoke,' Kitty turned the full force of her blue eyes on Patcheen but he could no more look directly into their depths than he could at the blazing sun which adorned the heavens. Modestly he bent his tousled grey head and sought refuge in the heather. Pius now knew for certain that there were exciting stirrings in the hearts that beat close by and that when the stirrings comingled there would be a rare song in the air.

'Wouldn't it be lovely,' Kitty whispered the hope half to herself, half to the twins, 'if this day could go on forever.'

The brothers were immediately arrested by the sentiment, impractical though it might sound.

'Yes, yes,' they whispered fervently, 'it would be lovely.'

For the remainder of the day Kitty helped with the making and clamping of the donkey stoolins and it was not she who cried halt as the shadows lengthened.

'If I don't eat soon,' Patcheen announced, 'my belly will never again converse with my gob.'

Taking each by an arm Kitty led them to a spongy passageway and thence to the dirt road which would take then to her home.

The summer passed uneventfully thereafter and then came the time for the drawing home of the turf. They made light work of the task and by the end of the second week in September the Doody shed was filled to capacity as promised. The turf was of the highest quality and properly utilised would keep the winter cold firmly in its place.

As usual the twins paid their biweekly visit to the pub at the crossroads and it was here one night that they overheard strange tidings which alarmed them no end.

'She'll pine for the ways of the city, you'll see,' a local farmer informed another, 'and it's my guess,' he continued, unaware that he had an interested audience only a few yards away, 'that she'll make tracks as soon as her year's mourning is down.'

'What makes you say that?' the second farmer asked.

'I say that,' said the first farmer, 'because she has stopped wearing the black at mass and when women stops wearing the black they gets anxious about the future and then they're likely to pull up stakes and to move or to marry as the humour catches them.'

That very night at the request of Pius the twins departed the pub after the second pint.

'Follow me,' he said, 'and don't ask no questions like a good man.'

Although slightly irritated Patcheen was curious. Silently he followed his twin into the night. Despite his best efforts he found himself unable to draw abreast of his brother. He wanted to ask why they were making a detour and why he had been obliged to forego half of his normal intake but could not catch up, so determined was Pius to reach his goal.

Eventually they found themselves at the gate which opened on to the Doody laneway.

'It's up to you now boy,' Pius confronted his brother, 'you better go in there and state your case or we might never see her again.'

'Look at the hour of the night we have!' Patcheen argued.

''Tis the right hour for what you have to do,' Pius insisted, 'and isn't there a light in the kitchen window which means she's still up.'

Patcheen hesitated. If he was to tell the absolute truth he would admit to having considered the precise manoeuvre on which his brother wished him to embark on many an occasion but implementing it was another matter altogether.

'I won't know how to put it,' he complained.

'It will all come to you when you face up to her,' Pius assured him as he pushed him towards the gateway. At that moment the door opened and Kitty appeared.

'Who's out there?' she called.

'It's only us,' Pius returned.

'I'm so relieved,' Kitty called back as she placed a shaking hand under her throat. The brothers stood silently side by side, Pius nudging Patcheen to give an account of himself and the latter temporarily tongue-tied.

'Is there anything wrong?' Kitty asked anxiously after she had advanced a few paces.

'This poor man has something wrong with him all right,' Pius pushed Patcheen forward, 'but he'll be telling you all about it himself for I would say that it's been playing on his mind for some time.'

'Oh dear!' came the sympathetic response, 'there is none of God's creatures without some kind of a cross.' So saying she bent her head meekly and went indoors, making sure as she did that the door remained ajar behind her. At the same moment Pius Mickelow turned on his heel and disappeared into the night.

'Sit up to the fire,' Kitty removed a bundle of knitting from a chair near the hearth and sat herself on a chair nearby, nearer his chair Patcheen noticed than she had ever ventured before. His heart soared but then it flopped awkwardly downward into its rightful resting place when he considered the unpredictable ways of the opposite sex.

So far as Patcheen knew, and it was also believed by other eminent authorities, members of the opposite sex for reasons best known to themselves did not always make themselves quite clear in matters of the heart.

Faced with this dilemma he bided his time. Caution was called for and he would be the first to admit that he had no experience in dealing with women.

So profound was the silence in the kitchen, apart from the ticking of the mantelpiece clock, that the only sound to be heard came from the gentle criss-crossing of the knitting needles which Patcheen had never before seen so speedily and skilfully employed. Thus they sat for what seemed ages. From time to time he adjusted himself on the chair but there was no move from his companion saving the bewildering complexities of the knitting fingers. As far as he could see she seemed to be in a jovial mood. However, limited and all as his experience was, he knew that females often tended to make their meaning clear too late in the day, with disastrous consequences.

Occasionally she would lift the blue eyes from her work and smile at him as if it was the most natural thing in the world that the two of them should be sitting together.

Then surprisingly she moved her chair nearer to his, so near that their bodies brushed whenever they adjusted themselves. It was a hopeful sign surely but she gave no other and as the night wore on it seemed that she might not move till dawn brightened the landscape beyond the curtained window.

'Unless I make a move now,' Patcheen told himself, 'I will never make one.'

'Do you know what I'm thinking?' he whispered confidentially.

'No,' came the conspiratorial reply.

'I was thinking,' said he, 'of what a waste it is to see two fires in two different houses when you could have just one fire in one house.'

'I know what you mean indeed,' she agreed, 'for it was often the same thought occurred to myself.'

'Waste not,' Patcheen recalled the first half of the ancient maxim.

'Want not!' she concluded it for him.

'Then there's the upkeep of the two houses.' He pressed his advantage. She nodded eagerly in accord.

'There's no telling the advantages,' he went on, at which she laughed and so did he.

'One of the houses would have to go,' she said.

'You mean for pour oul' Pius to stay here with us then?' he asked, hardly daring to believe his ears.

'We couldn't very well leave the poor creature on his own,' she replied, 'and isn't there a room to spare. We would have our room and he would have his, that's if he'll agree!'

'Oh he'll agree.' Patcheen assured her, 'there's nothing he'd like better.'

'That's good to hear.' She laid the knitting aside.

'All Pius ever wanted from the day he met you,' Patcheen informed her, 'was to see the two of us settled. He worries that you may go off and leave us and never come back.'

'I won't be leaving,' she whispered as she turned the devastatingly blue eyes upward and in so doing presented her pursed lips for approval. Only a man of iron would have by-passed such an opportunity. Kiss her he did, not once but several times and not just on the lips but all over her face and her throat and her nose and her nape and her ears. It was the blue eyes that he wondered at most of all. They seemed never to be without a sparkle and they were filled too with wonder or so it seemed every time he gazed into them.

When they had kissed their fill she laid the table for tea. They drank cup after cup and spoke for hours. Canon Mulgrave would have to be consulted. They both knew that he would approve, for was he not night and day vociferating his views about the absolute necessity for more marriages in the seriously depopulated parish and while discriminating pundits might argue that Kitty was past it, others would counter by insisting that where there was life there was hope.

As things turned out there would be no issue but otherwise it was as happy a marriage as one could find in the parish or the many parishes beyond. As for the arrangement with Pius, he treated his sister-in-law with the utmost respect and was at pains at all times to show her that he knew his place and could be trusted beyond words.

Certain of their immediate neighbours who believed themselves to be possessed of rare powers of prognostication let it be known that it was their belief that the bi-weekly visits to the crossroads pub and to other harmless activities would be seriously curtailed when the twins moved into the Doody homestead. They were to be proved totally wrong.

As always the pair showed up at the crossroads and they were to be seen at football matches and coursing meetings in the many enterprising townlands and villages which hosted such events in their seasons.

It was noted too by interested parties who had made close studies of the affairs of others on the grounds that it was beneficial to the community as a whole that the twins looked better, were sprightlier of step and were never without the price of a drink in their pockets.

Time passed and the old ways of the countryside began to undergo changes. Donkey and carts began to disappear from the roadways and the bog passages. Tractors and trailers began to replace them.

Small, serviceable motor-cars replaced the horse and pony carts and the family traps as a means of transport to mass and to village and occasionally to the town in the far away valley.

The twins Mickelow kept to the old ways for as long as was practicable but eventually, after years of subtle prompting from Kitty, submitted to the new craze and invested in a venerable Morris Minor which both brothers learned to drive.

From a financial point of view they were never as well off so the belated purchase of the car did not leave them in debt. All three had reached pensionable age before eventually deciding to invest in the Morris.

All around, other exciting changes were taking place in the villages and towns throughout the countryside. The old, musty, male-dominated public houses were being reconstructed and glamorous lounge bars began to replace them.

The crossroads pub, frequented by the twins, was among the last to conform to the modern style and the first female to accompany her men on a crossroads excursion on a Sunday night was the brave Kitty, wife of Patcheen Mickelow. In no time at all other females followed suit.

In short order came singalongs and dance music and even the

clergy for once, somewhat confused by the transition, kept their opinions to themselves and allowed the parish free rein in its appetite for modern entertainment.

The twins, lookalike as ever, grew frailer but retained both their rude health and appetite for enjoyment. Their tousled heads whitened in the face of the advancing years but their capacity for consuming stout declined not at all. Kitty kept the white and the grey at bay with various tints and lotions. The happiness the trio enjoyed from the day Patcheen married had mellowed into a pleasant contentment. Whatever the neighbours might opine they could never say that the Mickelows were poorly off. When the three old-age pensions were tallied they realised a considerable income.

Then, alas, Kitty took ill and after a short illness passed away. The twins very nearly succumbed to the grief which followed. In the course of time the sorrow would be assuaged a little but they might never have visited the crossroads pub again had it not been for what Pius would later term heavenly intervention.

It transpired that shortly before Kitty died she summoned Patcheen to their bedroom. She bade him be seated on the sole plush-covered chair which, up until this moment, had never been used to fill the role for which it had been designed. Coats, blouses, trousers and other articles of clothing had been draped across its back or dumped on the seat but it had never, in the course of its existence, been sat upon. It had none of the sturdiness of the kitchen chairs, was frail and rickety but was, after all, ornamental.

Patcheen sat awkwardly and listened intently to his wife's carefully prepared recital. She wished to be buried in the same grave as her late parents and she made him promise that when his time came for leaving the world he would join her there and Pius too if he so wished. He assured her that it would be their dearest wish. She next handed him a slip of paper with instructions for the smooth administration of her wake and funeral. On it was meticulously pencilled all that would be required in the line of drink and edibles. A silence followed. It was as though the business of briefing him had exhausted her. After a long pause she informed him that it was her wish to be laid out in her navy blue costume and white silk blouse.

'In the drawer over yonder,' she pointed weakly in the direction of the dressing table, 'you will find a blue ribbon to bind my hair.'

Patcheen nodded. Her wish would be carried out were the heavens to fall.

'In the bottom drawer,' she continued hoarsely, 'you will find two envelopes. In one which is marked wake money you will find sufficient to cover the cost of my wake and funeral and in the other which is addressed to Canon Mulgrave is the money to pay for the special masses for the repose of my soul and all the poor souls wherever they may be.'

During the long spring and summer which followed, the twins kept to themselves and were seen abroad only when they shopped at the crossroads or attended mass.

Despite the provision made by Kitty they found themselves in debt. Instead of the modest oak coffin for which she had allowed in her calculations they opted for the most expensive walnut with the most ornate trappings.

They found themselves faced with two choices: to sell the Morris Minor or abstain from intoxicating drink until the undertaker was paid. In the space of a year according to Pius's reckoning they should be free of debt and also free to resume their visits to the crossroads pub. Then came the heavenly intervention referred to by Pius.

It so happened that after the funeral mass when Patcheen approached Canon Mulgrave to pay for the mass the canon had expressed reluctance in accepting the extra money for the masses which would be said for Kitty and the poor souls.

'Now, now,' Canon Mulgrave said, 'there's no need at all for that. You've paid for the high mass and that in itself is sufficient.'

Patcheen would have none of it. Mindful of his wife's clearly expressed instructions he forced the envelope upon the canon and hurried from the scene.

Later that afternoon when the canon opened the envelope he was surprised at the amount therein. Normally he would have been gratified if a pound or two had been forthcoming but he was truly astonished when he beheld the neatly folded twenty-pound note. His conscience dictated that the money would have to be returned with the suggestion that a pound or two would do nicely in its stead. He knew for a certainty that the twenty-pound note was far and away beyond the means of the twins. He resolved to return the note intact at the earliest opportunity. Some time would pass before he did. He would agonise every time he looked inside the envelope which he kept atop the mahogany desk in his study. He dithered for several months. There were times when he told himself that the money had been given with a good heart and there were other times when he tried to convince himself that it would be against the spirit of the dead woman's intent if he did not accept the money. He decided that the masses should be celebrated without more ado and he also decided that further cogitation would be required before he finally decided on the destination of the twenty-pound note.

It turned out that shortly before Christmas the canon's letter box was flooded by a deluge of neglected bills. He withdrew the twenty-pound note from its envelope. With infinite care he smoothed it on top of his desk. It would go a long way towards discharging his debts. Then he manfully reminded himself that the Christmas dues would shortly commence to replenish the presbytery coffers. This left him with only one choice. The twenty-pound note would have to be returned.

He chided himself for his long-term tardiness and lack of Christian resolution. He sat in his car and drove to the abode of the Mickelows. Pius it was who greeted him at the door. The canon gracefully declined the invitation to enter.

The canon, like all the canons and curates before him, had long since given up the impossible task of telling the twins apart. However, as far as this particular mission was concerned, one twin was as good as the other.

Earlier that morning Patcheen had set out for a distant grove where he would cull a sufficiency of holly and ivy to decorate the crib and the kitchen.

'Now my dear man,' Canon Mulgrave held the twenty-pound note aloft, 'I must tell you that this note you see before you is rightfully yours. It was far too much and I am conscience-bound to return it.'

Mystified, Pius Mickelow gazed with open mouth at the money and when he had gazed his fill he gazed secondly at his visitor. When the canon thrust the twenty-pound note into the gnarled hand Pius decided to play along although his mystification had greatly increased and he was now convinced beyond reasonable doubt that the canon had succumbed to the dotage which few escape at the end of their days.

'Not a word now sir!' the canon raised an admonishing finger, 'not a word no matter what. This is strictly between you and I. The masses have been said so you can set your mind at rest. The money is yours to do with as you please. I'll be on my way now and I sincerely hope that you and your brother enjoy a happy and a holy Christmas.'

The canon would relish the forthcoming Christmas. His conscience had been salved. He had acted as a true Christian.

On the Sunday evening before Christmas the twins sat at either side of the hearth. They had sat for over an hour without exchanging a word. It was Pius who broke the silence.

'What say we go to the pub,' he suggested matter-o- factly. Thinking that he had not heard aright, Patcheen inclined his head.

'What's that you say?' he asked.

'The pub,' Pius threw back.

'And what will we use for money?' Patcheen asked sarcastically. Pius produced the twenty-pound note for the first time.

'Is it real?' Patcheen asked as he took the note in his hand. Satisfied that it was the genuine article he asked where it came from.

'I am not at liberty to say,' Pius answered solemnly, 'but it wasn't found and it wasn't stolen. The man who gave it to me made me promise that I would never tell.'

'Let's move,' Patcheen rose and donned his overcoat. Pius followed suit.

'And you can't say where it came from?'

'Can't say,' came the reply, 'but this I will say, 'it came from God through man and if it came from God you may be sure that Kitty had a hand in it.'

Spreading Joy and Jam at Christmas

Let him who can boast of no failing take a bow for he is a unique fellow. He is elite among the elite but I would not have his impeccable status for all the lamb on Carrigtwohill.

Carpers will ask why I open on such a vein, what arrant nonsense am I proposing to inflict upon them as winter deepens and Christmas draws near.

I am actually about to recall an outing which took place a week before Christmas, at a time when my hair was black and you'd get a pint for two bob. The hero of the piece is no longer with us but if ever a man was cut out to play Santa Claus, he was that man. He could, in fact, fill any role.

It is many years now since this Mayo friend of mine and I set out for his native county where we proposed to spend a few days carousing and visiting the friends of his boyhood.

As we left Tubbercurry one evening shortly before Christmas on our way into Mayo he recalled the school where he had spent, according to himself, a wasted youth.

His teacher had been a grumpy fellow who regarded my friend and most of the other pupils as irredeemable illiterates and he would warn them day after day that they would never be fit for anything but the most menial of tasks.

'O'Donnell,' he would say to my friend, 'all I want is to see you able to spell for when you go to England your people won't know where you are because you won't be able to write and tell them.'

Actually O'Donnell was able to read and write before ever he went to the national school but he realised that if this fact became known he would find himself out on a limb. His illiterate companions might have no more to do with him. Better, he felt, be a fool among other fools than a star whose brilliance might be his undoing.

When we arrived in Claremorris we stopped at a well-known hostelry. Outside the door we noticed a large van full of jam. There were crates of one-pound and two-pound pots from floor to ceiling. There was raspberry, strawberry and plum. There was gooseberry, marmalade and mixed fruit.

'It's a terror,' said my friend, 'to see so much jam exposed to the naked eye and half the world starving.' He shook his head at the injustice of it.

In the bar we treated ourselves to two amber deorums of Irish whiskey and while were sipping from same a young girl entered and approached my friend.

She had somehow mistaken him for the driver of the jam van. In fact he could be mistaken for anybody. He had that kind of face. A woman once gave him a pound to say mass. He had been wearing a dark suit on the occasion.

'Sir,' said the young girl, 'my mother wants to know would you have any cracked pot? Strawberry or marmalade or mixed fruit or anything at all will do.'

'Musha what do you want a cracked pot for?' my friend asked, 'and the van loaded with sound pots.'

'Can I have a pot so sir, a one-pound will do?'

'And has your mother a conveyance?' my friend asked.

'Oh she has sir,' said the girl. 'She has an ass and cart.'

'Tell her to load a few crates,' said my friend, 'but not to overdo it. Ye don't want to make pigs of yeerselves entirely.'

'Oh no sir,' said the girl and she ran from the bar, a transformed creature.

Shortly afterwards we left the pub and proceeded to our car which we had parked nearby.

There was no sign of the jam van.

We walked through the town and a delightful walk it was. I would recommend a walk through Claremorris for any and all persons down in the dumps. The friendliness of the people was matched by the cleanliness of the streets and the disposition of the town as a whole.

There were some who came forward and shook our hands, tendering to us the most profuse welcomes to Mayo and the town itself.

One old woman complained of dizzy spells when we enquired after her health. My friend took her pulse and asked if she was taking anything for her complaint. She recalled visits to several doctors and reeled off a long list of medicines. None had done her any good. She seemed to be growing worse rather than better. My friend shook his head as he listened.

'Do you take a lot of spring water?' he asked after he had heard all he wanted to hear.

'Only in tea,' she said, 'and mostly from the tap.'

'Drink plenty spring water,' he advised. 'Spring water never did anybody any harm.'

The old woman nodded eagerly.

'Eat plenty vegetables,' he went on, 'especially cabbage and take a drop of the hot stuff morning and night.'

'I declare to God and His blessed Mother,' said she, 'but I feel better already. It was God sent you this way. I'll pray for you.'

'Pray for us all,' said my friend and he strolled off in the direction of the mountains or more particularly in the direction of Ballyhaunis where he had a large number of relations from his mother's side. I was left holding the baby as it were.

'Is he a doctor?' the old woman asked.

'No,' I informed her, 'he's not a doctor.'

'A specialist then?' she asked hopefully.

'Yes,' I replied, 'he's a specialist.'

Of course he was a specialist, a specialist in cheering people up and a specialist in dispersing gloom.

Eventually we found ourselves driving out of town. A slight mist was drifting down.

In Mayo mists don't fall down. They drift down. We drove slowly. There was no need for words between myself and this natural dispenser of goodness.

'Glory be to God!' he exclaimed when we beheld an ass and cart on the left hand side of the road. At each side of the body sat a female. One was shawled and old. The other was young and beautiful. Their faces were radiant with happiness and contentment.

In the cart were two cases of jam; one was filled with one pound pots and the other with two pound pots. He lowered the window of the car and saluted the pair. The girl waved at him ecstatically. Turning to me he said: 'Were we to depart life now we would surely see heaven for the happiness we spread this day.'

The Voice of an Angel

A drunken Santa Claus is better than no Santa Claus. I heard the remark in the kitchen of a neighbour, a genuinely frustrated mother of seven whose spouse had not returned as promised from an alcoholic excursion downtown where, as he maintained afterwards, he had been waylaid as he was about to return home by some whiskey-sodden companions from his childhood. Sensing that he would not return in time Maggie Cluney, that was the unfortunate mother's name, looked speculatively in my direction but after a brief inspection shook her head ruefully.

In those days I was a lathy, bony youngster about seven stones adrift, especially in the midriff, from an acceptable Santa Claus. The only other person in the kitchen over the age of ten was Maggie's sister Julie Josie who had earlier intimated that she was drunk, which had given rise to the opening statement of our narrative.

After an hour's coaxing and two steaming hot whiskeys we convinced her that nobody would fit the bill as she would. Drowsily, giddily she rose and inarticulately informed us that she was returning to her maidenly abode so that she could sleep off the excess spirits to which she was unaccustomed. Before she managed to stagger through the doorway we ushered the children out into the backyard and burdened her with the Santa Claus outfit from false beard to long boots, from tasselled headgear to vermilion greatcoat and finally the bag of gifts, one for every member of the household.

No great notice would be taken of her in the streets. She lived around the corner and besides there would be many other Santa Clauses abroad in various stages of inebriation but most would be sober and composed, conscious of the sacred missions with which they had been entrusted. Our particular one, Julie Josie, made her way homewards without mishap and also made it upstairs to her single bed where she fell instantly asleep.

Soon the room was filled with gentle snores, even and rhythmical, sonorous and richly feminine, snores that somehow suggested that deep in her subconscious was the need of a male companion who might take the sting out of the frost of life and fulfil her in a manner beyond the capacity of seasonal whiskey. In her sober everyday world she would never admit to any need whatsoever and often when questioned jocosely about her single state she would belittle all members of the opposite sex with a vehemence that made some believe she protested too much. For all that she was a good sister and a good aunt and an even better sister-in-law for she would always present herself *in loco parentis* whenever her sister gave birth and was a great favourite with her nephews, nieces and brother-in-law for the duration of her sister's confinement.

The night wore on until the ninth hour and it was precisely at this time that Julie Josie rose from her unassailable bed. She betook herself to a downstairs room where she donned the Christmas paraphernalia. She slung the bag of gifts across her shoulder and made her way to her sister's house where she was warmly received by her brother-in-law who insisted that she fortify herself with a drop of whiskey before the distribution of the gifts. Then and only then were the children called from the two small, happily overcrowded bedrooms adjoining the kitchen.

The younger ones held back in awe whilst the older ones rushed forward to greet their beloved aunt, pretending as they did that she was really Santa Claus. Some people become imbued with the true spirit of Christmas when they don the red coat and Julie Josie was one of these. After the gifts were distributed they all sat around the fire, the children drinking lemonade and eating Christmas cake, the oldsters sipping whiskey and telling tales of bygone days when geese were really geese and Christmases were always white, when ghosts of loving ancestors whispered in the chimney and a tiny infant was turned away because there was no room at the inn.

Between the whiskey and the sentimental recall many a tear was shed. There were some in the neighbourhood who would say that Julie Josie shed enough tears at Christmas to float the *Titanic*. She was, truly, a sentimental soul, well meaning and generous to a fault. Several whiskeys after her arrival she announced that it was time to go home. She refused all offers of assistance and even more adamantly refused to hand over her Christmas gear. She knew her way home didn't she! Wasn't she going back there now for the thousandth time and anyway what could possibly befall anybody at Christmas when men's hearts were full of goodness even if their bellies were full of beer!

She was, alas, drunker than she thought for she by-passed the corner which led to her house and went downtown in the general direction of the parish church. Mindless of her error she hummed happily to herself staggering to left and right and executing one daring stagger of record proportions which took her first backwards and then forwards, then hither and then thither, until she had travelled the best part of a hundred yards. Had her ever-increasing momentum not been arrested by the parish priest, Canon Coodle, she might well have wound up in the suburbs or even on the bank of the river which circled the town.

Luckily for Julie Josie the canon was a man of considerable girth and without any great strain he steadied the drunken representation of Christmas which wound up in his arms. Although a moderate imbiber himself he always made allowance for those who took a drop in excess on special occasions. He might shake his great, leonine head reproachfully when confronted by extreme cases and he might deliver the occasional sermon condemning the evil of over-indulgence to the detriment of the drunkard's wife and family but he never got carried away. If he had a fault, poor fellow, it was that he suffered from absent-mindedness. This was perhaps why he failed to identify the party who had collided with him. He presumed, and who would blame him, that the creature was male so he did what he always did with unidentified drunks. He directed this one to a warm room over the garage as he had all the others over the years, placed the now incoherent Julie Josie sideways on the bed and left her to her own devices convinced that she was a man and would sleep off the drink in a matter of hours before returning to wife and children.

As he tip-toed down the stairs the reassuring snores convinced him that all would be well in the course of time.

Earlier that night another intoxicated soul was chosen at random to fill the role of Santa Claus although he had never done so before, having neither chick nor child.

His name was Tom Winter and indeed it would have to be said that he looked wintry even in the height of summer for the poor fellow had a perpetually blue nose and was almost always a-shiver.

It was widely held by authoritative sources that he was generally emerging from a skite or booze or bender, call it what you will. Those who knew him best would explain that he only drank at weekends but that he drank so much during those particular days he spent the following five days recovering.

He was the proprietor of a small hardware business specialising in such commodities as sweeping brushes, mousetraps and chamber pots and, of course, nails, screws, hinges and what-have-you. He carried a considerable amount of his stock on his person. His waistcoat pockets, for instance, would be filled with shoelaces and his coat pockets with scissors, penknives and screwdrivers while his trousers' pockets played host to less dangerous articles such as picture cord and pencil toppers. Whatever the customer needed, provided it wasn't a plough or a mowing machine, he would generally find it in a matter of moments on one of his shelves or in one of his pockets.

At six o'clock in the evening he closed his premises and partook of a large cheese sandwich and a double gin before proceeding happily to his favourite tavern where it was his wont to indulge until closing time throughout the weekend and on festive occasions such as Christmas, Easter and St Patrick's Day or, of course, any other special occasion which might provide him with a break from routine.

Tom Winter, for all his wintry features, was a warm-hearted chap, gregarious in his own fashion so long as he didn't have to converse with more than two persons at the same time. He always bought his round and he frequently stood drinks to those who were less well off than himself or seemed that way.

Often it would occur to him that he drank too much and that he was wasting his life. His conscience would prick him from time to time and suggest that he might more profitably pursue some health-giving pursuits but, alas, when a weak-willed man wrestles with his conscience all the weight is on his side and the conscience is the victim of an unfair contest. So it was on Christmas Eve that Tom Winter found himself in the heel of the evening sitting on a high stool with a whiskey-sodden companion at either side of him.

Then a tall, thin, coatless man with his long, grey hair trailing behind his poll and ears dashed into the premises and allowed his gaze to wander from face to face. The obviously demented creature shook his head in despair and then his eyes alighted upon Tom of the wintry dial. He raised an imperial finger which greatly alarmed Tom for he thought at first that the new arrival was either a ghost or a madman. After taking further stock Tom recognised the intruder as a refugee from the northern part of the town, a sober hard-working chap with a large family and an even larger missus who kept him on his toes and who no doubt had dispatched him on some impossible mission on the very eve of Christmas.

Tom's alarm grew even greater when he noticed that the hen-pecked unfortunate was beckoning him. It was as though he had been summoned by an ancient and pietistic patriarch of superhuman power for he found himself dismounting from his stool. For the first time in his life he began to feel how the twelve apostles felt when they were called from their various vocations to follow the man whose birthday was at hand. The grey-haired elder caught Tom Winter by the sleeve of his coat and led him out of doors. His companions were to say afterwards that Tom's normally wintry features had assumed a radiance that lighted up his head like an electric bulb. They would concede that it had been already moderately lighted by the intake of seven large gins and corresponding tonics but as he left the premises in the wake of the coatless messiah it seemed as though a halo was about to encircle his head and shoulders.

Outside in the night air the coatless one explained his predicament. His brother-in-law, at the best of times an unreliable sort, had promised to fill the role of Santa Claus and was now nowhere to be found. Would Tom, out of the goodness of his heart, do the needful and don the red coat so that the poor man's seven children would continue to keep faith with Christmas!

Tom was about to decline when the coatless wretch fell to his knees and set up such a pitiful wailing that only a man with a heart of stone could continue to hold out. A stream of semi-coherent supplications that would bring tears from a cement block assailed Tom's ears.

'If,' the kneeling figure was wailing, 'I don't come back home with some sort of Santa Claus she'll have my sacred life!'

Tom could only deduce that the grovelling wretch was referring to his outsize wife whose shrill voice could be heard above the wind and the rain during the long nights when fits of dissatisfaction soured her and she became discontented with her lot. She had been known to assault her terrified husband with rolling pins, cups, mugs and saucers and once with an iron kettle which necessitated the insertion of twenty-three stitches.

'Get up and behave like a man.' Tom Winter now adopted a wintry tone which had the effect of putting an end to the wailing. It was obvious that the poor creature was without backbone and if the right tone was adopted would obey any command. He struggled to his feet clutching wildly at Tom lest that worthy attempt to flee. Hope replaced the look of despair in his eyes as he babbled out his gratitude like a puling infant who has been lifted from the cradle.

On their weary way to the anguished fellow's abode Tom had the foresight to enquire if there was any gin on the premises.

'Gin!' came the echo.

'Yes!' Tom raised his voice and made several gin-swallowing motions.

'There may not be gin there now,' came the immediate and generous response, 'but there will be gin,' and so saying the greatly addled victim of wifely abuse dashed back into the pub and returned at once with a bottle of gin. Not only did he bring gin but under his other oxter was a bag containing several bottles of tonic water. Since he could not shake his hand for fear of damage to the bottles Tom Winter slapped him on the back in appreciation of his thoughtfulness.

When they arrived at the abode in question it was decided that they should use the back entrance so that the game might not be given away to the children. There, sure enough, hanging from a cobwebbed rafter was the Santa Claus coat, the Santa Claus hat and the Santa Claus beard. There were no long boots and for this Tom was grateful.

His companion acted as dresser and in jig time Tom was indistinguishable, boots apart, from any other of the numerous Santa Clauses who roamed the country that night. It was agreed that the man of the house should first enter and announce that he had seen Santa Claus in the vicinity and that they should prepare some gin and tonic for his arrival.

A liberal glass of gin was poured and some tonic water added. The lady of the house whose name was Gladiola announced that she had developed a pain in the back as a result of the stress she had endured because of the absence of Santa Claus. She was presented with an equally liberal dollop of gin.

'Hush!' Gladiola raised a silencing hand and then entering fully into the spirit of the business called, 'methinks I hear a step!'

Suddenly everybody from the youngest to the oldest was silent and indeed there was, sure enough, the sound of footsteps in the backyard. Then the back door of the kitchen opened and there entered with his tail in the air the family tomcat who had just returned from an amorous expedition to another part of town. He was followed by Santa Claus. The younger children hid behind their mother while the others crowded round their most welcome visitor and shook his hand and sang and danced and jumped atop the table while their father saw to it that their visitor was presented with his glass of gin into which, without delay, he made substantial inroads.

After the presents were distributed Tom sat by the fire and was prevailed upon to accept another glass of gin.

'I will. I will,' he replied good-humouredly, 'but only if the lady of the house is having one too.'

The lady in question was more than agreeable and soon there was a half-empty bottle where there had been a full one. Songs were sung and for all his wan, woebegone, winterish appearance Tom sang as warmly as any and since he was the proprietor of a soft mellow voice was much in demand as the night wore on.

For once the lady of the house did not resort to abusive language nor did she raise a hand in anger to her husband. Instead she addressed herself to the second gin bottle for which the man of the house had dispatched his oldest daughter. Did I say that he indulged in a glass or two himself? If I didn't let me say at once that he did and if I didn't say that he laughed and sang you may now take my word for it that he did and that he danced as well especially with the smaller members of the household.

The time passed happily and Tom Winter was obliged to admit to himself that he had never spent a better night. No sooner had the second gin bottle been emptied than the clock struck twelve. Declining all offers of tea and edibles Tom took his leave of the happy family in the fond hope that the pub he had vacated earlier in the night would be still manned by some of its staff for much as he enjoyed the household gin he, like all gin lovers, would, if asked, agree that there was no gin like the gin that comes across a bar counter. It is more natural for one thing and there is the unique atmosphere and there is the incomparable presence of drunken companions.

At the doorway, after he had made his goodbyes to the children, Tom Winter gave his word to Gladiola and her husband that he would do the needful without fail the following Christmas and during every Christmas thereafter while there was a gasp of life left in his body. Forgetting to disrobe, he turned his head towards his favourite watering hole. Although full to the gills with gin already he felt an insatiable desire to be reunited with the distinct camaraderie of that spot which had cheered him so often in the past. It is an astonishing aspect entirely of the toper's life that he most requires drink when he least needs it. No other thought now occupied Tom Winter's mind but the prospect of downing a glass of gin and tonic. Let the sot or the drunkard be mightily overburdened after his intake he will, nevertheless, always manage to find room for one more.

After many a skip and many a stagger he eventually arrived at his destination but there was, alas, no room at the inn, at least there was no room for Tom so early on the morning of Christmas Day.

In the eye of the drinker there is no sight so sad as an empty public house or worse a public house which has retained its maximum number of clients and is not prepared, for the sake of comfort and safety, to admit any more. He thought he heard the tinkling of glasses and chinking of coins in tills behind the closed doors, behind the shuttered windows. He had never in his life felt so lonely. It seemed as if the whole world had gone off and left him behind all alone.

Disconsolately he directed his steps towards his shop. Some time later, after it seemed that he had been walking all night, he realised that he had been going around in circles and it dawned on him that the reason for his aimless wandering might be because he really didn't want to go home. To begin with there was nobody there, no cat or no dog, not even a mouse for he had trapped them all in his many mousetraps. Again, more firmly this time, he directed his steps towards the shop but walk as he would he found himself no nearer his base.

Was there a superhuman force restraining him, keeping him away from calamity or was he so drunk that it was not within his power to focus himself properly? There came a time in his journeying when it seemed that he was destined to go on forever and then he fell into the benign arms of Canon Cornelius Coodle. At this stage he had been in the process of passing out.

'My poor fellow,' the canon spoke gently as he dragged his stupefied find towards the garage and thence to the warm room upstairs where he deposited him upon the bed already occupied by the first Santa Claus. Canon Coodle had been surprised to see the first Santa Claus. He had totally forgotten but was relieved that no harm had come to the creature. He was quite taken by the fetching snores, not at all like those to which he was accustomed. He satisfied himself that the second Santa was in no danger of suffocating and was pleased to acknowledge his first resounding snore. He stood for a while at the head of the stairs, listening intently, a rapturous smile on his ancient and serene countenance. He reminded himself that he must tell his curates about this remarkable phenomenon in the morning but wait! What phenomenon! He racked his brains for several moments and then it came back to him. It was the harmonised snoring. Never in all his days had he heard anything so agreeable. It was as though the pair on the bed had been training together all their lives such was the perfect complimentary pitch of their joint renditions. He was reminded of a lyric by Thomas Moore:

Then we'll sing the wild song it once was such pleasure to hear
When our voices commingling breathed like one on the ear.

Surely this was a phenomenon or was it more! Was it a minor miracle, an act of homage to the creator on Christmas morning! He hurried downstairs for his tape recorder. Alas when he returned the snoring had ceased altogether and the pair now lay side by side breathing deeply and evenly, their white beards rising and falling as the air expelled itself from their lungs. Again he thought of Thomas Moore but resorted to parody in order to suit the occasion:

Where the storms that we feel in this wide world might cease
And our hearts like thy snoring be mingled in peace.

Raising his hand he breathed a blessing upon the contented pair before finally repairing to his bed and to the sleep he so richly deserved. As the night wore on the couple on the bed resorted occasionally to bouts of the melodious snoring heard earlier. Then came the dawn and Julie Josie stirred in her bed but did not open her eyes. Her head, surprisingly, did not throb nor did her heart thump. She lay contented for a while in the belief that she was in her own bed. When the snore erupted from somewhere beside her, some place too close for comfort, she too erupted and would have taken instant flight had she not become aware of her apparel.

She stood astonished looking down at the figure on the bed. She crept close to the recumbent form and gently removed the beard. She could scarcely believe her eyes. She knew Tom Winter well, had shopped with him, had always purchased her hardware wants from Tom and Tom alone and she recalled how at that very moment four different pictures hung from walls in her home, hung by Tom's picture cord from Tom's nails, which he had himself driven, and found to be good nails. She also recalled how her late father had purchased the hammer which had driven the nails.

She knew Tom to be a gentle soul, a good-hearted chap who should not be judged on the strength of his wintry face alone. She decided to wake him. He raised himself slowly to his elbows and was surprised, to say the least, when he beheld Santa Claus standing by the bed.

'I'm sorry I didn't bring you anything,' the voice said and what a voice! It is surely the voice of an angel, Tom told himself. He had never heard an angel's voice but he had imagined such a voice ringing in his ear one day and calling him to heaven if he was lucky, if he was very, very lucky. The voice he had just heard was the kind of voice which had called him in his more hopeful dreams.

'Did we sleep together?' he asked falteringly.

'Looks like it,' she answered with a laugh.

'In that case,' said Tom solemnly, 'you must marry me. In fact,' he continued hardly believing himself to be possessed of such courage, 'I would marry you if we had never slept together. I have admired you many a time on the streets and in my humble shop which you have enhanced by your all too rare visits. Say you'll marry me and make my life into something glorious and good. Marry me and change my ways.'

She took his hand gently and was surprised to see that he was not in the least winterish at close quarters.

'We will talk about it some other time,' she whispered gently.

'I will give up the gin,' he promised, 'and never touch the accursed stuff again.'

'No need to give up all drink though,' came the pragmatic response. 'I firmly believe that a few beers now and then would stand you in better stead.' She looked at her watch and saw that it was twenty-five minutes to eleven.

'I'll have to hurry,' she said, 'if I'm not to miss mass.'

'So must I,' he told her.

'Have you any idea how we arrived here?' she asked. He shook his head. As they divested themselves of their Santa Claus coats she spoke again. 'There is something very strange about all this,' she ventured.

'I know. I know,' Tom agreed. 'It's as though we were destined to be together. I mean why else would God join us together in this most unlikely place without either one of us knowing the first thing about it. Neither of us have any idea how we came to be here.'

They never would because the incident would have slipped Canon Coodle's mind after his breakfast and it would never surface again not even when he would marry them in the summer of the following year. He would baptise their children too in the years that followed and they would both live to see their children grow up and their grandchildren and even their great-grandchildren so that it could be truly said of them that they both lived happily ever after.

A Tasmanian Backhander

'When you meet a bully,' Roger Wonsit thrust his hands deep into his trousers pockets and surveyed the class of schoolboys before him, 'you must not allow yourself to be cowed and you must not take to your heels like a coward.'

He paused and allowed his injunctions to sink in before proceeding. He took a turn round the classroom, his head held high, a steely look in his grey eyes. His captive audience, for the most part boys of seven and eight years old, listened with mixed feelings as the famous ex-boxer clenched and unclenched his fists.

Jonathan Cape, the second smallest boy in the class, was glad he wasn't a bully. On the other hand he doubted if he would be able to stand his ground for long should a bully suddenly confront him. Roger Wonsit was going on.

'I,' he said and he paused for a longer period, 'have met many bullies in my time and I have dispatched them thus!' Here he feinted and thrust a straight left into the face of an imaginary bully before demolishing the scoundrel with a right cross.

'There are other methods,' he went on belligerently, 'but the most important thing is that you must never allow anything or anybody to come between yourself and your particular bully.' Here he extended his arms and emitted a blood-curdling whoop that made the hairs stand on Jonathan's head. He looked around for an avenue of escape, convinced that the middle-aged man before him was about to dismember several members of the class. Instead Roger Wonsit seized the imaginary bully by the hair of the head and swung him round and round as though he were a wet dishcloth.

'When your bully comes into view,' he shouted at the top of his voice, 'what must you do?' The class waited eagerly for the great boxer to continue but Roger was not continuing. He was once more applying his tried and trusted psychology of allowing his words to sink in. After several moments he clapped his hands together and asked for the second time: 'What must you do when your bully stands before you?'

When no answer came, as expected, he provided one.

'You must go for his jugular. Forget the size of him and the weight of him. Just go for him and get stuck in. Now what do you do when you see your bully?' The class responded at once, even Jonathan Cape.

'You must go for his jugular and get stuck in.'

'Again.' Roger Wonsit lifted his outstretched palms demanding a more forceful response. This time the class went overboard as such classes do when given the slightest opportunity. Satisfied that he could elicit no more by way of vocal reply he executed a neat dance around the room, shadow-boxing and flooring imaginary assailants at every hand's turn. If asked, most of the boys' parents would be hard put to recall the championship bouts won by Roger Wonsit. They would remember him as an amateur boxer all right and they would remember that he was without peer when it came to weaving and to footwork and to wild swings, any one of which would have dispatched his opponent to Kingdom Come had it landed but they could not recall any knock-outs. The boys' teacher would agree but a number of the more gullible females in the parish had insisted that Roger be allowed talk to the boys.

The emergence, after a long period of relative peace, of several youthful bullies had prompted the action in the first place. The schoolteacher first approached his headmaster, an elderly chap justly famed for his sarcastic comments, and asked for his approval.

'Who did you say?' the headmaster asked in disbelief.

'Roger Wonsit,' his assistant informed him.

'Roger Wonsit,' said the headmaster wearily as was his way, 'would not beat a dead dog. In fact,' he continued, 'Roger Wonsit would not beat the snow off his own overcoat.'

Having rid himself of his daily spew of sarcasm he confided to his assistant that he had no objection to the proposal.

On his way home Jonathan dawdled as only schoolboys dawdle and have been dawdling since the first school was established. As he gazed through a confectioner's window he was joined by his friend Bob's Bobby, an unkempt lad with tousled hair and a wide gap in his upper teeth.

Bob's Bobby was of the travelling people. Confined now to the town's suburbs because of the severity of the winter they would stay put till spring came over the windowsill, as the song says. Then they would move into the countryside and Bob's Bobby's schooling would end temporarily and prematurely as it did every year.

Like most of his kind Bob's Bobby had little interest in schooling.

The teacher understood his feelings in this respect and left him alone for the most part provided he behaved himself.

Jonathan counted the meagre coins which he had withdrawn from his pocket.

'Come on!' He elbowed his friend and made his way into the confectioner's where he went directly to a blonde-haired, rather corpulent young woman who greeted him by his first name.

'A currant bun if you please Miss Polly.' Jonathan handed over the coins and if Miss Polly noticed that there was a minor deficit she kept it to herself and rung up the amount received on the till behind her back.

Outside the shop the boys stood silently examining the bun which sat invitingly on Jonathan's palm. With a skill beyond his years Jonathan managed to divide the bun into two fair halves. He handed one to his friend and if you think that they gobbled the halves down at once then you don't know boys. They consumed the delicate pastry crumb by crumb as only small boys can and when they finished they licked their fingers clean and they ran their tongues around their mouths lest a solitary particle escape. This is not to say that small boys do not wolf and gobble. Of course they do but there are times when the fare is scarce and it is at these times that they prolong the consumption of the delicacy although it must be said that they are not above retaining choice pieces for the very end and these they may well gobble like starving wolves. It is the way of all boys and many adults.

On their way homeward they spoke of many things and then there came the subject of bullies. They were agreed that bullies were best avoided and neither would subscribe to the way-out views of Roger Wonsit. His name, Bob's Bobby recalled, had often come up at night as the travelling folk sat around their campfire. It was Bob's Bobby's grandfather Big Bob who had mentioned the boxer's name.

'I saw him fight once,' the old man told the extended family as they savoured the heat from the glowing logfire. 'In those days he was called Killer Wonsit but I shall never know why for as far as I could see, he was not possessed of the power to kill a butterfly. On the night I saw him he was fighting a man called Crusher Kaly and I shall never know why for he would not crush a skinless banana. They fought for three rounds and not a single blow was struck although I must admit that both boxers left the ring hardly able to stand. I remember they made a lot of noises and they threw a lot of punches but they hadn't a scratch between them when the final bell sounded. The two together would not make one fighting man.'

The young friends parted at Jonathan Cape's front door. Sometimes Jonathan would accompany Bob's Bobby to the campsite and already Jonathan was well acquainted with Big Bob and other lesser-known members of the travelling clan. However, on this particular occasion, Jonathan made the excuse that he had errands to run. He did not say that the real reason was fear of meeting a bully. Truth to tell there was only one real bully in the community and he was newly emerged. He had not yet attracted any henchmen although there was one small, harmless boy who followed him about wherever he went. Already the bully whose sobriquet happened to be Pugace had beaten up several younger bullies and was in receipt of weekly dividends from a score or so of terrified small boys in whom he had successfully invested his time and intimidatory tactics. He didn't have to beat up these victims of his terror campaign. The fame of Pugface had spread throughout the town but only among the schoolchildren. It was their secret and even their parents were in the dark as to the identity of the wretch who was responsible for the sleepless, tortured nights of their offspring.

Pugface had threatened his victims with absolute dismemberment should they breathe a word of his existence to anybody.

Imagine the horror experienced by Jonathan when there was no response to his frenzied knocking just as Pugface, trailed by his satellite, came swaggering down the street. Jonathan's mother, if only he had known, was next door copying a yuletide recipe from her neighbour. Jonathan tried to make himself look smaller as Pugface drew near but failed utterly in his first attempt at self-diminishment.

'Got any money boy?' The question came from the uncouth, overgrown twelve-year-old who stood towering above him.

If only I hadn't purchased that bun, Jonathan thought.

'You deaf boy?' The second question was accompanied by a vicious wigging of Jonathan's left ear. When the bully let go Jonathan remembered Roger Wonsit's words. He withdrew several yards, to the bigger boy's astonishment.

'Go for the jugular!' That's what Wonsit had said. Jonathan did not know exactly where the jugular was situated but he suspected it must be somewhere downstairs or else he would surely have heard his mother use it. He bent his head and ran at his tormentor with a high-pitched squeal. Almost at once, after he had rebounded, he found himself on the flat of his back. Pugface lifted him to his feet by the hair of his head.

'You have my money ready for me next time we meet, you hear boy, else you won't reckernise yourself when you look in the mirror.'

'Sure!' Jonathan assured him.

'You won't forget boy!' Pugface was now wigging the right ear.

'I won't! I won't! I won't!' Jonathan promised. Later he might have told his mother or he might have told his father who had been a crack footballer in his heyday but a fitful sleep full of nightmares would pass before he confided in anybody. After school he informed his friend Bob's Bobby of the previous afternoon's disaster. Christmas was but three days distant and if Jonathan was to hand over his Christmas money there would be nothing left for presents. The friends decided that under no circumstances should any money be handed over. Bob's Bobby was emphatic especially since Jonathan had disclosed to him some weeks before that he intended buying him a Christmas present.

'And I'll get you one too,' Bob's Bobby had replied although after this impetuous promise he did not know where the money for such a luxury would come from. The travellers had little money and the little they had they needed for food and clothing and sometimes for medicine and professional treatment for their sick horses and ponies.

After school the friends decided on a circuitous way home. Bob's Bobby went first so that Jonathan would have time to beat a hasty retreat should his tormentor appear.

'He won't bother with me,' Bob's Bobby explained. 'I don't have any money and I don't have nowhere to get money.' Having escorted his charge to his front door and having waited till he was safely indoors Bob's Bobby hurried homewards, not because he was afraid of Pugface but because he wished to consult his grandfather before the old man departed to the next county where he planned to spend the twelve days of Christmas with his youngest daughter who happened to be married to a travelling man with a loose base in that part of the world. Bob's Bobby found the old man about to depart. First he asked him about the likely locations of red-berried holly trees and then he told him of Jonathan's predicament. Small bearts of red-berried holly sold at one shilling each and there was, Bob's Bobby reckoned, enough time left to him before Christmas to dispose of sufficient bearts to meet his financial requirements for Christmas.

The old man disclosed the whereabouts of three giant holly trees in the extreme corner of a distant wood.

'Cut your branches cleanly and then only the tiniest,' the old traveller warned. 'This way the trees will not suffer and other branches will grow in place of those you cut. For God's sake do not hack or bend or pull branches or the trees will suffer great pain.'

Bob's Bobby promised Big Bob that the trees would not be injured.

'Now,' said his grandfather, 'what was this other matter you wanted to talk about?' Briefly Bob's Bobby ran though the events of the day and the day before.

'I know him to see him,' Big Bob informed his grandson, 'and he's no different from any other bully except that this fellow is blubber from head to toe and will not last long in a scrap. Still he's big and blustery and by now he's used to scaring people so he thinks he's tough.' Followed by his grandson, Big Bob led the way to a small alder grove out of earshot of the makeshift canvas tents and other improvised shelters. There were caravans too, brightly painted down to the very wheel-spokes, canvas-covered as well and not at all unlike the covered wagons used by the early American trail-blazers as they pioneered their way across an undeveloped continent.

'This Pugface,' Big Bob lit his pipe and allowed the blue smoke to ascend through the branches overhead, 'will fall or maybe run the same as all his kind as soon as he meets anybody who'll stand up to him. As far as I can see your friend Jonathan is not this person although from what you've told me he does not seem wanting in courage. Courage alone is never enough when you're dealing with somebody twice your size so it seems to me that you are the very man to deal with Pugface.'

'Me!' Bob's Bobby could scarcely restrain the laughter which came surging from his throat. Ignoring the outburst his grandfather led him by the hand through the grove until they reached an ancient stile which led into an even more ancient graveyard.

'Your great-grandfather, who was my father, lies over there where the ivy climbs the wall near the corner. He was the smallest of all his brothers and some say he was the smallest traveller that ever lived in this part of the country. Yet, for all that, he beat four well-known bullies in the same day in four different places and at the end of that day they stopped being bullies for the rest of their lives. In many ways you resemble him. You have his eyes and you have his hair but now you must ask yourself if you have his wiles and above all you must ask yourself if you have his heart so what you must do is go over to his grave and ask him for the loan of his wiles and the loan of his heart. If a voice comes up out of the ground that says no it will mean that he doesn't want you to have them but if there is no answer by the count of three sevens it will mean that he has passed the things you need over to you. So long as you have his heart and his wiles you need fear no man. Off with you now and I will stand here till you return.'

Big Bob smiled grimly as he watched his nimble grandson leap from mound to mound towards the grave and at the same time, as his grandfather's smile grew grimmer, to his first brush with those who would deny him and deny his friends their natural rights. He watched as the skinny figure made the sign of the cross and he laughed aloud when, at the end of his supplication, he leaped into the air a transformed person. He arrived breathless at Big Bob's side.

'You feel better now?' his grandfather asked.

Bob's Bobby nodded.

'And you feel bigger now?'

'Oh yes. Much bigger,' came the reply.

'All you have to do now is walk up to Pugface in the schoolyard tomorrow and invite him to fight.' Big Bob made it sound as if it was a run-of-the-mill task. His grandson nodded eagerly.

'Now let us return to the camp and on our way I will tell you a few things which will make your job easier. Naturally you will keep these things to yourself or you'll lose your advantage before you begin.'

'Naturally,' came back the positive response. That night the newly infused champion of civil liberties slept soundly and did not awaken until his mother called him for school. His breakfast consisted of a pannyful of sweetened oatmeal porridge and he devoured it with a relish.

As usual during the lunch break the schoolyard was crowded. Pugface stood in the centre surrounded by his fear-filled followers. Bob's Bobby swung him around sharply and invited him to fight after school at a particular place where schoolboys had fought for generations. The venue was an ancient, tree-lined lane which led to the river bank. Mostly the place was deserted although when darkness fell courting couples would converge on the area, sometimes reclining in amorous embraces against the trunks of the giant beeches and, other times, when the moon was visible, walking the river bank hand in hand.

Pugface was temporarily at a loss for words and while he futilely instituted a search for same a crowd of schoolboys began to gather. All eyes were focused on Pugface. Bob's Bobby stood with his skinny legs apart awaiting an answer, his great-grandfather's burning eyes fixed unwaveringly on those of the school's most notorious bully, still speechless and under mounting pressure to make a statement.

The laughter which should have surfaced at the tiny traveller's outrageous challenge was stifled by the intensity of his glare and by the rigidity of his stance.

Only a few moments before a rumour had spread like wildfire through the playground. Bob's Bobby, for all his insignificance and despite his tender years, had killed a grown man with a single kidney punch, a Tasmanian backhander, during a summer altercation at the great fair of Puck in Killorglin in the county of Kerry. It was certain that nobody in the school, the teachers apart, knew the precise whereabouts of the kidneys and it was even more certain that nobody, the teachers included, would ever before have heard of a Tasmanian backhander and how would they when the now oft-repeated phrase had, until that time, belonged exclusively to the vocabulary of Big Bob the traveller who had created it only the day before.

The story of the Killorglin massacre, started initially by Jonathan Cape, had now spread to every corner of the school ground and still, after all this time, Pugface had not responded to Bob's Bobby's challenge nor had he even decided whether he should take the challenge seriously. Finally he spoke.

'After school,' he growled, 'I'll kill you stone dead. First I'll tear off your ears and I'll keep them for my cat. Then I'll tear out your heart and I'll keep it for my dog. Then I'll break your legs and your hands and your head.'

'After school.' Bob's Bobby joined his friend Jonathan who stood near the front of the onlooking throng. The pair decided to return earlier than usual to their classroom. 'We will take this puffed *sciortán* from your withers,' Bob's Bobby assured his friend, 'and that will be my Christmas present to you.'

It was his grandfather who had made the original statement regarding the *sciortán*, his final words, before his departure for his daughter's home in west Cork.

Through the branches of the great trees the sun's rays shed a mottled light on the riverside arena where two hundred schoolboys had gathered to witness the demolition of Bob's Bobby. They were not quite convinced that he had killed a man at the fair of Killorglin and, even if he had, it was certain that members of his clan were at hand to render assistance but every schoolboy would agree that the travelling folk were wily and fearless and there was no doubt about the fact that they would have a variety of ploys and stratagems to suit every occasion. They were most eager to witness, for the first time, the execution of the Tasmanian backhander. Some were sceptical but the majority would have seen the fighting men of the travellers in action at fairs and festivals where they would resort to the most outlandish stratagems in order to gain the upper hand.

'Right, make a ring!' The curt command came from a senior boy whose father was a teacher in the school. It was apparent that some of the father's authority had rubbed off on the son for a ring was created almost immediately and a great hush ensued while the self-appointed master of ceremonies raised his hands aloft and called upon the protagonists to enter the circle. First in was Pugface, shadow-boxing as he entered and snorting like a regular professional as he delivered deadly blows from every angle. The onlookers screamed and shouted at the tops of their yet unbroken voices. Bob's Bobby's entry was less dramatic than his rival's. His approach was indifferent and even reposeful especially when his supporters, and they were in a majority, cheered him until their lungs were fit to burst.

The master of ceremonies now took up his position between the opponents.

'Is it to be a fight to the finish?' he demanded in stentorian tones.

'Yes. Yes!' two hundred voices answered frenetically before either of the principals had a chance to approve or disapprove.

'I'll count to ten,' the master of ceremonies spoke shrilly, 'and when the count is concluded the fight will begin and it will be a fight to the finish.'

He pushed the waiting pugilists well apart but before he could commence the count Bob's Bobby took off his tattered shortcoat and folded it neatly before handing it to his second who chanced to be none other than Jonathan Cape. He then spat on his hands while the onlookers remarked that they had never in their lives beheld such a look in any man's eyes before. The burning orbs fixed themselves on those of Pugface who bent his head, unable to withstand the baleful glare of the tiny traveller. The taking off of the shortcoat had unnerved him. Worse was to follow.

Spitting on his hands a second time Bob's Bobby took off his frayed shirt and folded it neatly. Again he handed it over to his second. The wily traveller then removed his vest until he stood bare from the waist up. He flexed his wrists as an excited murmur ran through the crowd. Could this be the prelude to the devastating Tasmanian backhander? They were never to find out, for Pugface's courage, already wilting after the divesting of the shortcoat, went into sharper decline after the taking off of the shirt. A cold fear gripped him when the last garment of the upper body was handed over to a grinning Jonathan Cape. Why was Cape grinning? Why was the traveller so cocksure? Why did his own hands shake and why did his knees weaken? Why did he wish he was somewhere else all of a sudden and why did the traveller's eyes burn like glowing embers so that his own eyes were blinded and he was unable to see straight? With a cry of indescribable passion the young traveller sunk his teeth into the side of his lower lip. The red blood spurted forth and ran down his chin, coursed down his neck and spread itself over his chest. With a second even more unnerving shriek he rubbed the blood all over his face and arms. Several faint-hearted onlookers took flight. Others, unaccustomed to the sight of blood, fell insensible to the ground.

Bob's Bobby now presented an absolutely hideous sight. The blood drained from the drooling visage of his disintegrating opponent and, worst of all, the shrieking, demoniacal, blood-covered impish traveller was about to launch his first attack. Pugface staggered backwards uttering strange sounds made up of gasps and whimpers and sobs. Then suddenly he turned and ran for his life pursued by Bob's Bobby and Jonathan Cape and a score of other victims of his vile intimidation. They followed him through the streets of the astonished town until he arrived at his own door, a wretched figure still slobbering and sobbing. He disappeared indoors without a single, solitary look behind and was not seen in public for a full week. When he reappeared he was a different Pugface, kind, thoughtful, considerate and courteous to young and old. He would so remain for the remainder of his natural life and when he died prematurely trying to save a drowning cat his was one of the largest funerals ever seen in the district. The travelling folk said of him that he went straight to heaven and that he was embraced three times by St Peter at the pearly gates. After the fight Bob's Bobby, accompanied by his faithful friend, returned to the grave of his great-grandfather where he ceremoniously returned the wiles and the heart he had borrowed. He would never seek a loan of them again for to have these precious things once, even for a short while, is to have them forever. The Christmas that followed was the best for many a year especially for small boys.

Christmas Noses

There are more noses blown at Christmas than any other time of year and, believe me, noses need blowing just as their proprietors need Christmas.

Let me put it another way gentle reader. We don't blow our noses just to clear them or to make loud or rude noises.

There are many hard-faced gents abroad, especially during Christmas, with soft hearts. These unfortunates are slow to express their feelings until they have a certain amount of intoxicating drink aboard. Even then they are reluctant to express their more profound emotions.

What they do instead is to produce large handkerchiefs into which they blow their real feelings. One has to listen closely. Nothing more is required. The baying and the snorting and the trumpeting to which the listener's ears are subjected can be interpreted as expressions of love and concern as fond and as genuine as any which escape all too rarely from the confines of the human heart. How's that William Wordsworth puts it:

Thanks for the human heart by which we live
Thanks for its tenderness, its joys, its fears.
To me the meanest flower that grows can give
Thoughts that do often lie too deep for tears.

Nose-blowing becomes the elderly more than the young and this may well be because elderly noses are larger and veinier and hairier and pucer. Give me an old nose any day of the week before a young nose. There are no reverberations when young noses are blown. In fact you have to tell young folk that they should blow their noses. Old folk blow like nobody's business which is good for noses and old folk alike.

Then there are certain young gentlemen who blow their noses when there is no need whatsoever to do so. They believe that it matures them. They remind me, in many respects, of those young men who sport moustaches and even beards which they hope will make them look older.

These undeveloped nose-blowings have a false ring to them. They are hollow-sounding. They are easily identified by the experienced ear or by anybody whose parents or grandparents were nose-blowers. I could always distinguish my father's nose-blowing from other nose-blows and whenever I heard him in the distance I was instantly reassured that all was well with the world.

Then there are gents who blow their noses in order to make themselves look more manly but it never comes off. The sounds are like those made by baby elephants who have become separated from their mothers whereas the genuine article, the full male outpouring from the facial proboscis, has all the powerful vibrancy of a rogue elephant.

I recall too when I was a boy there were severe-faced old gents of irascible dispositions who would blow their noses at people to intimidate them. It worked in most cases but never when the nose was blown at another nose-blower.

A nose blown properly and from the correct angle often put a man on the right road just as surely as a kick on the posterior did. In order to realise maximum effect, however, the nose should be blown in quiet or hallowed places where silence dominates. A nose suddenly blown at full force in a silent room can send a surprised assailant scuttling for shelter.

There is only one occasion when I find nose-blowing to be extremely shattering and that is when I am the proprietor of a hangover. I always run for my life when I see a nose-blower approaching. Let him blow by all means as long as I am out of range.

On the credit side I heard of a nose-blower in a distant land who once blew a hole in his handkerchief when his prodigal son came home and another who blew off his own hat when he sneezed on Christmas Eve after his grand-daughter had told him she loved him.

I am of the belief that no house should be without a nose-blower. A good, snorting, rattling, bellicose nose-blow will frighten away intruders far better than a barking dog. The criminal will always know that a bark came from a dog but with a comprehensive nose-blow who is to say that the blower is not a polar bear or a tiger or even an elephant!

However, it must be finally said that a good nose-blow into a voluminous handkerchief is the last refuge of the inarticulate, especially those shy souls who long to tell of their love and concern during the glowing days of Christmas.

High Fielding

Jack Frost wasn't as cold or as pinched as his name might suggest. No, he was bluff and hale and hearty, always ostentatiously and good-naturedly slapping down a large-denomination note on the collection tables which were strategically placed Sunday after Sunday around the entrance to the church on behalf of some charity or other. Yet Jack wasn't popular. He wasn't half as well-liked, for instance, as Dinny Doublesay who contributed very little to charities for the good reason that he didn't have an awful lot to give. Of course, Dinny had played football with the local team when he was in his heyday and he had a way with the girls or so they said. Also he was trainer-in-chief of the highly successful under-14 team year in, year out, so that he was highly regarded by parents and youngsters alike. Jack Frost did not like Dinny Doublesay. He once confided to his wife that he hated the sight of him although when pressed for a reason he couldn't say why.

'Could it be,' she asked, 'because everybody else likes him?'

'It could be,' Jack replied peevishly, 'and it could also be something else like he's lousy and warty and picks his nose and he's always chasing after women.'

'But he's a widower,' his wife argued, 'and there's no restriction on widowers.'

'Shut up,' Jack Frost shouted at her and he drew the bedclothes over his head. Jack's wife laughed herself gently to sleep wondering how it was that there had never been an open confrontation between her husband and the man he despised. Certainly the town was small enough and how often did they drink in Gilhaffy's, the football pub where the game's players and aficionados gathered after every championship encounter!

She knew that Jack often tended to bide his time, always on the lookout for an opportunity to get even with somebody who had taken him down or with somebody he didn't like for reasons that he couldn't altogether explain.

She knew Jack Frost. She had been married to him and to the business for thirty years. Jack was sly for all his apparent heartiness and in business there was nobody as devious. He overcharged whenever he thought he would get away with it and as for giving proper weight and measure, well! All Jack's instincts would be opposed to such a dictum. Once when he had overcharged an elderly female for poor-quality sausages his wife had taken him aside and told him firmly that it was wrong.

'Of course it is,' Jack agreed, 'but it's also wrong for her to hide boxes of sardines in her cleavage every time she thinks nobody's looking and it's wrong for her to keep popping grapes into her mouth when she has no notion of buying any.'

The confrontation which Kate Frost had long anticipated and dreaded took place one late evening at the meat counter in the supermarket. Jack was, as usual, immaculately dressed in freshly laundered white coat and cap and greeted each and every customer as though they were long-lost relatives who had been sorely missed. His smile disappeared when he beheld Dinny Doublesay even though the latter had a twenty-pound note in his hand. Jack Frost accepted the note with a curt thank-you after he had wrapped and handed Dinny the four slices of lamb's liver for which he had declared a preference over chops, steaks and kidneys.

Jack placed the note in the till and then sweetly, smilingly and mischievously handed his victim the change out of a ten-pound note.

'I gave you twenty,' Dinny spoke matter-of-factly, not wishing to draw attention to himself.

'You're sure it wasn't a hundred you gave me!' Jack Frost threw out the question for the benefit of everybody within ear-shot. Dinny pursed his lips and availed of the silence which had imposed itself with deadly impact all round.

'I gave you twenty,' he spoke evenly, 'and you gave me the change out of ten which means you've taken me down for ten pounds.'

'Why don't you come in here and have a look at the contents of the till and then we'll see who's codding who?'

Jack Frost stood to one side in order to allow access to his accuser. A number of shoppers surged forward lest they miss the outcome. As the till drawers shot forward Dinny moved in to investigate but was forestalled by Jack.

'Let's have a pair of independent witnesses.' The supermarket proprietor raised a hand and intimated to a pair of females that they should come forward and authenticate the outcome.

Dinny in their presence instituted a fruitless search which would be repeated over and over, at Jack's urgings, by the pair of female witnesses who would declare that there was no twenty-pound note to be seen. There were numerous five- and ten-pound notes but not a solitary twenty.

'Satisfied Mr Doublesay!' Jack slammed the till shut and devoted his attention to the pair who had vindicated him. Dinny stood irresolutely to one side before shuffling his way towards the main exit. He was confused and embarrassed. He could have sworn that he had a twenty-pound note in his hand and that he handed it to Jack Frost. He decided to go home. His daughter would know for sure. Had she not handed him the money as he left the house!

In his wake Jack was escorting the two witnesses to the wine shelves where they would choose one of the more expensive vintages in return for their honesty and integrity.

'Witnesses' expenses!' Jack had laughed aloud as he beamed on all and sundry. Word of the incident would later spread but nobody believed, the witnesses apart, that Jack Frost was innocent. There were many who would recall similar experiences. When he reached home Dinny sat on his favourite chair. His daughter, sensing that something was seriously amiss, sat on hers.

'Did you or did you not give me a twenty-pound note when I left the house a while back?' Dinny asked.

'I gave you a twenty-pound note,' his daughter informed him.

Later in the back room at Gilhaffy's Dinny's many friends in the footballing world commiserated with him, three of his closer cronies in particular. These would be the Maglane brothers Johnny, Jerry and Jimmy who once formed the nucleus of the local football team. They played at left half forward, centre forward and right half forward respectively and when they combined as a unit there was no holding them. They specialised particularly in long passes by hand or foot which often saw the ball travel over distances of forty yards where one of the trio would have surreptitiously removed himself so that he would be in a position to gather the pass and send it over or under the bar for a vital score.

They were, according to local newspaper reporters, imaginative, innovative, accurate and mercurial but it was their passing from improbable distances that set them apart.

Often in the back room at Gilhaffy's followers of the code would ask each other to nominate the best player that ever togged out for the team and invariably the answer would come back – 'I don't know who the best player was but I know who the best three players were.'

The Maglanes were particularly close to Dinny Doublesay. Dinny was the team's full forward when the Maglanes were in the ascendancy. They put many a score his way, unselfishly passing from less favourable distances to where Dinny was disposed near the edge of the square.

'Combine!' Johnny Maglane was fond of saying before championship finals. 'Combine and nothing will beat us!'

'Submerge yourselves!' Jerry would counsel, 'and rise as one so that we will form an unstoppable wave.' Jerry was the poet of the Maglane family and in fact had composed several ballads about the exploits and triumphs of the team.

'A team that doesn't play together won't stay together,' Jimmy would say as the fifteen players primed each other before running on to the field fired with resolve and gleaming with embrocation.

Uppermost in the thoughts of all those congregated in the back room at Gilhaffy's was how to get even with Jack Frost. Violence was outlawed since the team's greatest successes were achieved in the face of violence by the expedient of not reacting and by playing the game according to the rules.

As well as being poetic Jerry Maglane was also the strategist of the team. It was he who laid out the plan of play and it was he who might suddenly order a change of tactics which often turned defeat into victory. There is no element of humanity as potent or as loyal or as dangerous or as compassionate towards each other as the survivors of a once-successful football team. There is that quiet confidence in themselves. There is the certain knowledge that when they present a united front they can achieve anything. That is why none interfered with Jerry as he figured out a way to get even with Jack Frost.

He sat, isolated, humming and hawing to himself, scratching his nose, his forehead and his jaw in turn. He pulled upon his ear lobes as though they were the handles of pumps which would send mighty ideas gushing to his brain. From time to time they surveyed him anxiously.

'Ah yes!' he announced triumphantly at the end of his deliberations, 'I see it all now.'

Johnny Maglane placed a pint of stout in his brother's hand. Nobody knew better than he of the strain to which Jerry had been subjected while he deliberated. None would ask him to reveal his plan. All would be known in due course and this made the prospect of restitution all the sweeter.

Later when the lights had been dimmed in the back room and only the nucleus of the town's best-ever team remained, Jerry told of his requirements.

'I will need,' said he, 'our two best fielders and our best long passer. No more will I say till the deed is done and our comrade's honour is avenged.'

Here he laid a hand on the shoulder of Dinny as a tear moistened his eye and the lips that issued many a stern command on the playing field trembled with emotion.

'All I will say to you,' he addressed himself to the former full forward, 'is that under no circumstances are you to buy a solitary item for Christmas nor are you to utter a solitary word to any man or woman until our business is done.'

The nights passed slowly thereafter and as they did the Christmas fever mounted until its spirit was everywhere abroad. Two nights before the blessed event there was an extension of shopping hours until nine o'clock.

Shortly before the extension ended Johnny Maglane and his wife Pidge arrived at Jack Frost's supermarket ostensibly to purchase some groceries to tide them over the Christmas holiday.

'I want you,' Johnny informed Pidge, 'to engage Jack Frost in conversation. Make sure that his back is turned to me at all times.'

Pidge nodded eagerly. She was well aware that there was something afoot and she was only too eager to be part of it. Dinny ranked high among her friends and she was as anxious as the other conspirators to see the score settled. Also she had no doubt about her ability to engage and absorb Jack Frost in a long and interesting conversation. Jack, for his part, had often cast a longing eye in the direction of the footballer's wife.

'Dang it!' he often whispered to himself, 'I will never understand how those danged footballers with nothing in their heads wind up with such good-looking women. I mean,' he would continue to confide to himself, 'what have they got that I haven't got and yet the best of women fall for these so-called athletes who, more often than not, kick the danged ball wide.'

It was a question that he would never successfully answer. When Pidge approached him and suggested they remove themselves to a quiet area he jumped at the opportunity and when they arrived at a secluded spot behind the dog-and-cat food pyramids he waited eagerly for some heart-lifting revelation. For a while she did not speak, for the good reason that she could think of nothing to say.

'Well!' Jack Frost moved from one foot to the other.

'Well!' Pidge echoed the question as she racked her brains for something to say.

'Oh yes,' she said in a confidential tone as though what she was about to say had slipped her mind and had suddenly presented itself again.

'I was wondering,' Pidge opened, 'if you would consider joining our drama society?'

Jack Frost was astonished.

'Me!' was all he could say.

'I don't see why not.' Pidge was in full flight now. 'I mean you have the appearance and you have the carriage. Carriage is ninety percent of acting. Then you're sharp. I mean you wouldn't have any trouble remembering lines. I'm sure you know the price of everything on those shelves and if you can memorise such prosaic things as prices you can memorise anything. Then there's your voice. It's so seductive and yet so resonant. Then there are your eyes, those come-to-bed eyes. Man dear you were born for the stage!'

It was at this stage of the conversation that the object whizzed by overhead.

'What was that?' Jack asked, looking up anxiously but seeing nothing.

'What was what?' Pidge asked although fully aware that something had passed by in the space above them.

'Never mind, never mind!' Jack dismissed the intrusion and wished only for his unexpected veneration to continue. It was, in fact, a ten-pound trussed turkey enshrouded in plastic wrapping which had passed. It had been thrown by Pidge's husband Johnny who had lifted it from a display case and, when he was certain nobody was looking, flung it a full forty yards out through the main exit where it was beautifully fielded by his brother Jerry who passed it at least fifty more yards to the third Maglane brother Jimmy who fielded it with great skill before placing it in the open booth of his car. There followed a ham, cooked and wrapped, and if the Maglane brothers had fielded well in their respective heydays they fielded magnificently now but the skills of Jerry and Jimmy were shortly to be put to an unprecedented test by the oldest brother who, for good measure, had lifted a bottle of Cuvée Dom Perignon 1985 from the wine shelf, had lovingly handled it feeling its weight and balance and dispatched it faithfully and accurately into the waiting hands of the much-lauded fielder, his brother Jerry, who flung it in turn to the third brother Jimmy, who placed it beside the turkey and ham in the car booth.

After the champagne had been flung Johnny Maglane decided that enough was enough. The three items which had flown through the air with the greatest of ease would more than compensate Dinny and by the time the story leaked and reached the ears of Jack Frost, the ham and the turkey would have been devoured. Christmas would have been toasted and the champagne swallowed by Dinny Doublesay and his darling daughter.

A Christmas Diversion

At seventy-one the Badger MacMew retained most of the brown, grey-streaked hair which had earned him his sobriquet. Otherwise he didn't look in the least like a badger. He was tall, slender, elegant and courteous which was more than could be said for some of the mischievous neighbours who privately compared him to the carnivorous mammal after which he was named.

'It isn't fair,' Mary Agge Lehone was fond of telling the few elderly customers who still frequented her tiny green grocery near the end of the long street which had seen better days.

'I mean,' Mary Agge would go on, 'he's so refined and he never badgers anybody. He brings me bags of kindling all the time and he never charges anything. It's all out of the goodness of his heart.'

Part of what Mary Agge said was true. The Badger MacMew, particularly during the long winters, would scour the nearby woodlands for the kindling with which the bright turf fires of the neighbourhood were started.

Though never full, the rickety turf shed at the rear of the Lehone premises was never without a horse-rail or two of turf, not top-quality black turf but sods of brown and grey which burned all too quickly. Black, bottom-sod turf, on the other hand, lasted from one end of the day to the other provided, of course, the fire was properly constructed in the first place.

The Badger's turf shed, several doors downwards from Mary Agge's, contained no turf at all. There was some timber and a modest heap of *bruscar*. Since the Badger lived off his old-age pension he could not afford to supplement his wood stocks with turf or coal. By careful management and skilful disposition of his *bruscar* his hearth was never without a small fire while he was indoors. Electricity was still waiting in the wings in those distant days so that it was to native timber and turf that the street's inhabitants turned to keep out the cold and boil the water and cook the food and wash the clothes and the faces and the hands and the bodies and so forth and so on.

Before we proceed further it must be said that it wasn't altogether out of the goodness of his heart that the Badger MacMew saw to the kindling wants of Mary Agge Lehone. The Badger had, all his life, shown a preference for the single state. Mary Agge's late husband Walter had expired suddenly some thirty years before while cleaning the family chimney. The exertions had proved too much for him and when he fell silently to the ground he was already dead. Mary Agge had been thirty-seven at the time and while she might have married during the intervening years she declined many a substantial offer for she was dainty, petite and some said good-looking in her own way. She also had her own home, fronted by the small green grocery. She knew how to cook and even her detractors would be forced to admit that she never put a hard word on anybody. She received the blessed sacrament every morning of the week and was one of the four select female trios who decorated the altars of the parish church, unfailingly, when it was their turn to do so.

The Badger, on the other hand, missed mass on occasion and received the sacred host but yearly. He was, however, it was agreed by most, not a bad chap at all and might well see heaven if he mended his ways ever so slightly. He suffered occasionally from severe twinges of arthritis but was otherwise healthy and mobile. He had been a trousers-maker until his sixty-eighth year when his arthritic fingers began to fail him and he was forced into retirement.

When Mary Agge's husband Walter died many felt that she would succumb to grief and die of a broken heart but surprisingly she rallied as most widows do and proceeded to live out her lonely days as content as any woman could be in such a situation. The Badger decided shortly after Walter's burial that he would contribute in his own small way to Mary Agge's upkeep. She would never be without kindling while he could visit the woodlands. Gradually he found himself falling in love with her but he resolved that she must never know. For one thing it might damage their friendship such as it was if he ever confessed his true feelings to her. Then there was the danger that she might be so deeply offended that she might sever the relationship permanently. He chose to keep his mouth shut and pray that she might deduce from the quality and consistency of the kindlings that he cherished her above all others and would do so till his last lopping crumbled silently into the ashes of her hearth. He dreamed of her last thing at night and first thing in the morning. He always maintained to himself that it was a small thing which would acquaint her fully of his love for her, some as yet unimagined occasion which would swing things in his favour, some incident or instrument of fate, some insignificant out-of-the-blue factor from which he might find her securely cradled in his arms, her soft hair brushing his ear lobes and her hazel eyes laughing into his.

In his dreams they travelled widely together, sharing the same tastes, revelling in the wild scenery where they would find themselves at the close of day in the presence of incomparable sunsets.

One would never dream from looking at the Badger MacMew that such romantic thoughts dominated his dreaming but such is the reality of life that we should never be surprised by the romantic aspirations of the most unlikely. All humans aspire through fantasy but nominating oneself for the ultimate honours in a close relationship was an undertaking fraught with hazards. That was the reason the Badger had become a perpetual bidder of time like millions of other no-hopers in every corner of the human world. He was well aware that others in the vicinity were desirous of advancing their causes through fair means or foul in the direction of his beloved Mary Agge. His worst fear was that she might suddenly be swept off her feet by a dark horse in a late surge while he dawdled and hoped for a miracle. In this respect there was one individual he feared more than any other. In his estimation the person in question was a loud-mouthed, scurrilous pervert by the name of Danny Sagru. Every street, he thought bitterly, had its Danny Sagru. He was, therefore, astonished one day to hear the very same scoundrel being described by none other than Mary Agge herself as not a bad oul' fella.

Not a bad oul' fella! He repeated the undeserved delineation to himself several times. Oh dear, oh dear! How naive was womanhood and how gormless was this unfortunate woman in particular!

Danny Sagru was, without doubt, the most unpopular man in the entire street, the entire parish. If you were to scour the highways and byways you would be hard put to find somebody with a good word to say about him. There were a number of reasons for this. He owned most of the land roundabout. He was wealthier than even Tom Shine the draper, Joe Willies the baker, Ned Hobbs the grocer.

Danny Sagru didn't carry his wealth well. He boasted about it. He rattled the silver in his trousers pockets and he regularly flicked the chunky wad of notes which he had no need to carry about with him.

If he ever gave a small boy a penny he would always charge the recipient to inform all and sundry that Danny Sagru had given it to him.

He never subscribed to charities and yet Mary Agge Lehone had publicly stated that he was not a bad oul' fella. He was an oul' fella all right, the Badger would subscribe to this. He was several years older than the Badger although he did not look as if he was. He had an appetite like a horse but wait, the Badger began a reassessment of his arch-rival.

If he was placed under oath the Badger would have to admit that the scoundrel possessed a certain degree of spurious loyalty. He would have to concede that Danny Sagru always purchased his vegetables from Mary Agge Lehone and from Mary Agge Lehone alone. Let the cabbage be wrinkled, the spuds watery, the turnips frostbitten. Let her parsnips be shrivelled, her carrots shrunken, her cauliflowers browning! It mattered not to Danny and there was another even more worrying aspect of his purchases. He never questioned her prices. There was an extravagance about him as he pressed the coins into the cup of her hand.

'Your change, your change,' she would call after him as he exploded through the shop door, cabbages in one hand, potato satchel in the other.

'Keep it, keep it,' he would call back as though it were a considerable sum, whereas in reality, it never exceeded a half-penny.

For all his wealth Danny Sagru had never forsaken the modest home where he first saw the light. The house, like all the others including Mary Agge's, was two-storeyed and two-bedroomed with a back shed, always filled to capacity with black, heavy sods. There was access from the shed to a long but narrow backway along which ran the seventy or more back sheds which housed the fuel supplies for the corresponding front or street houses. All looked alike, all with pitch painted corrugated iron roofs, all rickety and in need of restructuring, all save that of Danny, which was a model of its kind and which was crammed from bottom to top with turf sods as black as the ace of spades, heavy as lead and more lasting than coal.

Danny had several suppliers who were acquainted from long experience with his precise needs. Turf-cutters with horse-drawn, clamped rails of the precious bottom sods would arrive regularly at the Sagru shed and deposit their loads. There was a fixed rate and seasoned turf-cutters would say to novices, 'You don't renege on him and he won't renege on you. You'll get nothing extra but you will get your due.'

Then, as happens every ten years or so, there came a poor turf harvest. The less well-off suffered most. Danny Sagru suffered not at all. Widows and waifs in the vicinity might perish with the cold but Danny held fast to the sods he had. His poorer neighbours knew that it would be a waste of time to plead for a sod or two to tide them over till the bogs dried so that suppliers might gain access to their turf banks. Like the Badger MacMew they traversed the woodlands near and far for kindling.

The Badger led parties of youngsters to likely places where old logs had lain rotting for years. They sawed and hacked and somehow managed to acquire hearthfuls of fuel to see them through. All the while, through the long nights, Danny Sagru sat in front of his warm fire, occasionally adding to the brightness and redness of his ulcerous nose by the simple expedient of swallowing glass after glass of punch. None shared his hearth, no dog nor cat nor chick nor child nor neighbour nor friend. What he savoured he savoured alone.

Alas for Mary Agge Lehone her fires grew smaller but they never went out. The Badger MacMew saw to that. The Badger gave all he had until the frost silently laid its cold, white mantle over field and bogland, over street, backway and rooftop. The frost was but a day in residence when Danny Sagru was astonished by the inroads the bad weather had made into his turf. Instead of tackling his spirited pony to the gleaming trap as was his wont when he wished to visit an outlying cattle fair he hired a hackney car to transport him across the fifteen miles of roadway to the village where the fair would be in progress. With Christmas coming up in a few days and fodder in short supply there would be little demand for store cattle. It was a good time to buy and a man with fodder to spare and money to burn like Danny Sagru might profitably expand his existing stock at no great expense. He had done so many times in the past and, indeed, it was from such fortuitous investments that he built most of his fortune. As they drove towards the village Danny's attention was drawn to a moving vehicle which slowly descended a hilly boreen on its way to the main road.

'Pull up! Pull up!' Danny called to his driver. As the roadbound transport reached the cross which would take it to the village where the fair was in progress Danny emerged from the rear of the hired car and raised a hand, indicating that he had a desire to parley. Before him was stalled at the crossroads one of the largest, highest-clamped, heaviest loads of black turf ever to present itself before the greedy green eyes of Danny Sagru. The load was drawn by a powerful black mare, sixteen hands high and shimmering with muscle from crest to hock, a beautiful animal and worthy transporter of such a perfectly clamped cargo.

'How much?' Danny Sagru asked.

The turfman, squat and brown, looked over his merchandise as if he had only then noticed it and took stock of the prosperous-looking individual who posed the question regarding the price.

'One pound, two shillings and sixpence,' came the clipped response.

Danny advanced and circled the mare and rail, feeling individual sods as he proceeded with his inspection.

'If you'll be good enough to move out of the way now, like a good chap,' the turfman flicked his reins, 'I'll be on my way, for you see sir I have clients galore waiting in the village.'

'Hold it! Hold it!' Danny Sagru raised an imperious hand and blocked his way. The mare shook her shining harness and raised her shapely head with its sensitive nose and flickering ears.

'I'll give you your money,' Danny announced calmly, 'but you'll have to deliver to my premises in Ballyfurane.'

'Which is seven miles from here and seven miles back and which adds another shilling to the price, for this mare will be in sore need of oats by the time we deliver.' The turfman folded his arms.

'I won't quibble with you.' Danny located the money and handed it over.

'You'll give me a luck penny now!' Danny suggested to the turfman who was quick to point out that luck money only came into question when large sums were involved.

'Do you know me?' Danny asked.

'Sure don't the whole world know you,' the turfman declared.

'Ask any person you meet on your way into town and they'll show you where I hang out,' Danny informed him. 'The turf shed is at the rear of the house and 'tisn't bolted nor locked for as quirky and quare as my neighbours are they're too proud to steal. Off with you now and who knows but we'll do business again.'

'Ballyfurane is out of my way,' the turfman announced as he allowed the mare her head, 'but if the money is right I could see myself doing further business with you.'

The village of Ballyfurane consisted of one long main street and two small side streets. The windows of the small shops along the main thoroughfare were decorated with holly and ivy. Some boasted tinsel and fairy lights and a few sported homemade cribs representing the nativity.

With Christmas approaching there was an air of mild anticipation. Shoppers were plentiful and business, if not brisk, was reasonably good, which was just about as good as anybody could expect in a small place like Ballyfurane.

When the Angelus bell tolled in memory of the Incarnation, as it did every day at twelve noon, Badger MacMew found himself standing at the quietest of the village's four street corners. His hands were thrust deep into his trousers pockets and there was a faraway look on his unshaven face. He was, however, far from despondent. He had, but a bare five minutes before, delivered a bundle of high-quality kindling to Mary Agge Lehone and she had actually allowed her fingers to rest briefly on the back of his hand by way of appreciation. With recollection he concluded that it would be fairer to say her fingers brushed the back of his hand. Still it was a handsome advance on the smiles with which she had previously rewarded him.

As he looked into the distance he beheld for the first time the high-clamped rail of turf drawn by the black mare, guided by a turfman he had never seen before. He withdrew his hands slowly from his pockets and proceeded in a rambling fashion towards the oncoming transport. The Badger was possessed of the natural curiosity of all villagers everywhere except that in his personal case he was a curious fellow by nature and liked to know at all times what was happening in his bailiwick. As he drew near he was surprised when the mare drew to a halt at the behest of the turfman.

'Excuse me sir!' the turfman respectfully addressed himself to the Badger. 'I am looking for the premises of Danny Sagru.'

The Badger did not answer at once. The proprietor of the sought after premises was safely out of town and would not be back for some time, probably nightfall since he was partial to strong drink whenever he encountered fellow-members of the cattle-jobbing confraternity.

'Follow me.' The Badger turned on his heels and led the way to the by-way at the rear of the main street. He kept a distance of forty yards between himself and the turfman and he walked along the pavements rather than the roadway so that it might be clearly seen that the turfman and he had no connection with each other. Firstly he led the turfman to a lane-way at the back of which was a by-way which would take them albeit circuituously to the backway behind the main street where the many lookalike turf sheds stood side by side. The backway was deserted save for a neighbourhood tomcat who sat on the roof of a shed and took no interest in the proceedings beneath him. In the backway the Badger slowed his gait so that the turfman might catch up with him.

'This is the shed.' He indicated the rickety structure at the rear of Mary Agge Lehone's small shop. 'I'll open the door for you and you can heel it in.'

In no time at all the rail was empty and the turfman on his way homewards by an altogether different egress, indicated by the Badger. It was an egress which would lead him to a little-used boreen which would lead him past the village and on to the main route to his hilly abode. Later that evening he and his wife and family would invest the turf money in their Christmas shopping and a happy and holy Christmas would be had by all.

As soon as the turfman had departed the Badger took it upon himself to call upon Mary Agge. A beaming smile was the essence of her greeting as soon as he entered. They stood there without exchange of words or the need for exchange of words.

'You will find,' the Badger said after a short while, 'a little Christmas gift in your shed and I hope it brings you the warmth and comfort you so richly deserve.'

With that he departed and did not appear on the street again until Christmas Eve. It was nightfall as he walked past her door and at first he thought that the sounds he heard as he went by were the chortlings of a dove but no, it was Mary Agge calling his name, gently ever so gently and but barely discernible even though the street was still. When he entered she closed the door behind them and led the way to the small kitchen where a glowing fire spread heat from the hearth.

'You'll have a drop of whiskey,' she said with a smile, 'and so will I,' and so they did and she invited him back the following day for his Christmas dinner and there was no word from Danny Sagru about his missing turf for he was vain in the extreme and would never give it to say that he had been taken down. It would never occur to him, in a score of years, that the Badger had diverted the turf and that Mary Agge Lehone had burned it.

Indeed the Badger and Mary Agge shared all their Christmas dinners thereafter but not as friends or lovers or anything like that but as man and wife and there need be no worries about their living happily ever after because that was exactly what they did.

The Woman Who Hated Christmas

Polly Baun did not hate Christmas as some of her more uncharitable neighbours would have people believe. She merely disliked it. She was once accused by a local drunkard of trying to call a halt to Christmas. She was on her way out of church at the time and the drunkard, who celebrated his own form of mass by criticising the sermon while he leaned against the outside wall of the church, was seen to push her on the back as she passed the spot where he leaned. As a result Polly Baun fell forward and was rendered immobile for a week. She told her husband that she had slipped on a banana skin because he was a short-tempered chap. However, he found out from another drunkard who frequented the same tavern that Polly had been pushed. When he confronted her with his findings she reluctantly conceded that the second drunkard had been telling the truth.

'You won't do anything rash!' she beseeched him.

'I won't do anything rash,' Shaun Baun promised, 'but you will have to agree that this man's energies must be directed in another direction. I mean we can't have him pushing women to the ground because he disagrees with their views. I mean,' he continued in what he believed to be a reasonable tone, 'if this sort of thing is allowed to go on unchecked no woman will be safe.'

'It doesn't worry me in the least,' Polly assured him.

'That may be,' he returned, 'but the fact of the matter is that no woman deserves to be pushed to the ground.'

Polly decided that the time had come to terminate the conversation. It was leading nowhere to begin with and she was afraid she might say something that would infuriate her husband. He flew off the handle easily but generally he would return to his normal state of complacency after a few brief moments.

As Christmas approached, the street shed its everyday look and donned the finery of the season. Polly Baun made one of her few concessions to Christmas by buying a goose. It was a young goose, small but plump and, most importantly, purchased from an accredited goose breeder. It would suit the two of them nicely. There were no children and there would be no Christmas guests and Polly who was of a thrifty disposition judged that there would also be enough for St

Stephen's Day. She did not need to be thrifty. The hat shop behind which they lived did a tidy business. The tiny kitchen at the rear of the shop served a threefold purpose all told. As well as being a kitchen it was also a dining area and sitting-room. They might have added on but Polly failed to see the need for this. She was content with what she had and she felt that one of the chief problems with the world was that people did not know when they were well off.

'They should be on their knees all day thanking God,' she would tell her husband when he brought news of malcontents who lived only to whine.

Shaun Baun sought out and isolated his wife's attacker one wet night a week before Christmas. The scoundrel was in the habit of taking a turn around the town before retiring to the pub for the evening. Shaun did not want to take advantage of him while he might be in his cups and besides he wanted him sober enough to fully understand the enormity of his transgressions.

'You sir!' Shaun addressed his victim in a secluded side street, 'are not a gentleman and neither are you any other kind of man. You knocked my wife to the ground and did not bother to go to her assistance.'

'I was drunk,' came back the reply.

'Being drunk is not sufficient justification for pushing a woman to the ground.'

'I was told,' the drunkard's voice was filled with fear, 'that she hates Christmas.'

'That is not sufficient justification either,' Shaun Baun insisted. The drunkard began to back off as Shaun assumed a fighting pose.

'Before I clobber you,' Shaun Baun announced grimly, 'I feel obliged to correct a mistaken impression you have. My wife does not hate Christmas as you would infer. My wife simply discourages Christmas which is an entirely different matter.' So saying Shaun feinted, snorted, shuffled and finally landed a nose-breaking blow which saw the drunkard fall to the ground with a cry of pain. At once Shaun Baun extended a helping hand and brought him to his feet where he assured him that full retribution had been extracted and that the matter was closed.

'However,' Shaun Baun drew himself up to his full height which was five feet one and a half inches, 'if you so much as look at my wife from this day forth I will break both your legs.'

The drunkard nodded his head eagerly, earnestly indicating that he had taken the warning to heart. He would, in the course of time, intimidate other women but he would never thereafter have anything to do with Polly Baun. For her part Polly would never know that an assault had taken place. Shaun would never tell her. She would only disapprove. She would continue to discourage Christmas as was her wont and, with this in mind, she decided to remove all the chairs from the kitchen and place them in the backyard until Christmas had run its course. If, she quite rightly deduced, there were no chairs for those who made Christmas visits they would not be able to sit down and, therefore, their visits would be of short duration.

On the day before Christmas Eve the hat shop was busy. Occasionally when a purchase was made the wearer would first defer to Polly's judgement. This, of course, necessitated a trip to the kitchen. The practice had been in existence for years. Countrymen in particular and confirmed bachelors would make the short trip to the kitchen to have their hats or caps inspected. On getting the nod from Polly they would return to the shop and pay Shaun for their purchases. Sometimes Polly would disapprove of the colour and other times she would disapprove of the shape. There were times when she would shake her head because of the hat's size or because of its rim or because of its crown. Shaun's trade flourished because his customers were satisfied and the shy ones and the retiring ones and the irresolute ones left the premises safe in the knowledge that they would not be laughed at because of their choice of headgear.

As time passed and it became clear that the union would not be blessed with children Polly became known as the woman who hated Christmas. Nobody would ever say it to her face and certainly nobody would say it to her husband's face. It must be said on behalf of the community that none took real exception to her stance. They were well used to Christmas attitudes. There was a tradesman who resided in the suburbs and every year about a week before Christmas he would disappear into the countryside where he rented a small cabin until Christmas was over. He had nothing personal against Christmas and had said so publicly on numerous occasions. It was just that he couldn't stand the build-up to Christmas what with the decorations and the lighting and the cards and the shopping and the gluttony, to mention but a few of his grievances.

There was another gentleman who locked his door on Christmas Eve and did not open it for a month. Some say he simply hibernated and when he reappeared on the street after the prescribed period he looked as if he had. He was unshaven and his hair was tousled and his face was gaunt as a corpse's and there were black circles under his eyes.

Then there were those who would go off the drink for Christmas just because everybody else was going on. And there were those who would not countenance seasonal fare such as turkeys or geese or plum pudding or spiced beef. One man said he would rather an egg and another insisted that those who consumed fowl would have tainted innards for the rest of their days.

There were, therefore, abundant precedents for attitudes like Polly Baun's. There were those who would excuse her on the grounds that maybe she had a good and secret reason to hate Christmas but mostly they would accept what Shaun said, that she simply discouraged it.

There had been occasions when small children would come to the door of the kitchen while their parents searched for suitable hats. The knowing ones would point to where the silhouette of the woman who hated Christmas was visible through the stained glass of the doorway which led from the shop to the kitchen. One might whisper to the others as he pointed inwards, 'that's the woman who hates Christmas!' If Polly heard, she never reacted. Sometimes in the streets, during the days before Christmas, she would find herself the object of curious stares from shoppers who had just been informed of her pet aversion by friends or relations. If she noticed she gave no indication.

Shaun Baun also felt the seasonal undercurrents when he visited his neighbourhood tavern during the Christmas festivities. He drank but little, a few glasses of stout with a friend but never whiskey. He had once been a prodigious whiskey drinker and then all of a sudden he gave up whiskey altogether and never indulged again. No one knew why, not even his closest friends. There was no explanation. One night he went home full of whiskey and the next night he drank none. There was the inevitable speculation but the truth would never be known and his friends, all too well aware of his fiery temper, did not pursue the matter. Neither did they raise the question of his wife's Christmas disposition except when his back was turned but like most of the community they did not consider it to be of any great significance. There was, of course, a reason for it. There had to be if one accepted the premise that there was a reason for everything.

On Christmas Eve there was much merriment and goodwill in the tavern. Another of Shaun Baun's cronies had given up whiskey on his doctor's instructions and presumed wrongly that this might well have been the reason why Shaun had forsaken the stuff. Courteously but firmly Shaun informed him that his giving up whiskey had nothing to do with doctors, that it was a purely personal decision. The night was spoiled for Shaun. Rather than betray his true feelings on such an occasion he slipped away early and walked as far as the outermost suburbs of the town, then turned and made his way homewards at a brisk pace. Nobody could be blamed for thinking that here was a busy shopkeeper availing himself of the rarer airs of the night whereas the truth was that his mind was in turmoil, all brought on by the reference to whiskey in the public house. Nobody knew better than Shaun why he had given up whiskey unless it was his wife.

As he walked he clenched and unclenched his fists and cursed the day that he had ever tasted whiskey. He remembered striking her and he remembered why and as he did he stopped and threw his arms upwards into the night and sobbed as he always sobbed whenever he found himself unable to drive the dreadful memory away. He remembered how he had been drinking since the early afternoon on that fateful occasion. Every time he sold a hat he would dash across the roadway to the pub with the purchaser in tow. He reckoned afterwards that he had never consumed so much whiskey in so short a time. When he closed the shop he announced that he was going straight to the public house and this despite his wife's protestations. She begged him to eat something. She lovingly entreated him not to drink any more whiskey, to indulge in beer or stout, and he agreed and kissed her and then hurried off to surfeit himself with more whiskey. He would later excuse himself on the grounds that he was young and impetuous but he would never be able to excuse the use of his fist in that awful moment which would haunt him for the rest of his life. An oncoming pedestrian moved swiftly on to the road-way at the sight of the gesticulating creature who seemed to rant and rave as he approached. Shaun moved relentlessly onward, trying to dispel the memory of what had been the worst moment he had ever experienced but he still remembered as though it had happened only the day before.

He had left the pub with several companions and they had gone on to an after-hours establishment where they exceeded themselves. Shaun had come home at seven o'clock in the morning. He searched in vain for his key but it was nowhere to be found. He turned out his pockets but the exercise yielded nothing. Then he did what his likes had been doing since the first key had been mislaid. He knocked gently upon the front window with his knuckles and when this failed to elicit a response he located a coin and used it to beat a subdued tattoo on the fanlight and when this failed he pounded upon the door.

At length the door was opened to him and closed behind him by his dressing-gowned, bedroom-slippered wife. It took little by way of skill to evade his drunken embrace. She passed him easily in the shop and awaited him with folded arms in the kitchen.

A wiser woman would have ushered him upstairs, bedded him safely down and suspended any verbal onslaught until a more favourable time. She did not know so early in her married days that the most futile of all wifely exercises is arguing with a drunken husband.

She began by asking him if he saw the state of himself, which was a pointless question to begin with. She asked him in short order if he knew the hour of the morning it was and was he aware of the fact that he was expected to accompany her to mass in a few short hours. He stood silently, hands and head hanging, unable to muster a reply. All he wished for was his bed; even the floor would have satisfied him but she had only begun. She outlined for him all the trouble he had caused her in their three years of marriage, his drinking habits, his bouts of sickness after the excesses of the pub, his intemperate language and, worst of all, the spectacle he made of himself in front of the neighbours. Nothing remarkable here, the gentle reader would be sure to say, familiar enough stuff and common to such occasions in the so-called civilised countries of the world but let me stress that it was not the quality of her broadsides but the quantity. She went on and on and on and it became clear that she should have vented her ire piecemeal over the three years rather than hoard it all for one sustained outburst.

Afterwards Shaun Baun would say that he did what he did to shut out the noise. If there had been lulls now and then he might have borne it all with more patience but she simply never let up. On the few occasions that he nodded off she shouted into the more convenient ear so that he would splutter into immediate if drunken wakefulness. Finally, the whole business became unbearable. Her voice had reached its highest pitch since the onslaught began and she even grew surprised at the frenzy of her own outpourings.

Could she but have taken a leaf out of the books of the countless wives in the neighbourhood who found themselves confronted with equally intemperate spouses she would have fared much better and there would be no need for recrimination on Christmas morning. Alas, this was not her way. She foolishly presumed that the swaying monstrosity before her was one of a kind and that a drastic dressing-down of truly lasting proportions was his only hope of salvation.

Whenever he tried to move out of ear-shot she seized him firmly by the shoulders and made him stand his ground. Drunk and incapable as he was he managed to place the table between them. For a while they played a game of cat and mouse but eventually he tired and she began a final session of ranting which had the effect of clouding his judgement such was its intensity. He did not realise that he had delivered the blow until she had fallen to the ground.

Afterwards he would argue with himself that he only meant to remove her from his path so that he could escape upstairs and find succour in the spare bedroom. She fell heavily, the blood streaming from a laceration on her cheekbone. When he attempted to help her he fell awkwardly across her and stunned himself when his forehead struck the floor. When he woke he saw that the morning's light was streaming in the window. The clock on the kitchen mantelpiece confirmed his worst fears. For the first time in his life he had missed mass. Then slowly the events of the night before began to take shape. He prayed in vain that he had experienced a nightmare, that his wife would appear any moment bouncing and cheerful from last mass. He struggled to his feet and entered his shop.

The last of the mass-goers had departed the street outside. Fearing the worst he climbed the stairs to the bedroom which they had so lovingly shared since they first married. She lay on the bed, her head propped up by bloodstained pillows, a plaster covering the gash she had suffered, her face swollen beyond belief. Shaun Baun fell on his knees at the side of the bed and sobbed his very heart out but the figure on the bed lay motionless, her unforgiving eyes fixed on the ceiling. There would be no Christmas dinner on that occasion. Contritely, all day and all night, he made sobbing visitations to the bedroom with cups of coffee and tea and other beverages but there was to be no relenting.

Three months would pass before she acknowledged his existence and three more would expire before words were exchanged. Two years in all would go unfleetingly by before it could be said that they had the semblance of a relationship. That had all been twenty-five years before and now as he walked homewards avoiding the main streets he longed to kneel before her and beg her forgiveness once more. Every so often during the course of every year in between he would ask her to forgive the unforgivable as he called it. He had never touched her in anger since that night or raised his voice or allowed his face to exhibit the semblance of a frown in her presence.

When he returned she was sitting silently by the fire. The goose, plucked and stuffed, sat on a large dish. It would be duly roasted on the morrow. As soon as he entered the kitchen he sat by her side and took her hand in his. As always, he declared his love for her and she responded, as always, by squeezing the hand which held hers. They would sit thus as they had sat since that unforgettable night so many years before. There would be no change in the pattern. They would happily recall the events of the day and they would decide upon which mass they would attend on the great holy day. She would accept the glass of sherry which he always poured for her. He would pour himself a bottle of stout and they would sip happily. They would enjoy another drink and another and then they would sit quietly for a while. Then as always the sobbing would begin. It would come from deep within him. He would kneel in front of her with his head buried in her lap and every so often, between great heaving sobs, he would tell her how sorry he was. She would nod and smile and place her hands around his head and then he would raise the head and look into her eyes and ask her forgiveness as he had been doing for so many years.

'I forgive you dear,' she would reassure him and he would sob all the more. She would never hurt him. She could not find it in her heart to do that. He was a good man if a hotheaded one and he had made up for that moment of madness many times over. All through the night she would dutifully comfort him by accepting his every expression of atonement. She always thought of her father on such occasions. He had never raised his voice to her or to her mother. He had been drunk on many an occasion, notably weddings and christenings, but all he ever did was to lift her mother or herself in his arms. She was glad that she was able to forgive her husband but there was forgiveness and forgiveness and hers was the kind that would never let her forget. Her husband would never know the difference. She would always be there when he needed her, especially at Christmas.

PAIL BUT NOT WAN

One of my fondest memories of Christmas is a whistling milkman now passed on to that sweet clime where whistle the gentle winds of heaven. He would whistle louder, longer and sweeter at Christmas than at any other time of the year.

He must have been sixty when I first heard him of a Christmas morning many years ago. He was a curly-haired, chubby-faced fellow who looked only thirty years old, although in reality he was double that age. He was that kind of person. Age, it would seem, made no impression on him.

Without doubt his fountain of youth was his whistling. First thing in the morning after the cocks had crowed and the last of the crows flown countrywards his exhilarating serenading could be heard clearly for long distances as he cycled upon his rounds.

What a happy man he must have been! He never whistled a drab melody. He excelled most of all at the stirring march and he would generously empty his heart to all and sundry at no charge whatsoever. Romantic airs were meat and drink to him and he would give his all in an effort to strum the sweet chords of love which lie dormant in so many people.

Dour veterans of the marital confrontation would relent and turn in their beds to celebrate sweet sessions of amorous rapture and all because of his incidental input. No nightingale ever sang so sweetly as he. No skylark ever plumbed the soulful depths for sensitive melody. The early morning, ushered in by the waning stars, was merely the backdrop for his princely renditions.

He contributed more to the rescue of foundering marriages than any human intermediary could ever hope to. It often seemed that he was especially transported from some heavenly sphere for no other purpose than the upraising of downcast hearts. Even his lightweight warblings would fritter away depressions and lift up the human spirit to its loftiest pinnacles.

Surely the pipings of that yesterday milkman had their origins in heaven although it was the orifice of his contracting lips that modulated and measured the bewitching torrent of empyrean sonority which charmed and delighted all those who happened to be within earshot. There wasn't a child in the street who did not try to emulate that dear, departed milkman.

I remember once of an icy morning before Christmas he fell from his rickety bicycle, spilling the contents of both his pails and breaking two front teeth into the bargain. His lips, poor fellow, were brutally lacerated. The tears formed in his eyes as he witnessed the streams of freshly drawn milk coursing irredeemably to the nearest channel but how quickly did he transform misfortune into triumph.

Supporting himself on his right knee and placing his left hand over his breast he pursed his shattered lips, oblivious to the agonising pain. Then extending his right hand to his unseen public he gave the performance of his life. Long before had he finished, the under-employed lips of couples in that once dreary street were never so utilised in the pursuit of loving fulfilment. For the listening lovers in the silent houses it was a never-to-be-forgotten experience. Some had never even dreamed of aspiring to such unprecedented ecstasies. Many had waited a score of Christmases for such a development.

If only the world and its people could wait long enough everybody would eventually be kissed by someone, be loved by someone.

This piece is just an informal salute to Christmas and to the memory of a forgotten milkman who made life more harmonious on a far-off Christmas morning for those within his round.

The Good Corner Boy

This is the story of the good corner boy. As stories go it is as true as any. To some it may seem improbable but I can counter this by stating that most true stories seem that way anyway. Enough, however, of the preamble. Let us proceed without further ado.

On 20 December 1971, Madgie Crane withdrew some of her savings from the bank. A tidy sum was involved: two hundred pounds no less, but then as she might say herself she had many calls. There were sons and daughters and grandchildren. There were neighbours and there were friends and relations. Of husbands she had none. There had been one but he had passed on some years before and she had come to terms with her grief in the course of time.

As she turned the corner which would take her to the post office she bumped accidentally into another woman who chanced to be returning from the same venue. As a result Madgie Crane's purse jumped from the grocery bag where it had been securely wedged between a cabbage and a half-pound of rashers. It landed at the feet of the corner boy in residence and that worthy immediately fenced it between his waiting boots where no trace of it remained visible to the searching eye.

The minutes passed but no move did our corner boy make. He looked hither and thither from time to time but if there had never been a purse between his feet he would have looked hither and thither anyway and he would have looked up and down anyway but he would never have bent to tie his shoes for in all the years that I have spent studying corner boys I never saw one bend to tie his shoes.

As he pretended to look after his laces his delicate fingers quickly opened the purse and his drowsy eyes looked inside. Two hundred pounds if there was a penny! Deftly he flicked the purse up the loose sleeve of his faded raincoat and rose to his feet. Even if somebody had been watching, and he was sure that nobody had, his actions could not possibly convey anything of a disingenuous nature.

It was no more than a formality to insert his hands into his trousers' pockets with the purse still up his sleeve. A gentle shake of the sleeve in question and the purse fell downwards into the waiting pocket. It was precisely at that moment that he was addressed by Madgie Crane. There was a tear in her eye and a quiver in her voice.

'I suppose,' she opened tremulously, 'you saw no sign of a purse.'

No answer came from the seemingly mystified corner boy. It was as though she had spoken in a strange tongue.

'Every penny I had was inside in it,' she continued.

Still no response from the resident corner boy. He blew his nose and he looked hither and thither. He shifted his weight from one foot to the other and he looked secondly at Madgie Crane. He noted the weariness and the confusion and he watched without change of expression as the tears became more copious. Her brimming eyes discharged them aplenty down the sides of her withered face. His hand tightened on the swollen purse and he inclined his head towards the channel which ran parallel to the pavement.

Hard as he would try afterwards he would never be able to explain why he did what he did because he needed money at that point in his life as he had never needed money before. He needed it for his widowed sister with whom he lodged and he needed it for her children whom he loved and he needed it to pay his bills. He needed it so that he might embark on a comprehensive drunk for a day or two for he believed that this was his entitlement because of the season that was in it.

Having inclined his head towards a particular spot in the channel he moved swiftly in that direction and pretended to retrieve the purse. Lifting it aloft he enquired of Madgie Crane if this indeed was the missing article. Madgie chortled with delight and clapped her dumpling hands together soundlessly. She stood on her toes for the first time in twenty years and graciously accepted her property from the hands of her benefactor.

She opened the purse and she proceeded to count her money. Never was there such an assiduous reckoning and never did anyone count so little for so long. Assuring herself that every note was present and correct she instituted a second count and finally, when that was satisfactorily concluded, she started a third count. It was during the middle of this count that she moved off in the direction of the post office where she had deposited her grocery bag with an obliging clerk.

The corner boy stood amazed. He had been stunned and shocked many times in his life but he had never been amazed. It was a strange and unnerving experience for a man of his years. A giddiness assailed him and he collapsed in an ungainly heap at the corner where he had stood rocklike for so long.

A half hour later he woke up in a nearby public house just as an ambulance arrived on the scene. He refused all forms of aid and was told that a doctor was on the way. He declined the publican's offer to wait in the snug but he did not decline the medicinal brandy tendered to him by the publican's wife. Exactly forty-five minutes after his collapse he returned to his corner and took up his usual position.

Word of his good deed spread and the community was shocked to learn that he had received nothing by way of reward from Madgie. No wonder he fainted, some said, and he was right to faint, more said. An ad hoc committee was formed and a collection made. It amounted to eleven pounds two shillings and seven pence half-penny. He wrapped it in his handkerchief and instructed a neighbour who chanced to be passing to deliver it to his sister. For the rest of the day, because it was Christmas time, he answered all queries from passers-by, directing strangers to the post office, the banks and the churches, often accompanying them to the extremes of his bailiwick and imparting his blessing on all. Also because it was Christmas he led the old and the feeble across the busy roadway, cautioning them to alert him whenever they wished to cross back again. Only at Christmas do corner boys involve themselves in the activities around them.

Then a second giddiness assailed him but this time it was accompanied by a sharp pain in the chest. He fell to the pavement where he immediately expired. When word of his passing spread, all who knew him agreed he had been a good corner boy. He never scolded children and he was the last refuge of wandering tomcats who took shelter behind him at night when cross canines might tear them asunder. He was devoted to his corner. Those who knew him would testify that he lived for nothing else and that it was because of his corner he never married.

When drunkards fought or scuffled on their way homewards he never interfered, thereby assuring the impoverished and the curious of free entertainment, unlike others who spoiled the fun by coming between the contestants. His corner would never be the same again nor would we look upon his likes again. Truly it could be said that he died at his post and surely it would be right and fitting to call him the good corner boy.

SOMETHING DRASTIC

Canon Cornelius Coodle stood with his palms on the parapet of Ballybradawn bridge and surveyed the swirling, foaming flood waters below. The canon could never cross any bridge at home or abroad without pausing to inspect the waters that passed beneath. He had once been a salmon angler and was locally regarded as something of an authority on lures, particularly artificial flies and minnows which he frequently made himself. He was of the belief that every major river needed its own particular bait.

Generally speaking, suitable baits were to be found in shops which catered for the needs of anglers but because of the contours of local river beds and because of the related agitation of the changing waters the canon believed that one had to be specific. There were other factors too such as the light and shade peculiar to certain stretches of water influenced by the arboreal canopies at particular times of year. All of these and many other features, too numerous to mention, had to be taken into account when a man sat down to prepare his angling gear for the beginning of the angling season which was no more than ten days away.

Canon Coodle had not fished for several years. Now in his early eighties he lacked the sprightliness which once saw him vault the most formidable of stiles in his stride and leap unerringly from rock to crag to grassy inch where a false step might easily mean permanent immersion or at the very least a broken limb.

As he looked down the river's course he recalled doughty salmon which he had landed in his heyday. A happy smile crossed his face but was at once replaced by a frown for which he could find no apparent justification. This was the worrying part. His memory had started to fail him as well as his physical agility and he wondered what it might be that had occasioned the frown. In vain he tried to bring it to mind. He knew for certain that there was a problem and undoubtedly it was an unpleasant task and it would hang over him until it presented itself at the most unlikely and unfavourable time such as when he might be sitting in his study after dinner smoking his pipe or savouring a sip from the glass of port in which he sometimes indulged after a satisfactory meal. Then the forgotten obligation or predicament would intrude not because he would remember it of his own accord but because it would be thrust upon him by a reminder from his housekeeper or curates or by a visit from the person or persons involved.

Always when making a promise that he would perform a particular function he would start right away in the direction of his study to make a note of the business but by the time he reached pencil and paper he would have forgotten. He was a prudent enough man about the maintenance of his health so that when he found the chill of the river winds penetrating his overcoat he began his return journey to the presbytery.

Every evening before dinner he would walk briskly as far as the bridge and back again. He never dawdled on such excursions. The pangs of hunger and the prospect of an excellent dinner saw to that. It was the only business, apart from celebration of his masses, of which his housekeeper did not need to remind him. It was said of him that he had a good stroke which simply meant in the everyday idiom of the place that he was possessed of a healthy appetite.

Upon his return he knelt for a while in prayer. Then came the persistent tinkling of the housekeeper's bell. After a decent interval he joined his curates in the dining-room. Throughout the excellent meal the talk centred on Christmas duties. It was during dessert that the younger of the curates reminded the canon that he was expected at the local convent at two o'clock on Christmas Day where, as had been the custom for the eighteen years of his canonship, he would be expected to join the sisters for the Christmas dinner.

The curate had been waylaid by Mother Francesca, a towering figure of commensurate girth for whom both curates and their beloved pastor had a healthy respect if not regard.

'Was she born a reverend mother,' a wisecracking bishop had once asked, 'because,' he continued, 'I just cannot imagine her as a novice.'

It would be true to say, however, that Francesca was not as bad as she was painted. All she ever wanted was her own way and as long as that was forthcoming life could be tolerable enough for those who came into contact with her on a regular basis. So that was it then, the canon, relieved after a fashion, pushed away his half-finished dessert and declined the offer of coffee from the senior curate. At the mention of Francesca's name and the awful prospect of the Christmas dinner which he could not avoid he had instantly decided that instead of the glass of port to which he would normally address himself he would finish off the bottle which contained, in his humble estimation, at least three glasses. He felt it was his inalienable right in view of what he would have to suffer shortly as a consequence of parochial custom.

After the port he would go straight to bed for, as he well knew, he would be in no condition to go anywhere else. His curates no longer allowed him to go on sick calls after dark unless it was a special occasion and then only if one of the curates was available to transport him.

The younger men had noted his reaction when reminded of his unwelcome seasonal responsibility. They had both dined with Mother Francesca and they had both been obliged to resort to Vesuvian belches in order to get rid of the trapped winds and obnoxious gases which had built up to dangerous levels after the meals which Francesca insisted on preparing herself, especially if those invited to dine were members of the clergy. She had been brought up to believe that the clergy needed and were entitled to richer, meatier and generally more substantial meals than lay people no matter how pious. The official convent cook, Sister Carmelita, never interfered when her superior became involved. She had been tempted often enough especially during the preparation for the Christmas dinner but like all the other inmates she opted for the peaceful way out and kept her mind to herself.

Christmas, which was not the norm for Christmas days in that part of the world, broke mild and balmy and belied the time of year that was in it. The presbytery housekeeper had taken off at first light on her bicycle for her sister's home in the nearby hills and, after the masses, the curates would head for the homes of their families in the north and south of the diocese.

The canon would look after the sick calls, if any, and one of the curates would return before darkness to relieve the canon who would be in no fit mental condition to go anywhere, anyway, after his ordeal at the convent and it was to this venerable institution that he wended his way shortly before two o'clock on the appointed day to partake of the Christmas fare so lovingly prepared by Mother Francesca.

During Francesca's brief absences from the kitchen Sister Carmelita would furtively and speedily modify the more distasteful aspects of the reverend mother's preparations. 'Otherwise she might poison us all!' she told herself not without justification.

As Canon Coodle drew near the tree-lined entrance his steps faltered and he cast about him that sort of despairing look which was to be seen on the faces of condemned souls as they ascend the steps to the gallows. Although he tried to banish them, visions of the previous years' dinners began to take shape before his mind's eye. How could he ever forget the monumental heap which covered the huge dish so that not a solitary speck of the esteemed willow pattern was to be seen anywhere beneath. There was, to begin with, a mound of mashed turnips which would comfortably cope with the needs of a small hotel for the round of a day and there was a mighty heap of potato stuffing which would go a long way towards assuaging the hunger pangs of the average family with a grandparent or two thrown in for good measure.

There had been peas and beans, white meat and dark as well as the outsized thigh of the largest cock turkey that could be found in the countryside for miles around and all of this on the same plate, covered with fat-infused gravy. Worst of all, the victims were expected to consume every trace of food on their plates. The canon shuddered at the memory. Mother Francesca always took it as a personal affront if anybody failed to clear the plate. She eschewed containers for the different vegetables, stoutly maintaining that there was too much trouble involved and that, anyway, it was nothing more than grandiose nonsense.

All her charges from young postulants to elderly sisters who had all but forgotten where they originally came from had the foresight to cut down on food intake for days before and especially on Christmas morning with such a challenge looming in front of them. The canon had expressly foregone breakfast so that he would be capable of making inroads into Francesca's plate not to mention her specially enriched plum pudding which followed hot on the heels of the monstrous main course. The plum pudding in turn was followed by Christmas cake and several freshly opened tins of assorted biscuits which had to be liberally sampled and seen to be liberally sampled.

The saddest aspect of the entire orgy as far as Canon Cornelius Coodle was concerned was that not a single drop of intoxicating drink was on display although it would have to be said that this was not entirely the fault of the reverend mother. Rather was it the fault of the canon's predecessor Canon Montague and the reverend mother's predecessor Mother Amabilis.

The late Canon Montague, poor fellow, had the reputation of being the heaviest drinker in the diocese and would drink any other two clerics under the table, at any given sitting, without exerting himself. His friend Mother Amabilis was what locals would call an innocent sort, that is to say she was a trifle naive as far as the ways of the world were concerned. She would ply the late canon with his favourite poison, Hooter's Heart-throb whiskey, until, I turn to the locals again, it came out through his eyes.

Always, by the time the dinner ended he was incapable of negotiating the journey from convent to presbytery of his own accord. Before he expired at the astonishing age of eighty-nine from sheer senility and a perfectly functioning liver, he had consumed a veritable reservoir of Hooter's Heart-throb. On the Christmas of his eighty-sixth year he was so plied with his favourite tincture by Mother Amabilis that he was unable to perform his priestly duties for three whole days. Word inevitably reached the bishop of the diocese and, as a consequence, the mother-general paid a surprise visit to Mother Amabilis shortly after Christmas or to be exact on the afternoon of the feast of the Epiphany. She called her aside, as it were, and from that moment forth an embargo was placed on intoxicating drink within the confines of the convent. All existing stocks were transferred to the local hospital where they might be used in moderation for purely medicinal purposes.

Oddly enough Canon Coodle placed not a particle of blame on his otherwise illustrious predecessor or on the open-handed Mother Amabilis. There is none of us who does not suffer in some small way from the sins of our ancestors but the balance is nearly always redressed by the goodness they leave behind.

Canon Coodle, with apologies to none, fortified himself, to a limited degree, by imbibing two glasses of twelve-year-old whiskey prior to his departure for the convent and he now found himself flushed of face but sound in mind and limb, with no prospect of further drink, at the hall door of the convent. He was warmly received and it must be said that there wasn't a nun there, Mother Francesca apart, who would not have gladly lifted the cruel restriction given the authority to do so. There was no doubt but that Mother Francesca had the power to do so because the present incumbent of the bishopric would have yielded to any demand she might make rather than incur her ire.

Francesca, alas, had been born of drunken parents and since there are some who believe that it is better to be born in hell there was no way she would countenance the lifting of the ban on alcohol. Rather than possessing a genuine vocation for her calling the reverend mother was a refugee from the real world and like all refugees she was so thankful to be in a safe haven that she would rather die than invalidate an established procedure.

As the nuns tripped merrily into the spacious dining-room the canon trudged behind escorted by Mother Francesca. They sat according to rank and age along both sides of the table with the canon at the head and the reverend mother at the bottom.

All present then reverentially entwined their fingers and sat rigidly as they waited for the canon to start the proceedings with the Grace Before Meals. He had but barely concluded when the phone rang. All sat silently in the hope that it would go away but go it did not. Mother Francesca lifted her mighty frame slowly from her seat. What a rugby forward she would have made, the canon almost laughed aloud, if she had been born of the opposite sex, although as she bore down upon the offending phone she looked more like a battleship. A heated argument ensued. It was obvious that the person at the other end of the line was determined to have her way.

'Can't it wait a half hour?' the Reverend Mother shouted. Her frown suggested that the answer was in the negative.

'But he's just about to begin his Christmas dinner, poor man,' the Reverend Mother persisted vehemently. The anger on her face as she listened intimated that the caller did not really care what the canon was sitting down to.

'All right, all right!' the Reverend Mother called at the top of her voice, 'we'll let him decide for himself.'

Meanwhile Canon Cornelius Coodle, vicar general of the diocese and the eldest of its priests, had been an eager listener. Was the possibility of a reprieve on the cards?

'You are required for a sick call,' Mother Francesca spoke as if the canon was to blame, 'but I have suggested to this person,' she distastefully indicated the mouthpiece in her hand, 'that you be allowed finish your dinner first.'

The canon rose to his feet, touching the sides of his mouth with the large white napkin provided by his hosts in an effort to conceal his absolute delight.

'Find out where it is,' he asked gently, 'we must never keep a poor soul waiting.' He laid the napkin on the table and blessed himself although he had neither sipped nor eaten.

'You won't believe this,' the Reverend Mother turned her attention to the nuns who had been highly entertained by the exchanges, 'but they want him to go to the very top of Ballybuggawn at his age without a bite inside in him.' All the nuns tut-tutted obediently and reproachfully.

'I'll have to fetch my car.' The canon was already moving towards the door of the dining-room, his face alight with joy, a surging youthfulness in his step.

'Wait, wait!' Mother Francesca called after him. 'The sisters will drive you as far as your car and you can take your dinner with you.' Here she summoned the younger members of her community and in no time at all a pair of eager sisters appeared from the kitchen with a large wickerwork basket containing the delights already mentioned.

'No need, no need.' The canon raised his hands aloft. It required his best efforts to control his happiness. He wanted to leap, to shout, to dance while Mother Francesca lifted the white cloth which covered the massive array of goodies which they had prepared for him. He feigned inexpressible gratitude and announced that he would do justice to the fare before the night was out. Then he was gone, followed by the two nuns who bore the basket between them. They would deposit it in the boot of his car on his instructions and he would proceed airily to Flanagan's of Ballybuggawn and, if it was on top of the highest hill in the parish itself, he wouldn't have minded were it twice as high or the road twice as dangerous. He was a free man and, more importantly, a clergyman on his way to succour some unfortunate soul who desperately needed forgiveness. Otherwise why would he or she seek the services of a priest on Christmas Day?

Canon Coodle regretted that he would not be able to keep his promise about doing justice to the contents of the basket but he promised himself that it would not be thrown away untouched. With this in mind he drew to a halt near an iron gate which led to a green field half-way up the hill of Ballybuggawn. A large flock of crows had just alighted thereon and who better to consume and relish an unwanted meal than the birds of the air. Entering the field, basket in hand, he looked all around to see if anybody was watching. He need not have worried. Man, woman and child in the area were sitting down to dinner or had finished dinner and were resting.

Then, hastily, he unceremoniously dumped the entire convent dinner and returned each plate to the basket before going back to his car. Nobody would ever know and when Mother Francesca would ask if he had enjoyed his Christmas dinner he could truthfully reply that it had gone down well and there wasn't a single one of the crows, already gorging themselves with delighted squawks, who would contradict him. He stood contentedly, hands clasped behind back, surveying the snow-covered summit of Ballybuggawn. He brought his hands to his midriff and entwined them prayerfully as he expressed his gratitude to the Lord of Creation for his happy lot. If, at the end of his days, he should be asked to nominate the happiest day of his life he would have no hesitation in selecting the day that was in it.

At Flanagan's of Ballybuggawn he was well received. Here in this humble cot he was respected above all other men in the parish for his humility and saintliness. Joe and Sarah Flanagan, a childless couple in their late seventies, were mystified when the canon asked to be shown into the presence of the sick party. As the elderly pair continued to exchange baffled looks the canon announced that he would administer the sacrament of Extreme Unction without further delay.

'I'm afraid there's been a mistake canon,' Joe Flanagan forestalled him, 'there's nobody sick here.'

Joe's wife Sarah curtsied and spoke next. 'We haven't been sick a day thank God these fifty years canon,' she said proudly.

'And is there another Flanagan in the neighbourhood?' the canon asked politely.

He was informed with equal politeness that he was looking at the only two Flanagans on Ballybuggawn Hill from top to bottom.

'And is there anybody in need of a priest hereabouts?' the canon ventured. No. There was nobody sick in the vicinity thank God but might it not be some other Flanagan in some other part of the parish?

'Oh dear, oh dear!' Canon Coodle looked out through the small window of the kitchen and saw that the first stars were beginning to appear prematurely as dusk embraced the snow-crested hill.

'It's a long journey back to town canon,' Joe Flanagan reminded his parish priest.

'And a cold one canon,' Sarah Flanagan was curtsying again.

'Would you take a drop of something canon,' Joe Flanagan asked in a most respectful tone, 'a tint of the hot stuff now for the journey?'

'Or there's port,' Sarah put in, 'Sandeman's Five Star or there's brandy if you'd care for it?'

'Port,' the canon divested himself of his overcoat and took the chair which Joe had moved closer to the fire, 'a port would be much appreciated.'

An hour later after the canon had swallowed a large glass of port and eaten two boiled eggs with several slices of homemade brown bread the trio knelt and recited the Rosary after which the canon thanked his hosts from the bottom of his heart and assured them that he had never eaten such flavoursome eggs or such nourishing bread in his entire life.

The trio had concluded earlier that the canon had been the victim of a mischievous joke and privately the canon could not find it in his heart to condemn the mischief-maker if such indeed it was. Reluctantly he took his leave and promised faithfully that he would visit for his supper again when the snow had departed from the hilltop and the slopes brightened by the lengthening days.

That night in the presbytery sitting-room the canon sat with his two curates and housekeeper. Between sips of port he recounted the events of the day but made no reference to the convent basket or the delighted crows. He waxed eloquently about the simple but incomparable fare given with such a heart and a will by the Flanagans.

'There is nothing on the face of creation,' the housekeeper said solemnly, 'as good as a free-range egg, freshly laid.' Her listeners lifted their glasses in agreement while she rearranged the knitting which lay upon her lap. 'What crowns it all, of course, is fresh brown bread made with expert hands and Sarah Flanagan has years of breadmaking behind her.'

Again the listeners lifted their glasses, this time without drinking from them.

'But,' the housekeeper was continuing as she resumed her knitting, 'if there was home-made butter going with the brown bread you would have a feast fit for a parish priest.'

Here they all laughed, none more so than the canon. The housekeeper smiled to herself when the laughter had abated. She had made the call from her sister's phone and she had adopted a sharp Ulster accent in an effort to conceal her identity. There was no doubt in her mind that she had escaped detection. She had no qualms of conscience about the call. Her primary role in life was to protect her canon against all-comers whether bishops, mutinous curates, rampaging reverend mothers or whosoever threatened the canon's well-being. Other executives in the lay world had wives and secretaries to look out for them whereas Canon Coodle, on the threshold of infirmity, was easy prey for assorted parochial predators. She had watched him suffer over the years at the indelicate hands of Mother Francesca, a pampered virago who couldn't fry a sausage properly and who had burned more rashers in her time than any ten women in the parish put together. Of late the housekeeper had noticed a slight decline in the canon's health, especially during the days leading up to Christmas when she knew that the awful prospect of Francesca's cooking was about as much as he could bear. She had made up her mind irreversibly before she left for her sister's on Christmas Day. Nobody else seemed to notice the extreme distress of Canon Coodle. She resolved that something drastic should be done and that she was the one to do it. She knew Joe and Sarah Flanagan as well as she could know anybody. She knew of their genuine regard for Canon Coodle and she knew that the Flanagans would see to his welfare foodwise. She was proud of what she had done. She had won a reprieve for her lord and master and now that the precedent had been established she would ensure that he would never again have to endure the murderous concoctions of Francesca and thus guarantee a longer and less stressful life for her ageing parish priest.

THE WOMAN WHO PASSED HERSELF OUT

Jenny Collins had a philosophy about Christmas. She shared it with her friends and neighbours as she did with everything else she had.

'Christmas,' said Jenny, 'is like an egg. If you don't take it before its date of expiry it will turn rotten.' The trouble with Jenny was that she took her own words too much to heart. For instance she would send out greeting cards from the middle of October onwards. This would be acceptable if the cards were destined for such far-off places as Tristan da Cunha or Faizabad but the opposite was nearly always the case. Mostly the cards were for neighbours or for friends who lived nearby. Occasionally there would be one addressed to Dublin or Cork, places to where delivery was assured after a day or two.

'Jenny,' her father had said to her once after she served him his Christmas dinner at eleven in the morning, 'you are in mortal danger of passing yourself out.'

It was widely believed in that part of the world at that time that those who passed themselves out rarely caught up with themselves again. Jenny's father, who was in his eighties, would explain to his friends that she brought the trait from her grandmother who set out all her life for twelve o'clock mass at ten minutes past eleven and this despite the fact that the church was less than a hundred yards from her home. When the old lady eventually expired after a visit from the family doctor the latter was seen to shake his head in amazement when he was asked to pronounce her dead within the hour. He had predicted that she would hold out for at least a fortnight but true to form she had quit the land of the living fourteen days before her time. Her granddaughter Jenny had never been late for school and neither had any one of Jenny's three children, two girls and a boy who won every school attendance prize that was going and who were to be seen on all mass days with their parents in the front pew of the parish church at least a half hour before the priest and his retinue appeared at the altar. Others who were never in time for anything would shake their heads in disbelief at the folly of it all but Canon Coodle, the parish priest, was heard to say to his housekeeper that Jenny and her brood were to be commended.

'It is a holy and wholesome thought to pray for the dead,' the canon said solemnly, 'so that they may be loosed from their sins.'

Jenny's husband Tom was of the strong silent variety. As far as he was concerned his wife's injunctions were law and, anyway, he was a most devout person. As well as that he seldom spoke and rarely contradicted. Jenny, therefore, was free to do as she pleased without previous consultations, not that she was ever likely to do anything untoward in the first place.

Older, wiser matrons along the street felt that Tom Collins should exercise a little more control over his wife's comings and goings on the grounds that it was not altogether correct to give a woman all the rein, especially a young woman. Be that as it may, as the man said, Jenny and Tom Collins were never at loggerheads and the children were healthy and happy.

Jenny's father who resided with them since his wife's death was well looked after although from time to time he would issue cautions to his daughter about the dangers of presumption and presupposition not to mention the awful consequences of passing herself out. He would issue these dire warnings on a daily basis as Christmas approached but he was too old and too infirm to realise that Jenny would have long beforehand anticipated Christmas. She would have scoured the shops near and far during the post-Christmas and New Year's sales seasons in the hope of finding inexpensive but suitable presents for not-so-near relations and not-so-close friends. Then when the sales fever had worn off she would relax for a brief period but once St Patrick's Day had slipped by she would begin to feel the pressures of Christmas once more.

A suitable Sunday would be set aside so that she might engage two turkeys, one for Christmas and one for the feast of the Epiphany or the Women's Christmas as it was called thereabouts.

Sometime between the last week of March and the first week of April the entire family would fare forth on foot into the countryside as soon as the midday meal was consumed and the ware washed and dried. This particular excursion would always fall on a Sunday and so it happened that on the fifth Sunday of the Lenten period the family set out to the same farmhouse with the same Christmas order for turkeys, all five firmly wrapped against the wind and the rain. Jenny had seen to her father's wants before her departure and when she informed him of her plans he protested, insisting that there was plenty of time with Christmas more than eight months away.

'And how do I know,' his daughter informed him, 'whether turkeys will be scarce or plentiful this coming Christmas and how do I know,' she went on, warming to her task, 'whether or not some disease might strike the turkey population between now and then and who's to say but a plague of foxes will not descend on the countryside and devour half the birds or who is to say what may or may not happen so isn't it better be sure than sorry?'

'Away with you,' he laughed, extending his face for a kiss, 'you're every bit as bad as your grandmother.'

Secure in the knowledge that there would be turkeys for the distant festivities, Jenny Collins placed an order with her local butcher for spiced beef, standing close by to ensure that the order was properly entered in the appropriate ledger and that her name was spelled correctly.

Some would remark that it was just as well that she was not nearly so fastidious about other festivals. She would surely pass herself out altogether, they maintained, if she was. For instance she would not bother with shamrock for her husband's lapel or badges for her daughters' coats until the very morning before St Patrick's Day nor would she bother with sprigs of palm for Palm Sunday until that very morning whereas others would have it ready, cut and blessed for days before. The simple truth was that Jenny Collins looked upon all other festivals as mere diversions on the road to Christmas. Her father would agree.

'Jenny,' said he, 'sees the ending of one Christmas as the beginning of another. Personally speaking I do not wish to hear of Christmas until a week or so beforehand. It becomes diluted if it drags out too long. What's going to happen eventually is that they'll drag out Christmas so much that it will snap.'

Nobody took any notice of the old man and who could blame them! Had he not prophesied the end of the world three times and had not nothing happened! He was, it must be said, genuinely worried about his daughter.

'A lot of people do what I do,' she explained. 'It saves money and it saves time.'

He had shaken his head ominously at the time and would not be reassured. When Christmas finally came around Jenny became nervous and fidgety and began to natter to herself when she thought nobody was listening.

Most of the time when we talk to ourselves we merely indulge in harmless quotes or we hum and we haw and vice versa. We do not, as Jenny Collins did, remind ourselves about the future. Quite unexpectedly she began to purchase odds and ends for the next Christmas despite the fact that the Christmas being celebrated was not yet over. Her father became greatly alarmed and went so far as to suggest that what Jenny was doing was sacrilegious. Her children, for the very first time, became worried and her husband decided it was time to speak. Is anything more eagerly awaited than the utterance of a man who has steadfastly kept his mouth shut over the years whilst others all around are pontificating! Consequently, when Tom Collins cleared his throat with a view towards expressing what could well be described as his maiden speech there was widespread alarm in the house. Jenny, anticipating a statement of unprecedented importance, called for order by rapping noisily on the milk jug with a dessert spoon. All the members of the family were seated at the table quite accidentally on the occasion. Jenny's father sat at the head completing his favourite crossword while his son-in-law Tom sat at the bottom with a face like a slipper trying to contain two blood-thirsty greyhounds who have just sighted a hare. He was waiting for precisely the right moment to unleash his two words. At one side sat Jenny and her son while at the other sat the two girls. The old man placed his crossword underneath the milk jug. The two girls put aside the text-books with which they were involved. Son and mother jointly closed the history book which lay before them and Tom cleared his throat for the second time.

'Bad business,' he said solemnly and although he was given all the time in the world he would not add further to the little he had already said. A silence ensued. It was a long silence during which everybody exchanged looks except the man whose statement had occasioned them.

Everybody present knew what Tom meant. He was saying that while it was all right to plan one Christmas in advance it was not all right to plan two. The silence was allowed its allotted span before books were readdressed and the crossword resumed. They were a wise family in that they knew there would be no point in saying any more.

Time passed and Jenny Collins wisely decided to celebrate one Christmas without reference to the second but only for a while. The snows had but barely departed from the surrounding hills when a restlessness took hold of her. She was able to resist it for a while but when the daffodils put in their appearance she began to have brief glimpses of future Christmases. She turned to prayer but her powers of concentration were no match for the urgings which seemed to redouble their efforts and as April bestrewed the shady places with delicate blooms she found it impossible to subdue the Christmas feelings to which she always had yielded in previous years and yet she did. She was to discover, however, that it is wrong to over-subdue for when the urge can no longer be held at bay it reemerges with twice the power.

Jenny went on a Christmas buying binge all through the last week of April. It appeared that she was making up for the time she had lost, for instead of buying for just the Christmas ahead she bought for following Christmases as well. Surprised but considerate shop assistants would remind her that she had already bought certain items but she would explain that she was buying for an invalid friend. Normally she was not given to untruths but she would excuse herself on the grounds that it was inventiveness rather than strict lying. Her husband was aware of what was going on and when she became aware that he was, she was quick to point out that she wasn't squandering his money, that she would be spending it anyway sooner or later. He would say nothing. There would be no more pronouncements. The children took no notice. Adults could do what they liked and generally did.

As the summer sped by Jenny Collins bought more and more, inexpensive items mostly which she stored in the attic in an old chest.

'Not for the coming Christmas,' she explained to her father, 'nor for the Christmas after but for future Christmases.'

'But where's the point?' her father had asked.

'Better be sure than sorry,' she had answered and when he expressed dissatisfaction with such a reply she had merely shrugged her shoulders and asked what harm if any she was doing.

'Things have come to a pretty pass,' her father scolded.

Later that night he invited his son-in-law to join him in a drink. They chose a quiet pub at the farthest end of the street. Half-way through the first drink the old man rounded on his son-in-law and asked somewhat petulantly: 'Why do you condone it?'

'I don't condone it,' came the considered response. 'I put up with it because she has no other fault and I figure that a woman needs one fault at least if she is to remain normal.'

'That's all very fine,' the old man said, 'but where will it all end! If she's not stopped soon she'll be buying ten or even twenty years ahead of normal.'

There was no immediate answer from Tom. It was obvious that he had not contemplated this new aspect of the problem. He had no fault to find with Jenny but if what the old man had prophesied came to pass Jenny would have to be taken aside.

'I'll take her aside,' he promised.

'When?' the old man asked.

'One of these days now I'll get down to it.'

'Too late.' The old man shook his head ruefully and finished his drink. 'It is my considered opinion,' he looked his son-in-law in the eye, 'that she is in the process of passing herself out and, once they start, the trend becomes irreversible. I am not laying all the blame on you. I am also partly responsible.'

'What do we do?' Tom asked anxiously.

'We will have to take drastic steps, that's what we'll have to do,' the old man answered.

'What do you mean!' Tom asked anxiously.

'I mean,' the old man became deadly serious, 'we shall have to enlist outside help.'

'But who?' his son-in-law asked.

'The parish priest.' The old man was unequivocal.

While the barman replenished their glasses they sat glumly in the snug to where they had retired after some regular customers, renowned for their acute powers of hearing and insatiable curiosity, had established themselves. Upon receipt of the drink they took up where they had left off. This time the exchanges were conducted in whispers.

'But what can the parish priest do that a psychotherapist can't do?' Tom Collins asked.

'If word gets out that she's seeing a psychotherapist,' the old man countered irritably, 'she'll be the talk of the town and we'll never live it down. Anyway psychotherapists cost money whereas Canon Coodle will cost nothing.'

'But what does Canon Coodle know about such matters?' Tom asked.

'He's a priest,' came back the incontrovertible reply. From time to time there would be silence in the public bar. The customers had reverted to their normal roles of listeners. The pair in the snug responded with a corresponding silence. When the conversation resumed on the outside a deficiency became apparent to the pair on the inside. The latter would be well aware that one of those on the outside would have been delegated by common consent to eavesdrop on those on the inside. The volume of the conversation would be raised while the eavesdropper availed himself of the best possible listening position. Often juicy titbits would be picked up especially if the occupants of the snug were less than sober, titbits that could be profitably relayed to wives and sweethearts after the pub had closed for the night.

On this occasion the eavesdropper was to be cheated. The occupiers of the snug had clammed up. After a short while they finished their drinks and left the premises. Outside they dawdled on the sidewalk before moving on to the centre of the roadway where they strolled leisurely until they had assured themselves that their voices could not carry.

'Canon Coodle it will be then,' Tom agreed. 'When do you propose to see him?'

'I don't propose to see him at all,' the old man answered with a cynical laugh. 'She is your responsibility and I suggest that you see him now, right this very minute before you go to bed.'

Before Tom had time to reply he found himself being directed towards the presbytery. The old man had a firm grip on his arm and, although reluctant, Tom did not resist the pressure.

Canon Coodle listened most attentively to what his parishioner had to say. He posed no questions, preferring to stimulate his caller with encouraging nods and winks. It was his experience that, by listening and by hearing the person out, all would be revealed in the end. When Tom Collins reached the end of his revelations the canon expressed neither surprise nor dismay. He sat perfectly still for some time in case his caller might wish to add an overlooked item. When none was forthcoming he did what he always did after listening to unfortunates with puckers to resolve. He poured two large glasses of port and handed one to Tom Collins. They sipped for a while in silence while the cleric mulled over what he had been told. He knew Tom and his wife well; a model couple surely and a credit to the parish.

The cleric knew Tom's father-in-law, a domestic alarmist if ever there was one but a devout and decent man, nevertheless. The canon wondered if he might not be at the back of his son-in-law's visit. He would not ask. He would provide instead the counsel which was expected of him. Slowly the canon began to make up his mind and making it up he resolved that if the pucker could not be resolved by the parish with all its resources it would be a reflection on both the parish and himself.

'Before you think about seeking out expert medical advice further afield,' the canon opened, 'you might consider exhausting the capabilities of the parish first. I mean,' the canon continued in his homely fashion as he silently resorbed the last of his port, 'the solution to our problem could be in our own hands.'

'My father-in-law said something about sending for an exorcist,' Tom suddenly put in lest he forget the matter before the conversation ended.

Canon Coodle considered the question and as he did he remembered his last meeting with Father Sylvie Mallew, the diocesan exorcist, a saintly and upright cleric who, in Canon Coodle's private estimation, would be likely to do more harm than good in this case. He had first met Father Sylvie after an unsuccessful adjuration addressed to an evil spirit which had placed an elderly lady under its power.

'Could it be,' Canon Coodle's companion of the time asked, 'that he failed to exorcise the evil spirit because there was no evil spirit to begin with?' Canon Coodle was forced to concur that this indeed might have been the case. When both clerics encountered Father Sylvie in the local hotel he was in a state of total exhaustion after the fruitless but demanding rite. The local doctor ordered him straight away to the nearest general hospital where the ailing exorcist spent a month recuperating from his ordeal. It transpired that the real evil spirit of the piece was the daughter-in-law of the old lady who had failed to come up trumps with a spirit. It was the daughter-in-law who demanded the exorcist in the first place. Later she would admit that she had been driven to it by the exorbitant demands of the old woman, by her continuous nagging and whining and by the fact that they heartily detested each other. For this and for many other valid reasons Canon Coodle was totally against calling in an exorcist especially an exorcist with the track record of Father Sylvie Mallew. He was at pains to establish his position to Tom Collins.

'You may or may not know,' he explained patiently, 'that exorcism as such is governed by the Canon Law of the Roman Catholic Church. Before consenting to an exorcism I would be bound to seek authorisation from my bishop and even then before we could get down to brass tacks it would have to be proved that we are dealing with a case of real possession. Now, you and I both know that your wife is no more possessed than you or me so let us here and now dispense with exorcism. If we don't and if we are foolish enough to resort to it your wife may very well begin to believe that she is possessed and that is almost as bad as being truly possessed.'

'What should we do then?' Tom asked.

'First things first,' the canon replied, 'so let us deal with what we know and proceed from there. You told me earlier that your wife was of the belief that she had passed herself out, which is a common enough expression hereabouts. In my time I have met several people who passed themselves out to a certain degree but never to such a degree that they were not able to return to their normal selves after a certain period. I must confess,' the canon continued, warming to his task, 'that I very nearly passed myself out on a few occasions when my curates were indisposed. The fact that I did not pass myself out means that I do not take the matter seriously. Passing oneself out is really no more than an expression or at worst a flight of the imagination. From your wife's particular case we may safely draw the conclusion that she has simply looked too far ahead.'

'Years and years ahead,' her husband interrupted in an exasperated tone, 'and if she isn't stopped she'll soon be decades ahead and maybe even centuries and if that happens it is possible that she'll never return to her former self and it really means that I'll be married to a woman who isn't there at all.'

'Come, come!' the canon resorted to one of his favourite expressions. He used it frequently when somebody forced him into a corner.

'Don't you come, come with me!' Tom would never normally react in such a fashion to his parish priest but he had the feeling that the canon was a trifle too dismissive or at the very least was not prepared to take him seriously.

'Now, now!' said the canon.

'Don't you now, now me either!' Tom turned on him. The canon was taken completely by surprise. In every case the expressions he had used helped to mollify people, to calm them down and reassure them. The canon was about to say 'well, well' but changed his mind in view of the agitated state of his visitor.

The canon was now fully alerted to the fact that the time for meaningless expressions was past. He would have to approach the situation from a different angle. He would need to apply some home-made, countrified common sense.

'My wife is getting worse by the hour,' Tom was on the verge of tears, 'while we sit here talking nonsense.'

'Now, now!' The expression died on the canon's lips as he endeavoured with all his mental might to come to the aid of his parishioner. At the back of his mind's eye a picture began to form. It was a picture from the past and it was dominated by the figure of Big Bob the uncrowned king of the travelling people. It was well known to the canon that Big Bob was not accorded regal status because of his fighting ability although he had never been beaten in a fair fight. Rather was it because of his sagacity and diplomacy although some would prefer words like roguery and guile or scheming and deception. Whatever about anybody's opinion of Big Bob he was a man of his word and once given it was never broken. Women trusted him and children followed him when he walked through the town in his swallowtail coat and Homburg hat. He was part of the community and then again he wasn't. He was a travelling man but he honoured the outskirts of the town with his presence during the winter and early spring. Then he departed, as he was fond of saying himself, for the broad road.

The picture in Canon Coodle's memory had become better developed as he tried to placate his visitor with words of concern and understanding. The picture was still hazy and it would remain hazy for it had happened many years before and it had happened under moonlight so that an absolutely clear picture was out of the question. He remembered a woman, somewhere in her mid thirties, running in circles in the commonage where the travelling folk were camped. It was in that part of the commonage where the travelling folk trained their horses so that a dirt track of almost perfect circular proportions would already be etched. A man stood at the centre of the ring. From time to time he clapped his hands and called out to the woman. The calls were of an encouraging nature and the man who made the calls was none other than Big Bob. Later when they met accidentally near the big bridge which spanned the river the canon's curiosity got the better of him. He told Big Bob of what he had seen in the moonlight and the traveller responded that the canon had indeed seen a woman running in a circle under the light of the moon.

'She was my sister,' Big Bob explained, 'and after her tenth babby she lost the run of herself so I took her out to the ring and told her to run until she caught up with herself.'

'And did she?' Canon Coodle had asked eagerly at the time.

'Yes,' Big Bob had replied, 'she caught up with herself soon enough and she had no more children after that.'

The canon had been somewhat mystified but he felt as he looked across at Tom Collins that his sudden recall of the events in the commonage had a rare significance. By no means a superstitious man, the canon would testify under oath that Big Bob had no supernatural gifts but he would also testify that Big Bob was an extraordinary man with uncommon powers over his fellow travellers. It was also said of him that he had great power over horses. It was said of him too, by his detractors, that he had stolen more eggs and chickens in his heyday than any man alive but the canon did not believe this. His fellow-travellers, especially the womenfolk, would always vindicate him on the grounds that what he stole from the well-off was stolen for hungry children and if not for hungry children then for the aged and the infirm among his clan. Then there were things he would never steal. He would never steal money and he would never steal horses. He would never steal dogs but if a dog got the notion to follow the travellers' caravans that was another story. Judges liked him. In particular district justices would listen when he made a case for a young traveller who might have been engaged in fisticuffs or window-breaking or abusive language while under the influence. Whatever the charge Big Bob would guarantee that the wrong-doer's behaviour would undergo a change for the better if he was given a chance. The travellers said of him that he kept more men out of jail than Daniel O'Connell.

The canon was well aware that the settled community might not take too kindly to the proposal which he was about to make to Tom Collins.

'When all fruit fails we must try haws,' Canon Coodle opened. He went on to tell his visitor of what he had seen in the moonlight so many years before and of the exchanges between himself and Big Bob.

'You're not suggesting ...' Tom was cut off before he could finish.

'That is exactly what I am suggesting,' the canon said, 'unless, of course, you can come up with something better.'

All Tom could do was shake his head. He shook it for a long while before he spoke.

'Nothing ventured, nothing gained,' he agreed resignedly.

'That's the spirit,' said Canon Coodle. 'All we have to do now is wait for a moonlit night.'

'Tonight is a moonlit night,' Tom Collins pointed out to his parish priest.

'So it is. So it is!' the canon exclaimed joyously as he drew the curtains apart and gazed onto the gleaming lawn outside the window of his study. 'See how balmy and blessed is God's moonlight,' the canon was quite carried away by what he saw. 'Note how it silvers the land and softens the harsher features. How blessed is the balm it brings! How sublime its serenity!' He placed a fatherly arm around the shoulders of Tom who had joined him at the window. 'See where it struggles with the shadows for supremacy. How gracious is moonlight and how tranquil! See Tom where it transforms the grey of the slates on the outhouses to shining silver.'

'It's mid-winter canon,' Tom reminded the moonstruck canon.

'So it is. So it is,' the canon answered absently.

'Christmas is only four days away,' Tom pointed out.

'You mean,' the canon removed his arm the better to survey the anxious face before him, 'you are contemplating doing it tonight?'

'Pray why not?' Tom asked.

'Why not indeed!' Canon Coodle agreed.

'I will go and fetch Jenny.' Tom hastened towards the door.

'And I will locate Big Bob,' the canon announced, 'as soon as I can find my hat and coat.' After a lengthy search, during which Tom fretted and fumed, the hat and coat were located. They left the presbytery together.

The canon turned towards the travellers' encampment on the outskirts and the younger man turned towards the town.

'I'll see you at the entrance to the commonage,' Tom called over his shoulder.

'Please God. Please God!' Canon Coodle called back.

An hour would pass before the principals in the bizarre ceremony were gathered together at the entrance to the commonage. Big Bob, replete in swallowtails, Homburg hat and flowing white silk scarf, stood with Jenny at one side of the entrance while her husband and Canon Coodle stood at the other watching with undivided interest. Big Bob was speaking to the housewife. As he spoke her eyes became fixed on his. From time to time she seemed to nod her head as though she agreed with what he was saying. Not a word was borne to the watching pair although the depth and richness of the traveller's tone was clearly audible. Now and then Big Bob would raise a hand and in flowing movements would indicate the moon overhead and the myriad of stars that winked and danced in the December sky. All the time he spoke softly but all that was heard by the listeners was a purring monotone not unlike the *crónáning* of a contented cat. The listeners strained but still not a word came their way. They would never know because later Jenny Collins would say that she could not recall a single word no matter how hard she tried. She would explain that she knew at the time and that things were clear to her but all had been washed away.

Finally Big Bob closed his mouth firmly and, taking Jenny Collins by the hand, led her into the commonage where they stood for a while before he intimated with signs that she was to negotiate the circle hewn by the horses' hoofs. Big Bob took up his position in the centre of the ring and clapped his hands. At the sound of the clap Jenny broke into a lively trot. She completed several circles of the ring until Big Bob called out: 'Whoah, whoah, whoah girl!' at which she stopped. For a while she stood silently, her eyes fixed firmly on the travelling man.

The watching pair exchanged looks of wonderment and perplexity but no word passed between them. They were aware that something extraordinary was taking place and they sensed that what was now happening was beyond words and would be threatened by external or contrary movements.

Suddenly Big Bob clapped his hands a second time, at which Jenny proceeded to run backwards, her steps keeping time with the clapping. As the clapping slowed so did Jenny. She was now walking backwards to the slow but steady handclap, walking as though in a dream.

Her husband and Canon Coodle would say afterwards when recalling the ceremony that there was a very short period when she seemed to actually float backwards although both were realistic enough to realise that it may have been some form of illusion. As the handclap slowed altogether so did the steps of the woman who had passed herself out and it became clear that instead of catching up with herself she was allowing herself to be caught up with.

'Now, now, now is the time,' Big Bob cooed.

All were agreed afterwards that cooing was the best word to describe the sound of his voice.

'Now, now, now,' he cooed again as Jenny stood stock-still.

'Ooh ah ooh owowow ooh ooh,' she cried out in exultation as she assumed herself back into her being.

'Extraordinary!' Canon Coodle could scarcely believe his eyes.

'Most remarkable!' he exclaimed and then, 'most peculiar entirely!'

As for Tom Collins, the poor fellow was speechless. The tears ran down his face as Jenny approached and flung herself into his waiting arms. She was his wife again, his reliable, lovable helpmate, his pride and joy, his one true love. She would never pass herself out again and she would buy her Christmas gifts like everybody else. Uncaring and oblivious to all, Jenny and Tom Collins walked through the moonlit commonage hand in hand. They would eventually arrive home but not before they had exhausted the moonlight which they would remember forever and which they found to be romantic and enchanting.

'How can we ever repay you!' Canon Coodle asked of the elderly traveller. 'May the blessings of God rain down on you like this heavenly moonlight.'

'Not by moonlight alone doth man live,' Big Bob's apocalyptic tones rose with a great ring of truth over the commonage as Canon Coodle reached for his wallet. From afar, borne upon moonbeams, came the gentle laughter of Jenny Collins. It was the laughter of a woman who had been lost but had been found and she would remain found for every Christmas thereafter.

The Best Christmas Dinner

As Wally Pooley cycled through the countryside his faith in the goodness of his fellow humans began to waver. Wally had not eaten a bite in twenty-four hours. Hard to imagine, he thought, that the great festival of Christmas is not yet over and still there are men and women who turn the needy and the starving away from their doors.

Wally had expected the spirit of Christmas to burgeon rather than diminish as the prescribed Twelve Days slowly expired. The feast of the Epiphany, due to fall on the morrow, would see the sacred period draw to its official close and that would be that, Wally exclaimed bitterly to a fettered donkey which sought in vain for grass or vetch or any form of sustenance along the inhospitable margins of the roadway.

In many ways you and I are alike Mister Donkey, Wally concluded as he pedalled laboriously uphill; we search, often fruitlessly, for the fill of our bellies while the less worthy grow fat behind closed doors. It never occurred to him that it might be his calling that gave rise to the hostility he had experienced since setting out from his tiny house that morning. Then there was the indisputable fact that he was a townie, and townies, let them be saints in their hearts, were always suspect when they ventured into the countryside.

Wally Pooley was a process server with ultimate responsibility to the minister for justice although it is doubtful if the minister in question had ever exchanged the time of day with Wally or with any other process server, such was the gap that existed between the upper echelons of the ministry and the lower ranks.

Strictly speaking Wally was not obliged to serve summons until the Christmas period had passed but the pangs of hunger which had assailed him since he set out that morning might well not be assuaged until the processes were delivered and the affidavits of service signed. Then and only then would remuneration for his labours be forthcoming from the lawyers who employed him in the first place although in this instance there was only one lawyer, J. P. Holligan.

Before setting out that morning Wally had phoned his employer and acknowledged the several processes which he had received by post several days before Christmas, processes which should have been delivered immediately after their arrival but, as Wally pointed out to J. P. Holligan, he just did not have the heart to inflict so much misery on his fellow human beings with Christmas just around the corner. The truth of the matter was that Wally had been unable to rise from his lonely bed to admit the postman who would have been well acquainted with Wally's ways. When his knock failed to draw an immediate response the postman simply stood on his toes and dropped the mail through the partially opened window of Wally's bedroom. As the letters drifted downwards Wally cursed his companions of the night before, drunken wretches every one, who would not hear of his departure while he had the price of a round left in his pocket.

Wally did not rise at all that day. On the following day before departing for the public house he placed the letters carefully in the breast pocket of his shortcoat where they would remain until his last penny was spent and he would be forced to the road once more with the latest vile assortment of processes.

When he rang J. P. Holligan of Holligan, Molligan and Colligan and explained that he would need an advance so that he might purchase some simple necessities such as the fundamental bread and butter and a variety of non-luxury items such as rashers, eggs, sausages and black puddings, the lawyer had not been in the least sympathetic, not even when it was pointed out to him that the rigours of the itinerary awaiting his humble servant would tax the energies of a professional cyclist not to mind an underfed, famished creature about to brave the elements in the pursuit of justice.

'Spare me the gruesome details,' J. P. Holligan had cut in with some vehemence. The reference to food so early in the day had added to his queasiness which had built up over the Christmas period. Undeterred, Wally Pooley laid further claim to an advance by reminding the lawyer of tricky but successful assignments in the past involving considerable physical risk and debilitating fatigue but his pleas fell on barren ground. In the end, after he had exhausted all the coins in his possession on the public phone, he had set out without bite or sup, fairly confident that a cup of tea or a plate of soup might be forthcoming from some kind soul upon his route. There were still in that part of the world some tolerant householders who made allowances for process servers even when they arrived with scripts of woe.

'Ah sure someone must do it!' the more forgiving recipients would say whilst others, not many, would make allowance by saying that it took all kinds to make a world.

The vast majority of people, rightly or wrongly, looked upon these lowly minions of the law as renegades and outcasts and would often threaten them with physical violence. The more perverted wrong-doers who would be expecting a visit from Wally would threaten him beforehand with shooting or with hanging and drowning. In his time he had been threatened with leg-breaking, head-splitting, dismemberment and castration, to mention but a few of the punishments to which he would be subjected should he deliver one of his processes where it wasn't wanted.

Already that morning Wally had succeeded in delivering processes for such heinous offences as property trespass by animals and humans, for debt and for assault, for breach of contract, for attempted rape and for indecent exposure. Now, as he neared the end of his hazardous itinerary, only one process remained to be served. He knew the house well. He had called there in the past but not to fulfil his legal obligations. For years before his elevation to process server he had been interested in politics and whenever canvassing parties went into the countryside in search of votes Wally went along, chiefly because he had nothing else to do but also for the good reason that the party which claimed his support was out of power and he was needed to swell the ranks of canvassers to respectable numbers.

Then, unexpectedly, after a snap election the party was returned to power and a new government was formed. Mindful of Wally's past contributions a party hack put Wally's name forward for the position of process server. Despite strong opposition because of his drinking habits and general unreliability he was duly appointed. Most of his business came from Holligan, Molligan and Colligan. The first-mentioned of these was also a government supporter and a known skin-flint-cum-begrudger. The fact that he opposed the appointment of Wally Pooley worked in the latter's favour and brought him support he could not have otherwise counted upon.

The side road which led to the house where the last of the process recipients resided was seriously disfigured by potholes made doubly worse by recent rains. Wally had unhappy memories from previous visits. For one thing both the brother and sister who occupied the house were rabid supporters of the opposition and had set the farmyard dogs on Wally and his fellow-canvassers during their last visit.

As the house drew near the potholes grew larger so that Wally had the utmost difficulty negotiating them. Inevitably he was thrown from his bicycle and found himself seated in a hole full of muddy water. To add to his misfortune the three farmyard dogs appeared on the scene and proceeded to snap at him as well as bark hysterically. Quickly he rose to his feet shielding one side of his body with the bicycle and arming his free hand with a quantity of sizeable stones which he had started to gather the moment the dogs appeared. He aimed at the most savage of the three and sent him yelping to safety. The cowardly canine would continue with his intimidatory tactics while he was safely out of range. Before Wally had time to gather more ammunition the other dogs had joined the ringleader and proceeded with their criticism of the visitor from a distance.

During all this time neither of the proprietors of the great house put in an appearance. I could have been savaged to death, Wally told himself, for all they care. Shivering as he advanced along the narrow boreen, he began to feel the icy cold of the water on his rear quarters. With chattering teeth he told himself aloud that he would surely fall foul of pneumonia or worse if he didn't dry himself quickly. He shook the wet trousers gingerly but all he succeeded in doing was to send the freezing drops down the backs of his thighs.

'Oh God!' he appealed in loud tones to his maker, 'what did I ever do to you that you should treat me this way?'

As he proceeded on foot the pushing of the bicycle became an almost unbearable task. Cursing and crying he longed for the sight of the house where he might heat himself for a while by a fire. He recalled that there had been a warm range in the kitchen the last time he and his companions had managed to gain access to it. A pleasant anticipatory shudder brought him momentary relief when he remembered the glow of the fire which would shed its benign heat on him before he was much older. Even Wally's closest companions would concede that he was a poor subject for any form of hardship. Now in his forties it was certain that he had spent more of his two score years whining than celebrating. For a moment he paused and a look of alarm appeared for the first time on his face. The process! Was it still in his pocket or had he inadvertently handed it in with one of the others to the wrong recipient? His hand went instantly to his breast pocket where he kept all the letters. He did not withdraw the safety pin. His fingers found and felt the reassuring length of the legal epistle he would shortly deliver. With a sigh of relief he proceeded.

At either side of the ancient tree-lined road, once a stately avenue, the verdant acres stretched as far as he could see, an indication of the vast wealth enjoyed by the owners, reputed to be the best-off farmers in the parish. Well off they might well be but according to locals they were so mean that even the travelling folk did not consider it worth their while to call. They left their secret signs at either side of the gate which led to the house. These signs spoke more eloquently than any conventional language of the meanness and misery of the middle-aged man and woman to whom the house and lands belonged. Another sign told of cross dogs and yet another spelt dangerous bull for it was the practice of the ungenerous pair to release one of the more dangerous bulls on to the narrow roadway in order to discourage visitors, especially travellers.

At long last the house came into view but as far as Wally Pooley could see there was no sign of a human presence. Despite the reputation of its inhabitants Wally was glad to see the thin spiral of smoke which ascended from the kitchen chimney. He looked at his watch. The noon of the day had just passed and it was at this time that country people, farmers in particular, sat down to dinner. They partook of supper in the evening after the cows had been milked or alternative stock catered for.

There were no afternoons in the countryside, only morning, evening and night. Anything after midday was looked upon as early evening. Afternoon was a word used only by landlords in former more repressive times and it had no place in the local agricultural vocabulary. It had been discarded with other words which had never fitted properly in the first place into the native ambience.

The house which stood overlooking a spacious lawn was of prepossessing proportions. It had once belonged to an English landlord whose agent disposed of it for a fraction of its value when the British pulled out after the War of Independence. The present owners were the son and daughter of the original purchaser, a man so mean that he never ate more than enough to keep him alive and who, if he had his way, would have imposed the same abstinence on those who worked for him. His offspring were somewhat different. They made certain that they always dined well themselves but, if others were to starve, surely it was not their concern.

Wally knocked tentatively at the kitchen door. It would be unthinkable, even for the owners, to use the ornate front door with its ancient elaborate knocker so stiff that it could hardly be raised, much less used. When there was no response to his knocking Wally pushed gently upon the door and was relieved when it opened easily into the warm interior. The range stood gleaming as always, a bright fire glowing in its bosom, a promising assortment of dinner utensils chortling and steaming and fragrant on its surface. He made straightaway for the range to which he immediately turned his ice-cold posterior. The warmth ran through his buttocks and then through his limbs and all his other parts while he stood entranced, utterly captivated by the exquisite heat. Such was the pleasing glow which suffused him that he could have stood thus, without moving, for hours. The steam rose behind him from the soggy seat of his trousers until the life returned to him. He would have taken off the trousers and laid them across the bars of the rack over the range but it would have been an unbecoming pose for a process server even if he had an ancient football togs underneath.

As he relaxed he drifted into a standing slumber during which he dreamed of scantily clad damsels frolicking on foreign strands. He recognised several for, after all, he had encountered them in the same place on numerous occasions in the past. They recognised him too for they contorted themselves to the most extraordinary limits in order to provoke him. One in particular took him by the hand and led him to a cave underneath towering cliffs. Inside she raised a cautionary finger to her moist lips intimating that absolute silence was required for that which was about to follow.

'Wake up you dirty devil!' The voice which exploded in his ear did not belong to any of the exotic creatures on the foreign strand. They would never address him in such a fashion. The voice belonged to Miss Clottie, the lady of the manor. Wally had some difficulty in returning to reality. When he did he found himself being glared at by Miss Clottie and her brother Master Bob.

'What are you doing here!' The decidedly unfriendly query came from Miss Clottie. Master Bob took refuge in silence knowing if there was dirty work to be done the task could not be in more capable hands than those of his beloved sister. Blurting out the words, Wally explained his predicament and begged to be allowed stay a few short minutes until his trousers dried. He told them of the assault by the dogs which was a most serious matter in view of his position as a government-appointed process server. Indeed, if news of the assault reached the ears of the proper authorities there would be hell to pay. He was relieved to notice the look which passed between brother and sister. It was a look of mild alarm mingled with total derision but he knew nevertheless that his words would take heeding.

'Surely,' Miss Clottie was at it again, 'you're not trying to tell us that you have a process for us!'

'Yes for you, you pompous oul' jade,' Wally was tempted to reply. Instead he kept his mouth shut and awaited the same old response which his unexpected arrival always elicited.

'The very idea,' Miss Clottie was saying, 'a process indeed for the MacMullys of Cloontubber House! Did you ever hear the bate of it!' She turned to her brother who had grown strangely silent as she stood before him, hands on hips. This, Wally told himself, is the part of the business I enjoy the best. This job is distasteful to be sure but it has its moments and these are they. The power of authority surged through him. He could let them know what lay in store for them right away by handing over the process or he could play them the way a cat plays a mouse.

He could see, however, that while Master Bob was visibly affected by his arrival he had made no dent whatsoever on the uppishness of his sister. She was a snob from head to toe so she was and wasn't it always the same with those infected by the disease of grandeur. They believed they were so high and mighty, so much above the ordinary, so perfect in every way that even if there was a process in the offing nobody would have the gall to serve it. She placed a plate of steaming soup on the table before her brother but all he did was to stir it indifferently and after a while listlessly swallow the spoonfuls as though they were doses of unpleasant medicine. Suddenly Miss Clottie turned on Wally, this time with arms folded.

'No Missie, no, no, no thank you.' Wally let the words run mischievously out of his mouth before she could open hers.

'No thank you for what?' she asked, genuinely confused.

'For the soup you might be about to offer me.'

If she bridled under this most unacceptable jibe from a townie and a cheap townie at that she kept it to herself. She turned instead and removed the half-emptied soup plate from the table. She placed it in the kitchen sink never taking her eyes off the obnoxious creature by the range. She knew him well enough. She had seen him frequently in the town, mostly coming and going from pubs or standing in bookies' doorways when he wasn't searching for returns in bookies' windows.

'You can be on your way now,' she informed him. 'You seem to be dry enough for the road.'

'Just another minute,' he pleaded.

'Gather yourself my buck,' she threatened, 'or I'll give you a second dose of the dogs.'

'Oh dear! Oh dear!' Wally Pooley addressed himself silently once more. 'They think it will never happen to them but happen it will. Processes are there to be served and they stare everybody in the face just like the hereafter. There's no escape and just because you think you're a cut above your neighbour won't excuse you. I am your local process server and like your local undertaker I will have you sooner or later.'

Wally spoke the last part aloud.

'What's he talking about?' Puzzled, she turned to her brother for an explanation. Master Bob shrugged his shoulders while his sister's perplexity grew. Approaching the range she pushed the process server to one side and lifted one of the largest plates Wally had ever seen from the top of a pot of steaming water where she had earlier placed it so that it would be properly heated for her brother's dinner.

Intrigued, the visitor watched while she placed the items hereafter listed, on the plate: two peeled boiled potatoes, not too floury and not too soggy but precisely of the texture which had always endeared itself to the famished Wally; two medium-sized mouth-watering fillet steaks; one mound of boiled mashed parsnips; several fried onion rings, the size of small necklaces; and, finally, to cover it all, a pouring of the richest, brownest gravy ever seen by Wally . Smartly she turned and placed the plate in front of her brother. She raised a hand to forestall him lest he start the course in the presence of such a lowly creature as he who had returned his bottom to the glow of the range.

'Off with you now,' she commanded.

'I'll go when my business is done,' Wally Pooley informed her.

'Then state your business now,' she demanded.

'My business is with your brother,' Wally returned.

'Then I'll go,' she said, 'but I'll be back in fifteen minutes.'

After his sister had left, Master Bob, for all his listlessness up until that time, directed his full attention to his dinner. Wally looked on helplessly, his mouth watering, his tongue licking his lips as the head of the house lifted a forkful of choice fillet to his drooling lips. Watching him chew the juicy steak was as much as Wally could bear. Master Bob closed his eyes and raised his head the better to savour the fare. He was a slow eater. His mastications were thoughtful and deliberate. He seemed determined to extract the very last juices, the ultimate essence from everything that entered his mouth.

He should be on exhibition, Wally thought, if only to show people how much pleasure there is to be found in simple chewing. To an unobservant onlooker it might seem that he was teasing the less fortunate process server but this was not the case. Always when he masticated savoury chunks of fillet he became oblivious to all external activities. Swallowing the first forkful after what seemed, in Wally's eyes, to be an eternity, Master Bob refocused his eyes on the contents of the plate. Using both knife and fork he probed and prodded and finally settled for a gravy-enriched mouthful of mashed parsnips. He held it aloft on his fork for several seconds, first cherishing and then totally admiring this contrasting titbit before slowly opening his generous mouth and lovingly depositing the parsnip therein.

There followed such a sucking and a savouring that the gathering saliva shot forth unbidden from Wally's mouth. He decided that a time for action had come and without a by-your-leave sat on a chair next to the merrily masticating Master Bob. If the latter was aware of Wally's presence he failed to show it. He sat with his head slightly aloft, his jaws gently salivating the parsnip, his eyes closed, in a world of his own.

After the parsnip had departed to the same destination as the fillet Master Bob heaved a great sigh of satisfaction and burped appreciatively without a word of apology to the visitor. Burping secondly he reached out for a glass of milk which his sister had earlier poured for him. He swallowed noisily while the ravenous onlooker swallowed an imaginary mouthful in tandem. After the second invasion of his plate Master Bob decided the time had come for a break in the proceedings. He placed knife and fork on top of the appetising array yet to be devoured and rubbed his hands together, sighing ecstatically as he did. Then and not till then did he become aware of Wally's presence at the table. He was momentarily shocked by this outrageous breach of agricultural protocol but his annoyance slowly disappeared as he contemplated his next move.

Wally watched helplessly as the greedy eyes of his tormentor swept over the contents of the plate. Wally guessed that he would opt for an onion ring and was agreeably surprised when Master Bob decided to indulge in a second mouthful of the fillet. Carefully and lovingly he chose the section he desired, severing it neatly from the whole before impaling it on the fork prongs. Wally guessed rightly that he would wait until doomsday before Master Bob would proffer a solitary morsel from the plate where, in Wally's estimation, there was easily enough for two.

Normally Wally would not resort to the ploy which he had devised shortly before taking his place at the table but the pangs of hunger had multiplied since Master Bob had begun his meal.

Firstly he opened the safety pin which had secured his breast pocket. Secondly he withdrew the envelope which contained the process and thirdly he lifted it aloft the better to behold it and to contemplate its real value. It would also, undoubtedly, attract the attention of Master Bob but that very person was now looking out the window, having risen from his seat. He gave no indication that he had noticed the envelope. He was, therefore, in Wally's opinion, relishing the food he had consumed so far. Wally had done the same thing on the rare occasions when he had been presented with high-quality meals. Master Bob, he felt, would now be enjoying the interval between mastication and resumption. He would recall every bite he had eaten and would, no doubt, be considering an amalgamation of parsnip and potato or onion rings and fillet or even a medley of all four. After all, he had only barely begun and needed time to chew the cud as it were before resuming acquaintance with the constituents of his plate.

Again there was the irritating rubbing together of the hands and the even more irritating burps. When he sat again he took his implements in hand and, screwing his head this way and that, viewed his meal from every angle. The lull seemed to have sharpened his appetite for at once he uplifted a large lump of potato and parsnips, browned with an abundance of gravy.

Alas for Master Bob, the sapid composition would never reach his mouth. A polite coughing of the best drawing-room variety was sufficient to distract him. With a perplexed look he lay the top-heavy fork on the plate. Then with a quizzical look he turned his attention to the source of the coughing. It was, indeed, his unwelcome guest the process server, the very creature he thought he had browbeaten into respectful silence. The ominous epistle was still held aloft.

'Can't it wait,' Master Bob pleaded.

'Duty calls,' came back the firm reply.

'All right, hand it over then!' There was resignation in the once haughty tone. Slowly he opened the envelope and extracted its contents. There was only one sheet of paper but on that sheet were tidings that would drain the blood from its reader's face. As he read his hands trembled and, having read, he lifted the process secondly and reread. The second reading did nothing to restore his earlier sense of well-being.

The face was now ashen and the lips which had recently worked so feverishly and industriously were tightly drawn. Master Bob pushed his plate away and by good chance it ended nearer the hands of the process server than those of its rightful owner.

Wally's hands gently circled the plate without touching it.

'Have you finished with this?' he asked. No answer came from the sealed lips.

'You sure now!' Wally asked in a barely audible tone and yet no answer came. In that part of the world, as elsewhere, there were large numbers of people who believed that silence gives consent. Acting on this dictum Wally reached forward and seized the knife and fork which now lay idle at the head of the table. He made the sign of the Cross with the knife as he lifted the heavily laden fork and intook its cargo so that it might be free to fulfil its role as accomplice of the knife which by now was also free to mark out a choice square of tender fillet.

As the process server stuffed himself Master Bob lifted his head in alarm from time to time. He thought he heard barking or it could have been slobbering. Another time he was convinced that he heard a pig grunting but there was no pig only Wally, who was making mighty inroads into the surprise repast. As he neared the end Wally could not help but notice that Master Bob had buried his head in his hands. He availed of the opportunity to pour himself a full tumbler of milk. He wiped the plate clean at precisely the same time Miss Clottie returned with the cowardly dogs. She was shocked by what she saw at the table. She could scarcely bring herself to speak. Hurrying forward she lifted the process and started to read. In a matter of seconds her already grim visage underwent a grievous change for the worse.

Wally Pooley felt that his time for departure had come. He was already acquainted with the contents of the letter but nobody would ever hear it from him. Indeed the whole country knew that Master Bob would be contesting a paternity suit at the next sitting of the Circuit Court. Rising as graciously as he knew how, Wally succeeded in containing the belch which would have forced its way upward and outward without apology.

'Best meal I ever ate Missie.' He directed his thanks towards Miss Clottie but that unfortunate creature was incapable of acknowledgement. Wally gently laid the knife, fork, plate and glass in the sink and backed himself out through the kitchen door, nodding his head with maximum deference as he did.

Time, as only time could, would resolve Master Bob's dilemma. He would duly acknowledge the son which was undoubtedly his and he would marry the child's mother while Miss Clottie would marry a local farmer during the fall of the year and she would present her ageing husband with a son and heir nine months to the day after the knot was tied. Wally Pooley would always say that the dinner he had eaten on that eleventh of the twelve days of Christmas was the best fare ever to cross his lips. He took the full credit himself: 'For,' as he would confide to his drunken cronies many a time, 'I took my chance when it came and I delivered my process not a minute too early or a minute too late.'

The Long and the Short of It

Long Jason Lattally was not alone tall as a telephone pole but also thin as a lath, so thin, in fact, that it was a wonder he did not topple over altogether. He had a narrow jaw and he had a pointed nose and he had no lips to speak of. Consequently his eyes seemed outrageously large, as did his ears and his cheek bones. People who saw him for the first time announced that he had the boniest face they ever saw. Canon Coodle, the parish priest, put it another way.

'He has a very refined face,' the canon told his housekeeper, 'maybe a little bit too refined and we must remember that refinement is a quality sought after by many but acquired by few.'

Jason Lattally was well off by parochial standards. There was a time when he shared the family business with a brother but the poor fellow was whipped away one night by a storm as he walked along the banks of the estuary below the town. At least people presumed that he had been whipped away. In appearance there was little difference between himself and his brother Jason. If anything he was a trifle thinner and a trifle taller and a trifle hungrier-looking and maybe a trifle more lathy but for all that he was a likeable chap and when he was being transported to the graveyard on the day of his burial many notable utterances went the rounds in his favour.

Some months after his departure from the land of the living his brother Jason bought a new suit, a new shirt and a new pair of shoes and went here, there and everywhere looking for a wife. When he started out he believed that his task would be an easy one. He was now the sole proprietor of a small but successful grocery shop. The business was free of debt and contained modest living quarters as well as a back entrance which was regarded as vital to the running of a successful business in the main street of the town. Goods, for instance, might be delivered through the rear and so might fuel and it was through this rear egress that Jason exited every night to consume the few pints of stout which helped him unwind and contributed in no small way to the deep slumber which saw him wake up eager and refreshed each morning of his working week.

At first in his quest for a partner he enjoyed no luck at all. He was tempted to engage the services of a matchmaker but told himself that if he could not secure a woman through his own devices he did not deserve one. How wrong was Long Jason Lattally! Wiser men than he would testify with their hands across their hearts that a man needed all the help he could get in the isolating and securing of a suitable wife.

Time went by and at the end of a year Jason was as far from acquiring a partner as he had been when he set out. Then he was informed by a female neighbour who was aware of his plight that there was no need for him to search afar when he might pick and choose from the selection under his very nose. He had many female customers who were of the marrying age and, more importantly, of the marrying bent.

When Madame Lucia Palugi the famous Dublin fortune-teller came to town and set up shop for a week in the front room of a small house, several doors down the street from the premises of Long Jason Lattally, Jason decided to pay her a visit. She was a somewhat obese lady of indeterminate age but she had earned for herself an unrivalled reputation as a clairvoyant. After she had carefully read Jason's palm she informed him that he had a lifeline which suggested that he would reach the ripe old age of one hundred and two. She also informed him that he was unmarried and when he asked her how she could tell she merely pointed at the crystal ball which dominated the top of the table at which they sat. Peer though he did with all his might, Jason saw nothing in the crystal. The opposite was the case with the noted prophetess. She saw two women, one tall, thin and rangy and the other short and stocky. Jason informed her with mounting astonishment that he knew both women, that both were in fact regular customers of his, although he had never seriously contemplated either.

'That may be,' he was told amiably, and Madame Palugi went on to tell him that while he might not be enamoured of them they were most certainly enamoured of him, 'and,' she continued without a tremor in her tone, 'one or other of the pair will be the mistress of your abode before Christmas for I see before me in my crystal ball a pair of legs which are definitely not yours and these legs happen to be in position under your kitchen table. I cannot say whether the legs are long or short and I cannot see a trace of a face because my crystal is somewhat clouded but it is a fact that the owner of the legs will be your wife before Christmas.'

Madame Palugi had seen nothing in her crystal ball but she was well informed nevertheless. The lady who owned the house where

Madame Palugi foretold the future had filled her in as soon as Long Jason entered and, as he sat in the tiny ante-room awaiting his turn to be divined, much was revealed about his background and romantic aspirations. At the end of the session he was prepared to accept the fact that he would have a wife before Christmas and that she would be one of the two women mentioned by the fortune-teller. He decided after a sleepless night that his future wife would be the tall, thin woman and not the short, stocky one. The tall, thin candidate, by name Alicia Mullally, was less plain than the stocky candidate and besides that she was possessed of a considerable fortune, had already acquired some business acumen and had the reputation of being an excellent housekeeper.

The shorter woman, whose name was Elsie Bawnie, could fairly be described as being sober and industrious and had plenty too by way of worldly goods. She had a certain charm and came from a family renowned for its honesty although in that particular place at that particular time people hid their money and stowed away their valuables at the mere mention of the word honesty.

'I have never met an honest man with the exception of Canon Coodle,' Big Bob the Traveller was fond of saying, 'and I'm pretty sure that I never will. Even if a man is honest,' Big Bob would continue, 'he has already given a hostage to fortune because of his physical attachments and may not be trusted altogether.'

When Jason Lattally approached Alicia Mullally as she left the local greengrocers with a packet of birdseed she was quite taken aback and did not know whether to laugh or cry. She leaned her long frame forward like a heron about to snatch a sprat and would have flapped homewards straight off had not Jason seized her gently by the sleeve of her calico blouse and restrained her.

'Will you?' he asked.

'Will I what?' she responded as though she had not heard the first time.

'Will you marry me?'

When she remained tight-lipped he repeated the question and still she would not commit herself. It was not the first time that such a question had been put to Alicia Mullally. She had always answered in the negative in the past and had regretted her decision at least twice. At the time she had convinced herself that they would ask again and indeed they had asked again but not Alicia. What a strange place, she told herself, for a man to propose and was it, she asked herself, an indication of other strangenesses? Strangenesses were the last thing she wanted. Like all women she wanted a man she could depend on. She did not, however, say no. She tried to draw away but she did not try very hard. He still held her firmly by the sleeve.

'Will you or won't you?' he said and she deduced that if the answer was not in the affirmative there might not be a second offer. Their eyes met and she could see that he was deadly serious. He had paled almost beyond recognition and she guessed that he had built up his courage for some time before approaching her. When she spoke again her voice had softened and there was sympathy in her eyes. She laid a hand on the hand that held her by the sleeve.

'Why don't you call to the house sometime?' she whispered invitingly. 'This is no place to talk about marriage.'

Jason released his hold and assured her that she could expect him that very night when he would be hoping for a positive answer.

News of the proposal spread quickly. In the space of one hour the whole street was fully informed. In the space of two the town knew that Long Jason Lattally would be calling to the abode of Alicia Mullally that very night. It was believed that she would accept but not before she hummed and hawed her fill. She was of the breed of hummers and hawers and breeding will out.

'You will find breeding in turnips,' Big Bob the Travelling Man would say. 'Why man,' he would continue in his homely way, 'you will find breeding in the poll of a hatchet, in the handle of a scythe, in the straw of your thatch, in the spokes of your wagon.' He would go on and on until his audience drifted away.

The first thing Big Bob did when he heard of the proposal was to trim his flowing white mohal. The second thing he did was to visit his friend Bertie Bawnie, the father of the town's smallest woman but not so small as not to be marriageable. It was Elsie herself who opened the door.

'Small yes!' Big Bob silently said to himself, 'but ugly no.'

The travelling man was greeted warmly. It would not be in her breeding to do otherwise. Big Bob recalled her late mother who had been renowned for her generosity and courtesy. It was, therefore, inbred into Elsie. She ushered him through the small pork shop to an even smaller kitchen where her father sat snoozing by a bright peat fire. Bertie Bawnie had a round pink face atop a small chunky body. He rose at once to his feet when he saw who his visitor was. Expansively he indicated a chair and with a well-rehearsed motion of wrists and fingers indicated to his daughter that she was to fetch glasses and whiskey. Not until a glass of whiskey had been consumed in the most leisurely fashion by each of the elders was a word spoken.

'What brings you friend?' Bertie Bawnie asked as he replenished both glasses.

'I have come matchmaking,' came the solemn reply. The traveller was quick to elaborate.

'It has come to my attention,' he said, 'that Long Jason Lattally is about to propose to Alicia Mullally and it has further come to my attention,' he went on, 'that the daughter of this house would be far better suited to Lattally but I need that daughter's permission and I need her father's permission before I can make a case.'

An uncomfortable silence greeted the traveller's announcement. Big Bob had made a match or two in the past but mostly among the travelling people. If the truth were told he would be more of a consultant than a matchmaker. He would be fully versed in the lore of the countryside and would be aware of the failings and virtues of marriageable men and women along the roads which he travelled regularly. He would be cognisant of the background and breeding of likely partners and he always made himself available whenever vital information was required by professional matchmakers. He had a priceless stock of valuable knowledge and he was easy to deal with as far as consultancy fees were concerned.

The Bawnies, father and daughter, replied to his proposal in their individual ways and in their own time; the daughter by refilling the glasses as soon as they were drained and the father by asking if Big Bob would be interested in acting on his daughter's behalf. A considerable amount of whiskey was consumed before the deliberations came to an end. The chief worry entertained by Bertie Bawnie was that Long Jason Lattally might have already proposed.

'I think not,' Big Bob reassured him, 'for it has come to my attention that Alicia Mullally is a dawdler who finds it difficult to make up her mind. She should and could have been married years ago but she kept putting the matter on the long finger.'

Bertie Bawnie countered by saying that it was his belief there would be a Mullally/Lattally marriage before Christmas and that Christmas was almost down on the door.

'You may have made your move too late,' he concluded unhappily.

'Not so,' Big Bob answered. 'Now is the time to make the move for it has come to my attention that Long Jason is due to propose at nine o'clock tonight.'

'It is now eight.' Elsie Bawnie spoke for the first time and it occurred to Big Bob that she had the demurest way and the most subtle way of making a point.

'I'll go now,' he said in dramatic tones, 'and I'll state my case to Long Jason Lattally.'

Elsie followed him to the door and, taking him by the hand, thrust a ten-pound note therein.

'There will be ninety more,' she promised, 'if you succeed in your mission for if I can't have Long Jason I won't have anybody. He is all that's left of the Lattallys and I am all that's left of the Bawnies, barring my Da.'

As he drew his coat about him preparatory to crossing the street for his proposed confrontation with Long Jason, Big Bob was forestalled by the distant but resonant tones of the last remaining male Bawnie.

'There's another hundred from me,' the voice said, 'if the news is joyful.'

There was no question but that the Bawnies had great faith in the travelling man. There were few others who were possessed of the same faith and, surprisingly, one of these was Canon Coodle although it would have to be said that his faith was limited. Still faith was faith regardless of its consistency. Big Bob was fully aware that father and daughter trusted him fully and he was quite moved as a result. The expression 'faith can move mountains' was familiar to him. He had heard it often enough in church and had come to set great store by the ancient proverb. There had been an occasion of celebration around the campfire when the travellers would philosophise at length about religion and about the world at large. The happy group had just run out of liquor and the tragedy was that the combined finances of the travellers were not sufficient to purchase a single bottle of stout. Big Bob had volunteered to approach one of the town's public houses, where he would request credit.

While most of the publicans did not encourage the travelling folk to drink on their premises there were occasions when they could be depended upon to extend a small amount of credit. He had been a young man then and his listeners had scoffed at the very thought of his demanding credit from a publican.

'Oh ye of little faith,' he said at the time, whereupon a rival responded that travellers could not be expected to have as much faith as settled people, as past experiences would show.

'The Good Book tells us that faith can move mountains,' Big Bob countered, 'and it don't say what kind of faith so it seems to me that my faith is good enough for this kind of task.' The credit had been forthcoming but Big Bob could never be sure whether it was his faith or the fact that the publican was drunk at the time.

Now as he knocked on Long Jason Lattally's door he prayed for resolve. When he beheld his caller Long Jason presumed that the traveller had come a-begging. He thrust his hand into his trousers pocket and handed over a silver coin. The traveller accepted the money and expressed his gratitude but explained that he had not come seeking alms.

'I believe,' Big Bob said, 'that you intend getting married.'

Long Jason laughed. 'And what has that got to do with you?' he asked.

'If you'll be good enough to let me in I'll tell you everything,' Big Bob promised.

The long man consulted his watch and, seeing that he had the best part of an hour to spare, stepped to one side so that his caller might enter. Inside they both sat but there was no drink on view.

'Will whiskey be all right?' the long man asked, his bareboned face breaking into a smile.

'Whiskey is just what I need.' Big Bob moistened his lips.

Long Jason filled two glasses. Normally he drank only in a public house and always illegally after hours since he was of the belief like many of his neighbours that drink taken at home involved no risk and, therefore, lost much of its potency. He had on this occasion decided to make an exception on the grounds that he needed some sort of booster if he was to successfully propose to Alicia Mullally. Both men sipped their drinks for a while and exchanged well worn items of news.

'So!' Long Jason stretched his legs and awaited the pronouncement that would justify his visitor's intrusion.

'So!' came back the long drawn-out response. Big Bob rose to his feet and placed his hands behind his back. 'I have come,' he said solemnly, 'to ask if you would consent to a life-long traipse with Elsie Bawnie?'

'A life-long traipse eh!' Long Jason pondered the phrase. He had not heard it before and felt that it was not a bad description at all of the undertaking implied.

'And by whose authority do you present yourself here with such a proposal?' he asked.

'By the girl herself with the full approval of her father,' Big Bob answered.

'I had an inkling that she was that way inclined.' Long Jason pulled upon his jaw until Big Bob felt that he might pull it off altogether, so thin and finely pointed was it.

'It's like the bottom end of a sickle moon,' Big Bob thought. 'Are you interested?' he asked as he resumed his seat.

'She's small,' the long man replied, 'and she's nice, danged nice, but with me being so tall and she being so small we'd be a laughing stock.'

'For a short while only,' Big Bob assured him, 'and then only when the pair of you would be upright. You will never meet such a lady for charm, a lady that so knows her place. She would make a man happy and she would bear the finest of children.'

'I know, I know,' the long man found it difficult to contain his irritation, 'but the bother is that I have more or less contracted to propose to Alicia Mullally. In fact she awaits me this very night.'

'If you have any sense,' Big Bob spoke forcibly, 'you'll let her wait.'

'I can't do that,' said the long man.

'Those who have awaited,' Big Bob informed him solemnly, 'have been elated and those who have gone have been put upon.'

'What's that from?' Long Jason asked anxiously.

'That is from the book of travellers,' came the reply, 'verse one, chapter two.'

'Elsie Bawnie is a very small woman and I am a very tall man.' Long Jason was adamant.

'And what of Alicia Mullally?' Big Bob asked. 'Are not the pair of ye too tall for your own good and whoever heard of an equal pairing making a good match. For a true marriage,' Big Bob went on, 'you need opposites, the fair and the dark, the stout and the skinny, the stooped and the straight, the tall and the small. This tall dame could be the very death of you my poor man. She is not suited to you at all.'

Long Jason was impressed in spite of himself but he was determined to fulfil his tryst.

'Tonight,' he clenched his fists as he spoke, 'I embark on the most important mission of my life to date. Tonight I will open my heart to the woman who will one day be the mother of my children and I plan to have many. I would not be alone now if my mother had brought more children into the world so you see it's important that I get started without any more delay.'

'I was never a man,' Big Bob looked into the fire, 'to pour cold water on the plans of a lover but you could be starting on the road to ruin and I cannot in all conscience stand idly by while you destroy yourself.'

'What do you mean?' Long Jason grew more apprehensive with every passing moment.

'Did you ever ask yourself where is the windiest spot in the country?' Big Bob was master of the situation now. This was his field. He belonged where he was and he would make the most of it.

'The windiest spot in the country!' Long Jason was puzzled. He decided nevertheless to answer the question. 'They say,' he replied, 'that the right bank of the estuary about a mile below the bridge is the windiest spot of all.'

'Windy enough to blow the hair off a man's head?' Big Bob asked.

'Windier,' came back the instant response.

'Windy enough to blow a man's false teeth back his throat and out you know where?'

'Windier,' came the emphatic reply.

'Windy enough to blow a man away altogether?'

'Yes,' came the answer, 'and who knows it better than my poor self that lost his only brother in a south-west gale and he out walking for the good of his health.' Long Jason shook his narrow head in sorrow. The tears rolled down without hindrance because of the shape of his face. They fell on his freshly shone shoes and they fell on the floor and as he continued to shake his head they fell with a hiss and a fizz into the kitchen fire. When he had cried his fill he lifted the whiskey bottle and recharged the glasses. Before he raised his drink to his lips he olagóned his fill. It is the nature of this man to *olagón*, Big Bob told himself, and there is no point in asking him to desist for all his ancestors were *olagóners* and keeners and would raise their voices in the most melancholy fashion at the slightest opportunity. Eventually the *olagóning* came to an end and Long Jason raised his glass to the memory of his dead brother. Big Bob raised his and drained his and said what a pity it was that such a man should be swept away especially when he need not have been swept away at all.

'How's that?' Long Jason asked.

'How's what?' Big Bob returned innocently.

'You said that he need not have been swept away at all.'

'Did I?' Big Bob's voice was filled with surprise. 'Ah yes,' he reflected, 'so I did, so I did.'

'Explain.' Long Jason's request fell on receptive ears.

'What restrains the ship when the storm blows and the wind howls? Think before you answer.' Big Bob was on a familiar tack.

'Why the anchor restrains the ship,' Long Jason replied.

'And who is the last to yield in the tug-of-war?' Big Bob asked as he raised the back of his coat and toasted his posterior to the fire.

'Why the anchor-man of course,' Long Jason replied. It was clear that he was beginning to enjoy the questions-and-answers exercise, especially since he found no difficulty in answering. He awaited the next poser with confidence.

'What was your brother anchored to when he was blown away?' Big Bob asked.

'Why he was anchored to nothing,' came the response.

'And if he was anchored to something do you think he would be blown away?'

'It would have to be something mighty solid,' the long man replied.

'Mighty solid.' Big Bob paced the kitchen raising his empty glass and placing it on the mantelpiece over the fire. 'And do you think, for instance, if he had a long thin dame the likes of Alicia Mullally by his side that she would be solid enough to anchor him against the force of the wind?'

'She most certainly would not,' came the scornful response.

'Isn't it likely,' Big Bob was now standing in the centre of the kitchen, his hands joined like an advocate, 'isn't it likely,' he reiterated, 'that instead of your brother being blown away on his own that his companion would be blown away as well?'

'I don't have any doubt whatsoever about it,' Long Jason affirmed. 'In fact,' he concluded, 'any man who would go walking with such a female on the right-hand bank of the estuary should have his head examined.'

'Would you go walking with such a woman on the aforementioned spot?' Big Bob looked up the chimney from the expansive hearth. He noticed that it badly needed cleaning. He wasn't a sweep himself but he was not above holding a ladder for a modest fee.

'I certainly would not walk with her on the right-hand bank of the estuary.'

'There are other windy places,' Big Bob pressed on with his advantage, 'and no matter where you are you cannot write off the unexpected squall. Any time you walk with a dame as long and as thin and as light and as frail and as unsteady as Alicia Mullally you are putting your life at risk. Now let us suppose that you are out walking with Elsie Bawnie and that suddenly the wind rises and you find yourselves on the right-hand bank of the estuary with no shelter and nowhere to turn. What would you do? I'll tell you what you would do. You would hold on to Elsie for there is no squall and there is no wind and there is no storm that would blow her away. The heavens have yet to invent a gale that would bowl her over. I defy the blasts and the gusts that sweep in from the foaming sea. Let them rage and roar but they won't budge Elsie Bawnie one inch and I'll lay my hat and cloak on that and my old black mare plaited and ribboned and my painted caravan. I can see it all now in my mind's eye. I can see yourself and the long woman leaning into one another against the force of the storm and finding no purchase in yeerselves or anywhere else, here one minute and gone the next, gone and swept and carried forever in the belly of the blast, out past the headland and across the roaring sea to lands unknown, never to be seen again and may God in his mercy forgive you your sins in the name of the father, the son and the holy ghost. Then I see you in another calamity and the wind about to lift you like a paper kite when all of a sudden who comes along, who comes along I ask you? Come on man and answer me. Who comes along?'

'Elsie Bawnie comes along,' Long Jason roars aloud as though he were imbued by the spirit of the sou'wester.

'She takes your hands.'
'She takes my hands.'
'She holds you down.'
'She holds me down.'
'She wraps her arms around your legs.'
'She wraps her arms around my legs.'
'She leads you home to safety.'
'She leads me home to safety.'
'To your warm bed where she lies you down.'
'To my warm bed where she lies me down.'
'And ministers into you with all her holy powers.'
'And ministers into me with all her holy powers.'
'Forever and ever amen.'
'Forever and ever amen.'

Jason Lattally raised his long bony arms aloft. 'Forever and ever,' he called out and pushing his mentor to one side dashed through the door and did not draw breath until he found himself with the same long, bony arms around Elsie Bawnie to whom he proposed when he regained his breath and by whom he was accepted.

Big Bob, somewhat exhausted from his intercessory endeavours, laid hands on the bottle of whiskey which stood invitingly on the kitchen table. He raised it to his lips and swallowed long and swallowed hard until some of his strength returned. Then he sat and planned. There is much to be done, he told himself, and there is much coin to be made if I play my cards right and before this night is down I'll turn the trump in my favour not once but many times. He allowed himself another quarter hour of leisurely drinking before combing his mohal and rearranging his apparel.

Five minutes later he stood in the kitchen of the abode of Alicia Mullally. She was surprised to see him. She had been expecting another person entirely she told him.

'I have come,' Big Bob spoke with all the authority he could muster, 'on behalf of Bertie Bawnie, a man who loves you dearly, a man who will cater to all your needs and place his monies at your disposal and, although he is of small stature, were he to stand on top of his money he would be the tallest man in this town.' Big Bob went on as he had with Long Jason pointing out the danger from gales and squalls that lurked everywhere awaiting long thin victims. When he had finished

Alicia Mullally begged him to convey her love to the smallest man in the town, the anchor of anchors, Bertie Bawnie.

Giddy with the promise of another hundred pounds Big Bob arrived at the abode of Bertie Bawnie. The poor fellow sat by the fire caterwauling as no cat ever could while he lamented the imminent departure of his daughter who had just agreed to be the wife of Long Jason Lattally before the advent of Christmas.

Big Bob drew up a chair and stretched his legs towards the fire. Slowly and melodiously, for such was the timbre of his rich voice, he pointed out the benefits of attaching oneself to a woman with the length and suppleness of Alicia Mullally, with the leanness of her and the keenness of her and the slender yielding frame of her. He was at his most poetic when he described the pair as he envisaged them walking along the right bank of the estuary. Overhead the wild geese flew in stately skeins to their feeding grounds while seabirds of every denomination mewed and bleated. He saw them walk hand in hand towards a setting sun and suddenly from the south-west came great black stormclouds and in a matter of seconds all hell broke loose. Everything that was unattached was blown away, everything except Bertie Bawnie, and just as Alicia was about to be whipped away to God knows where by the all-conquering winds of the west she was seized around the midriff by her stocky partner and saved from a watery grave. He went on and on, inventing countless perilous situations where always the stocky partner was at hand when an anchor was needed.

After a full hour of Big Bob's blather Bertie Bawnie was on his knees imploring the king of the travellers to make a case for him. When Big Bob declared that the case had been successfully made Bawnie danced on the kitchen table and jumped like a stag over every chair in the kitchen, which was no small feat when one took his size into consideration. He willingly paid over the promised hundred for the successful pairing of Long Jason Lattally and his daughter Elsie plus another hundred for his negotiating the not-too-distant Christmas nuptials of Bertie himself and the overjoyed Alicia Mullally.

As Big Bob wended his unsteady way homewards the first flakes of snow alighted on his broad shoulders. It had been a great night's work entirely and to think that he might never have contemplated embarking on a matchmaking venture at all but for the fact that his old friend, the saintly Canon Coodle, had complained to him in the late autumn that the population of the parish was declining and that unless there was an increase in the number of marriages there was a danger that it would decline further.

'I haven't presided over a christening in three solid weeks,' Canon Coodle said sadly, 'and from latest intelligence reports I have deduced that it will be at least another three before there's any change.'

Canon Coodle always looked upon his housekeeper and sacristan as the intelligence officers of the parish and he knew from experience that their sources were impeccable.

Big Bob would never let the canon know about his efforts on the elderly clergyman's behalf. Was not virtue its own reward and was he not several hundred pounds better off than when he had set out that evening! He raised his great head to sniff the snow-laden wind and thanked his maker for his successes on the matchmaking front. Surely in a short while the cries of infants would be heard once more in the parish but first would come the bells of marriage and then, after consummation, the merry bells of Christmas.

Christmas Eruptions

There are more rows at Christmas than any other time of year but they are rows of shorter duration even if they are rows of greater intensity. Then, of course, I am a man who supports the theory that there can be no true happiness in any household without a flaming eruption now and again.

I am not talking about the joy that comes with the making-up, which is fine in itself. Rather am I talking about the dispelling of those noxious gases which gather over long periods of calm and lassitude. I refer too, of course, to subjugated feelings and dispositions which have turned evil over the course of time as well as all the other ups and downs which assail the human make-up. If these are not unleashed and if they are retained unnecessarily the human spirit will corrode and instead of relationships which are vibrant and vital there will be inevitable stagnation and you will never have the air-clearing, heart-warming confrontations necessary to the successful maintenance of the human system.

People tend to behave too properly at Christmas and where this happens an outbreak of one kind or another is inevitable. Too-proper behaviour is not natural in that it suppresses the mischief and blackguardism inherent in all of us, barring a sainted few.

If this natural mischief is not vented at regular intervals there can only be two consequences, i.e., stagnation or violence, and bad as the latter is the former is even worse because a stagnant home is no home and a stagnant marriage is God's greatest curse. The occasional verbal outbreak, therefore, is a vital ingredient in the successful marriage.

The most dangerous of the Christmas denizens is the common-or-garden senior male of the household. Nearly always he is likely to be a chap who is set in his ways and who may like to lie down quietly after the excesses of Christmas Day. The best treatment for this type of Yuletide invalid is to guide him to a secluded room and to place a Do Not Disturb sign on the door.

If he is suddenly awakened by some accidental intrusion it should be considered a wise manoeuvre to vacate the vicinity of the room where he rests.

Other dangerous denizens are senior married females who have been pushed too far all day and taken for granted over too long a time.

The bother here is that outbreaks are totally unpredictable because females tend to suffer silently and give little indication of the explosive scenes which can and do occur as a matter of course in every respectable household.

When these suppressed housewives erupt it is always wise for outsiders to make for the nearest exit until the cataclysm subsides.

Thankfully Yuletide outbreaks, whether male or female, tend to be of short duration. They should be encouraged up to a certain point, however, for the good of the persons in question and for the good of the family as a whole. One of the most devastating Christmas rows ever to occur in the street where I was born happened a short while before the Christmas dinner. We shall call them Tom and Mary.

Tom was sitting by the fire sipping from a glass of whiskey. Mary was sipping from a glass of sherry as was the wont with females at that time.

'Will you have peas or beans with your turkey?' Mary asked politely.

'It's immaterial to me,' Tom responded with equal civility.

'Make up your mind now like a good man for I haven't all day,' said Mary who had been on the go since daybreak attending to the myriad chores which needed her attention.

'I really don't care one way or the other,' Tom persisted.

'Dammit!' said Mary peevishly, 'will you make up your bloody mind,' whereat Tom told her what she could do with the peas and beans whereat Mary informed him that he was a thankless wretch whereat Tom smashed his glass against the floor whereat they harangued each other without mercy and without let-up for a quarter of an hour whereat they both grew exhausted and fell into each other's arms whereat all was peaceful again and instead of having peas or beans they had both peas and beans together and a happy Christmas to boot.

A Last Christmas Gift

The twins Wally and Carl Hern bore not the slightest resemblance to each other. Wally was several inches taller and several stones heavier.

From the day they could walk Wally was as easygoing as Carl was mettlesome. Wally's features were uniform and softly drawn against Carl's angled, almost severe lineaments.

Carl's nose was unusually long and pointed, his jaw jutting and hooked, contrasting sharply with Wally's chubbiness.

Wally's was a slow, lumbering gait whereas Carl's was precise and undeviating. Wally was a careless dresser. Carl was natty and orderly.

In temperament the difference between the pair was more marked. Wally was an amiable hunk of boyhood slow to rouse, easy to mollify.

Carl, on the other hand, angered easily, was ever alert for slights and took offence from seemingly innocuous banter. When this happened redress was immediate and painful. He was clever with his fists. Add to this the looming form of his twin brother continually dominating the background and it was easy to understand why he never lost a fight.

From an early age Carl was to grow more and more perplexed by his brother's cheerful disposition, his way with people, old and young alike, the ease with which he shrugged off affronts and other forms of disparagement which seemed intolerable to Carl. Inevitably the perplexity turned to resentment and eventually to jealousy but this was not to fully fester for some time. It would remain dormant for a period thanks to the intervention and shrewd good sense of the twins' mother Maisie.

There were five other children but the twins were the eldest. In their tenth year their father lost himself in the East End of London where it was said he had settled in with another woman. Maisie Hern made no attempt to locate her husband. She sent no word reminding him where his real responsibilities lay. She was too proud for that. Anyway where was the satisfaction in holding a man against his will! She simply readjusted herself and made the most of the situation.

She was quick to interpret the dark scowls and barely subdued mutterings of the smaller twin whenever Wally came in for any sort of favourable mention from neighbours or others. It was the concealed menace underneath Carl's surface discontent that worried her.

He became more snarly and vituperative at each recital of his brother's accomplishments.

One night his spleen erupted into a vicious physical assault. A furious fight followed. Maisie Hern, shocked, sat powerless until it ended. At first it seemed that the bigger, stronger Wally must yield to the passionate yet accurate onslaughts of the smaller twin. He took a severe pummelling in the early stages and was content to merely defend himself. He was, in fact, unable to do anything more. Then as Carl's fury slowly abated after the first murderous offensives the superior strength of the bigger twin asserted itself.

Carl clung to his brother for dear life knowing that if he let go he would be knocked senseless. Inexorably Wally forced him to arm's length and drew back his clenched fist preparatory to delivering a stunning chastisement. Slowly, however, he managed to gain control of himself. His whole body slackened, as did his grip on Carl. He opened his fist and looked at his hand in puzzlement, wondering how it had ever come to be closed in the first place.

Seizing his opportunity Carl made a last do-or-die attack but there was no strength left in him. He spent himself fully and futilely until he was forced to hold on to the table for support. Wally wiped his own face clean of blood and handed the cloth to Carl. Unperturbed, Wally went upstairs to bed.

Word of the fight spread. Maisie Hern had to confide in somebody and who better than a neighbour especially since her husband had deserted her. Maisie had fully recognised the value of the fight. It had shown her that Wally could contain Carl without physical domination. The neighbour suggested boxing gloves and undertook to instruct the boys in their use.

The twins were to fight many times after that first occasion but never privately. Encouraged by Maisie they were much sought after by pubs and clubs. Whenever there was a boxing tournament anywhere near they occupied a special place on the bill. Wally never won or never seemed to win but he did not mind that. There was always a bag of sweets or fruit after the fight. Deep down he knew that he must let Carl have his way. It was the only means of keeping his brother's insane jealousy on a leash.

Without the mollification of these public victories there was no telling what form the smaller twin's jealousy might take. The fights always followed a fixed pattern. Unlike the first conflict in the kitchen it was Wally who had the better of matters in the early stages of all the fights thereafter. He would, of course, be roundly booed by the crowd. After all he was nearly twice the size of his seemingly gamier, pluckier opponent. Acting to the prescribed pattern, Carl would feign hurt and injury as he allowed himself to be thumped and slapped around the ring. He was not above taking a count at times while the onlookers shouted themselves hoarse for his recovery.

At the end of the first one-and-a-half-minute round those who were unacquainted with the procedure would call upon the referee to discontinue the bout. The second round was but a repetition of the first with Carl at the time at the receiving end of what seemed to be countless callously delivered punches. Midway through the third and final round he would bring the crowd to its toes with an all-out, unexpected assault on Wally.

He would throw punches from every conceivable angle. There were flurries and combinations bewildering to behold. As the bigger twin wilted under the sustained barrage there was hysteria all around. When he finally fell to the canvas, unable to rise, the crowd went berserk. Carl beamed when, after the count, his hand was raised aloft. The blows had been real enough even if they had little or no effect on Wally. He lay there patiently until a second lifted him to his corner. He fully realised that as long as Carl was chalking up such victories there was an assurance of peace in the home. He was well content to play the role of underdog. He was worried by the fact that sooner or later they would outgrow this form of confrontation. He hoped with all his heart that such a day might never come. He hoped in vain.

Time passed and with puberty came the realisation that the fighting must end. Anyway they had ceased to be a draw. This sort of bout was strictly for children and children they no longer were. Despite her circumstances Maisie contrived to send them to secondary school. For the first few months all went well until both boys sat for a house examination. Unfortunately, Wally secured better marks. Neither did particularly well but the fact that Wally had shown himself to be the better of the two brought a return of the old anxiety to himself and his mother. They had not long to wait. Carl absented himself from school the very day after the results were made known. Every so often after that he would spend a day touring the countryside while Wally invented different excuses to cover his absence.

Came the next house examination and the positions were reversed. Wally had seen to that. Both boys fared poorly, so poorly that the president of the school, Father Ambrose, suggested to Maisie that it might be a more sensible course if the boys were apprenticed to trades. Being a deserted wife Maisie occupied the same status as a widow and as such had little difficulty in persuading two local tradesmen to take the boys on.

Carl was apprenticed to a plumber and Wally to a carpenter. In a short while Wally was making himself useful around the house. He showed an aptitude for woodwork from the beginning and although Carl was adapting himself without difficulty he was presented with no opportunity to display his developing skills. Inevitably the jealousy crept in. Wally wisely desisted from any further enhancement of the home. From that time onward he never even mentioned his work.

Eventually both boys completed their apprenticeships and were retained in employment by their masters. Then came the incident of the greyhound. Wally's master, in his spare time, was a respected breeder of coursing dogs and like all such devotees was forever seeking likely converts to the sport. Wally seemed to him to be an ideal candidate. He, therefore, presented him free of charge with a black greyhound pup on the final day of his apprenticeship.

Carl, not to be outdone, with the accumulated wages of several weeks went further afield and purchased a white pup of impeccable background from another breeder.

Carl's was clearly the better prospect for a distinguished coursing career. He was perfectly bred and shaped exceptionally well as a sapling. Wally's charge clearly lacked the style and class that were so evident from the outset in his brother's hound.

Then came the annual coursing meet when both dogs were entered for a stake confined to no-course duffers. Carl's dog started as a clear favourite and at the end of the day had effortlessly won his way to the final. Wally's also managed to scrape his way to the final course but was given no chance against his better-bred, lightly raced opponent.

It was at this juncture that Wally's master stepped in. An old hand at the doing-up of tired finalists, he took charge of the unfancied black. He set to work on the dog's back and shoulders with his powerful hands until the exhausted hound responded and started to show signs of gameness. From his hip pocket he extracted a flask of *poitín* and applied the stimulating liquid to the dog's pads. He poured a dram into his palm and forced it into the dog's mouth. After some initial spluttering the creature shook its head and pricked its ears, declaring its gameness for the coming course.

On his master's advice Wally refused the first three calls to slips and it was only when threatened with disqualification that he deigned to lead his dog to the start. Carl's white was meanwhile left to fret and whimper in anticipation of the hare's breaking. The longer he was kept at the slips the more would be taken out of him for the rigorous buckle that lay ahead. It was an old trick, frequently resorted to by handlers whose hounds needed time to recover their strength.

The slip was a fair one. The black carried the white collar, the white the red. From the moment they were slipped the pair were inseparable. The hare was a strong and stagy one and had been especially held over for the ultimate buckle. With half the course covered they had come within a length of the fleeing puss. The white hound seemed to forge ahead but then with a tremendous surge the black excelled himself and put his nose to the fore. He lifted the unfortunate hare effortlessly in powerful, murderous jaws. In a second the creature was being cruelly torn apart between the two dogs. The black had won. He had killed in his stride in text-book manner. If the dark look that overshadowed Carl's taut face spelt extreme disappointment, the look of alarm that crossed Wally's spelt disaster. He was, therefore, mightily relieved when Carl congratulated him on the win. It was only a temporary respite. He knew no good would come of his success and cursed himself for allowing his master to take charge of the handling.

In the morning when Wally went to the makeshift kennel to take the black for his morning exercise the hound lay stretched in a pool of blood, its throat cut. Without a word to anybody he located an old coal sack in which he deposited the bloodied carcass. He heaved it on to his back and made his way circuitously to one of the deeper holes in the nearby river, making certain that he was seen by nobody. On the river bank he added several weighty stones to the bag's gruesome contents and flung it far out into the dark depths. Returning, he scoured the kennel free of all traces of blood. Then he went into the kitchen where his mother and Carl sat at the breakfast table with the remainder of the family.

'How's the dog?' his mother asked.

'He seems to have run away,' Wally answered.

'Run away?' his mother echoed. 'Why would he run away?'

'Don't know,' Wally returned, 'all I know is he's gone.'

'Would he have been stolen?' his mother asked.

'It's a possibility,' Wally told her.

At that moment Carl arose and without a word left the kitchen. His sudden action made everything clear to Maisie Hern.

Shortly afterwards Carl sold the white dog to a local trainer. As if by agreement there was no mention of either dog in the Hern home after that. The people of the locality accepted the black dog's disappearance at face value. It certainly wasn't the first time a promising greyhound had been stolen and it wouldn't be the last. It was around this time that Wally decided he would have to leave home. It wasn't just the incident of the butchered greyhound. This was only one of many deciding factors, the chief of which was Carl's sudden obsession with any girl Wally might take it into his head to court. Carl simply had to have her as well but not all of Wally's dates were willing to co-operate. When this happened Carl would fly into a rage and frighten the girl in question. In so doing he also queered the pitch for Wally.

The girls might be forgiven for concluding that, because he was a twin, Wally was just as likely to explode into a tantrum as his brother. He knew that he would always be in danger of being tarred with the same brush unless he made the break. He discussed every aspect of the matter with his mother. She was forced to concede that there was no other course open to him. He promised to return for good some day but this was not his intention. He wanted to get as far away from Carl as possible and to stay away so that he might build an independent and natural life for himself. London he believed would afford him the anonymity he desired. Nobody would ever find him there. He would miss his mother and his younger brothers and sisters and, of course, Carl.

Despite the envy and the resentment he loved his twin more than any other member of the family, his mother excepted. He would keep in touch with all of them but he would not reveal his address. He would send his mother money on a regular basis and he would bring her for a holiday occasionally but the life he would begin in the city would be strictly his own.

It wasn't long before he invested in an ancient house in south-east London. In his spare time he restored it to its original appearance. The area he chose was singularly free of Irish emigrants. He didn't want anybody returning home with word of his whereabouts until his relationship with Carl assumed reasonable proportions. This might never happen but he dared to hope that one day it would. Until such time, however, as he could be absolutely certain that a normal relationship was assured he would keep the location of his house a secret. Then he met Sally. She was a midlander several years younger than he. After a brief courtship they married secretly. After a while, at Sally's insistence, Wally let his family know that he had taken a wife. He promised to bring her on a visit as soon as possible. Two years were to pass before he decided to present her to Maisie and the family.

Sally knew all about Carl. Wally had told her everything. Mercifully Carl accepted her as a member of the family. He too had married a few months previously and was, according to himself, as happy as any man could wish to be. There followed a wonderful holiday. Wally was amazed at the change which had come over Carl. He seemed to have recognised that he no longer had anything to be jealous about. His wife was a vivacious and lovely girl, far more attractive than Sally, highly desirable in every possible way. No man could wish for more in a girl. He had set up his own plumbing business and there was wide demand for his services. It seemed that in Wally's absence he had given his true character a chance to develop. Financially he was far better off than Wally who, after all, was only a clog in a wheel and hadn't the sort of initiative or drive to start off on his own. He would always be content working for somebody else.

Carl owned a bigger car, a bigger house. If he compared his lot with Wally's, and it was highly unlikely that he was any longer given to such a purposeless practice, there would have to be a glow of satisfaction when he considered his position.

When, on the eve of Wally's departure, Carl asked him if he could help him in any way, financially or otherwise, Wally's last remaining reservations vanished and he knew he no longer had anything to fear from his twin.

Wally thanked him profusely for the offer of assistance but declined on the grounds that he already had all he wanted. No sooner had he said this, however, then he realised that he might be giving

Carl food for thought. He realised that to suggest he had everything he could possibly want was a mistake. It was possible that Carl might not have everything he could possibly want, so to place himself at a disadvantage he asked Carl for a loan of twenty pounds until he got back to London. Carl was delighted to hand over the money and suggested that Wally keep it as a belated wedding present. Wally agreed to this. For the first time in his life Wally really knew what freedom meant. Always at the back of his mind while he was in London had been the fear that Carl might show up and wreck everything. That was all behind him now and he could breathe easily. He could also go where he liked in London and renew old friendships with other exiles.

At the end of four years of marriage neither twin was blessed with issue although there had been assurances from both family doctors that there was no apparent reason why this should be so. About this time Carl and his wife took a holiday in London. They stayed with Wally and Sally, both of whom took a week off from work so as to be fully at the disposal of their guests.

It was a week of non-stop activity. If Carl had accumulated a great deal of money it wasn't because he was miserly. He spent prodigally throughout the week. When at the end they left for home exhausted but happy, Carl declared that it was the most wonderful week of his entire life. For Wally it was much more. The normal brotherly relationship for which he had wished so devoutly for so long had manifested itself unmistakably for the length of the holiday. He began to experience a contentment and sense of fulfilment which brought a totally new dimension of bliss into his life. The ominous shadows which had hovered over his deepest thoughts up until this time were now irrevocably dispersed and had been replaced by an almost dizzying feeling of release. There were times when he suffered fleeting pangs of guilt so rich and full was his new-found situation. He resolved to adopt a truly charitable and selfless approach to life in return for the great favour which had been bestowed upon him. He no longer recalled the hideous events of the past nor feared in the slightest for the future. He relayed his feelings to Sally and she in turn revealed that she also felt a sense of relief.

Around this time Wally's firm secured an overseas contract as a result of which he would have to spend at least three weeks abroad. There was simply no opting out. If he were to decide in favour of such a course he could easily find himself looking for a new job. Sally assured him that she would be all right. She had her job and after all what were three weeks in a lifetime! The last of his reservations disappeared when she said that one of the girls in the office had volunteered to stay with her until he returned home. At the airport just before his departure he found himself quite overcome by a nauseating feeling of loneliness. It was as unexpected as it was painful.

'I didn't realise it would be like this,' he told Sally, who had taken a half day off from work to drive him to the airport.

'It's only three weeks,' she consoled.

'But I'll be so far away from you. Ecuador's almost half-way round the world.'

'Look,' Sally laid her hand on his arm, 'you don't have to go. It isn't as if we need the money and besides you can always get another job.'

'Too late for that now,' he said. 'I couldn't very well back out at this stage. They'd never find a replacement at such short notice. Then there are my mates. No! I have to go. It's as simple as that. I don't want to but something tells me I'd feel a lot lousier if I stayed behind.'

'It will be worth it all when you come home to me,' she whispered.

They kissed and he held her briefly in his arms. He released her without a word and walked off hurriedly to the departure area. She stood unmoving for a long while before turning towards the car park.

In Ecuador Wally lost himself in his work. Because of labour difficulties the job took longer than was anticipated. At night he wrote long letters to Sally. In these he told her how much he longed to be home and how much he pined for her. He received several letters in return but they arrived weeks late so that he could only guess at the existing situation. The letters were full of warmth and concern for him. Finally the contract was fulfilled and the time came to return home. He sent a telegram from Guayaquil indicating the approximate time of his homecoming. Because of various delays it took two days to complete the journey.

Exhausted but elated he set foot on English soil at eight o'clock in the morning. Immediately he hastened to the nearest phone booth. Sally never left for work before eight forty-five. He would have no difficulty in making contact with her. In the booth his heart fluttered in anticipation. He longed with all his heart to hear the sound of her voice. He was surprised and disappointed when she did not respond. The phone was ringing all right but nobody came to answer. He was not unduly alarmed. There had been mornings when she was forced to dash for work without breakfast. It was, therefore, quite possible that she was still slumbering. He smiled fondly at the thought of her lying beyond her time in their comfortable double bed. He replaced the receiver and left the booth. After a cup of coffee and a sandwich he decided to make a second call. He looked at his watch. There was still time enough to catch her before she left for work. Still the same mechanical response. He laid down the receiver, bitterly disappointed.

In the taxi he comforted himself with the thought that she had probably slept it out altogether. This had happened on one or two occasions when he had been away overnight on the firm's business. He could think of no other reason unless she had been taken ill. In this unlikely but remotely possible circumstance she would have gone to her parents' home outside Northampton. He ordered the driver to pull up at the nearest phone booth. It was Sally's mother who answered the call. No. Sally was not with them. The last time she had heard from her was three weeks before. She had sounded all right then. He told his mother-in-law about the calls. She advised him not to worry. Sally was certainly at home asleep in her bed. Where else could she be? He made a third call to his home but there was no reply.

As they drove through the empty streets the first feelings of disquiet began to assail him. He asked himself a number of questions. Where, for instance, was the girl who was supposed to be staying with Sally during his absence? Surely one of the two should have heard the phone ringing and answered it! Where could Sally be if she wasn't in her own or her parents' home? Why was she not on the alert when she knew approximately the time he would be arriving? There could only be one possible answer. She had slept it out. But what if she had not? What if she hadn't slept at home the night before or on previous nights?

All sorts of terrible conclusions entered his mind. The most dreadful of all he dared not contemplate. As the taxi neared its destination he grew more apprehensive until finally he reached a state where he dreaded the prospect of entering the house. Almost at once he chided himself for his lack of faith in a woman who had all her married life been an exemplary spouse. There had to be a perfect explanation for the lack of response to his calls.

When, at length, the taxi driver deposited him at his front door he hesitated. He fumbled for his key and located it. He was about to insert it in the lock but he changed his mind and rang the doorbell instead. He waited a full minute before ringing a second time. The second summons proved as futile as the first. He inserted the key and entered the hallway. Her name was on his lips but no sound came. Slowly he climbed the stairs to the bedroom they had shared for the past four years. The bed was empty, the room deserted. There was still the possibility, of course, that she might have just vacated the house in a scramble to reach the office on time. He decided to ring the office. After a short wait he was put through to her supervisor. His wife had not been in all week nor had she made any form of contact. The last time the supervisor had seen her had been the previous Friday afternoon. It was now Thursday. No. She could offer no explanation nor had she any idea of her whereabouts. He asked if he might speak to the girl who had elected to stay with Sally during his absence. She came on the line at once. Yes. She had stayed for the required period. She presumed that he had returned when he said he would. Sally had made no mention of an extension of the contract. He replaced the phone and sat on the stairs. Suddenly he became violently sick. He staggered into the kitchen for a cloth with which to clean the area where he had vomited.

The sheet of notepaper was pinned prominently to the kitchen cabinet directly over the sink. Despairingly he forced himself to read it. There wasn't much. It was signed Sally. It said: 'Gone with Carl. Sorry.'

All the old depressions which he had experienced since childhood came flooding back. He sat on a chair and started to sob uncontrollably. He crumpled the sheet in his hand and flung it at the far wall. It bounced on the tiled floor and landed at his feet. He became sick a second time. Afterwards he went upstairs and lay on the bed. Wave after wave of total despair engulfed him until he was all but suffocated. He had never felt so despondent in his life. What had happened was the culmination of all the worst fantasies he had ever experienced, the ultimate in sheer human hopelessness. He cursed himself for having ever left for Ecuador. He should have known that what had happened was always well within the bounds of possibility provided the proper set of circumstances presented themselves at a given time.

He could not find it in his heart to blame Sally. He saw her role as inevitable, as a necessary part of his destiny. He lay in bed all day but even after several hours he was still badly stunned by the shock of her departure. He tossed and turned until, from sheer force of fatigue, he fell into an uneasy sleep. When he awakened the phone was ringing. He rushed to answer it. His mother's voice greeted him. At once he burst into tears. She had guessed the worst when Carl had disappeared without warning the week before. She had known for some time of Wally's impending trip overseas and so had Carl. It required no great detective work on her part when Carl's wife arrived at the door in a distraught state a few days after he had gone off without warning. Wally was glad when his mother informed him that she intended to spend some time with him.

She arrived the following evening and stayed for a month. Anxiously she listened as he moved about the house long after she had gone to bed. Always it would be well into the morning before he eventually retired. Even then it was doubtful if he slept. His eyes were bloodshot in the mornings. He found it as much as he could do to drag himself to his place of employment.

For the first few days after his homecoming he absented himself from work but the days had proved too long and dismal and it seemed that they would never pass. He decided to return to work. It was better than mooning around the house where everything he touched reminded him of his absent wife. The weeks passed but no word came. Every so often he would ring her parents' home in the hope that they might have heard something. It was always a fruitless exercise.

Towards the end of the fourth week his sleep returned and so did his appetite. His mother was grateful for these symptoms of a return to some sort of normalcy. She told him that she had overstayed her leave and he accepted this. She bade him a tearful goodbye promising to return at once should he relapse into his earlier despondency. Carl's wife recovered from the loss and the shock at the end of the second day. She flung herself wholeheartedly into the business which she had helped her husband establish. The employees, instead of resenting a female at the helm, became her devoted followers and worked harder than ever to ensure that she should succeed. She played every card at her disposal, using every womanly wile with workforce and customers alike. Her desire to succeed was exceeded only by her hatred of her husband. She was determined never to forgive him. Let him return if he wished one day and he would find his business at least as successful as he had left it but he would find her as cold as stone. In this her resolve was rigid. It was the sheer detestation of him that kept her going during the first difficult weeks while she endeavoured to acquire a working knowledge of the business.

She felt no sorrow for Wally. He was after all the twin brother of the man who had forsaken her and what sort of witless weakling was he, she asked herself, that couldn't hold on to his plain Jane of a wife! She had little sympathy for Maisie Hern either. She found her guilty by association. By dint of hard work she would erase the memory of her husband. By ploughing a lone furrow she would become independent of him until one day he would cease to be an impression on her lifestyle. She knew she would succeed in this. It made her work, hard and demanding as it was, enjoyable and satisfying. She would be self-sufficient no matter what. This was the goal that sustained her.

Six months were to pass before Wally Hern found himself responding rationally to the life around him. The grief remained but it was now in a secondary stage, less painful although no less lonely than the first. It was a change from the all-consuming heartache of the first months.

His mother revisited him for a few days the following spring. She found him haggard in appearance but otherwise healthy. He stayed up late and rose early but there was none of the fretful pacing of the first visit. Her concern for him kept her awake into the small hours. Of all her children he deserved to be hurt the least. Repeatedly she asked herself how they had reached such a dilemma. Carl's envy was the obvious answer but it wasn't as simple as that. If her husband had played his rightful role they might never have found themselves in this deadly predicament. Typically, she refused to absolve her daughters-in-law, particularly Carl's wife, whose initiative she interpreted as downright bitchiness. She could not or would not blame herself. She had done her utmost. Granted, this was not enough but no mother in a similar set of circumstances could have done more. She left for home after three days. Wally promised faithfully he would spend the summer holidays with her. She knew, however, that he would never leave the house, not even for a day, while there remained the faintest hope that his wife would return.

Sally returned on Christmas Eve after an absence of fifteen months. Using her key she let herself in silently and stood in the hallway not daring to go further. Wally knew from the unexpected draught that the front door had been opened. Only one other person had a key. He rose unsteadily from his chair, his heart thumping, not daring to believe that she might have returned. Mustering his courage he opened the kitchen door and saw her standing there.

'Happy Christmas.' He managed to get the words out. He took her in his arms, smothering the apologies that sprung to her lips with loving fingers. Later, after they had made love, no matter how hard she tried he would not allow her utter a self-condemnatory word. For the first time since her absence he slept deeply. The morning after, he did not awaken till shortly before noon.

'We'll have to talk,' Sally said after they had breakfast.

'There's no need,' he told her. 'All that matters is that you're back.'

He steadfastly refused to hear any sort of explanation, reassuring her with kisses every time she tried to start. That night Carl arrived. Wally it was who answered the door. Carl brushed past him silently and went straight to the kitchen where he confronted Sally. Ignoring Wally, who had followed him, he pushed her on to a chair.

'Why couldn't you have told me?' He glowered down at her at though he were about to strike her. His hands hung by his sides, his fists clenched. 'Why did you sneak off like that?' he demanded.

'Watch how you talk to my wife,' Wally spoke menacingly.

Carl turned on him and spat on the floor at his feet.

'Your wife,' he scoffed, 'your wife indeed. I'm not talking to your wife brother dear. I am talking to my woman!'

He made every word sound more loathsome than the next. He raised an arm aloft but Wally seized him by both hands and held him in a vice-like grip. He forced him on to a chair. Carl fumed and ranted but he was powerless to move.

'You're leaving here now and you'll never return,' Wally told him. 'All my life you've wanted anything of value I ever owned, my dog, my peace of mind, my standing, my wife. There's an end to it now. You can take no more from me.'

'I can take your life,' Carl spat back at him.

'Be careful,' Wally warned, 'that I don't take yours.'

Releasing him he put an arm around Sally.

'Just walk out that door and go about your business. Let me to mine from this night out or you'll be sorry. Go now and a happy Christmas to you.'

Carl rose and addressed himself to Sally.

'Look me in the face,' he screamed. 'Look in my eyes and tell me I must leave.'

Slowly she raised her head until her gaze was level with his. She spoke calmly and unwaveringly. 'This is my husband,' she said, 'and this is my home.'

'Is it?' he asked, his face distorted with rage. 'Suppose I tell him what you've been to me, what we've been through together. You have no more right to this home any more than you have to him. You gave yourself to me willingly or was it a whore I held in my arms? Was it a whore? Answer me and I'll leave peacefully.'

'Say another word to her and I'll smash your face in,' Wally cautioned.

'Are you afraid to let her answer,' Carl taunted.

'You were warned,' Wally cried hoarsely as he smashed a mighty fist into his brother's face. Carl fell to the floor. Wally stood towering over him ready to knock him down again. The gun appeared as if by magic in Carl's right hand. Wally stood paralysed. He had never looked into the barrel of a gun before. On Carl's face was a look which sent the cold terror running through him. The finality in his brother's eyes was terrifying to behold. Suddenly Wally knew how it was going to end. He lunged forward in a despairing effort to restrain him but even as he moved Carl had turned the gun inward towards himself and fired it into his breast. The gun fell from his hand. The blood gushed outward in a spate as the force of the blast threw him backwards on the floor. Death came instantly. Wally knew the moment he lifted his brother's head that life had departed. Death had also removed the snarl from Carl's face and replaced it with a look of serenity that Wally had never before seen there. It was as though he had finally resolved the terrible enigma which had tormented him all his life.

The Urging of Christmas

You can't postpone the true urging of Christmas. You have to do it now. That's the acid test of the man who would be Christmas. If you're a drinking man go and have a drink and it will help you do the right thing. Even a roasting fire won't thaw a frozen heart but a glass of whiskey might. I've seen it happen.

I've also seen Christmas destroyed by whiskey for whiskey is a dangerous cargo without plimsoll line or compass. It must be treated as if it were dynamite.

Then on the other hand, imbued by the spirit of Christmas and a bellyful of booze, I beheld a man who normally would not give you the itch lift his phone and beg his estranged daughter to come home for Christmas. She came with a heart and a half and on both sides all was forgiven. He wasn't half as mean thereafter. So, my friends, taking Christmas by the horns can work wonders.

Don't ever be ashamed to be weepy or sentimental about Christmas because you might not get the chance during the year ahead to show your humanity to the world and what the hell good is humanity if it's suffocated by caution! That's what Christmas is for, taking from our natural stock of humanity and disbursing it where it will do the most good.

If you have to think twice about the impulses that move you to be forgiving and charitable and loving you'll miss the boat. Generosity diminishes the more one considers it. The milk of human kindness doesn't come from cows or goats. It comes from the human heart, that great institute of compassion and repository of human hope.

If a man only submitted himself once a year to the dictates of Christmas all would not be lost but we have some who acknowledge the birth of Christ by regarding it as a day, the same as any other, when they may kill and maim at will. However, no matter what they do, the spirit of Christmas will survive and they will be long forgotten.

The spirit of Christmas has survived the Stalins, the Hitlers and the Mussolinis and all those who have perpetrated injustices since the birth of Christ. It has survived human greed and human jealousy and every human failing one cares to mention.

All the moons that have waxed and waned since the birth of Christ will testify that nothing lasts like Christmas. Not all the inhumanity, nor all the greed, nor all the violence will reduce its message by a whit. It's here to stay and there's nothing that evil men can do about it and that's one great consolation.

Officially declaring Christmas non-existent can work only for a while. You can't keep Christmas down for long. It is the most buoyant of all festivals.

There are ways, of course, of destroying the Christmases of individuals, of families and of communities and the chief of these is to drive while you're drunk. You may drink after you drive but never before.

Just say to yourself: 'I'll enjoy a few Christmas drinks when I arrive at my destination but not before. This will be my Christmas gift to my fellow man.'

You can start a row in a pub or a hotel and upset the Christmases of legitimate workers who have enough to contend with during anti-social hours. You can upset your home and your family by being too drunk or too mean or too intolerant or, worst of all, by being indifferent.

These are but a few. There are so many more. However, I know in my heart that you, dear reader, will do none of those heinous things. You'll try to do otherwise. Just try and since God loves a trier you're halfway there already.

Don't think I'm pontificating. I'm not. I'm trying to explain what Christmas should be all about. It's a time of opportunity. The climate is perfect for revealing our better natures. Just as the spring assures growth of crops so does Christmas assure growth of love.

It is not possible for man, because of his very nature, to be charitable and compassionate all the year round. Let us, therefore, make the most of Christmas.

Heap on more wood! the wind is chill;
But let it whistle as it will.
We'll keep our Christmas merry still.

So wrote the great Walter Scott long before Dickens wrote *A Christmas Carol* which gives the lie to those who would say that Dickens invented Christmas as we know it. Christmas was never invented. It was born out of love and carries on out of love.

I once asked an old woman what she would do if there was no Christmas.

'I don't know,' she said, 'but I wouldn't be bothered with anything else.'

Personally speaking, I don't know how I would survive if Christmas were to be abolished. There would be no point in getting drunk because that would only remind me of Christmas all the more.

I could not imagine a more bleak world. I just cannot conceive anything of commensurate magnitude to replace it. We should, therefore, be down on our knees thanking God that it is there.

If there was no Christmas there would be no *Adeste,* no *Silent Night,* no carol singing, no Santa Claus. I could go on and on. There would be nothing without Christmas because it's the plinth on which the rest of the year stands.

Sometime when you are alone with nothing to do try to remember all the things that would never again be if we lost Christmas. There is nothing else with the power to move the human heart to its utmost capability. For God's sake don't take it for granted. If you haven't done anything about it yet for pity's sake do it now or you'll be guilty of the awful crime of trying to undermine Christmas.

The Fourth Wise Man

Canon Coodle sighed happily. It was Christmas. He had just finished hearing confessions and to clear his head from the fog of sin, or what his parishioners believed to be sin, he had decided upon a walk around the church grounds which were as extensive as any you'd find in the country. His thoughts turned heavenward as they always did after a session in the confessional. He would have liked a glass of vintage port but it was still bright. He looked at his watch and came to the conclusion that darkness was imminent. Perhaps when the dusk surrendered its diminishing claims to daylight he would indulge, just one glass, no more. Before retiring that night he would consume two final glasses and then graciously surrender himself to the arms of Morpheus. Canon Coodle had spent eighty-two Christmases in the world but had never really felt the burden of his years. 'I'll die in harness,' he informed his physician, 'because I would hate to end up as a problem for someone.'

'Oh you'll die in harness all right,' Dr Matt Coumer had assured him a few weeks earlier when the canon had called to the surgery for his bi-annual overhaul.

'Is there something wrong?' the canon asked matter-of-factly as though it did not concern him.

'Your blood pressure's up and your heart is tricky. I can think of no other word for that particular heart of yours. Apart from the fact that you should have been dead years ago there's little else the matter.' Dr Coumer put aside his stethoscope and indicated to his parish priest that they should both be seated. 'You have only one problem canon.' The doctor leaned back in his chair and looked his elderly patient in the eye.

'And pray what would that be?'

'Two days hence on St Stephen's day you will have bands of wrenboys calling to the presbytery as they have been doing since you first came here. Your predecessors cleared them from the presbytery door for all the wrong reasons. You changed all that and we admire you for it but in one way you might be better off if the wrenboys stayed away from your door too.'

'Never!' Canon Coodle rose from his chair.

'Please sit down,' Matt Coumer spoke in the gentlest of tones as if he were reproving a wayward child. The canon sat and listened.

'In the past you have been known to dance jigs and hornpipes with each of the bands on the steps leading up to the presbytery door. All I'm asking you to do my dear friend is to dance with only one band on this occasion. If you do as I ask there's a good chance you'll see one more Christmas at least. If you persist in dancing with all the bands you'll be in danger of a seizure. Promise me now like a good man,' Dr Coumer reverted to the gentle tones he had used earlier, 'that all you'll dance on St Stephen's day is one hornpipe and one reel. Promise.'

'I promise,' Canon Coodle forced out the words against his will. He rose and shook hands with his physician who, in turn, placed a protective arm around the old man's shoulder.

As the canon recalled his visit he regretted the promise he had made. Round and round the church grounds he walked as if he were competing in a race. 'Promises were made to be broken,' he recalled the saying and then he smashed the fist of his right hand into the palm of his left, 'but not by Canon Cornelius Coodle,' he concluded in triumph with the voice of a man who had never broken a promise.

He decided to return to the warmth of the presbytery sitting-room and therein to partake of his ration of port as he termed the measure. Later there would be the Christmas Eve Masses and later still there would be a Christmas drink or two with his curates and two of the most amiable chaps imaginable he considered them to be. They would tease him of course about the flawed full forward line of the Ballybo Gaelic football team. The canon had first seen the light in Ballybo 'and is he proud of it!' the curates would tell their families when asked what sort of priest was Canon Coodle.

When they finished with Ballybo they would start about Celtic and their run in the Scottish League. The canon's first curacy had been in Glasgow. He would be a Celtic fan till the man above blew the whistle and called him from the field of play. He always favoured a melodramatic turn of phrase when arguing football with curates. It was what they expected of him and he would never let them down.

As the trio savoured their drinks in the brightly lit sitting-room they were joined by Mrs Hanlon, the housekeeper, who drank not at all but who, the curates suspected, would play her customary role of timekeeper as the clock ticked merrily on towards twelve. On Christmas night and New Year's eve, of all the nights of the year, she would stand benignly by, as Canon Coodle put it, and suffer silently the yearly massacres of 'Danny Boy' and 'The Last Rose of Summer' as the canon also put it, by himself and his specially invited colleagues from parishes near and far.

She sat now silently and most reposefully while the sacred hour approached. It was her favourite time, a time to savour, above all other times, for the birth of Christ was at hand and downstairs in the kitchen her turkey was ready for the morning oven with bread stuffing and potato stuffing close by, with ham cooked and glazed, with giblet stock prepared for soup and gravy, with the primed fortified special trifle at the ready and the plum pudding waiting to be steamed. It could be said that her cup was running over. Her drowsy eyes blinked but barely when the glasses of her three charges clinked.

'It's the sort of night,' she reminded herself, 'when a drunk is bound to show up at the front door looking for the canon or one of the curates to drive him home. Only six miles. Couldn't get a taxi. Wife and kids at home with no one to fill the role of Santa. On the other hand it might be an even more drunken wretch looking for a priest to give the last rites to a mother who was far healthier than he was.'

As ill-luck would have it the presbytery's inmates would not be left in peace until the sacristan rang the warning bell well in advance of first mass on the morning of Christmas day. A surprise lay in store.

'Now lads!'

Mrs Hanlon raised first her head from near her lap to where it had drooped with the weight of drowsiness and secondly her body from the chair which was ever so narrowly withdrawn outside the priestly triangle round the fire.

Canon Coodle was reminding his listeners of the time his uncle, a country schoolmaster, had shared a public house counter for a short period with Hilaire Belloc while the latter had been visiting Dublin.

'The poor man,' the canon continued with a chuckle, 'never spoke about anything else for the rest of his life.' The canon suddenly rose, extended his right hand and quoted from his uncle's acquaintance:

Dons admirable! Dons of might!
Uprising on my inward sight
Compact of ancient tales and port
And sleep and learning of a sort.

As the trio rose the housekeeper faded into the darkest corner of the room from where she would emerge to see to the fire and lights after the priests' departure to their upstairs rooms. The canon led his curates to the foot of the stairs, both hands extended now as he quoted once more from Belloc:

I will hold my house in the high wood
Within a walk of the sea
And the men who were boys when I was a boy
Will sit and drink with me.

Before they exchanged goodnights the trio said that it was the gentlest night of Christmas ever spent by any of the three. They had, they felt, effortlessly introduced the real spirit of Christmas into their midst and prepared themselves for the feast day that was to come.

No sooner had Canon Coodle eased himself into his bed than the housekeeper appeared at the bedside after first knocking on the bedroom door. On a tray she bore his nightcap, a small measure of whiskey topped up with boiling water and flavoured with cloves and lemon. She waited till the very last drop was swallowed, after which she drew the curtains and waited for the first low-key snore of the night.

As the canon slumbered so did he dream of his mother. She had passed on to her eternal reward shortly after his ordination. He was still young enough at the time to shed abundant tears for many months after her burial. Then with the passage of time as the grief melted into fond recall he could recall their times together without sorrow. She had once asked him, not long before his ordination, if there was a girl. He had shaken his head but of course there had been a girl. Hadn't that been the case always and wasn't it the case for many years thereafter but these were merely girls of the mind and with these phantom creatures all men must contend before sleep dulls the senses. Always the canon would spend his last waking moments thinking of his mother. Other nights he would dream of Gaelic football when he saw himself soaring above the heads of his opponents, reaching into the heavens where only the doughtiest and most agile of footballers soared in search of the pig-skin as it was known in country places in the days when Corny Coodle could out-field any man in the seven parishes. He was denied a place on the county team but only because his alma mater, Maynooth College, frowned upon high level commitment on the grounds that the sweet taste of physical glory might out-weigh the spiritual and the mystical. It happened all too often and it was believed by many that those who surrendered the spiritual to the physical turned their backs on the Roman collar and would always be deficient in outlook and aspiration.

'Hogwash!' was the only comment Canon Coodle would offer when such opinions were aired.

He would remember a classmate in his final year, one Tommy Henley, who withdrew from the race within weeks of his ordination because of pressure to stay away from county football. He had played under a variety of assumed names but when the college authorities discovered this duplicity they determined that he would abide by the rules or withdraw. He had opted for the latter.

Canon Coodle fondly remembered Tommy's marriage to Mary-Anne Fogarty. It had been a joyous wedding and were there not now twelve Henleys from that glorious union, all doing well in the world and was not one of them ordained. Canon Coodle stirred in his sleep. He found himself tussling for a ball with a Corkman named Tyers. The ball eluded both at their first attempt but Coodle got a hand to it to stop it from going over the line and wide. It fell to Tyers to raise the ball into his grasp with his right foot and so it went on until blows were very nearly exchanged. It was precisely at that moment that the canon opened his eyes to find himself being manhandled by his junior curate.

'Wake, wake, for God's sake canon!' the curate cried out.

The canon sat upright in his bed wondering if he was playing host to an unwelcome dream.

'It's the crib canon!' the curate threw both hands high in the air at the monstrosity of the entire business.

'What about the crib!' the canon asked calmly, 'is it on fire or what?'

'No, no, no!' the curate was screaming now. 'They are trying to wrest the boy scouts' box from the wall beside it.'

'But dang it!' the canon exclaimed disbelievingly, 'the boy scouts' box is part of the chapel wall.'

'Well they have a pick-axe and they have a hammer and chisel and they're hacking away like hell and they're drunk to boot.'

The canon had moved himself to the side of the bed where he sat momentarily.

'And where is the senior curate?' he asked.

'Fr Sinnott is on sick call,' he was informed by a now more composed junior curate.

'Where is Mrs Hanlon?' the canon asked fearfully.

'She's rung the civic guards,' he was at once informed, 'and now she's keeping an eye on the robbers till help comes.'

'Well help is at hand,' the canon raised his great voice and demanded his dressing-gown.

'Follow me!' he called. The canon would have been happier had the junior curate's role been reversed with that of his senior. He had seen Fr Sinnott on the football field, a tough customer who revelled in rough play and was not above planting the occasional consecrated wallop on the jaw of a would-be blackguard.

'Ballybo forever!' Canon Coodle shouted out the war cry of his native place as his six feet two inches, fifteen stones and eighty-two years bore down upon the sacrilegious wretches who dared tamper with his boy scouts' box, a veritable treasure chest which was now held in the arms of an emaciated cut-throat on his way to the door which he had earlier broken in. He was followed by two henchmen armed with pickaxe, hammer and chisel.

'My strength is as the strength of ten.' Canon Coodle issued the warning before crashing headlong into the wielder of the pick-axe. The wielder fell, winded and semi-conscious. The bearer of the chisel and hammer was to suffer a worse fate for as soon as he intimated that he meant business he was struck to the floor and rendered unconscious by Fr Sinnott who had just entered via the sacristy. At that moment the canon challenged the gang's ringleader.

'Drop that box,' he warned, 'or suffer the consequences. By the double dang,' the canon went on as he raised himself to his full height, 'you're for an early grave sir unless you yield.'

Yield the scoundrel did but it was not because of the canon's command. Rather had his trusty housekeeper edged her way behind the ringleader and embedded her knitting needle in his unprotected posterior. He dropped the boy scouts' box as though it were a box of adders and ran screaming into the night, leaving his henchmen to the tender mercies of an enraged Fr Sinnott. When the civic guards arrived as they did almost immediately after they had been summoned their main worry was the containment of the senior curate. It proved to be no easy task for Fr Sinnott was as strong as the proverbial horse. After a while, aided by the canon's mollifying tones and the housekeeper's tender words, they managed to seat him in a pew. Then and only then did the junior curate appear. He had taken up his position in the crib, next to St Joseph from where he had hurled sacred candles at the invaders.

It transpired that the box held several hundred pounds. The civic guards took the money with them for safe-keeping as they did the leaderless rogues who would have denied the boy scouts the summer holiday which the generous subscriptions of the parishioners had guaranteed them

'Coodle is the truest boy scout of them all,' the middle-aged sergeant of the civic guards announced to his two companions as they opened a bottle in the barracks to celebrate the capture. Later the ringleader would be happy to give himself up as the cold of the night proved itself to be the master of his mettle.

In the presbytery the triumphant foursome were content to reoccupy their warm beds and sleep the sleep of the blessed. Word of their exploits spread and would-be raiders gave the church and presbytery a wide berth from that sacred morning forward.

Christmas Day was a happy day as was the night that followed. The parishioners one and all commented over their Christmas dinners on the text of Canon Coodle's sermon. In it he had praised exceedingly the closeness of the family and the power of the family when beset by the force of evil. He was referring, of course, to the Holy Family of Jesus, Mary and Joseph but when he went on to suggest that all who shared the same roof were, in a sense, families too they knew that he was referring to the inmates of the presbytery and the role they had played in defending each other and their property when unity was needed.

In spite of this the younger curate was bestowed with a sobriquet which would stay with him even when he left the parish. He became known as the Fourth Wise Man. Nobody knew who was responsible for the nickname but almost everybody in the community was agreed that it was a wise move indeed to seek the sanctuary of the holy crib when confronted by hostile forces twice his size and armed to the teeth.

The achievements of the others guaranteed lasting veneration. The Fourth Wise Man went on to become a parish priest in the course of time and Fr Sinnott the senior curate ended up a monsignor. The occasion would be remembered as the night of the Fourth Wise Man.

As Christmas drew to a close Canon Coodle sat in the presbytery sitting-room with his housekeeper. 'If there is one sound,' he told her after he had sipped from his glass of port, 'that I love above all others it is the distant pulse of the *bodhrán,* the drum of drums, the native drum of Ireland. If tomorrow is as fine as the forecasters have promised we will be able to hear it from great distances.'

In the canon's study a sensitive goat-skin drum, beloved of wrenboys and stepdancers, hung from the ceiling to remind him of the days when, as a youngster, and indeed as a young man, he roved the countryside with his companions of the Ballybo Wrenboys Band under their captain the Tipper Coodle. The Tipper, uncle to the young Corny Coodle, was so called because of his preference for the bare knuckle over the *cipín* or wooden drumstick with a knob at either end.

Every band of the time would have an equal number of drummers and tippers, the tippers favouring the knuckle, the drummers favouring the *cipín*. Often the tippers would play even when the blood began to show on the backs of their bare hands such was their zeal in the pursuance of perfection.

'I tell you now with no word of a lie,' the canon confided to his housekeeper, 'those tippers could make the *bodhráns* talk and my dear uncle, God be good to him, could play and dance at the same time especially when he had a few whiskeys inside of him.'

'You're a fair dancer yourself canon,' Mrs Hanlon spoke out of a sense of appreciation rather than from a sense of duty as she recalled the canon's exploits at the front of the presbytery on previous St Stephen's days.

'He would dance with every group,' she informed her sister Bridgie whenever she visited the family home in the hills at the southern end of the parish, 'and out of his own pocket would come a ten-pound note for every band. I remember when it was a ten-shilling note but a ten -hilling note then was as good as a tenner now.'

The money, of course, would go towards the purchase of drink and edibles for the annual wren dances, several of which would be held all over the parish until the month of January expired. The previous canon would have nothing to do with wrenboys, labelling them drunkards and scoundrels and turning them away from the presbytery door. In the end they by-passed the presbytery altogether but all changed dramatically when Canon Coodle was appointed as parish priest.

The canon's face darkened a little when he recalled the terpsichorean restrictions imposed upon him by his physician. Never downcast for long he raised his great head and smiled at the prospect of the two dances which had been permitted to him. He resolved to invest more concentration and commitment into these than ever before and, please God, he would have his fill of the dance before the day was out.

As they sat, the canon reminiscing, the housekeeper deftly used her knitting needles to complete the cardigan which she had undertaken to knit for her sister. The bright needles moved like lightning in her practised fingers, one of them the same needle which had perforated the vile rear of the robbers' ringleader. The wound inflicted needed medical attention and when Dr Coumer called to the barracks on the morning of St Stephen's Day to re-examine the sore he was able to tell Sergeant Ruttle that it would take several days to heal.

'You'll have a drink before you leave,' Sergeant Ruttle insisted.

'I have a call to make,' he said.

'It can't be that serious.' The sergeant took a bottle of whiskey from his desk.

'I assure you,' said Matt Coumer at his most emphatic, 'that it is likely to be the most important call I shall make this day.' So saying he closed his black bag and made straight for the presbytery where he was immediately shown into the august presence of his parish priest.

'You can leave your coat on canon,' he announced warmly, 'for I have not come to examine you.'

'And why have you come my dear Matt?' the canon asked solicitously.

'I have come,' Matt informed him, 'to restore your licence.'

'And pray what licence would that be?' the canon asked, a look of anxiety appearing on his face.

'Your dance licence of course my dear canon,' Matt informed him, 'you may dance as much as you please and if my ears don't deceive me I believe I hear the sound of *bodhráns* so get your dancing shoes on. I'll stay to watch and enjoy a drop of your whiskey while I do.'

A Christmas Come-uppance

Canon Cornelius Coodle heaved a great sigh and ran gaunt fingers through his heavily silvered hair. At eighty-two he was still one of the more presentable priests in the diocese. Certainly he was the most distinguished-looking. When he spoke people listened. Nobody fell asleep during his sermons.

'Oh he calls a spade a spade sure enough,' the older farmers in the parish's hinterland were fond of saying, 'even if he does throw back a drop or two in excess now and then.'

'All he takes is a drop of port for God's sake,' the farmers' wives would respond defensively.

Removing his hands from his head Canon Coodle examined his smooth palms as though he might find in them a solution to the problem which had so recently been relayed to him on the phone. The voice at the other end had been that of his bishop.

'Bad news Corny,' the bishop had opened. He went on to inform his right arm, the name by which he always referred to the canon, of several distressing sightings of one Fr Tom Doddle, ecclesiastic-in-chief of Cooleentubber, a struggling parish in the easternmost part of the diocese. 'He was seen only last evening,' the bishop informed the right arm, 'vainly trying to negotiate a simple street corner. When a friendly civic guard came to his assistance he ranted and raved over the stupidity of an urban council which dared to place such abominable obstructions in the path of an innocent wayfarer.

'I tell you Corny,' the bishop continued, 'that if this insufferable staggering doesn't end at once we'll all be disgraced.'

'What can I do Pádraig?' Canon Coodle asked gently. Only the canon, at the bishop's behest, was permitted to address the diocesan leader by his Christian name.

'What I want you to do Corny is get him to go off the drink right away or, failing that, get him to reduce his intake – but most of all I want you to stop him staggering in public.'

There followed a silence. After a short interval the bishop resumed where he had left off. 'A staggering clergyman,' he told his canon, 'is a parody of the priesthood, a degradation of all we hold sacred, an abomination to the eye.'

While the bishop's litany continued Canon Coodle brought up to mind the only occasion he had ever staggered. He had been a green curate at the time. He had accompanied his parish priest Fr Willie Sidle to a Station mass. After the celebration of the mass both priests sat at a table, already partially manned by four local dignitaries, strong farmers all. After breakfast the talk turned to Gaelic football. The young curate was astonished at the inroads made into three bottles of Powers Gold Label as the morning matured into noon. For his part, after declaring his preference for port, he downed a mere half bottle. It was he who later guided the docile mare home while Fr Sidle issued a running commentary on the football prowess of the many farmers and labourers they encountered on their way back to the presbytery.

As they both untackled the mare from the parochial trap Fr Sidle paused in his labours in order to tender some advice to his curate. Earlier the parish priest had been surprised when the curate had indulged in a mild stagger as they departed the Station house.

'Observe!' he instructed his junior, 'my carriage and my disposition. I do not stagger under drink for two reasons. First I know to the drop what I can consume and secondly I would rather be hung like a dog before I would give it to say to any man that I am a staggerer. My drinking habits, as long as I don't show drink, are between me and my liver. I like football. I've seen you play Coodle and you're a decent half-back. I've seen you ship many a hard tackle but you never went down because you wouldn't give it to say that you were hurt. Go now and drink your moderate quota of port on occasion but stagger no more like a decent fellow.'

'Are you there Corny?' The bishop's exasperated tone brought Canon Coodle back to the time that was in it.

'You're not to worry.' The canon spoke with what he hoped was canonical assurance.

'That's good to hear Corny.' The bishop sounded mollified but he wasn't finished.

'Dang it,' he went on, 'I served under priests who could drink Lough Lein if they had the price of it but I never saw one of them stagger.'

The first thing Canon Coodle did after his bishop had hung up was to toast his late mentor Fr Willie Sidle. Fr Sidle had been his model during those formative early years.

'Fr Willie,' his parishioners boasted, 'always drinks his nuff at weddings, wakes, Stations and the like but he never drinks more than his nuff.'

Finishing his port the canon folded his once mighty hands over his ample paunch and pondered his problem. Desperate ills he told himself require desperate remedies and with this precept as his guide he began to formulate his plan.

Now Cornelius Coodle was not an envious man but if there was to be a momentary visitation from the deadliest of the seven deadly sins the man he would most envy would be Simon Tabley. Simon was a friend, however, a close and trusted one as were most of the teachers under the canon's management. Simon could carry his liquor. He drank during weekends only.

'He drinks like a fish,' a local wag once told his cronies, 'but the difference is that he don't make no splash.'

What the wag said was true. Simon, a childless widower in his late fifties, was principal of the Boys' National School. His only interest in life after his video camera was his devotion to whiskey consumption during weekends. His wife had been the victim of a youthful speedster's erratic driving. Simon had been lucky to survive and was in receipt of generous insurance. 'I would forfeit every penny,' he once confided to the canon, 'if I could hold her in my arms for a minute, a single minute my dear friend.'

The canon had nodded, his ancient face flushed by a port-induced rufescence. At the time Simon was quite taken by the angelic expression on the old man's face. A translation from the Gaelic came to him from memory:

As sacred candle
In a holy face
Such is the beauty
Of an ancient face.

When the pair met the following weekend Simon contained his curiosity as best he could. He had brought with him a bottle of vintage port and before he could sit down he found himself with a glass of whiskey in his hand. His entry to the canon's sitting-room coincided with that of the two curates.

'I'm off canon,' the senior curate informed his superior, 'you will be called, I hope, for ten o'clock mass in the morning.'

'What a personable chap,' the schoolmaster commented after he had taken a tiny sip from his unwatered whiskey. The canon showed his gratification with a benevolent nod. He had, after all, taught his assistant most of what he knew.

'And the other one?' Simon asked.

'Excellent young man, a beer perhaps when he is off duty, nothing while he's on.'

The preliminaries over, Canon Coodle addressed his visitor. 'There is,' he began, 'in this very diocese a floundering philanderer of a clergyman who seems to be quite incapable of walking in an upright manner while under the influence of drink. In fact,' the canon continued sarcastically, much to his visitor's surprise, 'he inflicted his undesirable presence on this very parish quite recently and literally passed himself out with a variety of hitherto-unaccomplished staggers. In short my dear friend he disgraced himself on the streets of this very parish, my parish. I understand his housekeeper drives him here on a regular basis and when she's finished her shopping mercifully drives him off again. Apparently he presents a soberer mien at his own front door as it were.'

'How's he otherwise?' Simon asked.

'Otherwise,' the canon grudgingly conceded, 'he seems to be all right.'

Simon found himself somewhat perplexed. The canon seemed to be stepping out of character a little. It must be his aversion to staggering he told himself.

'How can I help?' he asked.

'You can help by making a short video of one of his performances when he next intrudes in my bailiwick.'

'I don't know that I can do that canon,' Simon informed his friend.

'Oh you can do it,' the canon assured him, 'you have no choice. You don't want to see the children of the parish scandalised. A clergyman staggering through the streets of this town is the last thing any of us wishes to see. Suppose it was a teacher?' the canon suggested.

Simon decided not to rise to this bait. He personally knew several teachers who staggered occasionally when under the influence and even if they weren't always discreet about it Simon failed to see the harm in it unless it happened in the school or on the school grounds.

'Who would see this video?' he asked.

'Well,' the canon paused for a moment, 'there wouldn't be any point in the exercise if the star of the show didn't see it. I would see it and you would see it but nobody else. The idea is to show the poor wretch the error of his ways and then we'll destroy the evidence.'

'I'll do it because I know you mean well,' Simon agreed, 'although I have certain misgivings.'

'I'll never be able to repay you.' The canon gratefully replenished his friend's glass and returned to his armchair.

'Will it be difficult?' he asked.

'Shouldn't be,' Simon assured him. 'I know our quarry fairly well and I know his runs. Generally he arrives in town about three o'clock on Monday afternoons. I've spotted him on my way to the post office after school, calls to the hotel, to Brady's, O'Grady's, Mulligan's, Brannigan's and Crutley's, commences to stagger after leaving Brannigan's, shortish staggers really more like mis-steps until he emerges from Crutley's, his final port of call. Then the comprehensive staggers commence, be a piece of cake, nobody minds me on the streets, especially with my video. They're well used to me. I'll do the job and with average luck I'll have the finished product here on Monday night, a week before Christmas.'

'And I'll have my man here the following morning,' the canon promised.

The friends had another drink before parting, Canon Coodle to his bed and Simon to Brady's Bar or more precisely to the back lounge or inner sanctum of the widely revered premises. There he would sip until Mrs Brady gently reminded her special customers that it was time to go home.

True to form Fr Tom Doddle, parish priest of Cooleentubber, erupted from the ornate doorway of Crutley's Bar on to the main street where he collided with several passers-by. He escaped any form of derailment or injury himself. His victims were not so lucky. One young man who had been somewhat unsighted in the first place was knocked to the ground. He arose, none the worse for his encounter, dazed and badly shaken, after a short while. On his feet he assumed a fighting stance and challenged the onlookers to a fair fight. When no one took up his offer he wished all and sundry a Merry Christmas and sat on an adjacent windowsill in order to confirm his bearings.

As Fr Tom Doddle staggered onwards in ever-increasing lurches he was videoed front face, side face and rear by Simon until the schoolmaster was satisfied that he had captured a true portrait of the wayward cleric.

Time passed and at the appointed hour the film was set in motion by Simon. With mounting annoyance the canon followed the erratic progress of Fr Doddle. He cast a side glance now and then at his friend but that worthy merely sat with folded arms, expressionless and impassive.

'What's this?' Canon Coodle asked in alarm as his eyes returned to the small screen.

The question was followed by gasping sounds of disbelief and by various exclamations of astonishment. 'Oh no!' Canon Coodle covered his face with his hands. 'Can that awful parody really be me?' he asked, his voice broken, his face anguished.

'Have I seen myself as I really am Simon or is this video a distortion of my true self?'

'The video doesn't lie canon, not this time anyway. You've just seen yourself at a bad time and that can be unnerving.'

'Did you do this deliberately Simon because if you did I'm most grateful for giving me a look at the horrible old windbag I really am.'

'Not deliberately canon. You just happened to be in the vicinity.'

'But I look awful,' the canon cried out. 'I look drunk, trampish, farcical, infinitely worse than that poor priest.'

'No canon. You just look a bit weary that's all. You're no chicken you know.'

The canon raised his eyes aloft. He remembered the occasion clearly now. He had been on his way home from his pre-Christmas visit to the convent where his good friend the reverend mother had plied him with vintage port. He remembered saying to himself on his way home that he was a little unsteady on his feet but then he admitted, 'I often am and I need not have a single port taken. I remember I had my hat in one hand and my walking stick in the other just like we saw there,' the canon laughed, happily now, 'and my scarce, grey locks blowing in the wind like Lear but he had only a crown whereas I have a Roman collar. I've seen the light Simon. I was fast becoming a whining old hypocrite. I missed the mote in my own eye but I'll never make the same mistake again. I'm so grateful to you my boy. I wish you a happy, holy and wonderful Christmas and now will you please do something about our empty glasses so that I can celebrate my escape from hypocrisy.'

ANGELS IN OUR MIDST

Never pass an acquaintance, or indeed any man or woman, without conferring upon them that most inexpensive of all gifts – the common-or-garden salute. This applies especially at Christmas when people of all ages wish each other happy Christmases, holy Christmases and merry Christmases. Sometimes those with generous dispositions or with time on their hands also wish all and sundry a happy New Year. I believe this to be a commendable practice and I am glad that I find the opportunity in this collection of yuletide tales to indulge in my favourite eccentricity as my beloved wife sometimes calls it.

When we salute people, no matter how enlightened or well intentioned the sentiments, we must always be prepared for rebuff. When we wish other people happy Christmases we should try to realise that some are incapable of being happy because they enjoy being unhappy. Some enjoy being morose while others like to be churlish. I once had a distant cousin, now even more distant, God rest him since he expired in a fit of pique a few Christmases ago. He saw a group of people laughing hysterically on his way home from church and was overcome by disgust. Promptly he fell down and died poor fellow.

Another relation of mine, still with us, would faint upon beholding a radiant face and then there was a friend who never returned a salute. He would respond with grimaces and rude sounds. In case you are asking yourself why the preamble to this tale, if tale it can be called, I will not keep you waiting any longer. I am simply trying to ready the gentle reader for the unexpected.

On the most recent Christmas Eve at precisely twenty-five minutes past eleven I decided to go for a stroll through the streets of my native town. Before I left the house I underwent a wifely inspection. She approved of my shoes and my socks, rearranged my scarf so that no part of my throat was left uncovered. She removed my cap and replaced it with a heavier specimen as well as feeling the texture of my gloves and the quality of my overcoat. She already had a more than nodding acquaintance with the texture of the garment but habit dies hard and I would have to admit that nobody has my welfare more at heart than that gracious, glorious, lifelong companion.

'Try not to indulge in liquor until tonight,' she said, 'and then we can all have a few together.' I agreed or maybe it was the accumulated wisdom of three score and ten that made me fulfil the obligation without a second thought. Outside the air was crisp. There was a frosty nip and the sky overhead was blue. What more could a man wish for at the beginning of his daily peregrinations unless it was the occasional flurry of snow to emphasise the season. No sleet thank you for the good reason that sleet can't make up its mind whether its snow, rain or good round hailstone – hailstone, blessed ambassador from the court of winter. I will now proceed with my tale and won't be waylaid again.

The streets were bright and festive with the trappings of Christmas and everywhere could be heard the joyful exchanges of the season. On a personal basis I was greeted on countless occasions and was quick to return the compliments. When I had exhausted the main streets I briefly visited the town's two squares where further seasonal exchanges were the order of the morning.

Then I took myself to the side streets and thence to the back-ways, almost always favoured by the middle-aged and the elderly because of the absence of bustle. It was here I encountered a doughty middle-aged damsel who held the centre of the back-way against all comers. She also moved at an alarming pace despite being burdened with two large bags of groceries. She had, on her flushed face, a look of intense determination. In an earlier age with a sword in her hand she would have put to flight any foe foolhardy enough to challenge her. My sixth sense, which I always keep handy, warned me that I might be better advised to forego the normal Christmas wishes and continue on my way as though she did not exist.

My sixth sense is rarely wrong but I am a man who has always cherished the belief that passers-by are there to be saluted or greeted or whatever.

'A Happy Christmas!' I ventured.

There was no verbal response but she threw me a look which suggested that she had little time for frivolities. She barged by, her sturdy steps a challenge to anyone who might dispute her right to the middle of the back-way. All the other people I saluted on that resplendent morning returned the greeting with interest.

It was around that time that I began to feel peckish so I decided upon a short-cut home. There is truly no place like home when the pangs of hunger announce their arrival so I set off with a cheerful heart to the pork chops and mashed parsnips which awaited me.

I have often thought, since that eventful morning, how we fail to take account of the possibility of disaster when we find ourselves on the crest of a wave. How beautifully Robbie Burns put it when he ploughed the mouse's nest:

The best laid schemes of mice and men
Gang aft a-gley
And leave as nought but grief and pain
For promised joy.

A flight of starlings, dipping and soaring, chirping and chatting, flew by overhead while sturdy sparrows fed on motes and grains, impervious to the passing human.

Suddenly, for a second time, I braced myself as the doughty damsel bearing the grocery bags hove into view once more. It was obvious from her demeanour that things had not been going her way all morning. Ever a believer in the power and goodness of salutation I tendered the compliments of the season again. This time she stopped and looked me up and down without reply. Then she placed her bags on the ground and looked me in the eye.

'Bad cess to you,' she spat, 'with your Happy Christmas. How could I be happy and my husband drunk in some dive and me with no way of getting home?'

I was about to say something but could think of nothing appropriate. She then sent me about my business with a four-letter word followed by one of three.

For all that, the sun still shone down and the white frost faded on the roof-tops. None the worse for my encounter I stopped and bestowed the compliments of the season on a trio of people I thought I knew.

'You have some gall to salute us after what you and your crowd did to this poor girl here.'

The rebuke came from the woman probably in her late thirties, obviously the mother of the girl allegedly wronged by myself and my crowd. But who were my crowd and what had we done to the innocent who stood before me? Her husband stood idly by and made no attempt to speak and why should he with a spouse as articulate as the woman beside him. As I recall, although no word escaped his lips, he had adopted a supporting attitude.

'How did I wrong this girl?' I asked.

'The poem,' came back the prompt reply.

'What poem?' I asked.

'The poem she entered for your competition,' she answered.

'What competition?' I asked patiently.

Suddenly the words burst forth, one forcing the one before forward until a great spate of language told me that the competition had been organised by a food manufacturing company with a head office in London and that her daughter had managed to qualify for the final stages but had been deprived of her just rights by myself and my evil cronies. She went on to say that we would never have an hour's luck and that we would never die in our beds after which we would rot in hell and be damned forever without hope of redemption.

I explained that I did not belong to the organisation she had mentioned and had never, in fact, any dealings good, bad or indifferent with the food group in question, at which she spewed verbal fire in all directions so that even her husband's face began to register alarm.

The victim, a shy creature on the verge of her teens, seemed as if she was going to burst into tears. I pointed out that I had once been a judge in a poetry competition sponsored by Listowel Writers' Week but had never been involved with any other.

It was as though I had slapped her face. She rounded on me once more and berated me as if I was the scum of the earth. When she had exhausted herself I extended my hands and apologised profusely for the perfidy of dishonest judges everywhere. I infused the last dregs of my drained compassion into my tone but she was having none of it. Suddenly I altered my course as it were. I remarked on the singular beauty of the morning and how it was a shame that the fine weather had not come sooner. I then veered in the direction of their Christmas dinner and enquired if they had invested in a hen or a cock turkey or maybe like myself they had opted for a goose. She replied by swinging her umbrella at me. I was, of course, totally innocent of the charge laid at my door and begged her to take note of the facts. It was only then I deduced that the creature was intoxicated. At that moment a countryman passed and asked what was wrong. I had seen him before. His face was always belligerent.

'This girl,' my tormentor pointed out, 'sent a poem to this man's competition and they sent the poem back saying it was too late for entry.'

So the charge had taken a new twist and it was possible that on this occasion she was telling the truth, except that it wasn't my competition.

'Well,' I explained, 'the rules are there and when an entry is late it is returned to the owner.'

'Scandalous isn't the word for it,' said the new arrival, the hostility rampant in his attitude.

'And suppose,' said the mother of the victimised poetess, 'that it was Shakespeare sent it would you return it? Indeed you would not for if you did you'd have no Shakespeares and you'd have no omelettes.'

At least it sounded like omelettes but of course she meant *Hamlet* but had dropped her haitch having spent a period working in London before returning to Ireland. The gentleman who had stopped to ask what was wrong had passed a disparaging remark about poetry and was now at the receiving end of the umbrella. He crumbled like a gangly puppet and rolled to safety without a whimper. My time had come too. I felt I had suffered enough but how's that Shakespeare puts it:

When sorrows come, they come not single spies
But in battalions.

When I arrived home I was informed that my beloved wife had accepted a lift to the funeral of a distant relative in an equally distant village. As always she had left my dinner in a covered plate on a saucepan of hot water but on this occasion there was nothing in the nature of a dinner to be seen. Apparently a handyman had called to sweep out the back-yard and he presumed that the dinner was for him and why would he presume otherwise when, on so many times in the past, he had found his dinner waiting as mine had been waiting, until he came along. According to a friend of my wife's who had called to deliver a religious magazine to which we unfailingly subscribed and unfailingly never read, the handyman had bolted my dinner in jig time and declared it to be the best so far.

I settled for a snack as I recall and, not for the first time, decided to rediscover the fine flavour of a lightly-mustarded ham sandwich.

The ham was totally rotten so I decided upon a cheese sandwich but there was no cheese. At this stage I was about to fume but instead I sat down and composed myself. Slowly but surely I began to realise what a fortunate fellow I was. Here I was, unscathed after wading through a sea of troubles. I began to rejoice and when I went out into the backyard still brightly lit by the winter sun and showing the sickle of distant Ramadan materialising in the heavens, I raised my hands aloft and thanked God for my happy lot and for allowing me to share Christmas with the less fortunate. The trials I had experienced were merely joys in disguise and the people I met were surely angels in our midst for they reminded me of my happy lot and is this not the brief of angels! For the moment farewell dear friends and a Merry Christmas and a Happy New Year to all of us.

THE RESURRECTION

The widows of the deceased footballers blessed themselves and rose as one from the Marian shrine where they had offered an open-air Rosary for the success of the living footballers who would represent the townland of Ballybee on the following Sunday. On their coats, blouses and frocks they proudly wore the black and yellow colours of the Ballybee Gaelic football team. For the first time in twenty-four years Ballybee found themselves in the final of the junior championship.

None was more surprised than the players themselves. Rank outsiders at the beginning, they had played their hearts out in pulsating game after pulsating game until they reached the ultimate stage of the Canon Coodle Cup. Nonie Regan, mother of the team's youthful captain Shamus, prophesied from the beginning that the cup would come back to Ballybee.

'They have the youth,' she pointed out solemnly, 'and you won't beat youth at the end of the day.'

Before the first round of the championship she found few to agree with her but how different it was now! The team had grown in wisdom and experience and her son Shamus was being mentioned for the county team. It was widely believed by experienced non-partisans that the up-and-coming midfielder had the beating of his opposite number on the Ballybo fifteen, the redoubtable Badger Loran, a veteran of seven finals, five of which had been annexed by Ballybo. Despite the rise and rise of the opposition they were still money-on favourites to hold on to the crown.

Canon Cornelius Coodle after whom the cup was named had been a formidable footballer in his day and although extremely cautious in his footballing prognostications was inclined to favour Ballybee, 'but,' he cautioned his two curates, one from Ballybee and the other from Ballybo, 'there will be very little in it in the end and I wouldn't be at all surprised if it turned out to be a draw.'

On the morning of the game he gave one of his more memorable sermons, recalling his own footballing days and emphasising the need for sportsmanship when tempers flared and caution was likely to be thrown to the winds. He recalled sporting encounters from the past and congratulated the six other teams representing six townlands who failed to make it to the final.

'In many ways,' he explained, 'you are just as important as the finalists and with luck there might have been a different outcome in many of the games. You played like men and you behaved like men when the final whistle was blown. You shook hands with the victors and you withdrew gracefully from the scene to ready yourselves for future encounters when the day may be yours.'

The canon then addressed himself to the finalists in particular, pointing out that the children of the parish would be watching on that very afternoon and it behoved the players from both sides to set an example of sportsmanship and discipline. 'Moderate your language at all times,' he urged, 'and take into account the feelings of the referee when you feel like upbraiding him. He is only flesh and blood like all of us and he has a wife and children like many of you so be sure to take his delicate position into account before you threaten him with fist or boot. Remember that there will be songs about this great event, songs which will be sung rousingly in years to come when the combatants have passed on. What matters most is the game so see to it that you abide by the rules and in so doing you'll bring glory to your townlands and to your parish. It is my duty also to warn blackguards and thugs that the football field is for football and I shall be keeping a close eye on the goings-on at all times.'

Canon Coodle went on about excessive drinking and displays of drunkenness on the streets which scandalised young folk in particular. 'To me has fallen the honour of throwing in the ball and I hope the players from both sides will shake hands as gracefully at the close as they did at the beginning.'

Later in the day he would throw in the ball after the referee had called him on from the side-line and then he would withdraw to his cushioned chair where he would maintain a dutiful silence until the game ended.

Let us now look at the captains, firstly the Badger Loran, a forty-year-old midfielder, gnarled and bony and tough as wax, reputed to have broken more bones than a butcher and closed more eyes than any sleeping potion. A strong farmer unmarried and independent with a shock of grey hair which is why he was nicknamed the Badger in the first place. He entertained romantic feelings for the Widow Regan especially since her husband died but had never made his notions known for fear of rebuff. He played with distinction for the county team in his twenties but was still a force to be reckoned with at this level despite his age.

'He's no thoroughbred,' his supporters would tell anyone who cared to listen, 'but the Badger will still be in the running when the thoroughbreds are spent.'

Shamus Regan the Ballybee captain was of average height but physically he was gloriously realised and the fleetest of the thirty players who would contest the leather that day. He could go higher for the ball than any mortal in the eight townlands that made up the ancient parish. Barely gone eighteen he would need a little more weight and a little more muscle if he was to advance to county honours.

'When he's nineteen or twenty,' Canon Coodle informed his curate, 'he'll be a far tougher proposition.'

Shamus because of his blonde, curling locks was instantly recognisable wherever he went and was often a target for the scoundrels mentioned in Canon Coodle's sermon.

'They'll never nail him.' The canon wagged a finger at his assistants. 'He's too elusive, too speedy and built to ride the hardest tackle.'

'Wait till the Badger's done with him,' the curates cautioned humorously.

'He'll annihilate him,' said one hoping to draw the canon's fire.

'He'll pulverise him,' said the second hoping to do the same.

'And I'll pulverise you two,' the canon countered with a laugh, 'if you don't get out of here this very minute and start hearing Confessions.'

In truth the widow's blond-haired son could do with an extra year but he was well compensated with speed and skill.

From an early hour the supporters began to arrive in town. Most made straight for the pubs which had early openings and extended openings for the occasion. Restaurants and sweetshops did a roaring trade and the contrasting colours were quickly sold out, the black and yellow of Ballybee and the red and white of Ballybo.

Mental Nossery the poet had been in the throes of competition for several days. 'Mental isn't his right name at all', the canon would explain to visitors but the locals like to nickname those they don't fully understand. Mental, a still-gangly chap of middle age, stood on a barrel in Crutley's pub and read an appropriate verse from the epic he had started as soon as the finalists were made known.

'No talking now,' Fred Crutley ordered as he smote upon the bar counter with a large wooden mallet. Mental Nossery might be mental and he might be an odd-ball but the part of him that was a poet was sacred and must therefore be respected.

'Order now please,' Blossom O'Moone, barmaid for the day, called. Slowly an uncertain silence began to make itself felt. It was neither the time nor the place for poetry but Blossom would agree that a poet was a poet and might not be available the day after or the day after that or for indeed many a day especially this poet for he had received the annual rent for his leased farm only the day before. That was part of the agreement which both parties had signed, payment on the day or the nearest working day prior to the final of the football championship.

Fortified with three freshly consumed whiskeys and one pint of stout the poet raised a hand and prepared himself to read from the leaflet which fluttered in his shaking hand. He first explained to the somewhat disinterested clientele that he would be omitting most of the verses from the fourth book of the epic on account of the introductory nature of the contents, 'as for instance,' he explained to his restless listeners, 'the many verses necessary to depict the arrival of the aficionados and the names by which they are recognised locally.'

'Get on with it,' a loud voice called. It came from a whiskered elder who happened to be sporting the black and yellow colours of Ballybee. He was immediately shouted down by several raucous young gentleman who wore the red and white ribbons of Ballybo.

Without further preamble Mental Nossery started. Dramatically he extended a long lean hand to encompass his listeners as it were and with the other hand held the pages closer to his eyes: 'They came in coracle, punt and raft,' he intoned:

And every make of outrageous craft
The drunk, the doting, the damned, the daft
The lewd and the low and the lofty
On mule and jennet, on horse and ass
On pony and cob through ford and pass.
Pensioner, puler, laddie and lass
And the crass and crude and crafty.

Mental judged from the humour of the crowd that he might be best advised to move on to the names of those who would be present on the side-lines: 'Mottled McMahons and fair McEntees,' he raised his tone:

Black McAlackys and hairy McMees,
Bald-headed Bradys and brindled O'Deas
Committed to common obstruction
In bevvies and levies and staggering skeins
Black-toothed Bradys and buck-toothed Maines
Foxy-haired Finnertys, bow-legged Kanes
Fermenting to foster destruction.

'And now the ladies' – Mental Nossery was always mindful of the opposite sex. He often boasted that they would never be neglected while he drew breath.

'What do you think of it?' Blossom O'Moone asked of Toben the schoolmaster.

'Well,' said he, 'considering that we're landlocked here and only a small river for water, the punts and rafts and coracles show how mental the poet is.'

The clientele, those who could fully hear him, were impressed but they were not entertained. Nevertheless like any poet worthy of the name he referred to the female breeds likely to be in attendance. His rendering became pacier now as he reeled off:

Delia Dan Donies and Tessie Tom Ned's
Minnie Matt Minnie's and Freda Mick Fred's
Delectable damsels for marital beds
But presently prey to confusion
Julie Jack Josie's and Josie Jack Jim's
Katie Tom Katie's and Tessie Tom Tim's
Malignantly whetted by virginal whims
And curdled for want of collusion.

This verse, alas, proved too much for a hot-headed male member of the Freda Mick Fred family who denied that his breed were ever prey to confusion. He retaliated by knocking Mental from his barrel and would have throttled him had not Blossom spirited him out of doors and sent him on his way to a safer hostelry.

As match time drew near the pubs began to disgorge their crowds and soon there was a steady stream heading towards the sports' ground where the local brass band was playing. Then suddenly there was silence as the band struck up the national anthem. After the anthem a loudspeaker was placed in the now-steady hand of Mental whose true Christian name was Indigo.

'Now, now now!' the canon raised his hands aloft for silence, 'our Laureate will regale us with a verse or two.'

The canon withdrew a step leaving the stage to the poet. For his part Mental Nossery held forth with what he believed was the kernel of the poem.

'I see Mars in the sky or to be more exact in those black clouds that have gathered to the west of us. I now formally invoke the aid of the Holy Spirit and call for ten seconds' silence after which, by the grace of God, I will commence to versify:

Up above Mars waits for the bloody fare
The lightning brightening his burnished hair
As he madly treads on the trembling air
And prises the heavens asunder.
Now he raises his hands than the welkin higher
His nostrils belching and billowing fire
As his voice rolls over the land entire
With its terrible tones of thunder.

Harken now to the words I say
Let the lines be drawn for the coming fray
Let there be no quarter this glorious day
Let each wound another nourish.
Let the game flow fast, let the blood flow free
Let the ball know elbow, boot and knee
Let knuckles white set the molars free
Let the warrior spirit flourish.'

The canon applauded loudly but there was to be no more, for the referee's whistle had sounded and the game was on. The play flowed freely, then savagely, then wickedly, then beautifully and gracefully as Shamus Regan sent over the opening point for Ballybee. Ballybo responded quickly when the Badger fielded high and sent a long pass to his forward-in-chief who split the posts for the equalising point. There followed for the hour similar exchanges while the crowd roared their approval. Never had they seen such a final. Never had so many passionate tempers flared and died and flared again. Never were there so many accurate points and never before in the history of the competition were dynamic goals scored, one for either side by the captains of either team. The Badger lost his head and flayed his opponents but Shamus kept his and won a free kick which was to be the final one of the game the referee warned.

The sides were level as the Ballybee captain placed the ball, sixty full yards from the Ballybo goal. A tricky wind had crept into the proceedings towards the end of the game which made free-taking extremely difficult. Add to this the acute angle of the space between ball and posts. A mortifying silence descended. The day would belong to Ballybee should the ball go over the bar. Shamus bent his head and looked not at the far-off posts. He would estimate with closed eyes before he opened them to kick the ball. Over it went and the crowd went wild. Then a scuffle broke out and when Shamus tried to intervene he was felled and kicked in the head. The Badger threw his great body across the youth to save him from further kicks.

Later in the hospital the doctors concluded that Shamus was in a coma and might well remain in that suspended state for a month or a year or forever.

Blossom O'Moone lived on the side of the street in a small house which fronted seven acres of arable land. The cows which grazed her pastures were never hungry nor were they ever smitten by disease. Blossom's maxim was that cleanliness was the answer to all ills. The milch cows, five in number, provided half of her meagre income. Odd jobs such as white-washing, scrubbing and part-time barmaid-cum-cleaner at Crutley's public house provided the other half. If she was liberal with her favours, as they said, she was also choosy. Her liaisons were short-lived and those who boasted loudest about ravishing her had never even spoken to her. Those who did not boast at all and those who kept their minds to themselves would be more likely to have received her favours or so the wise men of the locality were fond of saying.

'Not so at all,' Mrs Crutley held opposing views, 'Blossom is just a hot court. If she was anything else she would not be working under this roof.'

The house and land had been willed to her by her grandfather.

Blossom's mother had succumbed to the ravages of tuberculosis in an era when there was no redress for victims of the disease. Her father's identity was a mystery.

Blonde and wispily formed she was possessed of what locals were fond of calling a quaint face. Rather was it a quizzical face. She seemed to be forever in search of mystical fulfilment although precisely what kind of mystical fulfilment no one was prepared to say. If they had been more observant they would have noticed that the quizzical look was replaced with one of concern whenever she found herself looking into the bright, blue eyes of Shamus Regan, captain of the Ballybee football team. Although twelve years his senior she felt that there was more than a mild interest. The fact that he also blushed unreservedly confirmed her suspicions. She stored him in a certain secret place in her memory and vowed to resurrect him at the earliest opportunity and she knew, however far-fetched it might seem, that opportunities always presented themselves, even on the most unlikely occasions. Presently, however, it seemed highly unlikely that there would be a moonlight tryst between them.

A small but vibrant river ran by one of the tiny fields at the rear of her house. She had planned to lure him there, to a sheltered grove near a small pool and there to bathe with him and run through the moon-lit fields with him till they fell exhausted into each other's arms but this would never happen now. It seemed certain that he would never waken from the coma in which he found himself.

The night frost had descended on the fields as she walked and whispered to herself: 'This very river flows under his window in the hospital in the town and were I to strip now down to my pelt and wear just a garment like that old fur coat Mrs Crutley gave me twelve months ago this Christmas and were I to tuck it inside my corduroy trousers and were I to pull on my wellingtons what would stop me from straying along the river bank to the hospital and then to that small room at the back which overlooks the river. Without disturbing the drip which sustains him, slip out of my things and slip in beside him. He has no hope of coming out of the coma anyway and what harm would I be doing if I held him close and kissed his lips and stroked his curls till he stirred maybe and yielded to me? Why shouldn't I do it when there's no other hope for the poor boy? I know I have it in me to waken him. I feel a great force in me and it's driving me towards him.'

Blossom was shocked by her resolve and her intensity. Later as she moved gracefully along the bank of the shining river she recalled the many times since the football final in the summer she had made the same journey but on those occasions it had been to worship from a distance and to pray for the still creature in the lone bed of the dimly-lit ward.

'She mightn't be the full shilling,' Dr Matt Coumer told his wife as they sat drinking one night after-hours in Crutley's, 'but she has mystic qualities. In another age, in another place she might have been a priestess or a sorceress.' Blossom had just served them with a drink and bestowed upon them a most mystical smile, the smile that others called quaint and quizzical. Matt shook his head after he had sipped from his glass. 'There's more to Blossom than flesh and bone,' he concluded and then he dropped the subject as they were joined outside the counter by Fred Crutley and his wife.

Blossom had little difficulty negotiating the stone steps which carried her from the river-side to the window of the ward where lay her golden boy. From a safe distance she could see all that was happening in the ward. Shamus Regan's mother sat at one side of the bed and, wonder of wonders, the Badger Loran sat at the other.

Blossom liked the Badger. He was tough, uncompromising and gnarled like an ancient thorn tree but he was respectful and in Blossom's eyes that was what mattered in a man when all was said and done.

After a while Mrs O'Regan rose and withdrew a hair brush from her coat pocket. The Badger lifted the young man's head and held it gently while Mrs Regan brushed the beautiful locks of her son's damaged head.

Blossom bent her own head over her hands and pressed her cold fingers against her forehead. A feeling of unbearable sorrow seized her as her entire body began to tremble. Then came the tears and with them a series of gentle but profound lamentations that helped to ease the pain within her. She dried her eyes with her cold hands and, still trembling, drew the fur coat tightly round her bosom.

In the ward the Badger was weeping. She had often heard people say of him that he was incapable of tears, that he could not express himself when sorrow assailed him, that's if it ever assailed him they said. If only they could see him now, Blossom thought. He sat on the side of the bed and shook his great shoulders helplessly when the widow placed tender hands thereon. She helped tease the anguish out of him. She had been taken by surprise, never having seen him shed a solitary tear until that very moment. 'It's good to cry,' she whispered and allowed her hands to caress the sides of his craggy face.

As she watched, Blossom declared to herself that such a woman would bring great ease and solace to a man and to the Badger in particular for he had held on to his feelings for too long a time and they had become frosted and crusted but Blossom sensed that he would never surrender to despair again, not with Nonie Regan by his side to comfort him.

After a long, long spell she noticed how the Badger's powerful body began to compose itself once more. Blossom knew that every person who walked the earth was possessed of a sorrow that wreaked havoc on the human heart. Age often alleviated it and so did companionship but love, mostly, was the antidote although traces of it would always remain and visit the spirit, reminding the victims of long-forgotten sorrows stored in the memory.

The Badger heaved a final sigh indicating that he had put his grief behind him. Then with a flourish he produced the most voluminous handkerchief Blossom had ever seen. He trumpeted several times into its deep folds and returned it to his pocket. Then he rose and steadied himself before taking the Widow Regan in his arms. As they clung tightly to each other Blossom felt the last of her sadness leave. Then the couple bent and kissed the lifeless form in the bed. The Badger would compensate in so many ways for the illness which had destroyed all forms of normal communication between mother and son.

After they left the ward Blossom stood stock-still for a while. She had learned enough about the dark to know that it could throw up anything when one least expected it. She might well be under secret surveillance from some unknown source, good or evil. Such was the way of darkness. From the distant streets of the town came the strains of Christmas carols, gentling and purifying her spirit.

I will go now to his bedside she told herself and if it is in the power of a human heart to raise the siege of silence and lifelessness that overwhelms him it shall be done and no one will ever know what befell.

In the ward he lay still, his blonde curls still shining after his mother's ministrations. Making certain that the corridor was empty she readied herself for the loving task ahead of her. He lay still while she whispered words of endearment and womanly passion into his ear. She kissed him and caressed him and she called his name in rich whispers and then a secret smile appeared on her face. It was an expression of triumph, of surpassing achievement, a jubilant rejoicing for having attained the unattainable, for defying all the odds, for restoring life to where there had been no life and no hope of life. There should have been somebody in the wings, she felt, to emerge and ask her to take a bow. She had never in her life felt so elated. She had suddenly been transformed from a general factotum to a healer and if she never did anything else in her life this was sufficient in her eyes to justify her tenure in a world that sometimes just did not care but, mercy of mercies, sometimes did care.

As she drew her fur coat round her she heard voices in the corridor; one belonged to the matron and the other was the property of the poet Mental Nossery. Mental intoned in deep euphony the words of an ancient hymn. If the truth were known the composition wasn't ancient at all. It was Mental's latest. 'It was composed,' Mental Nossery informed the matron, 'in the year eleven hundred and ninety by the court jester on the death of his sovereign, Frederick Barbarossa.'

Suitably impressed the matron led the way into the ward where her most prized patient was sitting up in bed. If the matron had entered a few seconds earlier she might have witnessed Blossom make good her escape through the ward window, a window which she closed discreetly behind her before embracing the soothing moonlight which awaited her without. She received it eagerly and watched as the matron and Mental Nossery recovered from their shock.

The resurrection of Shamus Regan was the talk of the parish for evermore. Only two people knew the truth, Blossom and Mental Nossery.

Mental had arrived at the hospital only moments after Blossom but whereas she had entered by the back entrance he had entered by the front. When he arrived at the door of the ward he heard strange sounds, sounds which he would normally associate with another place in other circumstances. In the half-light of the ward he deduced that there was an extra body in the bed, most certainly, judging from the sounds emerging from her lips, a female.

Later, as Mental Nossery left the hospital grounds he was waylaid by Blossom. He told her what had happened.

'I was about to enter the ward,' he explained, 'when I heard the unmistakable sounds of wild oats being sown. There were two participants in this wonderful activity so I presumed that Shamus had awakened or been awakened from his long sleep. The great thing is that he'll be all right from now on or so the matron and the two doctors who arrived hot-foot assured everybody.'

'It's a wonderful night entirely,' Blossom exclaimed with delight. She took Mental by the hand and led him to the river-bank, by which secret route they journeyed hand in hand to the abode of Blossom. First they walked her small fields under the light of an indulgent moon and then they withdrew to her cosy kitchen.

They married the following autumn and Mental Nossery no longer rented his lands. His proud wife who was an accomplished farmer in her own right saw to his verdant acres as well as her own. After some time Blossom produced a young son and not long after that Mental Nossery finished his epic. Canon Cornelius Coodle wrote the ten-thousand-words introduction and the poem was hailed far and wide. In that same summer Shamus Regan received his call for the county team and just before the September equinox of the same year the Badger Loran and Nonie Regan walked up the aisle together. As they left the church after the ceremony they were greeted by a jerseyed guard of honour consisting of members from the football teams of Ballybee and Ballybo.

DOTIE TUPPER'S CHRISTMAS

When Dotie Tupper retired from the fowl business at the age of eighty-four she decided to take a holiday. The first thing she did when she arrived at her home on the very day she gave up work was to immerse herself in a bath of warm water and remain there for the best part of an hour. In so doing she was merely following the habit of a life-time. There were no toilet facilities at her place of work save an antiquated WC frequented solely by Sam Toper. She avoided it as if it was an execution chamber. Whenever she felt overpowered by the offensive stenches in her work-place or felt in need of a wash she made the short trip to her modest home a few doors down the lane-way. Her boss Bustler Hearne never objected. He knew that Dotie would more than make up for any time she was likely to spend off the premises.

Bustler was a bully, a rude, crude and highly aggressive employer who made life hell for two of the three members of his staff, Sam Toper, fowl executioner, plucker-in-chief and trusser extraordinaire, and Mannie Kent, dispatcher and part-time cleaner. Dotie Tupper was in charge of sales, wages and supervising. She also helped out when her staff found themselves unable to cope with the pressures of work or illness.

Her boss, Bustler, spent of most of his time in the countryside within a radius of ten miles of his business location. Before he left in the mornings in his horse-drawn crate-clamped dray and after he returned in the evening with crates of assorted fowl he made his presence felt by verbally and physically abusing his plucker-in-chief and by roundly cursing his cleaner. Never once during the long years that Dotie spent in his employ had he been known to direct a single harsh word at her. He also paid her a decent wage and why wouldn't he, his detractors would say, and she coining money for him on all fronts. Certainly it would be true to say that she had made him a wealthy man. She also made a name for him as a supplier of high-quality produce. She was courteous to customers and when part-time staff were taken on at Christmas she taught them how to truss and pluck. In an emergency Dotie could wring a chicken's neck in a flash and on occasion in a matter of minutes had been known to dispatch an entire crateful to their eternal rewards if such other-wordly consolation is granted to the souls of departed fowl.

Dotie was a deeply religious person and with the canon's housekeeper, the redoubtable Mrs Hannie Hanlon, was in charge of the floral arrangements behind the church altar, was a chorister in the parish choir and an esteemed member of the Trallock Parish Amateur Drama Group sometimes known as the Trallock Players. It could be said that Dotie was a participant in the game of life and not a mere looker-on. She gave herself unstintingly to all worthwhile causes and when she gave Bustler a month's notice on the first of May he went on his knees before her and begged her to remain. She shook her head firmly even when he offered her a substantial raise, shorter hours and longer holidays as well as bonuses, bribes and assorted perks.

'I am eighty-four,' she announced firmly, 'and I am no longer able for the work.'

Fortunately for Dotie, Bustler had contributed to a personal pension scheme on behalf of himself and his prize employee of over sixty-eight years. She had started off her poultry career with Bustler's father Toby, brought him from the verge of bankruptcy and set his son firmly on the road to prosperity.

Bustler was a hot-tempered, intemperate thug or so it was claimed by those who maintained they knew him. He was possessed, however, of one virtue. He was a generous man and when Dotie departed she did not go empty-handed. During the years as an employee she managed to present a spotlessly clean appearance to the world. Not so her fellow-employees, Mannie Kent and Sam Toper. Sam's Sunday suit was mottled with the stains of partly erased fowl droppings and tiny traces of down and feathers while his workaday overalls had changed from light blue to off-white over the years.

Mannie also carried traces of down and other fowl specks from her place of employment on her everyday clothes. On the other hand Dotie, even while at work, presented a shining image to the public. Small and spare, she had a capacity for endless work. Without fail, no matter her disposition at the time, she always had a bath after work. When showers became the mode she showered on Saturdays and Sundays. She spent her summer holidays in the nearby seaside resort of Ballybunion. She always stayed at Collins' guesthouse and went for a hot seaweed bath every day of her richly deserved fortnight.

'Regular bathing,' she once told her life-long friend Mickey Mokely, 'is the only antidote for the job I'm in.'

For years before she retired she was invited by her dear friend Hannie Hanlon, Canon Coodle's housekeeper, to spend the Christmas holiday at the presbytery. Hannie had free rein at the parochial house but nevertheless thought it prudent to consult with the canon beforehand.

'She's as near to an angel,' the canon had noted at the time, 'as anyone we're likely to encounter in this world.'

So it was that in her eighty-fourth year she was still a welcome guest at the presbytery for the Christmas period except that this time she would stay for the extended sojourn of the Twelve Days. In the town she was a popular figure. Young and old called her by her first name, Dotie. 'Ah she's a dotie girl to be sure,' Fr Sinnott the senior curate announced when he frequently picked her up, placed her under his arm and laid her on the bottom step of the stairs after doing the rounds of the presbytery with her. Her bright presence brought joy and goodness wherever she went and yet deep down she carried a great hurt. Hannie knew about the hurt and the absent-minded canon had his suspicions. Absent-minded the canon might be about inanimate things but when he cared for people he was ever ready to listen to their woes and extend the hand of compassion where it was needed.

'There is a message clearly written on Canon Coodle's face,' Fr Sinnott once informed his bishop, 'and what it says is this – "I am here for you my friend no matter how high up or low down you are. I don't care what you have done. I am always here for you".'

'I've seen it,' said the bishop, 'and I thank God that it's there for all of us.'

The pair were returning from the all-Ireland Gaelic Football Final in Dublin chauffeured by a junior curate who neither drank nor smoked. He had been specially chosen by his parish priest, an astute gentleman who had seen both the bishop and Fr Sinnott play football and remarked more than once that he was truly grateful to his maker that he had never crossed the path of either on the playing field.

Among his other virtues, the junior curate in question was also possessed of sealed lips and subscribed to the ancient Chinese adage that a shut mouth caught no flies. If his Lordship and Fr Sinnott had a failing it was merely a shared love of an occasional indulgence in a few pints of stout, well, a good few pints of stout but not on a regular basis. Hence the necessity for an abstemious and close-mouthed driver.

On the Christmas of her eighty-fourth year Dotie arrived at the presbytery as usual. She was glad to be leaving her home for a while although a bright and cosy home it was and a home which she hoped to share with her dear friend Hannie should Canon Coodle pass on as indeed he must some day but as Hannie would say, 'let us pray that it's a far-off day and that I will be there to look after him until such time as that day comes'. At the canon's insistence Dotie always had her meals in the parochial dining-room.

On the Christmas Eve of that eighty-fourth Christmas Dotie was, according to Hannie, down in herself.

'Well then,' said Canon Coodle, 'we must do all in our powers to cheer her up.'

The topic of conversation at the tea-time table had been the return of the presbytery cat, a battle-scarred chap who had, from the looks of him when he returned, surely forfeited his penultimate life of the nine lives granted to all cats. Fond of a scrap and fiercely possessive of his many female friends it was inevitable that he would meet physically more accomplished toms during his ramblings on moon-lit roof-tops under starry skies when only cats are abroad. He slunk into the dining-room and rubbed his racked body against the canon's left shoe.

'Ah my friend,' said Canon Cornelius with a grim smile, 'what a mighty confession you could make at this moment.'

It was the first genuine laugh that Dotie had enjoyed in several weeks. Her woes had really begun when it began to dawn on her that she would never see her father again, not in this world anyway. Always, up until her eighty-fourth birthday, she cherished the faint hope that he would one day return. She remembered him only vaguely. She had been six years of age when he disappeared a month after her mother's death. There were ugly whispers abroad that while he was of unsound mind after his bereavement he might well have eased himself into the flooded river in the belief that he might be united with the woman who had been the love of his life. Then there were rumours that he had been seen in places as far apart as Glasgow and Chicago. Each night, from the age of six onwards, Dotie prayed for his safe return. At first she could not believe that he had walked out on her. She had missed her mother terribly at the time but with the passage of the years it was for her father she longed. She had seen other girls out walking with their fathers. She had bitten her lip in anguish when she saw small girls being lifted into the air by the one man they loved above all others in the world. She had cried herself to sleep on countless nights. Her aunt who had come to look after her and who slept in the adjoining room would silently slip into the bed beside her and do her best to console her. There were times when she thought she saw her father but it was always from a distance so she could not be certain.

'I don't have any doubt,' the district inspector of the RIC had made clear at the time. 'His behaviour was strange to say the least for days before his disappearance. He was seen by the river-side at a point where once in, it would be impossible to change one's mind. He knew what he wanted to do and he did it. That is my conclusion and it is the conclusion of all the other investigators involved.'

Dotie steadfastly refused to believe that her father was not coming home and now at eighty-four she knew in her heart that she would not see him again.

'One would imagine,' she told herself, 'that I would be over it by now but I will never be over it,' she cried out in the confines of her kitchen. The worst was that she could not remember sitting on his lap while he sang.

'I remember the pair of you well,' her aunt recalled, not realising how deeply wounded Dotie became at mention of her father. 'He used to sit on the old rocking chair on the porch and you would climb aboard his lap. He had a light tenor voice but he never sang after your mother died. He never meant to leave you. He wasn't himself the Lord be good to him and how could he after his terrible loss? We must pray for him. We must always pray for him.'

All through the years from the age of six to eighty-four she simply could not reconcile herself with his disappearance. In the early years she convinced herself that he was a victim of amnesia. She invented other excuses when the long decades went by and he failed to show up. At length she resigned herself to the sad fact that he was gone forever.

'He would be a hundred and twelve years of age next Saturday week.' She forced a laugh as she disclosed the information to Hannie

Hanlon. Hannie had remained silent not knowing what to say.

'I was reading lately in one of the Sunday papers,' Dotie continued, 'that the oldest man in the world was one hundred and eleven years of age. I was going to write to the editor and tell him that if my father was alive he would be the oldest man in the world and then I thought how foolish I would look if he decided to publish the letter.'

Still not knowing how to respond Hannie waited for her friend to continue. Dotie's voice was no longer steady as she spoke. 'Imagine it took me all those years before I finally realised he was well and truly dead and not coming home any more. I always cherished the hope that he might somehow make his way back to me but at a hundred and twelve it would be out of the question. I still have his photographs, one in particular, the one taken before he shaved off his moustache. My but he was handsome and so tall. I don't know where they got me because my mother was a tall woman too. If I could be sure I would see him again, see the two of them again somewhere someplace, I would die happy.'

Hannie placed a hand around her friend's shoulder but she could not find the proper words of consolation so she steered her out of the room and into the hall-way.

'I don't remember sitting on my father's lap while he sang to me and that's the hardest part.' Dotie was weeping now. 'I know for a fact that my aunt saw me sitting with him but I have no recollection of it.'

Dotie had just reached the age of sixteen when her aunt died, a victim of tuberculosis, the same disease that accounted for her mother. Relatives and friends decided that it would be best for Dotie if she emigrated to the United States where her only surviving aunt was settled but when Toby Hearne offered her a job Dotie had no hesitation in accepting. Neighbours and friends feared for her well-being at the hands of such a man but Dotie had no qualms. She was possessed of that rare quality which always brought out the best in people and like so many others Toby quickly fell under her spell. When he would rant and rave at others Dotie would look on in amusement knowing that his rage would expend itself in a few short minutes. Over the years she managed to temper his and Bustler's outbursts and around the time she decided it was time to retire Bustler's nature had assumed a mellow side which eventually won out over his dark side. She went so far as to suggest to him that he retire. The business was but a shadow of what it used to be but Bustler had made his money particularly during the period of the Second World War and he had invested it wisely always acting on Dotie's advice.

Rather than sell the business he closed it on his ninetieth birthday and retired to a local old-folks home where he spent the remainder of his days. He regularly visited the premises where he spent his entire life and when he died his last will and testament revealed that the sole beneficiary from his estate was none other than Dotie.

When Bustler withdrew from his business the same notion of retiring occurred to Canon Cornelius Coodle – but he quickly dismissed the thought when it dawned on him that he would be contributing to the unprecedented scarcity of priests in the diocese. He told himself that he would be the last man to leave down the side.

'I'll die in my harness,' he told the wrinkled face which confronted him in the mirror of his bedroom.

After late mass that night he withdrew to the sitting-room with Fr Sinnott. The canon raised his brimming glass of port and wished his senior curate the compliments of the season. Fr Sinnott responded and sipped from his tumbler of Jameson.

'Ah!' he exclaimed as Dotie and Hannie entered, 'the ladies are with us.'

Both priests rose and toasted the fresh arrivals who returned the seasonal compliments by touching the extended glasses of the clergymen with the delicate sherry glasses shapely and brimming. As they settled into their chairs the canon began to reminisce about past events in his life as was his wont on Christmas Eve. He noted, for all his preoccupation with other days, that all was not well with Dotie. It was Hannie who explained that Dotie was facing up to the fact that she would not see her father again and worse still that she could not remember sitting on his lap when she was a little girl.

'What age would he be now if he was alive?' Fr Sinnott asked with no little amazement.

'One hundred and twelve,' Dotie replied without a moment's hesitation as the tears flowed down her face.

Fr Sinnott extended his hands in her direction after placing his glass on the floor beneath his chair. Dotie handed her glass to her friend Hannie and a new hope surged within her. The senior curate's powerful hands were still extended towards her, the same hands that had subdued countless ambitious full forwards and the same hands that once held aloft the county championship Gaelic football trophy which was his inalienable right as captain. In his lap Dotie looked up into his face and in a little girl's voice asked the question which had been troubling her so much in recent times.

'Will I see my dad again?' she asked.

'Of course you will,' Fr Sinnott assured her

'But will he know me?'

'Will he what!' Fr Sinnott shouted, 'you'll be sore for six months woman for the squeezing he'll give you.'

A radiant smile adorned the tear-stained face of Dotie.

'And my mother!' she directed the question at Canon Coodle.

'Of course, of course,' Canon Coodle assured her, 'she'll be there at the gates of heaven by your father's side and the three of you will enter heaven together.'

Dotie's eyes were closed in bliss. Fr Sinnott rose with his charge cradled in his arms. He walked round the room a few times humming softly and paused in front of his canon's armchair. 'You take her for a while,' he said, 'and I'll fill another drink.'

Canon Coodle placed her carefully on his lap and gently kissed her on the forehead. A succession of reassuring and audible murmurs escaped him before he cleared his throat and crooned a lullaby from the Gaelic. It had been his grandmother's song when he was a small boy.

A Christmas Gander

There's many a regal gander no more than a skeleton in his pelt. How often did goose buyers find it out in the past to their cost? It's different these days when geese and ganders arrive on the Christmas market deprived of their downy raiments, their feathers and their wings. One can easily tell the elderly from the prime and if they are mass-produced itself the buyer will not be duped and if they lack the true flavour of pasture-land geese at least the flesh can be eaten if boiled or roasted properly.

Country people used to believe in those distant days that the shore gander was the best proposition of all because of his delightful flavour. His diet, apart from grass and his daily saucer of yellow meal, consisted mainly of molluscs, cuttle fish, slokawn or sloke and laven-worth. Is it any wonder there was such demand for shore ganders! It was also believed that the soup from boiled ganders of the seashore species was a priceless antidote for scrofulous diseases as well as being a proven booster for middle-aged and elderly males whose romantic input into their marital obligations was declining. After a few plates of shore-gander soup they generally excelled themselves.

Every time there is a Christmas in the offing my thoughts unfailingly turn to geese. Some people prefer turkeys while more have a preference for ducks and drakes and cockerels but it's the goose for me, the roast stuffed goose preceded by giblet soup. My mouth waters as I summon up remembrance of bygone ganders. Just before this very Christmas I engaged two from a country cousin, a woman of impeccable credentials in the matter of geese and ganders. In dark moments and troublesome times I think of these very geese, browned and roasted, and my heart soars like an uprising lark.

If you have ever been taken down in the purchase of a goose, that is to say if you buy an old goose thinking it to be a young goose, you will never again engage geese hastily nor will you buy at random from any Tom, Dick or Harry. To be quite candid I would put the same amount of preparation and planning into the purchase of a goose as I would into the robbing of a bank. Too many times in the past I was taken down by otherwise honest people. In the countryside it was never considered a dishonest act to dispose of elderly or decrepit geese to gullible townies. Old geese must be sold and who better to sell them to than townies. Few townies knew the identities or dwelling-places of goose producers so the producer is generally safe from retaliation. In addition nearly all people who sold geese looked alike. That is to say they were possessed of kind, honest faces especially these who foisted off ancient birds on the unwary and unsuspecting.

In my boyhood Christmases you would always find the rogue producers in that corner of the market where the donkey and pony transports were thickest and the smiling saleswomen would always call you sir, even if you were the biggest rogue in the world. Luckily for me I have now, near the end of my days, accrued some experience in the engaging and purchase of geese.

At the tender age of twelve I was sent to the market-place in my native town having been commissioned to invest in a prime goose for an elderly neighbour who should have known better. She was too old to go herself and even at the age of eighty she still had a good deal of faith in humanity. It was foolishly presumed at the time that I was street-wise. The word had yet to make its way into our everyday vocabulary. Crafty was the word used in those days but unfortunately I was not crafty enough to match the wily and seasoned dealers anxious to dispose of ancient geese.

Earlier that morning I received a short instruction in the ways of geese. Old geese, for instance, like their human counterparts were somewhat listless. Their eyes too were lack-lustre. Their beaks were worn down and were of a darker hue than those of young geese. The laipeens were wrinkled and coarse. These were some of the better-known defects to be found in geese and ganders of advanced years. This information was conveyed to me by the husband of the good lady who liked a goose for Christmas. He reminded me too that young ganders were aggressive, raucous chaps who liked to flap their wings and intimidate people going about their lawful business. Armed with this vast array of knowledge and clutching two florins in my trousers' pocket I entered the market. In those days trousers generally accommodated only one pocket and the lining was never truly trustworthy. Holes infiltrated and coins disappeared. Heartbreak followed and hunger too and all sorts of deprivation especially if the sum was substantial.

Great was the clamour of geese and turkeys in the market-place not to mention ducks, drakes, hens and chickens. For once there were more women than men. It was held by even the most hostile of males in those days that turkey money was female money and should be used by females as they saw fit but the truth was that most of the money was spent on special commodities which would sweeten and brighten Christmas in the home.

As I moved here and there I was obliged to pick my steps. Ass- and pony-rails cluttered the scene. Everywhere bargains were being struck and satisfied clients were departing with cross-winged braces of prime fowl. So numerous were the geese on every side that I hardly knew where to begin. I was almost overcome by the great and colourful array of transports and country folk, by the quick-fire exchanges of notes and silver, by the back-slapping and hand-slapping as bargains were struck and by the many minor altercations which eventually came to nought. It was almost too much for me and I fervently wished that I hadn't been saddled with so much responsibility.

'Ah!' said a friendly voice behind me. 'It's yourself is it' – with that he thrust out his hand and almost shook it free from my elbow joint with the shaking he gave it. I had never seen him before in my life but the more I examined his friendly face the more I began to recognise certain familiar traits. I didn't know it then but what I recognised were constituents common to the universal face of roguery. It was the friendliness of his smile that disarmed me and exposed my defence.

'I know what brought you,' he said, 'you're looking for a turkey for your mother.'

'No,' I told him, 'I'm looking for a goose for oul' Maggie Sullivan.'

'If you are,' said he, 'you'd better draw away from here,' and he winked in the most conspiratorial way you ever saw. I followed him past rails of gobbling turkeys, quacking ducks and hissing ganders.

'Half of these,' my new-found friend announced, indicating the owners of the fowl all around us, 'would nick the eye out of your head or,' said he in a loud whisper into my ear, 'if you was innocent enough to stick out your tongue that's the very last you'd see of it.'

He stopped at a corner of the market where an elderly, shawled woman with a wrinkled face was attending to an ass-rail of geese. She had, I recall to this very day, the kindest and homeliest face one could wish to see. Her voice was soft and sweet and as near to Gaelic in sound and rhythm as English could be. More to the point she had geese for sale.

'Stall-fed, every one of 'em,' she boasted, 'and not one of 'em that isn't a Michaelmas goose for sure.'

I had heard of Michaelmas geese or Green geese before this. What the term meant was that they had matured and would have been ready to eat at Michaelmas which falls on 29 September. However for extra substance and flavour they would have been confined to stalls or small out-houses till it was time for the Christmas market. The confinement meant that they would be unable to move about as much as geese normally do in the grazing area out of doors. Consequently the thighs would be less muscular and far more edible when cooked and also that the breast would be possessed of more meat and would be more succulent.

My newly acquired friend was now standing in the rail conducting a closer inspection of its occupants. They hissed and honked as he lifted them one by one to make sure that there was no impostor among them. When he had concluded his examination he explained my predicament, how my purchasing power was restricted to four shillings and how I had been warned about dishonest vendors who would think nothing of fobbing off an elderly goose on an innocent townie.

'Oh may the good God succour us all,' said the old woman, 'and may God in his mercy preserve us, the young and the old and the innocent, from them that would wrong law-abiding people. May the flames of hell singe their yalla hides and may St Peter turn 'em back at the gates of heaven and keep them waiting for a hundred years.' She made the sign of the cross with her Rosary beads and would have continued with her excoriation had not my friend raised his hand to his lips to remind her that the evening light would soon be fading and there was a long road home.

'This man is a townie,' he explained, 'and you may be sure he has other business that needs looking after.'

'What about this one?' my friend was asking.

'No, no, no,' she was quick to reply, 'that oul' codger only came along as a companion so's the others wouldn't be too nervous on the journey. There's a sweet young gander over in the corner,' she went on, 'in the peak of condition and only out of the stall this morning.'

'Is this the lad?' my friend asked as he lifted aloft a large, hissing specimen for my approval.

'Oh the weight of him!' he cried, 'and the tenderness of him! How much are you asking for him?'

'Oh he can't be sold at all,' said the old woman, 'he's engaged by the superintendent of the civic guards.'

'Tell us what you're asking for him anyway?'

'I'm asking four shillings,' she replied reluctantly, 'but 'twould want to be handed over straightaway in case the superintendent comes along and demands what's rightfully his.'

'Sealed!' My friend extended a grimy hand for my two florins and when they had been transferred to his I found myself with the gander in my hands. My friend hurried me out of the market by a circuitous route lest, as he put it himself, I wind up in the dungeon. All the time he kept his eyes open for the presence of the superintendent and his minions.

'We'll do 'em yet!' he kept shouting, 'we'll do 'em yet!' and so we did for in a very few minutes I found myself at Maggie Sullivan's door clutching my prize.

'May God comfort us this night,' she cried out when she beheld the gander. She stood back from the pair of us to have a better look at my purchase.

'He's one age with myself,' she wept, 'if he isn't older and look at the beak worn away by him.' She called her husband and between them they set up a frightening lamentation. There was nothing for it but to return to the market, recover our two florins and invest in a younger specimen. In the market I led Maggie and her husband to the corner where the old woman had her rail but there was no sign of her. We searched the three other corners but she was nowhere to be seen. The bother was that all the old women we saw wore shawls and all had wrinkled, innocent, homely faces and you'd never believe from looking at them that any single one of them was capable of fobbing off an elderly gander on an innocent townie.

The Hermit of Scartnabrock

Dr Matt Coumer could hardly believe his ears. The man who stood before him, as far as he knew, was the sanest and soberest in the parish. Matt had known him for most of his life. Gerry Severs lived in a small cottage by the river. He lived alone since his wife Pegeen had slipped away on him. That was the way Gerry, with his quaint turn of speech, put it whenever he was asked how his wife died. 'She slipped away on me', he would answer mournfully and then he would move hastily on lest further elaboration be required.

Matt had risen to his feet the moment Gerry entered his surgery.

'Well Gerry?' Matt asked as he proffered a hand to the young man. Not that much younger he thought, seven years, no more and no less, twenty-five years since he taught him how to cast a line and what a pupil he had been! He could land a fly in Matt's extended cap as they fished either side of the river.

'Sit down and I'll take your blood pressure.'

When Gerry failed to respond to the offer Matt countered by assuring him that there wouldn't be any charge.

'It's not blood pressure that's troubling me.' Gerry vacantly studied an anatomy chart on the wall opposite and searched for the opening words which would eventually disclose his unusual dilemma. Should he begin by telling his friend that his late, lamented wife Pegeen had been the scourge of his life from the day he had married her, that she had reviled him, spat on him, even beaten him, yes beaten him and savagely at that and that he had never reacted physically, never once. He had accepted every taunt and every jibe with resignation in the hope that she would change back into the gentle girl she had been before they married.

'I know all about Pegeen if that is what's troubling you or,' Matt paused, 'at least enough about her to know that you have suffered more than your share in your marriage.'

Gerry without turning felt for the chair he knew to be somewhere behind him. Locating it he gratefully sat and waited for the sudden giddiness which had visited him after Matt's revelation to disappear.

Matt sat behind his desk and waited until some of Gerry's composure returned. After a decent interval he informed his friend how some of Gerry's neighbours who chanced to be patients of his had asked him to intervene.

'She's a street angel and a house devil', one of Gerry's elderly neighbours had been the first to mention Pegeen's vicious behaviour. Others would follow before Matt decided to move. On that afternoon several years before as he and Gerry were fishing Matt asked him if all was well in his marriage.

'Couldn't be better,' Gerry had answered breezily.

'I'm told,' Matt would not be deterred, 'that there are serious rows.'

'A marriage without a row is like an egg without salt.'

It was the light-hearted way his friend answered that eased Matt's worries and, of course, there was the fact that neighbours exaggerated especially when they had nothing better to do.

Then one March morning earlier that year when the river was in flood, Pegeen stood barefoot on a parapet and threw herself into the swirling waters below.

'Christmas was her worst time,' Gerry spoke matter-of-factly. 'There was never a Christmas dinner but there was no scarcity of abuse. She heaped it on all through the twelve days and I took it.'

The disclosure was followed by a long silence.

'How long is she dead now?' Matt wondered if it was the right question.

'Nine months and three days,' came the forthright answer, 'and I'll tell you this Matt, I've never had such peace or at least I never had such peace until last night.'

'What happened last night?' Matt asked anxiously.

'I saw her,' came the prompt reply.

'You saw Pegeen?' Matt prompted.

'That's right,' from Gerry.

'Tell me about it.' Matt studied his friend's face for signs of instability, anything that would tell him about his mental state, studied the averted eyes for tell-tale indications of derangement and his hands for tell-tale jerks or contractions. There was nothing whatsoever to suggest that Gerry was anything other than the same, solid citizen he had always been.

'It was about half-twelve,' Gerry recalled, 'I could not sleep so I took a stroll down by the river. On my way back I felt a cold shiver all over my body. I often heard about cold shivers but I didn't believe about them until last night. A cold shiver is a nasty visitor but it's not as bad as an unnatural tremor because that's exactly what I felt shaking hands with me next.'

'An unnatural tremor you say?' Matt savoured the expression.

'Exactly,' Gerry went on, 'and on top of that I felt as if somebody had tugged at my coat but when I turned around to have a look there was nobody there or at least nobody near enough to have touched my coat. The nearest person to me at the time was a female standing under a lamp-post. My heart missed a beat Matt because she was dressed exactly like Pegeen.'

'How far away was she exactly?' Matt asked.

'Forty yards to be exact,' Gerry answered without a moment's hesitation, 'and I ought to know because I played centre forward long enough to know the distance. It was then I started to shake all over. I was like a cob-web in a breeze and when I lifted my left leg to get out of there fast it wouldn't move and neither would my right leg. I was stuck there. Then a black cat came slinking out of the shadows and he passed by where the woman stood or ghost or demon or whatever because I didn't know for sure who it was at that stage. As the cat drew near the power returned to my legs but by then a courting couple had entered the square and a car also drew up close by so I felt the terror quenching itself inside of me. I said to myself I'll have a look at this woman because I'm Gerry Severs and if you ask anybody in this town what sort of bloke I am they'll tell you I'm as sound as bell metal and that I don't spin yarns. I made my way towards the dame under the pole but when I drew near to her she turned her head away. I couldn't make out her features but then the lights of the car shone full on her face and the next thing you know I was staring into her two weepers. It was Pegeen. One minute it wasn't her face and the next minute it was and when her features were exposed by the car lights there was no doubt in my mind. The blood drained out of my body and the whole square seemed to start going round in a circle. I found my balance deserting me and the sight seemed to leave my eyes. Then I began to stagger and then I fell out on my face and eyes. Look, there's a bump on my forehead and there's a cut on my poll.'

When Gerry came round he was sitting in a chair in the kitchen of a neighbour. The courting couple had seen him lying on the ground and had seen the woman walk away and had partially revived him, enough to be able to drag him to the nearest cottage in the laneway which led from the square to the river.

Matt leaned back in his chair and closed his eyes in concentration as Gerry proceeded with his tale. Satisfied that there was no mental problem and that Gerry had been the victim of some minor hallucination which might well have been induced by the flashing car lights, he prescribed some sedatives and told him he would expect him to call around the same time on the morrow. 'And by the way,' Matt went on, 'I will expect you to join my wife Maggie and myself for Christmas dinner, that's if you're free on the occasion.'

'Oh I'll manage to fit you in,' Gerry laughed, grateful of the offer because he always felt at ease in the presence of Maggie Coumer and Matt was a trusted friend of long standing. That night Matt told the whole story to Maggie.

Normally he would never disclose the contents of any exchanges whatsoever between his patients and himself but Maggie was herself a professional having qualified as a nurse many years before. 'There's no doubt but that Gerry saw a girl but there's also no doubt she could not have been his wife because if you remember it was I who laid her out when her body was recovered and it was I who helped coffin her and she was as dead as mutton you can take it from me. I'll make a few enquiries tomorrow and I'll get to the bottom of this as sure as my name is Maggie Coumer.'

That night Gerry slept soundly thanks to the sleeping capsules which his friend had given him. In the Coumer household the good doctor and his partner whispered into the morning, careful not to awaken their three young children in rooms nearby.

'I remember years ago,' Maggie recalled, 'to have been sitting in the commercial room of the Manklefort Hotel in Dublin with my brother Thady and his girlfriend. The lights were low at the time and we could barely make out each other's faces. The lights had been dimmed on the instructions of the night porter who warned us to keep our voices down because members of the garda síochána were on the prowl for illegal patrons. Shortly after he left, a passing car threw its lights through a gap in the window curtains. A shaft of this light fell on my brother's face and suddenly his features were transformed into those of my father who had died the year before. If I didn't know better I might have imagined that he had returned briefly from the dead to be with us. Then the lights were gone and the image disappeared. I remember I had never been so lonely after that brief glimpse of his face.'

'Well you're not lonely now.' Matt gently placed his arms round her and drew her close.

On the following evening after Maggie had questioned all her sources she placed her findings before her husband. He neither hummed nor hawed until she had put the facts before him. It was her wont to persevere with all her narratives without pause and instead of being bored or disinterested as some might be, Matt found himself well informed at the end of the proceedings and entertained as well.

Maggie never lingered over her revelations no matter how interesting or how salacious they might seem. Matt would settle himself at the outset and on this occasion he was well pleased for she was a woman who never lied. Of course he would have to admit that he found a certain unique musicality in her voice that he found in no other. There was also a deep warmth and never, that he could recall, had there been the least stridency or harshness. It had occurred to him on a number of occasions that it might be his affection for her that made him feel so enraptured. Still he remained convinced that an independent adjudicator would give her full marks if there was a competition for housewives' tales.

She had, apparently, discovered the identity of the mysterious woman whose face in the car light had brought about Gerry's fainting spell. The woman was a first cousin of Gerry's late wife Pegeen and had returned home to her native parish a few short days before in the hope of meeting the man for whom she had pined since the day her cousin had married him. She had not come home for the funeral as she felt that it might have been an intrusion on her part and besides there was the protocol involved. If Gerry's affections were to be successfully transferred from his late wife to that wife's cousin then a period of at least six months should be allowed to pass. Consequently she had postponed her return until she could bear her burden no longer. She had been mortified when Gerry had collapsed after her face had been revealed to him. She had hoped that he would stop and chat or even take her in his arms but that had been a wild dream or so she admitted.

'What I propose to do,' Maggie confided to her husband, 'is invite her here for Christmas dinner and allow herself and Gerry to renew their relationship. I know, I know what you're going to say. You're going to say that it wasn't much of a relationship to begin with but my answer to that is that you cannot quench a love that burns as brightly as Noreen Meeke's and, on the other hand, Gerry will die from loneliness if he doesn't find a partner soon.'

Maggie folded her arms as she waited for her husband's appraisal. It must be said here, however, that there were many in the town who regarded Maggie as a consummate busy-body and a fully-fledged meddler. There were others, and this body included her husband, who saw her as an incurable romantic and an amateur matchmaker whose only aim was to bring lonely people together in holy wedlock. By way of arbitration Matt took his wife on his lap and kissed her gently as he complimented her on a fine afternoon's work, 'for,' said Matt, 'you have accomplished two important things. You have solved a mystery which might well hang over us for many a year and you have sown the seeds of love. What more could you do on behalf of the ignorant and the lonely, on behalf of all the unfulfilled in love and knowledge? How blessed I am to have for a wife such a wonderful creature.'

Maggie beamed and blushed although she was well aware that her husband often used flowery language when he paid homage to her.

Christmas dinner at Coumer's was a rare success. Noreen Meeke was an instant success with the children and Gerry, always a favourite, added to an afternoon of unpremeditated joy. By the time the Christmas and New Year festivities ended the relationship between Gerry and Noreen was on a firm footing.

Although both were people who might be fairly described as reserved they were soon linking arms in the streets and boreens of the parish and by the time the first salmon started to run before the beginning of the fishing season there was talk of a Christmas marriage. The good doctor and his friend Gerry were unusually successful, landing a ten- and twelve-pound salmon respectively with two-and-a-half inch blue minnows. The water was right for the colour and the size of bait and on the second day of legal fishing Gerry landed a second fish with the same lure. This salmon was presented to the parish priest Canon Coodle, himself a retired fisherman but now too elderly for the vicissitudes of flood-waters and gravelly streams. Long tradition obliged the first angler who bagged his second salmon of the season to present it to the parish priest. In cases where the angler might be in need the canon always paid the going rate but Gerry would not countenance financial reward.

'Tell the canon to say a prayer for me,' he informed Mrs Hanlon after she had accepted the fresh fish on her master's behalf.

'I'll do that Gerry,' she had promised, 'and I'll say one myself as well.'

The spring and summer went by and in the middle of September Gerry found himself gainful employment in Folan's timber-yard. Shortly afterwards he became engaged to Noreen Meeke and a fortnight before Christmas, to the day, the pair were married free, gratis and for nothing by the legendary Canon Coodle himself.

'Don't forget in my obituary,' he wagged a cautionary finger at his friend Matt Coumer, 'to tell them about the eighteen-pounder I landed in Shanowen the very day after I was made canon of this parish.'

Matt promised the outstanding catch would be resurrected for the occasion but added the rider that should roles be reversed the nineteen-pounder he bagged at the Black Stick on his second day out must not be excluded. It was not the first time it occurred to the canon that anglers were inordinately proud of their catches and why wouldn't they be he thought defensively to himself when the average weight of a spring fish was roughly eight pounds.

As Christmas drew near the love and compassion, often buried out of sight in men's hearts, began to flow so that by the time Christmas Eve came round there was an unmistakable air of goodwill and generosity all over the parish. The dour became cordial, the gripers grew cheerful, the grim grew gracious and so forth and so on until it seemed that a Christmas of untold joy was at hand. Every household radiated happiness, except one.

It had come to pass that Noreen Meeke the blushing bride of Gerry had ceased to blush, the laughter to which she had been addicted before she married vanished from her lips after marriage. In short Noreen was anything but meek and poor Gerry who was surely entitled to his fair share of marital bliss became once more a martyr to the matrimonial state. She had begun to natter early one morning as he dressed for work. The morning was dark and gloomy enough as it was without the addition of human woe to drag it down further. Gerry said nothing. He went to the side of the bed and he kissed his babbling bride to silence. Afterwards he went straight out the door to his place of work at Folan's timber-yard. He prayed that by the time he returned for his lunch she would be her old self once more but it was not to be.

There was no lunch but down from the room came a powerful verbal barrage which made Gerry believe for a moment that his late wife had been reincarnated. Trembling he opened the bedroom door and was gratified to see that it was his new wife who occupied the bed from which she was still holding forth. All the abuse wasn't directed at Gerry although it would be true to say that the greater portion of it was. She excluded none of his friends or neighbours reserving the choicer profanities for Matt and Maggie Coumer but most heinously of all she announced in a powerful voice that the flames of hell were not hot enough for Canon Coodle, his housekeeper and the two curates, a quartet, incidentally, on whom until this time nobody had laid a hard word.

Vainly Gerry tried to calm her. He spoke with the utmost tenderness and reassured her of his undying love. He spoke of the wonderful Christmas they would have and of the happy times after that. He endeavoured to calm, cajole and canoodle her but all his physical efforts were rejected and all his blandishments fell on deaf ears. He spent his entire lunch break with her. That evening Matt paid her a visit and prescribed some medication.

At ten o'clock that night, without a word to anyone, Gerry betook himself to an ancient water-keeper's lodge above the river bank. It was situated about two miles outside the town and was hidden from every approach by dense natural growth. He made several journeys during the course of the night and early morning until he had accumulated sufficient clothing and utensils to meet his needs. He prepared a fire from some timber and tinder he had brought with him. He slept until noon and when he had breakfasted he spent the remaining day-light hours walking along the river bank. He had brought his rods and lines and lures with him on his final journey to the lodge. He would spend the weeks ahead preparing his fishing gear.

In the course of time Noreen recovered fully but she never mentioned her husband's name or responded to queries about his welfare. If one was to judge by appearances one would have to conclude that no happier soul existed in the parish. She was well pleased with her deserted wife's allowance and declared it to be more than adequate.

Gerry, for his part, collected his dole money by arrangement from a small shop where he would purchase all his wants for the week. The shop stood near a cross-roads about a mile from where he resided but it might as well have been a hundred for the terrain was rough and dangerous and a resort of badgers whose rooting and grunting could be heard all night. Compared to the verbal broadsides of Noreen Meeke the sounds of the wilderness were music to Gerry's ears. Any salmon he bagged was taken to the crossroads shop which acted as an agency for a Waterford city fish buyer. Gerry ignored the other anglers who fished the waters contiguous to his domain. When saluted he grunted an acknowledgement and no more. On a few occasions from the undergrowth he spotted Matt Coumer circling the lodge but he never emerged. He blamed Matt's wife for landing him in a second disastrous marriage and wanted no more to do with her. He allowed his beard to grow and grow it did down to his naval, grimy, grey and gruesome. He became known as the Hermit of Scartnabrock.

After ten years in the wilderness he eventually fell foul of the wet and the damp and brought pneumonia upon himself. When he failed to appear for several days his friends Matt Coumer and Sergeant Ruttle went in search of him. He lay gasping his last breath on a damp bed when they found him. He managed a smile when he recognised them. It was a smile that touched Matt to the very quick of his being.

The funeral was poorly attended save for the salmon and trout anglers who fished the river from source to mouth year in, year out. They carried the coffin on their shoulders from the church to the graveyard where Canon Coodle spoke of the kindness Gerry had shown in his healthier days to younger anglers and to strangers who were not well versed in the ways of the river. The canon spoke of Gerry's attachment to all rivers great and small and explained the influence the river had on himself especially when the dead man and he fished together in the past. He spoke about the tributaries which brought their own special flavour to the river. He spoke of the different tunes the river sang depending on the highs and lows of the ever-flowing waters. He explained how the river never sang the same song twice, how the casual listener might easily be duped into believing that river-song remained the same for days on end until the floods came or the waters dropped in dry seasons to rock bottom. This was not the case at all he told them. There was a subtle difference every day guaranteed by the ever-changing flow. He explained how Gerry knew these things and he told how he himself could never pass a river without stopping to inspect the water and listen to the particular tune of the river in question. Afterwards the anglers went to their favourite watering hole where they toasted the dead angler and drank their fill in his memory.

Noreen never attended the funeral. After a month she packed her bags and returned to England where she married a man who passed by a great river every day but never looked at it. That then is the sad tale of the Hermit of Scartnabrock who so unsuccessfully fished in the waters of matrimony but managed to land a few whoppers in the river of his dreams.

Johnny Naile's Christmas

It had always been Johnny Naile's ambition to play the role of Santa Claus. He had nearly succeeded once. He had the appropriate garments on. He hadn't put a drink to his lips all day. He had stayed indoors from four in the afternoon. He had shaved, washed, cut his toe-nails and then his finger-nails. He had trimmed his red beard and would certainly have been the only red-haired Santa Claus ever to be seen in the village of Cushnalicka.

Cushnalicka had its assortment of cottages and bungalows, forty in all, at either side of the road-way and there were two extra houses, the presbytery and the vicarage. The new vicar, a dapper figure, spare and lean and Church of Ireland, was smiling and pleasant which immediately made him suspect.

'Anyone,' the Catholic canon's housekeeper was fond of maintaining, 'who smiles non-stop isn't right in the head.'

The canon and parish priest of Cushnalicka and several surrounding townlands rarely smiled. Neither did his curate Fr Bressnan. 'He's too weak to smile', some of the less charitable of the Catholic parishioners were fond of saying when the curate's lack of condition would be the prevailing topic.

'Mrs Topp,' they would say maliciously, 'don't believe in feeding curates. Signs on they're never the same after a year or two in Cushnalicka.'

'It's a wonder to me,' said Hannah Toben, the schoolmaster's wife, 'that they don't fade away altogether or collapse entirely or be capsized by a gale.' When she spoke in this disparaging fashion she always made sure that there was no sign of Mrs Topp in the vicinity.

Mrs Topp, a large, ambling, stern-faced widow, was the first to see Johnnie Naile as he attempted to make his way unseen through what was once described by a deceased postman as the most inquisitive resort in Western Europe. Johnnie, in full regalia, was as inconspicuous as his parish priest in full canonicals on Confirmation day. He was heartened as he drew near the presbytery that there was no sign of the housekeeper but then, suddenly, she appeared with a sweeping brush in her hand in pursuit of a heretical tomcat which had entered the sacred precincts without any invitation whatsoever.

George Cudd, the local civic guard who was also the only limb of the law in Cushnalicka, was heard to say that those who credited cats with an understanding of human language weren't too far wrong. 'I mean,' he confided to Mrs Toben, 'how else would the cat hear that the presbytery was full of mice unless it was a member of our species that let it drop.'

'They say,' Mrs Toben returned with equal confidentiality, 'that all the mice of the parish does have their meetings there.'

'I've heard of stranger happenings,' the civic guard nodded.

No sooner had Mrs Topp sent the tomcat about his business than she uplifted her brush and intimated in no uncertain terms that the pathetic representation of Santa Claus which was defiling her pavement was to come to a halt forthwith. Johnny Naile's apologetic smile revealed a mouthful of mixed molars, half of them as black as pitch and the remainder brown as hazelnuts. He was about to proceed on his way to the vicarage where he was expected when Mrs Topp confronted him a second time by forcing the head of the brush against his chest.

'I'll be late,' he pleaded. 'A promise is a promise missus.'

'A promise,' she called out to the street at large, 'sure no one would expect the likes of you to keep a promise.'

'This woman would,' he blurted out and suddenly covered his mouth with the palm of his right hand while he endeavoured to deliver a gentle hand-off with his free hand to the resolute housekeeper. The move made her all the more difficult to shift.

'You'd better make way for me woman because I'm comin' through,' Johnny shouted the warning while Mrs Topp braced herself.

Suddenly she changed her tack. Lowering the sweeping brush she forced a syrupy smile to her lips. Johnny Naile was more curious than disarmed. If Johnny's teeth were black and brown Mrs Topp's dentures were as white as snow but with the same tendency to shift. Shift they did with every word she spoke.

'Ah Johnny,' she was at her most cajoling now, 'be a good lad and tell me who the damsel is that you're meeting?'

'Can't do that missus.' Johnny was adamant.

Mrs Topp thrust a hand under his arm and endeavoured to guide him towards the front door of the presbytery which was still ajar after the cat's eviction.

'No, no, no missus,' Johnny held firm, 'what about the canon? What would he say if he caught me in the holy presbytery? I'd be excommunicated for sure with maybe jail on top of it.'

'The canon is gone to Limerick paying his sister her Christmas visit so you need have no fear of him. Come on now,' she wheedled and leaned her considerable rump against him to misdirect him indoors.

Johnny Naile realised that if he was to escape he would be obliged to knock the housekeeper to the ground and while he was reasonably sure that nothing would happen to her because of her abundant natural padding he could not be certain.

'Come on,' she whispered. 'I'll pour you a nice glass of the canon's own whiskey the likes of which you never tasted in all your born days.'

At the mention of the word whiskey Johnny could not make up his mind whether to run or submit.

'One drop of whiskey won't do all that much harm,' he told himself.

As he stood hesitantly he remembered his promise to Mrs Trupple the vicar's wife. 'Wait until just after dark,' she told him, 'you'll find the hat and coat will fit nicely. You'll find the bag of gifts in the pantry. You'll find the back door will be open. All you have to do is push it in. We'll be in the living-room. You'll get your five shillings when the presents are handed over.'

'Is there boots with the outfit?' he asked.

'Those you have on will do nicely,' she assured him. Johnny looked downwards doubtfully at the turned-down wellingtons which were the only footwear in his possession. After her departure he went over her instructions and cursed himself repeatedly for not asking her to go over the instructions a few more times.

'And what the blazes was a pantry?' he asked himself. He solved that one by asking a passing schoolboy to enlighten him.

'A pantry is it?' the schoolboy had asked.

'Yes,' Johnny answered, 'a pantry. What exactly is a pantry?'

'Why,' said the schoolboy, 'a pantry is nothing only a bedroom.'

'Upstairs or downstairs?' Johnny asked.

'Upstairs of course you ignorant eejit,' the schoolboy called out as he ran off.

In the kitchen of the presbytery where he had allowed himself to be conducted, Johnny raised the canon's special whiskey to his lips and downed it in its entirety at one swallow.

'Another drop!' Mrs Topp poured a liberal dollop into the empty glass.

Again, because of fear of the canon and the unfamiliar surroundings, he swallowed the contents of the glass without taking it from his lips. A great sigh of satisfaction escaped him. If the first glass hit the spot then the second glass travelled all over so that a mighty shudder seized him and rocked him to the very tips of his toes.

'Relax,' Mrs Topp advised him as she directed him towards a vacant chair. 'Now,' she demanded, 'what's that wan up to?'

'What wan?' Johnny asked drunkenly.

'Now,' said Mrs Topp as she held the snout of the bottle over his glass, 'will you be so good as to tell me the name of this damsel you're meeting?'

'Ah God help us,' said Johnny Naile, ''tis no damsel. Sure 'tis only Mrs Trupple the vicar's wife.'

'Are you doin' Santa for her then?'

Johnny nodded and raised his glass to the snout. This time he divided the contents into two swallows. At the conclusion of the second he was visited by a deep drowsiness. Sensing that no further information was available and that there was a danger her visitor might fall asleep she assisted him to the door-way and sent him rollicking down the street in the general direction of the vicarage.

She had made an unwise investment. The scandal which she hoped would materialise out of Johnny's disclosures never did. She had long cherished the hope that something juicy would come her way and that she might bring that Trupple wan, as she called her, down a peg or two. What harm but she had been prepared, when the vicar and his wife first arrived, to let historical bygones be bygones and initiate the younger woman into the tricky rituals and formulas of village life. She had been prepared to take her under her wing despite the fact that she belonged to a different faith and spoke with a cultivated accent.

The young Mrs Trupple had not exactly ignored her. It would be truer to say that she simply wasn't aware of the older woman's standing in the community and tended to treat her the same as everybody else.

Mrs Topp saw herself as the leading female representative of the Catholic Church in the parish, as the third in command behind the canon and Fr Bressnan, the curate. She often felt disappointed that the Pope had never dubbed the housekeepers of the world's countless presbyteries with any sort of formal title. For instance, she frequently told herself, nuns are called sisters and high-up nuns are called reverend mothers and young nuns are called novices. But there was no title of any kind for the parochial housekeeper who carries responsibility for the entire parish and fills in for the parish priest in so many unseen ways and who often keeps wayward clerics on the straight and narrow. Even the young scallywags who serve Mass are called altar boys and the parish clerk has the finest title of all, that of sacristan.

Sacristan, she often repeated the title to herself. Wouldn't sacristaness be a nice name now! Sacristaness Topp! She imagined herself being introduced by a master of ceremonies on formal occasions such as an episcopal visit or wearing a black mantilla being conducted on a Vatican tour by a slender, dark-haired monsignor and then the final part of the proceedings with voluptuous organ music shutting out all other sounds followed by silence as she hears her name being called out in that sexy Italian accent: 'Your Holiness may I present to you the Sacristaness of Cushnalicka.'

She quickly reverted to reality and drew a coat over her shoulders before heading off in the direction of the vicarage. Johnny had obviously disappeared indoors or else had fallen into the road-side drain. She concealed herself beneath the shade of a large evergreen just across the road from the vicarage. The minutes passed and then a quarter-hour. She was about to depart when, unexpectedly, from an upstairs room across the road-way came a scream, loud, clear and terror-filled the way a good scream should be or so Mrs Topp felt. Other screams followed and then shouts and other alarms. Down the street came George Cudd, the civic guard, portly and ponderous and puffing like a steam engine, vainly endeavouring to pull up his trousers and button his tunic at the same time. He came to grief after a few steps but resolved both problems where he sat after his fall.

Mrs Topp rubbed her palms together in high glee. She choked a scream of pure, unbridled joy lest her presence be given away. The minutes passed and from the vicarage a large group emerged with Johnny Naile at the forefront, held firmly by George Cudd the civic guard and followed by the vicar and his wife and their three children.

Johnny Naile, deprived of his red coat and hat, was a sorry sight. Clad only in his shrunken vest and raggedy long johns and still possessed of his turned-down wellingtons he tried to explain his case but nobody would listen. George Cudd became so incensed with his proclamations of innocence that he kneed him forcefully several times in the behind. He even went so far as to draw his baton and threatened to use it if his prisoner continued with his vociferation. By this time a number of villagers had joined the motley assortment outside the vicarage.

'What's he done George?' asked Mrs Topp who had crossed from the other side to join the commotion.

'What hasn't he done?' George Cudd replied as he kneed his prisoner lest he make further protestations. George had just been joined by two precious if burly reinforcements in the shape of his wife Molly and her partly deaf friend and neighbour Hannah Toben the schoolmaster's wife. Several adult topers from the village's two public houses joined the growing crowd. Blossom O'Moone wearing only her nightdress appeared in her doorway but did not join the throng. Blossom, according to numerous sources not all reliable, was the most accommodating girl in the village of Cushnalicka or for that matter in the entire parish or any other place you might care to name.

'But what will you be charging him with?' It was Mrs Topp again tugging at George Cudd's tunic.

'I'll be charging the wretch with attempted rape,' he informed those within earshot as he once more kneed his under-dressed prisoner, 'and I'll be charging him with resisting arrest and I'll be charging him with burglary.'

'What did he say?' Mrs Topp who was now out of earshot asked the person next to her, who happened to be Hannah Toben, who happened to be hard of hearing at the best of times.

'He'll be charging him with buggery,' Hannah Toben replied in the exaggerated tone she used when she believed she was dealing with people who were as deaf as herself.

'Buggery.' The word carried to the outskirts of the crowd. Some laughed nervously. Others were shocked. Buggery was something that happened elsewhere.

'String him up,' came a drunken call from behind a parked car pressed into service as a temporary latrine.

'Johnny Naile is a lot of things but he's no bugger and he's no rapist neither.' Blossom O'Moone it was who had spoken and after she made her views known there was silence the whole way to the barracks of the civic guards.

'What a story I'll have for himself when he comes back from his sister's!' The whispered words came from the thin lips of the Sacristaness of Cushnalicka. 'I won't say anything about the whiskey though and that's for sure,' she told herself.

Christmas morning presented itself without hail, rain or snow. The parishioners of Cushnalicka trooped to the earliest of the three Masses being celebrated on the sacred occasion. As always the canon was celebrant. Several years earlier he had resigned from a major parish in the south of the diocese. Unable for the heavy work-load and with an unprecedented shortage of priests he explained to the bishop that he would not retire. What he would like was a small parish, very small if possible, with just one curate to help him. The bishop had duly obliged with Cushnalicka which made everybody happy, especially Mrs Topp. Housekeeper to a priest was a fine thing but housekeeper to a canon with his tasselled hat and twenty or more scarlet buttons down the front of his soutane would make her the envy of the parish.

After Mass the congregation gathered in groups outside the church. The subject of conversation was the buggery and, of course, the attempted rape of the night before. The canon had only half listened as the housekeeper informed him of the terrible events that happened in his absence. As he was wont to do he doubted the veracity of all such tales and came to the conclusion that the housekeeper had been experimenting with his whiskey again. He never minded. She never took more than a glass or two and being a truly charitable man he concluded that she was as much entitled to the whiskey as he was provided she knew where to stop.

Despite the outrageous contents of his housekeeper's story he nevertheless took it upon himself to ring his friend the vicar. After the exchange of Christmas greetings and a promise to share a drink later in the day the vicar enlightened the canon regarding the events of the night before. Apparently when Johnny Naile arrived at the vicarage he was somewhat inebriated and mistook the master bedroom for the pantry.

The canon expressed no surprise. 'Johnny Naile,' he told the vicar, 'wouldn't know a pantry from a pea-shooter.'

Despite the fact that he was alcoholically incapacitated Johnny Naile made no noise as he entered the vicarage by the rear door and climbed the stairs to the master bedroom. Had he been wearing boots he would most certainly have been heard. Add to this the fact that the children were fast asleep having been out and about all day and would have dutifully pretended to be asleep anyway with the expectation of a visit from Santa Claus. The vicar had been preoccupied with his typewriter as he endeavoured to piece together a sermon for the following morning.

When Johnny arrived at the master bedroom he found the door open and the lights ablaze. Never before in his existence had he beheld such a bright and beautiful place. For a few hallucinatory moments he thought he might be in heaven but then he remembered the presents. Mrs Trupple had said they would be in the pantry and was not this the pantry! He tried high and low without success and then he was overcome by the heat of the place and by his exertions as well as the influence of three glasses of unwatered whiskey on an empty stomach. He fell across the large double bed and in a moment was fast asleep.

Alas, the vicar's wife lay reclining in her bath next door to the bedroom. Finishing her ablutions she rose and, totally oblivious to the happenings in the bedroom, entered that hallowed spot dragging a towel behind her and wearing only her birthday suit. The screams that followed were of a variety and pitch never before heard in the village of Cushnalicka. They were heard in every house. Those who slept were awakened and those who were awake wished they had been asleep. Prowling tomcats scurried into dark corners and the canines of the parish excelled themselves. The howling and the yowling would put a banshee to shame. Donkeys brayed in nearby fields and the moon raced for cover among the tattered clouds.

Johnny was released from custody just in time for last Mass on Christmas Day. He had no recall whatsoever of the previous night's events. The vicar had called earlier to the barracks and explained everything. George Cudd, having listened to his prisoner for most of the morning, had already deduced that he was holding an innocent man – if holding is the term, for the solitary cell where Johnny was incarcerated was without a bolt or lock.

When Mass was over he was showered with offers of Christmas dinners for word had spread that he was innocent of all charges. The only offer he accepted was the one from Blossom O'Moone.

MACKSON'S CHRISTMAS

Aenias Mackson, amiable as ever, kind and considerate, gave up his comfortable seat on the train. There were others who might have done so but they closed their eyes rather than look at the old lady with the large suitcase who had just come aboard. Christmas or no Christmas they had decided after they paid for their tickets that they would not surrender their seats on this occasion. Many would have done so in the past and felt that they had made their contributions, paid their dues so to speak and should be allowed to travel undisturbed, especially those going as far as Trallock one hundred and fifty miles down the line. Other male passengers who might have given in to the fragile figure so patently overburdened had varying reasons. Some would say that it was no concern of theirs, that if the old lady really wanted a seat she might have arrived earlier or travelled on the morning train.

One middle-aged man made an attempt to rise when she deposited her bag on the corridor by his side. He would have risen to his feet eventually. He had an elderly mother who had grown feeble in recent years and he wouldn't like to see her standing or so his conscience prompted him. He knew Aenias, had seen him several times in hotels and public houses in the city and would have laid a pound to a penny that he would volunteer his seat without a second thought. Not only did Aenias give up his seat to the old lady but he also saw to her luggage which consisted of the aforementioned suitcase and some small packages. Finding room for the suitcase presented problems as the overhead racks were already full. By removing his own smaller suitcase he managed to place the larger one, somewhat precariously, atop all the other luggage. In order to accomplish this he managed to stand on some toes and succeeded in brushing a lady's hat from her head.

'Do you mind!' she exclaimed in stentorian tones.

'That's my foot you know,' said the man on whose toe he had stepped unwittingly.

Aenias apologised profusely which was the only way he knew how to apologise. Having secured the old lady's possessions he found himself faced with another problem, the safe disposal of his own suitcase. The man with the toe pushed it down the corridor with his good foot as far as it could go and then firmly closed his eyes and folded his arms signalling his annoyance with Aenias.

'There's nothing in it,' this from the lady whose hat had fallen off. She lifted the suitcase and laughed as she announced its probable contents to her fellow passengers.

'More than likely a toothbrush,' she jibed and as she shook the case, 'a razor, possibly a bottle of hair oil or cream and a pair of sweaty socks I bet.'

Her remarks were greeted with laughter that was neither derisory nor hurtful. It was a Christmassy laughter. Aenias Mackson joined in while he rattled the suitcase good-naturedly as he made his way to the bar. He had promised himself earlier that day that he would avoid the bar on the journey down. He had drunk his fill the night before and had spent the morning in a pub adjacent to the station loading up against the hang-over which the night had bequeathed him. He had promised his mother on the last occasion he had visited home that he would never arrive drunk again.

'I would rather,' she said tearfully, 'that you didn't come home at all.'

Well he wouldn't arrive home drunk this Christmas Eve. He would go to the train bar and nurse a few bottles of stout until he reached Trallock. He was well into his second bottle when the lady who had commented on his bag's contents entered.

'Are you going to buy me a drink?' she demanded.

'What would you like?' he asked gently.

'Gin and tonic,' she replied.

When he returned with the drink they located a place near the door-way.

'That man,' she said, 'on whose toe you stood made a pass at me.'

'Oh dear!' was all Aenias could say.

'Is that all you can say?' she asked. 'Anyway,' she continued, 'was I right about the contents of the bag?'

'More or less,' he answered. He did not tell her that while in the pub that morning he had opened the suitcase and in the true spirit of Christmas, as he might say himself, had given away the seasonal presents within to a poor family who had been occupying a nearby table when he had come in earlier. The presents were for two younger sisters and a brother at home in his native town and, of course, there was the headscarf for his mother. His father had died when Aenias was eight years old. He told his friends that he had never been the same afterwards.

'No matter what I do,' he confided to a friend, 'I'll never be the same. He was my world, my whole world.'

'A man who makes a pass at a girl he's never seen before this,' his new companion informed him, 'should be thrown off the train.'

As they sped towards Limerick City and then to his native Trallock she held his hand.

'The only reason I'm holding your hand,' she explained, 'is that I feel sullied after that man's pass at me. Well I suppose you could also say that I'm a little drunk and alone and maybe afraid too if the truth was told.'

They sat silently for a while, neither anxious to shatter the repose their companionship had brought them.

'I have to go,' she said, 'Limerick's coming up.'

He rose when she did and walked with her to her seat where she recovered her bags and her coat. He took the bags in hand and made his way towards the exit.

'Will I see you again?' she smiled embarrassed by her courage.

'I hope so,' he answered.

'Have you got a biro?' she asked.

As he wrote her Dublin phone number on a slip of paper he spoke without raising his head. 'I hope you'll be in when I ring you,' he said.

'If I'm not,' she said, 'you must ring again and again.' Then she was gone.

He found a vacant seat and a place for his suitcase and drifted into an uneasy slumber from which he did not waken until he arrived in Trallock. He looked at his watch. 'Time for another drink,' he said.

His mother never went to bed before midnight. His sisters and brother would be awake expecting him. Despite many lapses over several Christmases their faith in him never wavered.

In a downtown pub he joined with a party of friends from his boyhood. After midnight had passed he reminded himself that he should go home. He was fully aware of the pattern into which he was falling. It was exactly the same as the past several Christmases. He was forced to admit that while he had a shilling in his pocket he was a compulsive avoider of home and family. He knew that his relationship with his mother was on the line and yet when he was asked by his friends if he was having another drink he confirmed that he was. He often asked himself if he was an alcoholic but he would always provide himself with reassuring answers. He could, for instance, go off the juice any time he wanted. He was popular with his friends. He had a good job in the Department of Industry and Commerce. His superiors had no complaints to make about him. Okay, so he owed a few pounds. He owed money to his mother. Frantically he searched his pockets. The presents which he had purchased and given away had taken their toll on his finances; so had the drinks he purchased.

In recall he realised that nobody had brought him a single drink all day, not until now. His needless extravagance with total strangers had left him with no more than a few pounds. Thank God he had purchased a return ticket. He remembered one very large order for which he had paid that morning in the pub near the station. A group of friends had joined his poor people at the next table. Introductions followed and he found himself paying for their drinks. He had been shocked at the price but he had insisted despite the protestations of the recipients. Phrases like 'ah you're too decent!' and 'he has a heart o' gold' started to drift back to him through the alcoholic excitement of the morning. Now he was left with a single five-pound note. Aenias had had eighty pounds starting out. He might not be an alcoholic but he was without doubt a wanton spendthrift. It would have to stop. He recalled the previous Christmas when his mother discovered he was broke and that this was the reason he stayed in bed over the holiday.

'I'm not being hard on you Aeney,' she told him, 'there's no need when you're so hard on yourself. You're just like your father, spending all you have on strangers and no thought for your own. How nice it would be for your brother and sisters if you took them to the pictures. If you had a car you could take us all for a drive.'

He had laughed bitterly but inwardly at this. A car! That was rich when he couldn't even afford a bicycle. The man behind the bar counter was calling time. Aenias looked at his watch. Mother o' God! Five o'clock in the morning! Where did the hours go! All victims of the season he told himself, the same as his money. As he walked home with his suitcase rattling he insisted to the stars overhead that he was just a creep. He found the key of the front door and tiptoed upstairs to bed. There was no sound in the house.

Later when he woke it was still dark but his watch told him that it was the darkness of the afternoon of Christmas Day. Why had nobody alerted him! The least they might have done was to call him for the mass or for his Christmas dinner. Downstairs his brother and sisters assured him that they had called him repeatedly but that he had been in a stupor every time. They placed his Christmas dinner in front of him. It was still hot but the pain in his head saw off his appetite. He pecked at the food and asked about his mother. When he didn't wake she had rented a cab and gone to her sister in the country. She might not return for a few days. She had not been feeling well. They were careful to lay no blame on him.

He told them how he had agonised about their presents and that he had no money either. He was truly ashamed of himself but they gathered round him and told him they loved him. They still had their Christmas monies, presents from neighbours, from aunts, uncles and cousins, dollars from America and English pounds galore. They heaped it upon him and to give him his due he faithfully recorded every penny he borrowed. The fact that he already owed them never entered the picture. In a few weeks he assured them he would repay every penny. He would go off the drink and he would never embarrass anybody again, particularly at Christmas. They told him he never embarrassed anybody in his life and that the money they gave him was a gift and that he was to forget about it.

They went for a walk round the deserted town stopping at each of the three churches to visit the sacred cribs where the infant Jesus lay, serenely, in his cot. The sisters Rita and Fiona, fifteen and fourteen, linked arms to their older brother throughout while Tom, the younger brother, brought up the rear. After an hour they returned to the family home where Aenias managed to finish most of the turkey and stuffing he had been unable to stomach earlier. Afterwards the foursome played cards and still later Aenias regaled them with city tales, largely humorous but sometimes unbearably sad. As the night wore on Aenias began to look at his watch with increasing regularity. His listeners guessed that his anxiety for drink was getting to him.

'Why don't you two go for a drink?' the older sister suggested to the brothers.

'Well now,' said Aenias with a chuckle, 'that would be the very last thought in my head.'

'Me too,' Tom put in, 'but if my mother finds out life won't be worth living for the rest of the year.'

'There's nobody here going to tell her,' Fiona assured him, 'provided of course ...' and she left the phrase hanging as Aenias looked speculatively from one sister to the other.

'Provided what?' he asked.

'Well,' Fiona explained reluctantly. 'He puked into the kitchen sink the last time and never cleaned up.'

'I promise I won't ever again do that,' Tom assured her. 'I was green then.'

'Of course you were.' Aenias clapped him on the back. 'I puked in the kitchen sink myself when I was seventeen and you can be sure that very few sinks have escaped a good puke at this time of the year.

'What time will you be back?' the younger sister asked.

'We'll be back in an hour at the outside,' Aenias promised.

'We'll wait up then.' The older sister's tone carried a trace of uncertainty. As the brothers left Aenias kissed both sisters and promised he would be as good as his word but again the pattern remained unchanged except that Tom had more than enough by the time midnight came round. Aenias would follow much later. He fell in with his companions of the previous night. They were pleased to see him. Those in big groups who failed to buy their rounds eventually found themselves isolated. It had been an established fact for years that Aenias always saw to his round and generally bought more than his share. Aenias left the premises where he had spent seven consecutive hours at six o'clock on the morning of St Stephen's Day or the Wren's Day as they still called it in the locality.

Aenias did not rise on the following day. The same dull headache assailed him when he awakened at noon. He declined all offers of food or drink and fell into a deep sleep from which he did not wake until nine o'clock that night. He missed the colourful wrenboys' bands with their spotless white uniforms, their tinselly, peaked caps and their painted moustaches as well as all the traditional singing and dancing for which they were justly famous.

Aenias crept round the room on tiptoe and located his trousers. He searched the pockets and found only a handful of silver. The pockets of his coat were not nearly as productive. He went back to bed.

He could not face the group, who would surely be in the public house by now, without the price of a round at least. He realised that his brother and the girls were waiting downstairs but he did not have the heart to face them. Filled with self-loathing he reminded himself for the umpteenth time since he came home that he was nothing more than a creep.

'I'm gone beyond redemption,' he said in a whisper, 'and that's a terrible thing to say at Christmas.'

He woke several times during the night. It was still dark when he started to get ready for the train. As he shaved he winced at the smell of rashers frying downstairs. He prayed that his mother would still be away. Hardly home yet he told himself. She would have confronted him already. He could have spent another day at home, even two days, but his time had come. No money and no zest and no hope.

He put on a brave face as he went downstairs. He rushed out to the back kitchen when he beheld the enormous display on his plate. It was colourful as it was plentiful with cubes of black and white puddings, sausages nicely browned, a little burning here and there which was the way he liked them. He didn't deserve such sisters. Then there were tomatoes in abundance each sliced into equal parts, and liver. Where the blazes did they get the liver on a holiday morning and at such an hour! Gently he embraced sisters and brother, relishing their healthy appetites as he tinkered with the toast for which he had asked.

At the station the four Macksons stood dejectedly together. Aenias leaned over and whispered to Tom. 'I am the sole owner,' he said, 'of the worst headache any man ever had.'

'I'll pray for you,' Tom whispered back. 'From now on I'll pray for you all the time.

'Pray for me!' Aenias was about to laugh but then it came back to him, something his mother had told him one day that last Christmas they spoke together. 'Tom's teachers believe he has a vocation for the priesthood,' she had told him proudly.

As they moved towards the train which had silently entered the station Aenias whispered a second time to his brother. 'I could do with a few prayers,' he said. He found himself shivering uncontrollably as the sisters handed him the suitcase. He felt like a man deserted and degraded as they stepped backwards, their eyes brimming with tears. The suitcase contained infinitely more on its return journey. There was a heavy pull-over and a shirt from his mother, socks, underwear and towels from his sisters and *The Oxford Book of Irish Verse* from Tom.

The Greatest Wake of All

Sam Toper always looked forward to Christmas. Sam's wife and family did not. Sam looked forward to Christmas because it was a time of free drinks. If one chanced to be in the right bar at the right time one was always sure to meet merry old gentlemen and, indeed, younger gentlemen who insisted in buying drinks for all and sundry. They would even buy drinks for people they had never before seen in all their lives. Sam couldn't understand it but because it was beneficial to him he totally accepted it. You wouldn't have any business explaining the spirit of Christmas to Sam and need I add that expressions like 'peace and goodwill' or 'come all ye faithful' would be meaningless to him.

Down deep he understood that there was an inexplicable chemistry at work, a chemistry which ordained that stingy oul' codgers who otherwise would not give him the time of day were prepared to press free drink on him at this particular time of year. If you were to suggest to Sam that he might more fully enter into the spirit of things if he himself bought drinks for people who were worse off than he was, Sam would be certain to double over in convulsions of laughter. From the look on his face after the laughter had subsided you would gather that it was one of the more preposterous proposals he had ever heard. Those who knew Sam well such as his wife and family and, of course, his neighbours were all agreed that Sam was a lousy creep, that he would not give you the itch if he had nine doses of it and that the idea of returning a favour was nothing short of reprehensible.

His employer, one Bustler Hearne, would have sacked him immediately after taking him on but for the fact that he could get no one else to work for him. Bustler Hearne was a bully and had beaten the daylights out of most of his previous employees for heinous crimes such as being late five minutes on wet mornings or for suggesting a rise in wages. It must however be taken into account that nobody else would employ Sam Toper because they couldn't motivate him the way Bustler could.

Bustler's business consisted of plucking and trussing fowl, particularly geese and turkeys, during the run-up to Christmas. For weeks before he would purchase his Christmas requirements from the fowl-rich countryside within a radius of ten miles. Of his regular employees, a Miss Dotie Tupper aged eighty-four was in charge of cash sales and another, our friend Sam, was fowl dispatcher and plucker-in-chief. Extra staff were taken on during the Christmas period. There was no such structure as a regular wage. One was paid for the number of turkeys plucked in the round of a day and woe betide the man or woman who damaged birds while plucking.

Sam was a model plucker when he put his mind to it and because he was possessed of an insatiable appetite for pints of stout he plucked like a man possessed, often earning three times as much as ordinary pluckers. Sam's wife Moya and their seven children had no great regard for Christmas. They loved their mother and each other after a fashion but because Christmas had never been kind to them they were never generous in their praise of it. There was no scarcity of food. The requisite share of Sam's weekly wage was put aside for Moya and would be collected by one of the older children when it fell due. Sam kept the balance so that he might satisfy his outrageous thirst.

'If,' said Canon Coodle the well-beloved parish priest, 'there is even a solitary half-penny missing from Moya's share of your wages I will raise you aloft and turn you inside out after which I will truss you and singe you and cast you into the depths of the quarry.' It mattered not to Canon Coodle that there was no water in the quarry hole nor had there ever been. It was the way he used his deep voice that made the hair stand on Sam's head.

There was another reason why the young Topers had no great affection for Christmas. They were constrained by their father to work as part-time goose and turkey pluckers during the Christmas holidays when other youngsters were roving the countryside in search of holly and ivy for the family cribs. They were made to work from dawn till dark and deprived of their rightful wages by their drink-crazed father. It was too late when Sergeant Ruttle heard about it but when he did he presented Sam with three deep and accurate kicks on his booze-fattened posterior and threatened him with life imprisonment if such a malpractice ever occurred again.

After that the children started to enjoy Christmas especially when Canon Coodle found them suitable employment for a few days before Christmas. The money would be spent on inexpensive gifts before their father found out about it and demanded that it be handed over so that he might slake his unquenchable thirst.

When the three older children arrived into their middle and late teens they made contact with aunts and uncles in England and the United States and eventually wound up in New York where they found gainful employment. They would save most assiduously from their very first wage packet with a view to bringing the entire family, father excluded, to New York where they might start life afresh.

Naturally the three eldest went first. They kept their departure a secret from their father. When he found out he locked the remainder of the family out for several nights. They found refuge with neighbours until Sergeant Ruttle was informed. On this occasion, although by no means a violent man, the sergeant doubled the number of posterior kicks normally implanted. Afterwards Sam took a pledge against drink which lasted for twenty-four hours.

Life went on and then an elderly neighbour died. He was one of two brothers, pint-sized cobblers who eked out the most meagre of existences in a tiny, one-storeyed house five doors up the lane-way from the Toper abode. People who came with shoes to be repaired had difficulty in telling the brothers apart. They were aged seventy and seventy-one, always slept in the same bed, never argued, were invariably kind to each other and never missed eight o'clock morning Mass in St Mary's church in the centre of the town. Let there be hail, rain or thunder, let there be sleet, snow or storm the brothers faced the elements each morning with happy faces and cheerful hearts.

The Toper children spent much of their spare time during the winter months huddled around the diminutive peat fire in the cobblers' shop listening to the many folktales which had been passed on from generation to generation and which now reposed in the fabulous memory of the compact cobblers of Cobblers' Lane for it was by this name that the lane was known.

All would change in a few short years. The last of the cobblers passed on to that happy clime where wax and heelball, thongs and laces were as plenteous as the green grass on the lush pastures of planet earth and where the shining steel of lasts and awls lighted the surrounds as far as the eye could see. People no longer slept on straw mattresses and there would be no more fleas. Urban councils everywhere would provide sturdy homes with baths and toilets and sufficient rooms for modern families. But there would always be people who would look askance at houses for the poor, holidays for the poor, subsistence for the poor and enough to eat for the poor.

The cobblers of Cobblers' Lane went by the names of Mickey and Mattie Mokely. It was Mattie who died one night in his sleep. When Mickey felt the cold form he knew that something was amiss. He called his brother gently by his name and when that failed to elicit a response he tapped him gingerly on the shoulder. He slapped him on the back but there was no reaction so he rose from the bed and lighted a candle which he held under Mattie's nose and then under Mattie's mouth but not the least flicker did the flame design. The younger brother donned his clothes, for now there was irrefutable proof that his brother was dead. As soon as he was dressed he bent over his brother's ear and recited the final act of contrition. Then he called the neighbours, one of whom went for the doctor while two went for the priest because it was the custom that a lone man or woman should never go for the priest unless there was no one else available. It was believed that a lone person might be more susceptible to the wiles of the devil and might be diverted from the presbytery where the priest was always available. Old people would recount instances where loners were found drowned in nearby rivers and streams while others fell foul of unseasonal mists and were tumbled inexplicably down precipices and into crevices where they might be found many years later or not found at all. On the other hand a pair of stout men with goodwill in their hearts and rosary beads wrapped round their fingers were known to be proof against all evil.

Despite the poverty of the times Mattie Mokely was waked well with three different varieties of whiskey, with port, sherry and rum, with Dutch gins and imported snuff. If memory serves me correctly I remember once to have overheard that vodka had yet to make its presence felt in the lanes and streets of Ireland. Mattie was laid out in his Sunday best. This consisted of his Clydesdale-blue suit, his low shoes or slippers as they were called. These had the brightness of polished ebony thanks to the ministrations of Mrs Hanlon, Canon Coodle's housekeeper. She admitted afterwards that she would perform such a chore for nobody else – the canon excepted.

'Mattie Mokely,' said she, 'was always a gentleman and I would be remiss if I didn't send him shining to the gates of heaven.'

During the wake, food was handed round. All would be paid for without fail when the obsequies were over and every penny would come from the life-savings of the Mokelys. Seven pigs' heads boiled almost to jelly were sliced and sent upon the rounds. There was ham, lamb, ram and jam the neighbours boasted afterwards. There were barm bracks and seed loaves and home-made scones by the score all provided by generous neighbours to whom the Mokely brothers would have shown kindnesses over the years. Credit was always extended to the hard-up and no one went without a pair of half-soles just because he was temporarily penniless. In spite of this there was little or nothing owing to the Mokely brothers. Only one man abused their generosity and failed to meet his commitments. That man you know already but his wife and family would do their best in the course of time to cancel his debts.

Sam's wife and family were held in high regard by all who knew them whereas no one was held in lower regard than Sam and yet it was the very same Sam who, in the early stages of the wake, consumed three times as much whiskey as anybody else and who, may God forgive all gluttons, devoured two heaped plates of pigs' head, plates which were destined for other folk who were too considerate to look after themselves. When Sam had eaten his fill and drunk his nuff he retired for a few hours to his abode where he stretched himself on his bed so that he might be prepared later on in the night for a second assault on the booze and comestibles.

Many people in Cobblers' Lane and further afield had predicted for years that Sam would have a bad end, that he would simply burst one day and that would be the end of him. Dr Matt Coumer knew better. Once when Sam had a drunken fall and needed some stitches the doctor, without Sam's consent, conducted a thorough check on this money-on candidate for a speedy demise. Matt was amazed by his findings which he passed on to none save a few select colleagues. Blood samples had been taken, pulse and blood pressure checked and rechecked, heart and lungs exhaustively recorded for flaw or failure but at the end of the day Matt was obliged to concede that for his age, weight and debauched habits Sam was the nonpareil of the local medical scene.

While the wake continued unabated Sam slept soundly and snored not at all. It was the practise of the period for poor people to set aside money on a regular basis for a decent wake and funeral lest they be disgraced in the eyes of the world. They would be able to say afterwards that they had met their obligations. 'We waked him well,' they would say or, 'we waked him dacent God be good to him.'

They would see to it that none of the mourners left the house in a sober state or with an empty stomach. To this end Mickey Mokely had spent every last shilling of his and his brother's savings. It never occurred to Mickey that should he pass on prematurely there would be little or nothing left to pay for his wake and funeral. The county council, of course, would provide enough to pay for a coffin and he would be in a position to share a free grave courtesy of his brother but there would be no drink and there would be no food. The way Mickey saw it was that he would survive long enough to put aside the cost of a decent wake and funeral for himself.

As the night wore on the more magnanimous grew the tributes to the dead man. These would be forthcoming anyway whether the deceased was a good man or not. They cost nothing and it brought some degree of consolation to the relatives. The praise came mostly from the elderly female neighbours who sat near the deathbed. With nodding heads they counted their beads between glasses of sherry or port. The ritual recital would go on for hours. When one group had exhausted their superlatives, another group would take over.

The words of praise had replaced the lonely keening which dominated such proceedings from time immemorial. The keeners were drawn from certain families who were held to be more professional than genuine mourners who might let down the side by not crying at all, who would be too stunned by the loss to give vent to any sound save an anguished sighing which could hardly be heard. Others would be too shy or too backward while others still were too heartbroken. There were more who felt that prayer heaped upon gentle prayer for hours on end was the appropriate method of mourning. The keeners had nothing against prayer. What was keening after all but a form of chanted or sung prayer! True professional keeners would shed tears when ever required and assume facial expressions so tragic that the very sight of them would trigger off fountains of tears from overcrowded wake-rooms. Some cynical mourners would argue that it was no bother at all to cry when one's gut was filled with whiskey or wine but the truth was that these were exceptional women and in the old days a wake without their ilk was like a bastable without a bottom.

As the night drifted into morning at the Mokely wake people began to drift away to their homes so that when the hour of one struck only a handful remained. These, for the most part, would have been immediate neighbours, one or more of whom would be expected to sit up with the corpse until morning when the normal activities of the lane and nearby streets resumed.

One of the last groups to leave the wake-room was the Toper family which consisted of Moya and her four children. They made their goodbyes to Mattie and went out into the night. They tiptoed silently downwards to their home where the head of the family was just beginning to stir having spent three hours of unbroken sleep in his bed and might well have spent several more had he not been awakened by the cold of his own waters which would not be restrained such was the earlier intake of liquor by their proprietor. He hurried from the little back room where he generally slept alone only to be confronted by his family who happened to be entering the house as he was leaving it. He issued a stern lecture about late hours and cuffed the children. As Moya passed hurriedly inwards he drew a kick at her but he was caught off balance and fell out on to the street where small clusters of mourners were still gathered. Smiling benignly at those who spared him a glance he increased his normal gait to a frantic run lest all the wake-room liquor be consumed.

His fears were groundless. The wake-room was empty and all he could see was the corpse clad in his Clydesdale and good shoes. He immediately lifted a whiskey bottle to his head and sought around for a bottle of stout which would serve as a chaser. He was delighted to see that a full crate of bottled stout occupied an honoured position under the deathbed. He would guard it with his life as he would the mortal remains of Mattie. As he sat a handful of neighbours silently entered, looked around, smiled knowingly and made no comment. They would return later and dutifully perform their stint by the corpse.

Sam ignored them and was pleased to observe that they had not interfered with the crate beneath the bed. There was many a man of proven courage and many a truly pious man who would face a raging bull rather than sit alone with a corpse. For Sam, however, the remains beside him on the deathbed presented no problem. Mattie had presented no threat in life and should therefore present even less of a threat in death. Anyway Sam was never a man to be intimidated by the hereafter or by the thought of the hereafter or so he said himself. His only fear in life was that some disaster might befall the world and close down the breweries and distilleries thereby leaving him threatened by the long thirst which he had always feared.

'As long as I have a bottle of stout in my hand,' he once declared to a neighbour, 'I have no fear of the hereafter or the hereunder but as little. Let 'em come at me sideways or downways or upways and you'll find me standing my ground. You can keep your guns and your swords and put a bottle of whiskey by my side, preferably a bottle of ten-year-old Jameson, and we'll see who'll come out on top.'

He drank contentedly for an hour and then he recalled the offspring who had reduced his income by high-tailing it to the United States. He never made vocal threats when he was alone. Instead he liked to growl at the absent faces of those he believed to have wronged him. People who had been privy to this growl would declare afterwards that they had never heard a sound like it, that it resembled nothing on the face of the earth. They would solemnly swear that no animal, domestic or wild, was capable of such spine-chilling utterances.

Dr Matt Coumer once heard the very same sounds emanating from the local grave-yard on a fine summer's night as he rambled through the suburbs with his wife. She had stopped dead and would not budge an inch. Matt would be the first to admit that he was not the bravest man in the community but he allowed his curiosity to get the better of him. Assuring his wife that there was nothing to fear he followed his ears to the horrific noises. After a brief search he noticed the human form rolled up against the side of an ancient tomb.

'I was reminded of Shakespeare,' Matt informed his friend the Badger Loran with whom he was drinking in the back lounge of Crutley's. 'You remember the ghost in *Hamlet?*' Matt recalled.

'Why wouldn't I?' responded the Badger, who had never even heard of *Hamlet* not to mind the ghost.

'You remember where the ghost describes the secrets of his prison house?'

'Course I do,' the Badger answered with a wink at Mrs Crutley.

'How's that it goes again?' Matt pondered. 'Ah yes indeed. I have it now,' and he went on to quote the relevant lines:

would harrow up thy soul, freeze thy young blood,
make thy two eyes, like stars, start from their spheres,

thy knotted and combined locks to part,
and each particular hair to stand on end,
like quills upon the fretful porpentine.

'Well that's exactly how I felt my friend as I studied the crumpled heap of humanity before my eyes. At first I thought it must be a bear which had somehow escaped from a distant zoo but I had second thoughts and realised that it must be some truly formidable member of the ape family. I was about to depart and report the sighting to my friend Sergeant Bill Ruttle but then the creature leaped to its feet and looked me between the eyes. I wouldn't give tuppence for my life at that moment but then I noticed the face and the unmistakable whiff of stale whiskey. The creature had stopped sounding off at this stage. It was when the growling stopped that I knew who stood before me. It was the one and only Sam Toper. When he recognised me he resumed his former position and commenced his out-pourings once more.'

Matt admitted to the Badger that he was utterly overcome by laughter. He hurried to the grave-yard gate and informed his nervous wife of all he saw and heard. She accompanied him to the tomb where Sam had changed his position and was now sitting on his behind with his head resting on his knees. The awesome growling still continued. Matt and his wife laughed loud and long and indeed laughed loud and long for many nights afterwards.

As Sam sat near the deathbed he thought he heard a sound coming from that unlikely place. He took no notice and readdressed himself to the bottle of whiskey. After a goodly swallow he felt the pangs of hunger assailing his whiskey-drenched saliva. He stumbled around the wake-room in search of suitable sustenance. A milder growl escaped him. It was a growl of satisfaction for he had located an unfinished plate of pig's head. He devoured it like a starving lion, grunting and gasping as he did. Then and not till then did the corpse sit up on the deathbed.

At first Sam could not believe what he saw. He placed the pig's head and the whiskey on the ground and rubbed his eyes. He had often been confronted by strange apparitions before but he had always been able to trace them to the excessive consumption of whiskey.

'I'm not that drunk,' he told himself, 'so it can't be whiskey.'

Slowly he took his knuckles from his eyes. The corpse was now sitting on the side of the bed and it was speaking.

'What's the hour Sam?' the corpse asked politely.

Sam replied with an ear-splitting scream. Other screams and assorted spasms followed as he bounded over the deathbed and disappeared into the starry night.

'Save me, save me!' he called pitifully.

Outside awaiting their turn to sit up with the corpse were the three neighbours who had entered earlier. They made no move for they could see nobody from whom Sam might be saved.

'Save me. Save me,' he shouted as he ran through his own front door, knocking it from its rusty hinges. He ended up under his bed and did not reappear until Mattie was safely buried later in the day.

It would be some time before the truth emerged. Shortly before the figure sat up on the bed Sam had stolen forty winks. While he snoozed, the corpse's brother, Mickey, found himself unable to resist the advances of sleep. Too much drink added to extreme physical exhaustion had driven him into a trance-like state so he did what he always did. He drew back the clothes and lay in the bed beside his brother. After a short while he felt the chill. With a few heaves and pushes he succeeded in dumping the corpse on to the floor. Mickey dropped off and slept for two hours by which time the intrepid Sam had instituted his search for suitable nourishment.

After the funeral an air of gloom hung over the lane-way. Most of the houses were left in darkness out of respect to the dead man. After a few days the pall lifted. Mickey re-opened his shop and was visited on an hourly basis by the neighbours. They brought him broth and they brought him pies and they brought him pancakes in their turn. One or more sat with him all day long and little by little he began to accept the sad fact that he would face the remainder of his life alone. Neighbours were fine and neighbours cared but in the last analysis neighbours had other priorities.

Nobody ever told the true story to Sam Toper. All concerned came to the conclusion that he was better off the way he was. It would be wrong to say that he wasn't the same after his experience but it would be true to say that minor changes occurred in the years that followed. He stopped kicking Moya for one thing. All he did now was slap her face and throw the occasional punch at her midriff. Other times he would rise from his couch in the middle of the night when the injustices he had suffered over a life-time surfaced and prevented him from going to sleep. After a spell of teeth-grinding and other rasping noises from mouth and throat he would commence his growling. He would never enter her room which she shared with the children. He would reduce himself to all fours outside her bedroom door and embark upon a long and highly varied session of hostile natterings and intimidatory mutterings. These were but the prelude to the spine-chilling snarls and warning snorts which were at the very centre of Sam's discontent. Moya and the children generally slept throughout unless, in a specially malignant fit of pique after too much liquor, he might throw the entire family out into the street. Almost immediately one of the neighbours would alert Sergeant Bill Ruttle who shepherded the family back indoors after which he never failed to implant several stinging, bone-shaking kicks on Sam's rear. These worked wonders with the temperament of Sam and never failed to reduce his growling to pitiful sobs and whimpers.

Bill took it upon himself to enlist the remaining boys of the Toper family in the Trallock boxing club. At fifteen and fourteen respectively Fiachra and Conn Toper were regarded as likely prospects although the sergeant never intimated that they should one day use their skills against their bullying father unless, of course, in self-defence.

Sam was the kind of fighter who, if he knew he was capable of defeating an opponent, would beat him senseless whereas he would run a mile from a better man. One might be tempted to ask why a better man or men were never called in to balance the situation. It was chiefly because there was an unwritten law at the time that the head of the household was the unquestioned master of his domain. Fine if Bill booted him around now and then but for a layman to intervene would amount to an invasion of the home and the home above all other things was regarded as sacred by church and state. Then there was the awful prospect that Sam might be injured or even killed if the security of his home was breached. Who would provide for his wife and family and who would pay for his funeral?

Sam survived and never changed his tyrannical ways. Time passed and a white Christmas presented itself for the dazzlement and delight of young and old. There had not been a white Christmas in the parish of Trallock for nine years. The flakes arrived first in faint flurries and rarely alighted on the ground. Instead they drifted around the streets and lane-ways, moving slowly westward and increasing slowly in density all the time. Four days before the great feast the snow began to come down in real earnest, whitening the roof-tops and the surrounding fields, brightening the hearts of the young folk and recalling for the older people happy days of childhood when somehow the snow never seemed as cold. Then just three days before Christmas a great event took place. A tall handsome man well-dressed and well-made alighted from the mid-day train at Trallock railway station. Immediately he commissioned two local bag carriers to take charge of his luggage which was considerable. He preceded the pair to the town centre where he entered the town's only travel agency. When his business was concluded he instructed his carriers to follow him to the poorest quarter of the town. The carriers showed no surprise. Often over the years and especially as Christmas drew near they would have been hired by well-off strangers to transport luggage to unlikely destinations. The lone strangers, it invariably transpired, would have been local men who had made good abroad, especially in England and America and occasionally in Australia. All these successful homecomers represented only a very small percentage of those who were forced to emigrate in the first place. Not everybody succeeded in their places of exile and not everybody who did remembered to come home.

As the party arrived at the corner which led to Cobblers' Lane they were ambushed by a cheerful party of snowballing youths and children who had grown tired of snowballing each other. The tall young man returned fire and instructed his carriers to do likewise. There followed a joyful exchange of snowballs which goes to show, if it ever needed showing, that bag carriers as well as visiting gentlemen are all children at heart. A man who does not know this, as Canon Cornelius Coodle might say, knows very little.

The four unexiled Toper siblings who were at the head and tail of the ambush went by the names of Fiachra, Conn, Aedh and Fionnuala which were the names of the Children of Lir, the great mythical sea god who married Aobh and had three sons and a daughter who were changed into swans by Lir's second wife Aoife. It was Mental Nossery the poet who suggested the names to Moya after the poet had found her wandering in tears round Trallock grave-yard with marks on her face one summer's morning a few weeks before she gave birth to her fourth child. The child was called Fiachra.

It was Fionnuala, the youngest of the Toper children, who recognised the tall handsome young man. When he followed her and lifted her in the air she screamed and then smiled when she saw the laughing face of her oldest brother Frank. Great rejoicings followed but these were eclipsed by the total joy of Frank's revelations that he had tickets to New York for his mother and the four other members of the family. All were sworn to secrecy for the good reason that Sam would be within his rights to prevent his younger children from leaving home before they reached legal age. When Sam arrived home late that evening he was partially covered in feather and turkey droppings. He acknowledged Frank's presence with a grunt but then realising that Frank would surely be well heeled he invited him out for a drink. Drink was the last thought in Frank's head but he agreed. His father needed to be humoured lest he deduce that he was being duped for the second time. In the public house Sam Toper called for a glass of whiskey and a pint bottle of stout.

'Pay for that!' he instructed his oldest son.

More drinks followed, all paid for by Frank. Sam drank his fill and almost slept out the following morning which would never do, he reminded himself, with hundreds of turkeys and geese still waiting to be plucked and no wages forthcoming until the bare pelts were singed and trussed. He gulped down a cup of tea and rushed out the door to his place of employment. If he was a solitary minute late he would be docked an hour's wages by the eighty-four-year-old timekeeper Dotie Topper who, according to all the employees under her supervision, could see around corners and had eyes in the back of her head as well as an ear-splitting bell which sounded off whenever the only door to the plucking quarter was opened.

When Sam returned home for his lunch at one o'clock the first thing he noticed was the cold and the second was the absence of any form of appetising odour such as that of beef stew or bacon and cabbage or roast chicken. All cockerels and pullets badly damaged in the plucking were available to staff at half price and there would be many of these at Christmas. Sam's suspicions were aroused when he finally became aware of the profound silence. He hurried through the house calling out his wife's name and then the names of the children. Panting he ran out the door and never slackened his pace until he reached the railway station. Its only occupants were the pair who had carried his son's suitcases to Cobblers' Lane the previous afternoon. Their lines were carefully rehearsed, their stories convincing. Yes! The children and the mother had all boarded the Dublin-bound passenger train at half-past nine that morning. Sam hurried to the barracks where he was interviewed by Sergeant Bill Ruttle. He demanded the return of his children without delay. He threatened the sergeant with legal proceedings which could cost him his job if he didn't get a move on. Bill guessed that the Topers were by now on their way by bus from Limerick city to Shannon airport. Later he would question friends and neighbours in Cobblers' Lane.

The children had looked elegant in the new clothes Frank had brought with him from New York and the neighbours would swear in any court of law that a more contented group of people never left Cobblers' Lane. Sam did not die of a broken heart. He did not love his children and he did not love his wife. The only person he loved was Sam. He questioned the neighbours but they had seen nothing, heard nothing and were too busy in the first place minding their own business.

As time passed Sam began to come to terms with his loss. He had extra money for drink and he lived out of tins. Sardines, beans and bread and butter were his basic diet. He thrived but his growling had entered a new phase. He now betook himself to the grave-yard for a few hours every evening. It afforded him the isolation he needed to indulge in his now-demented growling activities. On the rare occasions when he was visited by outlandish urges he would climb on the flat roof of an ancient tomb and hold forth loudly and at length, slobbering and whining, pillalooing and yelping sometimes savagely and sometimes gently. All his complaints were directed at his absent family.

Then a surprising development took place. He began to attract the attention of dogs. These were, for the most part, good-natured mongrels who indulged him and who followed him around in the hope that he might unearth something out of the ordinary. In time they ignored him but there still remained a few disciples who trailed him when they had nothing better to do. Alas one day while he held forth from an all-fours position on a large limestone flag at the farthest corner of the grave-yard he found himself confronted by two vicious Alsatians who savaged him beyond recognition for having the temerity to growl at them. They had returned to the town after an unsuccessful sheep search in the nearby hills. Well known for their murderous onslaughts a look-out had spotted them as they passed through a large upland field. The look-out had raised the alarm and in a short while several armed sheep farmers appeared on the scene. The killers, however, with that particular canine cunning common to sheep killers, had disappeared. The grave-yard had proved on occasion to be a source of food. Lazy, uncaring vandals from the locality would dump occasional carcasses over the grave-yard wall in the dead of night. Chiefly these would be aborted calves or dead cats and dogs. Sometimes there would be chunks of rancid meat and other times flitches of bacon with a tangy taste due to insufficient salting. Canon Coodle, the parish priest, had roundly condemned these sacrilegious practices on many occasions but the grave-yard was convenient and there was little or no likelihood that the dumpers would be identified.

The Alsatians were near to starving when they entered the grave-yard. They lifted their heads high and sniffed the cold air when strange sounds drifted towards them from the far corner. Excitedly they bounded in that direction. They were at first mystified when they beheld the strange creature on all fours. Beyond doubt it was of the human species but on all fours it was fair game. After the first onslaught the savage canines became hysterical. The blood of the victim indicated more substantial fare to come. Frenziedly they dragged the screaming Sam into an area overgrown with whitethorn.

It was some days before a passing mourner, on his way to the isolated grave of a deceased relative, discovered the remains. He alerted Sergeant Ruttle who took charge of the investigation. An inquest was set in motion and under cross-examination the sergeant informed the jury that when he arrived at the scene he found that the body had been mutilated by animals which had since been destroyed. Some of Sam's ribs had been gnawed away and much of the flesh had been removed from the upper part of the torso. Pressed by the coroner, Sergeant Ruttle revealed that rodents had consumed some of the victim's flesh.

Sam's wife Moya and their seven children flew home for the funeral. They never saw his remains. Once the coffin was closed it would never be opened again. Neither would Sam's family ever be seen again in their native place but first they would wake their father as a father had never been waked before.

The little house was crammed for the occasion. Although the wake had a sluggish start it turned in the end into the most enjoyable extravaganza in the long history of parish obsequies. The paid mourners and the ordinary mourners were hard put to find a good word for Sam. Not one could show a tear and remember that between them in their lifetime they had shed enough tears to float the *Titanic.* Drink and goodwill circulated freely but there were no kind words. It was left to Fionnuala, the family's youngest member, to set the eulogistic trend for the evening.

'God be good to my poor father,' she opened.

'Amen! Amen!' responded all present.

'We all know he blackened my eyes,' Fionnuala went on, 'and we all know he pulled out my hair. We know too he thumped me for no reason. He walloped me when I didn't deserve it. He growled at me and he howled at me and he scowled at me but he never bit me.'

'Amen! Amen!' sang the mourners.

Frank, the oldest son, spoke next.

'He broke my two legs once,' Frank recalled.

'He fell on top of me from a ladder when he was drunk but he never complained.'

'Amen! Amen!' sang the mourners.

Entering into the spirit of the thing Moya spoke next. Her voice was broken but she managed somehow to hold it together so it wouldn't fall apart. 'God grant that poor man a silver bed in heaven!' she cried out fervently, 'for he had no bed of roses down here. He suffered from a life-long thirst you wouldn't raise in the hobs of hell but he never complained. He just drank and drank and drank until that thirst was cured. There was never a man like him.'

'There was never a man like him,' everybody chorused.

'I recall well the time Frank broke his legs,' Sergeant Ruttle remembered in a fractured tone. 'Sam Toper never reported it to me and he never reported it to any other civic guard. He just put up with it because he was that kind of a man.'

'Amen! Amen!' came the assenting voices.

'And he never reported it to me either,' Dr Matt Coumer recalled. 'He took it on the chin like the proud father he was. We coffined a man today who will go down in history.'

'Down in history!' the mourners echoed to a man.

The wake was now buzzing. Drink in all its forms flowed freely and no man or woman went hungry on that memorable night. Holding Moya's hand in one of his and his wife's Blossom O'Moone's in the other Mental Nossery rose unsteadily to his feet. His voice was hoarse with emotion when he addressed the mourners. He nodded his head in the direction of the coffin and spoke: 'This was the noblest Toper of them all,' he cried. 'I knew his brothers Jack and Mick and he'd drink the two of them under the table. And is it not he who is responsible for this banquet here tonight? There would be no wake without him. This surely is the greatest wake of all and I swear to this by the six breast nipples of the three musketeers. I say to you once and I'll say no more. I say to you that there was only one Sam Toper and no more.'

'Amen, amen!' sang Moya and her sons and daughters.

'Amen, amen,' sang Mental Nossery and his wife Blossom.

'Amen, amen!' sang out the great assembly of mourners while in the full-moon sky abroad in the night a lone star with a lengthening tail of silver whirred across the winking heavens to prove without doubt that another soul had arrived at the gates of heaven.

THE SEVEN-YEAR TRANCE

This is the story of the strange disappearance of Hiccups O'Reilly. He did not disappear forever, only for seven years. 'They felt like a day,' he told his wife when he came home.

He was missing from Christmas Eve 1959 to Christmas Eve 1966 which was the very same day that Canon Cornelius Coodle landed the record-breaking thirty-four pound cock salmon in Pudley's Pool near the big bridge.

Hiccups' wife Delia did not believe him when he told her that he vanished while chasing a hare. He had been wearing a waist-coat made from the skin of his favourite greyhound bitch when he rose the hare in question on the slopes of Crabapple Hill overlooking the town. Hiccups was not called Hiccups because he was given to hiccupping. He was so called because he looked like a hiccup. Personally I do not know what a hiccup looks like. It's my guess, however, that it doesn't look good, that you wouldn't hang it on a wall for instance or you wouldn't give it to your children to play with.

Delia Hiccups' brothers, three in number, were built like tanks and made similar noises. Not once had they been seen to smile or laugh and whatever about Hiccups' story of disappearing while chasing a hare the whole town and countryside would be on one word that the surest known way to disappear was to be in receipt of a mature, well-timed upper-cut from any single one of the six overgrown fists of the three aforementioned brothers, Mick, Dick and Slick.

Since Hiccups had already disappeared once he felt it would not be in his best interests to disappear twice so he stuck grimly to his story no matter the degree of incredulity it induced in his wife or her brothers Mick, Dick and Slick McCraw. Some believed his story, others did not. They said that Hiccups was a professional liar and that it was just the sort of tale they would expect from him. His friends and neighbours believed him or at least they said they did.

The story really began when Hiccups was presented with a beautiful greyhound bitch as a Christmas present by his uncle Ned. She was fawn in colour, moved like lightning, swerved like a footballer and could not resist the sight of a hare. The name they gave her was Flash. On her first outing she won the Trallock Bitch Sweepstake which qualified her for a trip to the track in Limerick city for the final of another important stake. She won it easily and went on to win ten more big races before she was retired for breeding purposes. Alas she was never to breed because of an injury. She died soon after and so overcome with grief was Hiccups that he made a waist-coat out of her skin which he wore till the day he died. In fact, his enemies would say that it was the very same waist-coat he was seen wearing when he left Trallock railway station on that fateful Christmas Eve morning when he disappeared for seven years. His female companion was also wearing something, a perfectly fitting blonde wig which ran down to the small of her back. Nobody knew who she was, that's if she ever existed, but Hiccups' enemies insisted she was a voluptuous dame with false eyelashes and a well-developed bosom. Hiccups' friends would point out afterwards that there was no female missing from the parish or its surrounds so that the female seen with Hiccups – if seen – was no more than a casual acquaintance in whose vicinity he chanced to be prior to his departure.

I should have explained earlier that Hiccups was not warmly received by his wife after his long absence. In fact she locked him out and but for the intervention of Sergeant Ruttle and Canon Coodle he might never have seen the insides of his house again.

A week after his return his three brothers-in-law arrived at the house and demanded an explanation. They sat around the kitchen table and insisted that Hiccups join them. Hiccups knew that if his story was not accepted he would be beaten senseless so he wisely suggested to his would-be executioners that perhaps a sojourn in a nearby public house, such as Crutley's, might be more conducive to storytelling. The suggestion drew neither a hum nor a haw from Mick, Dick and Slick. When Hiccups intimated that he would be paying for all the drink consumed the brothers-in-law consulted with each other and with their sister who was not averse to a dollop of gin on occasion and they agreed that a public house might be a better proposition. The five proceeded to Crutley's at nine o'clock and found a particularly pleasant and secluded corner of the bar for the forthcoming revelations.

According to Hiccups he set out on the morning of Christmas Eve for open country, the morning it was alleged he left Trallock railway station with the wigged woman seven years before. He brought with him an elderly greyhound bitch for company and also in the half-hope that they might rise a hare. He made his way to the slopes of Crabapple Hill and arrived there at noon. The day in question he reminded his brothers-in-law and their sister was a fine one with a wide blue sky and no sign of rain or storm, just a mild frost which saw their breaths, his and the dog's, rise in foggy plumes into the clear air where lark and linnet sang loud and high in praise of the weather. At this juncture Hiccups caught Fred Crutley's eye and signalled a refill.

While Fred did the needful the party spoke of the quality of local potatoes, coming down strongly in favour of Kerr's Pinks. They spoke of the spiralling price of beef and butter and of many other topics which affected their lives. They accepted the drinks gravely and without thanks and when they had the table to themselves they looked at their storyteller and waited for the resumption of his tale. Hiccups cleared his throat and licked his lips.

'Where was I?' he asked

'There was linnets singing,' his wife said.

'And larks,' the oldest of the brothers Mick reminded her gruffly.

'There were larks of course,' she agreed in the most conciliatory of tones.

'Correct on all counts,' Hiccups announced happily. 'I will never forget that day,' he went on, 'and not just because it was such a fine Christmas Eve but because of what befell me for I swear that there was magic involved. Didn't the hairs all of a sudden stand up on the top of my head the very same as darning needles and didn't they tingle with music in the weak breeze that was just beginning to rise. After a while the bristles softened a little and were like what you would see on a coarse brush. The wind freshened all the while and sang in the heather.'

According to Hiccups the elderly bitch in his company suddenly sat down and refused to budge. He coaxed her but she whined and pined and whimpered which was most unusual because up until that time she was a brave and a game bitch without fear. The bitch then began to howl in a louder tone and the whole area at the western slope of Crabapple Hill brightened as though highlighted by spot-lights. It was then that the bitch rose unsteadily to her feet and raised her front paws aloft in the direction of her master, indicating that he should quit the scene if he knew what was good for him. He endeavoured to mollify her a second time but all she did was drop her paws and turn her back on him after which she galloped off yelping, down Crab-apple Hill at breakneck speed. She was not seen again for a very long time.

By now Hiccups was becoming a trifle apprehensive and when he heard the faint music of fairy pipes in the breeze he was between two minds whether he would stay on the hill or make for low ground. Ever a curious chap and coming from a long line of courageous sportsmen, he proceeded to the very top of the hill where the sun shone as if it was the very height of June instead of Christmas Eve. Then for the first time he felt his waist-coat tensing and pulsating as though it was a living creature. There was silence now all over and then came a faint female voice, the most melodious and haunting ever heard by Hiccups.

'It wasn't the banshee,' he explained to his listeners, 'and it wasn't the sheegwee and it wasn't a *lorgadán* and it wasn't the man in the moon. I have heard in my time,' Hiccups continued, 'female singers from every part of the globe, sopranos, mezzo-sopranos and contraltos but none to match the bewitching tone that seemed to emerge from the very heart of the hill.' According to Hiccups he very nearly swooned and would have, he was sure, had it not been for the exceedingly fresh breeze, not a gale mark you, nor a wind but a refreshing breeze which filled him with extraordinary vitality. The strains of incredibly beautiful pipe music were now pouring forth from every crack, every cave, every hole and every cicatrice, every hollow and every dip on the vast hillside. All the while the fairy voice sang its haunting tunes. They tugged at the heartstrings until it seemed they must wilt and wither. They filled the mind with unworldly thoughts and the feet with a mad desire to leap and fly and dance. Even the heather at his feet seemed to be tugging at its roots such was its desire for escape into the skies where it would be free. Then, without warning of any kind, there was no sound save the fairy voice which now circled around his head and finally around the waist-coat fashioned from the skin of his favourite bitch of all time, the one and only Flash, Flash of the lightning turns and the speed of the fastest gale, Flash that had never been bested by a hare. Now the voice was calling a name.

At this exact stage when the tale was at its most gripping Hiccups caught the very watchful eye of Fred Crutley – Fred who was never still, who never rested, who never seemed to take a break, who like the great barman that he was always hovered and never once intruded.

'Same again Fred!' Hiccups informed him.

During this interlude there was no small talk. His listeners including his wife were caught up in the story. The four came originally from a household in the far-off hills where there was more thought of a man who could tell a ghost story than there was of any professional man or any craftsman or any musician. Their faces were hungry for more for there was also an innocence underneath all the toughness and churlishness and the lack of good manners and it was on this basic innocence that Hiccups was depending for his physical welfare. While the innocence rose above the lesser traits and dominated their out-look and thinking he was safe. When the drink was served Fred moved out of ear-shot and swept the bar with his wary eye lest some unfortunate be denied his basic right to intoxicating liquor.

'Now!' said Hiccups, 'where was I?'

'They was calling Flash,' his wife informed him.

'They were not!' Hiccups was emphatic.

'Well,' said his wife, 'if they was not they was very near to calling her.'

'Don't argue woman!' Dick the second of the brothers cautioned her.

'Don't argue woman!' echoed Slick the youngest of the brothers.

They lifted their glasses and swallowed heartily. Then they directed their baleful eyes at their storyteller.

'This voice which was circling all around,' Hiccups resumed, 'was calling the name of my late greyhound bitch, my beloved Flash whose waist-coat I wear around my heart. "Flash, Flash, Flash," the voice called and I could feel the waist-coat trying to free itself off my body. "Flash, Flash, Flash!" it called again as the waist-coat struggled in vain to free itself.'

Then according to Hiccups the fairy voice materialised into a white hare. The hare hopped to and fro and danced provocatively in front of Hiccups and his darling waist-coat which was now trying to rip its buttons so that it could take off after the white hare. Failing to do so, the waist-coat took off anyway with Hiccups wrapped inside and with no say over his movements. He was obliged to follow the hare and his inadequate legs were doomed to chase wherever the hare decided to run. It ran, first of all, slowly up the hill as though it was giving the waist-coat a chance to catch up. It dawdled insolently as the waist-coat with Hiccups wrapped firmly inside tried to make up ground. All to no avail. The white hare, known far and wide as the fairy hare, lived in the depths of the hill, far, far underground, far from the sounds and sights of mixed-up humans. The hare now sat on its hind legs and started to call the waist-coat as though she was calling a cat.

'Peesh, peesh. Peesh, peesh,' she called.

Now nothing so infuriates a greyhound as comparison with a cat and Flash the greyhound bitch was no different. The waist-coat with Hiccups inside bounded up the hill and quickly gained on its tormentor. The hare was lucky to escape as Hiccups' legs worked overtime. As he tried to slow down Hiccups made the fatal mistake of digging in his heels. He turned several somersaults before coming to a halt. When he recovered and drew breath he saw the white hare sitting on a clump of heather far below him. He took off at once unable to restrain the waist-coat which was now at the height of its form and bent on nothing else but the tearing of the hare to shreds. As Hiccups bore down upon the hare the creature suddenly turned and went uphill again. Hiccups followed with no say over his movements. The waist-coat strained with all its might and its jaded owner had no choice but to follow. The hare took off in another direction when Hiccups drew near. The creature ran abreast of the hill along a lengthy level course. Now the hunt was on in real earnest.

The waist-coat started to bark as it neared its quarry. Hiccups found his own jaws directing themselves downwards, snapping and chopping and slobbering. His teeth almost seized upon the backbone of his would-be victim but all he got was a mouthful of white hair. The hare changed its course once more and now decided upon a rapid downhill run, avoiding nothing on its path, neither briar, nor nettle nor furze nor stream nor hole so that Hiccups was covered with scratches and blood and mud and drowned to the skin when the hare decided to stop for a breather half-way down the hill.

The waist-coat decided otherwise so that Hiccups found himself heading for a deep, soggy bog-hole at the bottom of the hill. In vain did he try to brake but the impetus was unstoppable. He roared at the top of his voice. He screamed in terror and cried out for the help as the moon started to rise over the top of the hill. Nobody answered his call. There was pipe music in plenty still coming from all sides and there was a great wailing and a great pillalooing coming from everywhere at once. Hiccups braced himself as the bog-hole drew near. He undertook a mighty leap in the hope that he might clear the obstacle and land at the other side. He landed, alas, right in the middle of the bog-hole with an almighty splash which sent frogs and newts and beetles scurrying for cover. So too did nesting wild ducks take off into the moon-lit skies as did freshly awakened larks, while stoats and rabbits and rooting badgers fled for their very lives. When Hiccups sank he was convinced he would never surface again but he reckoned without the waist-coat.

At this stage Hiccups beckoned to Fred who was now drinking a pint of stout in the company of Dr Matt Coumer, a routine to which he was addicted every single night of the week.

'Same again Fred!' Hiccups called as he examined the faces of his listeners.

They were enraptured not having heard a decent ghost story since their childhood. For the first time since his return Hiccups noticed a smile on his wife's face. It was a smile of sheer delight and it was directed towards her errant husband. The smile said that she was still mindful of his amorous skills and would not be averse to an embrace or even a kiss or even a hug or even a squeeze of longer duration culminating in a major make-up. She was still a fine-looking woman and he often wondered why he had stayed away seven years. The answer came to him at once. Too many black eyes from the brothers as a result of her infernal complaining about him. If her smile was anything to go by she would desist from such reckless behaviour from now on.

When the drinks were delivered he found his hand being shaken by Matt Coumer who congratulated him on his safe return. There were others too who came forward and patted his back and spoke about the sad effect his absence had caused in all quarters.

'I hope you won't be as long away the next time you go,' said an innocent who had just entered. He retreated quickly due to the ferocity of the snarls and growls escaping from the porter-stained mouths of Mick, Dick and Slick. When all the well-wishers had retreated the storyteller and his listeners made themselves comfortable. They quaffed from their fresh drinks and gave the nod to Hiccups indicating that he was to proceed with his tale.

'Where was I?' he asked as he scratched his head.

'You was in the middle of getting drowned,' his wife reminded him.

'And were you drowned?' asked the three brothers in unison.

Hiccups did not answer at once. The wrinkles furrowed his forehead as he tried to accurately record the occasion.

'Ah yes!' he said to himself, happy that he remembered where he had left off.

'There I was at the bottom of forty fathoms of bog-water, not able to swim, not able to see an inch, my lungs bursting for air when the waist-coat somehow inflated itself and brought me to the surface of the bog-hole.'

Apparently when Hiccups surfaced he found his hands paddling towards shore. The night was now master of the scene and the full moon played its role in lighting the hill and bog-lands. The stars twinkled over-head and it was at this stage that Hiccups found himself shivering with the cold. What with his wet clothes and the frost all around he concluded that pneumonia was inevitable.

'We have no time for that now,' the waist-coat seemed to say as it tensed and shook the water off before restarting the chase. Off they went, all three, at a frenetic gallop, the hare ahead by a yard or two all the time and Hiccups in hot pursuit with beads of sweat slowly replacing the beads of water on his brow. He began to huff and to puff and to fall and rise and roll over and tumble like an acrobat so fierce was the determination of the waist-coat at whose mercy he found himself.

Now came a furrowed field which they traversed at phenomenal speed. Now came a river which they leaped as though it were a rill. Now came a gate, over which they jumped as though they were steeple-chasers. Now came a hollow, deceitful and deep. They descended like steeple-jacks and when they hit the ground they sped over a mushy swamp till they were fit to collapse with exhaustion.

Then of a sudden the white hare stopped without warning of any kind. The waist-coat stopped as well. She was enjoying the hunt too much to move in for the kill at that stage but the white hare seemed genuinely spun out. Feeble, heart-rending cries, almost human in their intensity, escaped her sagging mouth. Waist-coat and man looked on in amazement as the hare began to call a name. The place where the hare had stopped was rich in the most luxurious, multicoloured growth, heavily scented and of druggish potency so that waist-coat and wearer were very nearly overcome.

The name that the hare was calling was that of the queen of the local fairies Been-been of Coolnaleen. A long tongue of fire arose from the over-grown spot and a cave opening was revealed. The fire gave off no heat, merely a sleep-inducing warmth and an incense-like odour. Then bells began to tinkle all over the hill behind them, wraith-like under the moon's pale glow. It was an enchanting time if ever there was an enchanting time. As the white hare seemed to fall into a deep trance the waist-coat came to life and would have moved in for the kill had not a tall stately female of indeterminate age but of blinding beauty and disarming manner appeared near the very spot where the white hare lay. Weak as the creature was the whispered name of Been-been of Coolnaleen still carried from its lips.

The freshly arrived fairy, for fairy no doubt she was, placed a finger on her lips intimating to man and waist-coat that they must preserve the silence which now dominated the land. She withdrew from her garments a satchel woven from golden threads and the like of which Hiccups had never seen in all his travels. Even the waist-coat was stilled as the glow from the golden satchel cast its mellow light on the sleeping hare. She stroked the creature gently behind the ears until it began to purr like a kitten. Then she placed it in the satchel and cautioned Hiccups and his waist-coat.

'Nevermore will ye hunt on Crabapple Hill,' she told them. Her tones were far from being stern but there was a finality to them that made the hair stand on the head of Hiccups.

'The hare ye have chased,' she told them, 'is really a princess who was deprived of her human form by an evil witch who reigned on the hill until she was blasted by thunder and lightning and destroyed for evermore. The princess will regain her human form when the wild geese return to the flat lands of Coolnaleen and that should be very soon since they have been sighted close by for some time and it would not be any great wonder were they to appear next year or the year after.'

So saying she commanded a circle of fire to surround her as she disappeared into the hill-side. When she was gone there was no sign that the place had been visited by flame or by a queen from the other world or that a brave white hare had vexed a human and his hound that very day. As soon as she was gone the dawn, pale as death, came slowly to life and tinged the eastern sky with a multiplicity of delicate pastels. Hiccups fell to the ground and remembered not a single thing, and he gave his word on this, until he woke up in the middle of a fairy rath seven years later.

'Fred!' he called, 'be bringing us another round like a good man.'

Fred landed shortly thereafter and placed the drinks on the table. Then he withdrew with a trayful of empty glasses and the price of the drinks. They quaffed from their glasses and toasted the courage and endurance of the white hare.

'Now!' said Hiccups, 'where was I?'

'You was after waking up in the middle of a fairy rath,' his wife told him, 'although 'tis a mystery to me how you stayed alive for seven years.'

'I was in a trance woman,' he explained.

'What do you think boys?' Mick asked Dick and Slick.

'I'll say nothing against fairies,' said Dick, 'although this man has the face of a born liar and I'll say that our brother-in-law wouldn't know the truth from a rumble in his belly.'

'As for me,' said Mick, 'I'll say nothing until we drink more, for the way I judges is to judge when I'm sober and then when I'm drunk. I've already judged sober and it will take five or six more drinks before I'm drunk. I will say his tale was uncommon enough and worth hearing out but I'll have to wait till I'm soused.'

After that the drink flowed freely but never once did Mick or Dick or Slick test the material of their trousers' pockets so that the monies therein, if monies there were, were in no danger of being jingled or removed.

As soon as Mick had consumed the six extra pints he belched like a fog-horn and announced that he was about to pronounce judgement. 'I found the defendant guilty as hell for the first part of his story while I was sober and for the second part of his story while I was drunk I find him not guilty which is a blessing to our sister for she went very close to being a widow.'

'And the verdict?' his sister asked.

'The verdict is that he tells us a story once a week from this day forth in this very pub for the remainder of his natural life. Otherwise all charges against him are dismissed and he may go home with his wife to have and to hold from this day forth, wet or dry, windy or still.'

Hiccups' wife threw her arms around him and thanked her brother Mick and the good God too. When Dick and Slick started to *crónán* and grumble they were silenced by Mick.

'We must forgive,' he said, 'especially since the twelve days of Christmas are not yet over. A ram has returned to the fold and for this we should be truly thankful.'

Awlingal Princess of Cunnackeenamadra

'Do you know what they remind me of?' Sergeant Bill Ruttle addressed his companion, Garda Sam Ruane, in low tones. The sergeant was referring to the brothers Mick, Dick and Slick McCraw who sat at a nearby table with their sister Delia and her husband Hiccups O'Reilly.

'What do they remind you of boss?' Sam asked out of the side of his mouth so that nobody would hear save the party for whom the question was intended.

'They remind me,' replied Bill, 'of three starving mongrels waiting for their scraps.'

Sam laughed loud and long, not out of loyalty to his sergeant but because he found the sergeant's comments in nine cases out of ten well worth laughing at. As Sam's guffaws subsided Fred Crutley approached the brothers' table with a tray upon which sat four pints of stout for the menfolk and a gin for Hiccups' wife Delia.

As always the drink was paid for by Hiccups who was fulfilling the conditions laid down by the brothers on the very same night of the previous year which was the night before New Year's Eve. The conditions were that Hiccups would purchase all the intoxicating liquor that might be required to make the night a tolerable one and that he and his wife would meet with her three brothers once a week over their life-time for no other purpose than the telling of stories especially those relating to the time Hiccups spent on Crabapple Hill while under a so-called trance.

'To date,' Bill confided to his friend, 'he has told fifty-one stories and it is my understanding that his three brothers-in-law are not at all pleased with the contents. On that first occasion this night last year he told a colourful and compelling tale and was acquitted of infidelity, absence without leave and what have you. Since that time,' Bill continued in a sad vein, 'the quality of the stories has deteriorated and the brothers have come to the conclusion that his version of events on Crabapple Hill is nothing but a collection of outrageous lies. They will surely kill or maim him unless he pulls one out of the hat tonight.'

'Well he won't be killed or maimed while we're here,' Sam assured his superior.

'Agreed, but the problem my dear Sam is that we won't be

around all the time and our beloved superintendent is of the belief that placing a bodyguard on Hiccups would be a waste of time and money. He is convinced that the very most that can happen to Hiccups is maybe a fractured jaw or a few kicks on the rump or a black eye.'

'How does he know what will happen,' Sam asked, 'can he see into the future?'

'Exactly my friend.' Bill was serious now. 'As I see it those McCraw boys are capable of anything, maybe not outright murder but how many times have we seen bad beatings turn into killings! We'll play it by ear Sam and see what happens.'

'Maybe he'll come up with a masterpiece tonight,' Sam suggested.

'Don't bank on it my friend.' Bill's voice was filled with foreboding.

At Hiccups' table there was an air of unease. The brothers Mick, Dick and Slick were jumpy to say the least. Their brother-in-law Hiccups was desperate. If his performance on this occasion was a flop like all the others in recent weeks the jig was up and it could well be the end of him.

Hiccups was a wealthy man, having inherited several substantial fortunes from uncles and aunts in America. If anything happened to him the money would go to his wife which was as good as saying that it would go to her brothers. Hiccups' wife Delia sat apprehensively by her husband. In the intervening year they had grown closer. She had forgiven him the long absence although she did not believe a single word about his ghostly sojourn on Crabapple Hill. She had to concede however that he had been a perfect husband since his return. He had showered her with presents. She had her own account in the bank and her weekly allowance was more than adequate. He was a loving and caring husband but she suspected that he had also been loving and caring with many other women. When Delia first found out about his philandering a few years into their marriage she had carried her troubles to her late mother who consoled her at the time by informing her that all men were the same in this particular respect, that it was the way they were made and if they did not behave thus there was something seriously wrong with them.

The couple were not blessed with children but Hiccups had promised her faithfully that if he did not raise a flag before the end of the springtime he would consider adopting a child. This had pleased

Delia no end but it had not pleased Mick, Dick and Slick who felt that they had special claims to Hiccups' considerable wealth. Hiccups traded in horses and cattle when he was not at race meetings or football matches. Very often he took Delia with him but of late she had expressed a fancy for housekeeping and intimated gently to her sports-loving husband that she was readying the house for a very special visitor.

Hiccups, against his will, was obliged to employ his brothers-in-law in a part-time capacity as cattle drovers and horse breakers on his large farm but so long as they did not intrude too much on his private life he suffered in silence. Now they were becoming out of hand but he reckoned that the arrival of his adopted son would change all that. The brothers would know exactly where they stood when his son and heir took up residence.

Just before Hiccups was about to commence his fifty-second instalment of the Crabapple saga his friend and sometime confidant Mental Nossery the poet arrived at Crutley's with his wife Blossom. The pair nodded civilly at the occupants of Hiccups' table and sat on a stool within a few feet of their friend. With snorts, scowls and other hostile emissions the McCraw brothers thumped their table and let it be known that they would prefer if the newly arrived couple sat elsewhere. The Nosserys ignored the brothers and ordered a drink from a passing barmaid. The pub was soon filled to capacity. The spirit of Christmas was still abroad and there were many seasonal holiday-makers on the premises.

When Mick thrust his empty glass under his brother-in-law's nose Hiccups was on his feet instantly and managed to attract the attention of one of the two circulating barmaids on duty. When the drinks were served Hiccups cleared his throat and started in a tone audible only to the occupants of his own table and possibly in a garbled manner to a limited few who sat close by. 'The last creature I saw when I walked down the slopes of Crabapple Hill a year ago this Christmas was the queen of the fairies, the one and only Been-been of Coolnaleen. She barred my way and told me I was never to set foot on the hill again. I promised that I would do her bidding and to this day the heather up there, if it could talk, would tell you that Hiccups O'Reilly never sets foot there. She stood there for a while and passed her hand over me, not touching me but so near to my body that my flesh tingled and the hair stood on my head with each single rib extending itself and curling itself till it seemed that a thousand tiny antlers occupied my crown. It seemed to me too at the time that she was removing the spell that had been cast upon me at the beginning of my seven-year disappearance.'

When Hiccups paused to rejuvenate himself with a substantial swallow from his brimming pint the others did likewise. Hiccups took advantage of the lull to point a finger at Mick, the oldest and most superstitious of the three brothers.

'Beware,' said Hiccups in chilling tones, 'that you tread not on that part of the hill where I was waylaid by Been-been of Coolnaleen.'

'And why shouldn't I?' Mick asked as though he cared not in the least about fairies, be they queens or commoners.

'I'll tell you why you should care my good man,' said Hiccups in hollow tones. Hiccups went on to explain that Been-been, when she had fully removed the spell, placed her cold hands on his shoulders and looked with her flashing orbs into his own dazzled eyes. She then told him not to tell anything of what befell him unless his life depended on it.

'She told me that those who questioned my version would come to bad ends.'

When asked by a fearful Mick what sort of bad end Hiccups told him that according to Been-been the heads of doubters would be cut of by freak accidents such as falling on scythes or upright saws or electric wires. Mick McCraw dreaded threats from the other world more than any threat in this. He vowed to himself he would remain silent for the rest of the episode.

'Who else besides all those other wretches you told us about did you meet while you was up there?' The question came from Slick who was already yawning at the slowness and drabness of the Crabapple saga.

Hiccups paused for a moment to swallow from his glass and permitted himself one of the few smiles of the night. 'I'm downright glad you asked that question,' he responded, 'for on my third day under the spell and under the hill, as it turned out, who did I meet but a vet. He was surely three hundred years old with hair down to his boots back and front and it woven into a three-piece suit which fitted him like it was tailor-made. Wasn't he the very same veterinary surgeon who treated the cow that jumped over the moon when she landed back on terra firma. He was a fine decent man with a smell of whiskey off his breath all the time which he claimed was as good as any antiseptic when one was around animals.'

Hiccups swallowed from his glass and availed of the opportunity to see how his tale was going down. There seemed to be a positive revival of interest and he had been aware of several intakes of breath at the mention of the cow that jumped over the moon. The cow in question had intrigued the McCraw brothers for many a year. The remainder of the rhyme they felt was preposterous and should not be taken seriously.

For instance they had been training cattle dogs all their lives and they had never once seen a dog laugh not to mention little dogs or pups like the one that laughed in the rhyme. As for the dish running away with the spoon, well that was complete nonsense as was the idea of a cat playing the fiddle. The one part of the rhyme that made sense to the McCraws was the cow that jumped over the moon. The McCraws might not know their oats as their neighbours might say and they certainly would not know their catechism which their teachers would verify and they knew nothing at all about women as any self-respecting woman in the parish would contend without fear of contradiction. But there was one creature they knew better than any other authority in the entire region and that was the bovine quadruped known far and wide as the cow.

But what kind of cow was it that jumped over the moon! It could not have been a mature cow at the peak of her milking output. She would be carrying too much fat and too much milk. Neither could it have been an in-calf heifer. She would not have the strength to jump over a decent hedge if she was carrying a calf. They had always felt that the cow that jumped over the moon was a heifer and a young heifer at that. However they could not be certain, not until now at least. All their lives they had chased other people's heifers, contrary creatures capable of jumping Beecher's Brook if the notion caught them, capable of clearing dykes and drains, ditches and hedges, gates and stiles, shrubs and bushes no matter the height. The McCraws firmly believed that a young heifer was the most contrary creature in the known world. They had grown old before their time on the trail of lost heifers and now at last there was the hope of confirmation that it was a heifer and not a cow that jumped over the moon. They resolved to find out in their own circuitous fashion.

'What sort of chap was he?' Slick asked.

'What sort of chap was who?' Hiccups returned.

'The vet you fool.' Slick banged the base of his empty glass on the table.

'He was a nice chap if you liked chaps that picked their noses all the time and if you liked chaps that would fall asleep if you asked him more than two questions in a row.'

'Was he good on cows and heifers?' from Mick.

'He was.'

'Would he tell the age of a heifer just by looking at her?' Dick enquired.

'He would, he would,' Hiccups replied as he wondered what the brothers were driving at.

'Had he a wife and children?' Delia asked innocently.

'Shut up you fool,' her brother Mick shouted and gesticulated as though he would strike her.

'All right,' Slick was continuing, 'was she light in weight, the heifer?'

'Light enough,' Hiccups assured him.

'It wasn't a cow that jumped over the moon then was it but a heifer,' Slick suggested thrusting his thumbs inside his galluses as if he was a barrister.

'It was a five-year-old cow,' Hiccups informed him.

'You're a liar sir,' Slick roared. It was the first time that Slick had addressed Hiccups as sir. He hadn't yet shed his barrister image.

All the brothers were shouting together now but the essence of all the tumult was that it was not a cow that jumped over the moon.

'How,' they asked 'could a five-year-old cow jump over the moon?'

'There is no way a five-year-old could do it,' Mick was insisting, 'and you're insulting my intelligence by saying so whereas,' he went on, 'whereas, whereas ...' he repeated the word, never having used it before and very much liking the sound of it. For Mick finding a new word was like an embattled soldier finding a new and deadly weapon.

'Whereas,' Mick rose to his feet, 'it would be no trouble to a two-year-old heifer to jump over the moon especially if she was on the road to a fair in the early morning and especially if she had never seen anything but hedges and grass before her outing. I've seen heifers jump over low clouds when the mood caught them.'

'Me too,' said his brother Slick pounding the table, 'I seen a bony heifer one morning jump over myself and I'm six feet.'

Dick was next to enter the controversy. 'Anyone,' said Dick heatedly, 'what says it was a cow jumped over the moon should have his nose broken and maybe his jaw.'

'That settles that then,' Slick concluded. 'The court finds,' he announced as he placed an ashtray on his head, 'that it was no cow jumped over the moon but a heifer and he's a dead man that says otherwise.'

Hiccups felt that if he had known what his brothers-in-law were driving at he would have said that it was a heifer that jumped over the moon and not a cow. Under the glare of the inquisition however he had lost his composure.

'Now that I come to think of it,' put in a pale-faced Hiccups, 'I think the veterinary surgeon said that it was a heifer jumped over the moon and not a cow.'

'Too late to back-track.' Slick placed a beefy hand around the slender neck of his brother-in-law and held him like a vice.

'We've heard what you said. You said it was a five-year-old cow, not two, three or four but five. A cow is what you said you rotten liar what wouldn't know the word of truth from a sneeze.'

Mick was next to cast judgement. 'You're a registered liar, a department liar, a perverted liar and if you lied in one thing then you lied in all things. You never spent seven years in a trance you sacrilegious belch. You spent seven years hooring and touring in England and France and maybe America and Australia too. You soon got tired of that peroxide blonde you took with you and you took up with others and left our poor sister in the lurch.'

'Well we're happy now,' Delia trembled as she said her piece.

'Let him go,' Mick instructed his brother Slick. 'My glass is empty and there's no way he can call for a drink while you have a hold of him like that.'

While the drinks were being delivered Sam Ruane addressed his sergeant in a whisper: 'I don't like it boss,' he said.

'Neither do I Sam,' said Bill, 'but I wouldn't worry too much. We'll bide our time and play the tune by ear when the last dance is called.'

'These birds have changed,' Mental Nossery whispered into his beautiful wife's ear after he had first nibbled its lobe. 'Ever since word went out that Hiccups and Delia were thinking of adopting a baby,' Mental continued, 'the brothers McCraw have assumed a different air of menace. If a new baby comes in, it means that they go out, and sooner or later Hiccups' life could be in danger.'

Blossom seized her husband's hand, her poet's hand. 'You mean that they might kill him!' she asked tremulously.

Mental whispered into his beloved's ear a second time but left the lobe alone. It was not an occasion for levity and Mental with his poet's insight sensed that there were dark clouds on the horizon.

'I'll tell you this and no more,' he told her, 'wherever there is disputed land you can't rule out a killing.'

'What can we do?' she asked fearfully.

'Worry not my pet, my peach,' Mental told her after the fashion of poets through the ages. 'Hiccups is not without friends as you shall see. He who rides the white steed of chivalry will carry the day and the sun will shine on a better world.'

'You're so brave my warrior poet,' Blossom whispered.

Blossom Nossery, formerly the lovely Blossom O'Moone, liked Hiccups. He never made passes, having too much regard for her husband Mental. Once he had given her his umbrella in a downpour and told her it was an honour. He had been corner forward on the cherished Ballybo team which won two titles in a row and most important of all he was godfather to her oldest son and his wife Delia was godmother. She watched him now as he looked with a mixture of terror and hope at her bardic warrior, her writer of epic poems, her shield and her champion, her sweetheart and her lover.

After Fred Crutley had deposited the fifth round of drinks on the table he was asked by Hiccups for the correct time.

'There is plenty of time my friend,' Fred informed him.

'Are you going some place?' Slick asked with thinly veiled sarcasm.

Before Hiccups could answer Mick posed a second question: 'What are you hatching Hiccups? It isn't eggs and that's for sure and you are hatching for I seen that look on a goose many a time.'

'Maybe,' Dick broke out into a rare laugh, 'he's catching a train and don't want to be late!'

'Another blonde maybe!' Slick guffawed.

Hiccups was sorry for his wife. The embarrassment showed clearly on her face. He wished he could place his arms around her and assure her that he would never again leave her but the brothers-in-law were demanding another round of drinks.

Most of the patrons had already left the bar. With New Year parties in the offing they wanted to be fresh for the festivities. One by one they drifted out into the night. A sickle moon hung limply overhead and a magnificent array of stars twinkled in the heavens.

Normally Fred would approach Hiccups' table on the stroke of midnight and remind the occupants that they could no longer stay. Tonight it was different. When Slick asked if there was any hope of another round of drinks Fred told him that there was every hope. The only reason that Slick had asked for drinks in the first place was because he thought he would be refused. He instructed Hiccups to pay up or else.

Those who remained on in the bar were strangely silent. Not even a whisper was to be heard. Mental and Blossom still remained as did Bill Ruttle and Sam Ruane; so too did the Badger Loran and his wife Nonie. Maimie Crutley had earlier joined her friends Badger and Nonie at a table near the main doorway. A few regulars sat discreetly out of range of the main table which was occupied by Hiccups and his tormentors. The only absentee of note was Dr Matt Coumer. Earlier in the evening he had been seen driving out of town at a pace far faster than usual.

'It couldn't have been a patient,' the observer said, 'because Matt would never drive like that on his way to see a patient. It must have been something really important.'

All of a sudden the lights were dimmed in the bar and the sound of eerie music drifted downwards from somewhere in the ceiling. It was undoubtedly the soundtrack from a horror movie.

'What's it from Sam?' Bill asked his colleague.

'It's from *Dracula's Daughter Meets the Werewolf's Son*,' Sam answered without a moment's hesitation.

'All knowledge is useful,' Bill pointed out as he lifted his glass and concentrated his vision on the main doorway.

Just then the bar lights were extinguished altogether and the pub's only spotlight shone on the doorway which seemed to hold so much interest for the sergeant. The music ceased and a roll of drums sharpened the interest of everybody present, most notably the three McCraw brothers. Cowards at heart they dreaded the darkness even when surrounded by other humans.

The roll of the drums intensified and there was the sound of a protracted scream from the doorway. The pub cat, a fat and less than frisky tabby, shrieked her way out of doors and was not seen for days. Silence again prevailed.

Nervously the McCraw brothers raised their glasses but lowered them untouched when a low and ghastly moan came from the direction of the doorway. Enter a dark stranger. He wore a black beard and moustache and was garbed like an Elizabethan gentleman. Slung over his shoulder was a large satchel woven from golden threads. When he laid it on the floor one couple could plainly hear the mewing and the bleating and the aforementioned moans coming from within.

Delia slipped silently from her chair on to the floor in a dead faint. Her exit from consciousness went unnoticed so absorbed was every watcher by the unbelievable goings-on at the doorway.

The table where the McCraw brothers sat began to shake as the trembling wretches transmitted their terror to the lifeless wooden surface where the glasses now tinkled and jumped and rolled over as though electrified. The brothers could have exited in a flash but so overcome were they by terror that their legs refused to move. On the other hand Hiccups was elated and quite carried away by recent events.

Hot on the heels of the Elizabethan satchel-carrier came a tall, stately if somewhat gaunt woman dressed completely in black with a ruff round her neck and a silver comb thrust deep into the bun of her tightly drawn hair.

'Is she ...' Mick asked in terror, his voice shaking, 'is she Been-been from Coolnaleen the queen of the Crabapple Hill fairies?'

'None other!' came the proud response from Hiccups.

'And is the creature in the satchel,' Mick asked, 'the same hare yourself and the waist-coat coursed that first time you climbed Crabapple Hill?'

'She is one and the same hare!'

Again there was pride in Hiccups' voice.

'And, and, and,' Slick asked brokenly, 'will she be changed tonight into a princess.'

'Yes. Yes,' Hiccups answered impatiently.

'Hear ye! O hear ye!' came the awesome and ponderous voice of the Elizabethan satchel-carrier. 'Behold the transformed white hare of Crabapple Hill.'

The words had no sooner left his lips than the queen of the Crabapple fairies knelt on one knee and opened the golden satchel. Extending her hands she commanded the creature in the satchel to come forth. Forth she came, a dazzling and beautifully shaped young lady with a glittering diamond tiara on her brow and golden slippers on her shapely feet.

'Behold!' said the Elizabethan satchel-carrier, 'the Princess Awlingal, rightful sovereign of Cunnackeenamadra and all parts west.'

The McCraws could not contain their shuddering and agitation. When Mick spoke his speech was slurred and broken.

Meanwhile Hiccups had noticed his wife's plight and placed her on a chair beside his own. He poured brandy into her mouth and she regained consciousness. They looked into each other's eyes and wondrous smiles appeared on their faces.

'What in God's name are you blabbering about man?' Hiccups with a newly discovered confidence asked his distraught brother-in-law.

Mick McCraw asked if the woman at the doorway was the same Been-been from Coolnaleen he had met on Crabapple Hill and if the transformed hare was really Awlingal the sovereign Princess of Cunnackeenamadra and all parts west.

'That's who she is for sure,' Hiccups answered still growing in confidence from watching the abject terror of his brothers-in-law.

'There is one sure way to find out,' Slick put in as he found his coherency returning to him.

'And what way would that be?' asked Dick who had been frothing at the mouth in fear a few short moments before.

'You remember,' Slick reminded his brothers, 'how Hiccups here told us he bit the back of the white hare as they coursed over Crabapple Hill and how he brought a clump of hair away with him. Now if that be so there surely has to be a mark on the back of the princess.'

As though their words had carried to all within the room the spotlight was turned off and the full bar lights turned on. Led by the Elizabethan satchel-carrier the queen of all the Crabapple Hill fairies and the Princess of Cunnackeenamadra and all parts west marched towards the table of the McCraws, the stout heels of their knee-length leather boots striking the timber floor in unison and bringing a sense of majesty to the occasion. The Elizabethan satchel-carrier raised a gloved hand imperiously and spoke in ringing tones: 'Hear ye! Oh hear ye!' He cast his stern countenance in the direction of Slick.

'Rise knaves!' he commanded at which the three brothers struggled terror-stricken to their feet and doffed their filthy caps in the direction of the royal pair.

'Now speak lest I draw my blade and disembowel the three of ye,' the Elizabethan satchel-carrier commanded. The cowardly trio at once began to blame each other and denied having any interest in seeking the hidden evidence which would prove forever that the Princess of Cunnackeenamadra was indeed the rightful sovereign of the territories attributed to her. Suddenly there was a flash of steel as the satchel-carrier withdrew his sword from his scabbard. He pointed the blade at the Adam's apple of Slick and informed him that he would cut his head off if he did not speak.

'All I want to know sir,' said the cringing Slick, 'is whether or not there is a mark on the back of this girl, a mark made by human teeth to be exact?'

'On thy knees thou most disrespectful of wretches where my hungry blade may relieve thee of thy head.'

'Nay, nay!' said the princess in voice most melodious and with that she raised her dress and revealed a scantily clad but shapely posterior without blemish of any kind. A gasp escaped the audience. It was not occasioned by the undeniable shapeliness of the royal rump but rather by the fact that there was a dark red disfiguration on the small of the back just over the the right cheek of Princess Awlingal's rear.

'What say you now sir?' asked the Elizabethan.

'I say was it caused by the teeth of a human?' Slick was surprised at his own audacity.

'If I may!' Sergeant Ruttle rose to his feet and handed his cap to Sam.

'My Lord!' he addressed himself to the Elizabethan who graciously acknowledged his presence with an economical but respectful curtsy.

'I am obliged to say at the outset,' Bill opened, 'that the mark on this most attractive area was not caused by human teeth, by teeth yes but not by teeth that grow in the mouth of a human. Rather was the mark made by these.' He extended his hand towards Hiccups who extracted his dentures from his mouth and handed them to the sergeant. Bill ordered all the interested parties to gather round the Princess of Cunnackeenamadra. He held Hiccups' false teeth aloft and slowly lowering them placed them over the disfiguration at the top of the right buttock.

'Are they a fit?' Slick asked.

'They are,' said the sergeant triumphantly, 'a precise fit and that concludes the evidence My Lord.'

Bill and the Elizabethan exchanged the most civil of nods.

When it dawned fully on the McCraw brothers that their brother-in-law had proven connections with the underworld they pushed their chairs back from the table in order to put as much distance between themselves and the *lorgadán* as possible. They eyed their sister with suspicion and for the first time began to perceive out of their fear and ignorance underworld subtleties and fairy-like fragilities transforming her placid features. Slowly, noiselessly, stealthily they rose from their seats and stood momentarily transfixed. Then at a signal from the oldest brother Mick they ran from the bar, overturning chairs, tables and stools and beseeching the great God of their fathers to save them.

In Crutleys there was unconfined delight. The participants in the charade turned out to be members of the Trallock Amateur Drama Group with the following cast in order of appearance:

Elizabethan Satchel-carrier	Matt Coumer
Been-been Coolnaleen	Roseanna Ruane
Princess Awlingal	Bridget Ruane
Counsel	Bill Ruttle
Producer	Maggie Coumer
Lighting	Canon Coodle
Stage Manager	Dotie Tupper
Music	Tom Mackson
Costumes	Mickey Mokely
	Dotie Tupper
Front of House	Fred Crutley
Concept	Mental Nossery

In the years ahead the brothers gave Hiccups and Delia a wide berth and covered their faces with their hands whenever they met lest they make contact with the eyes of either and be consigned forever to supernatural botheration.

When the two adopted sons of Hiccups and Delia reached boyhood a reconciliation was effected and the McCraw brothers devoted their lives to their nephews' upbringing.

The Sacred Calf

If you were suddenly to leap from behind a furze bush, seize my throat in both hands and threaten me with strangulation if I didn't tell you the truth, I could hardly tell a lie could I!

If you were to ask me as your grip tightened which was the most memorable Christmas in the history of our parish I would say without hesitation that it was the Christmas of the sacred calf. You will no doubt have heard and read of sacred cows but I'll lay a fat goose to a starving sparrow that it's the first time you've come across a sacred calf; golden calves yes, castrated calves yes, fatted calves yes, but sacred calves no!

The calf in question was born on St Patrick's Day, a spindly, knock-kneed chap the image of his grandfather and this is where the catch comes in. The father, if you get my drift, was suspect or if you like he was rejected for procreational purposes by an inspector from the Department of Agriculture on the grounds that his shoulders were exaggerated and he was also, alas, possessed of a somewhat contracted rump, features indeed which were often highly prized in his human counterparts by certain females, at least in this parish or so it is claimed by those who should know. Although the sacred calf himself suffered from no such so-called defects he might nevertheless be branded as undesirable for breeding purposes.

The sacred calf's owner, one Jackeen Coyne, was undecided about the creature's future. 'I could,' he told his wife, 'deprive him of his population stick and turn him into a prime bullock in the course of time or I could hold on to him and let him take his chances with the inspectors from the department.'

'You could sell him in a few weeks for veal or you could hold on to him until Christmas when he'd be just right for baby beef. Baby beef is all the go now,' his wife reminded him, 'but by that time he might be shaping towards a passable bull so you wouldn't have anything to lose.'

Jackeen, like most of the farmers in the district, always paid heed to what his wife suggested. Wives had no vested interests like butchers or calf-jobbers. They listened to the agricultural programmes on the radio and had a fair idea of what was going on. So it was that Jackeen opted for baby beef.

It had all begun the previous summer when a scrub bull or a Walkeen Aisy as he would be known locally entered the scene or rather broke into the well-fenced acres of Jackeen. The owner of the marauding scrub was a happy-go-lucky sort, one Mickey Martin, who rarely mended his fences and might never have done so had not Jackeen threatened him with the law on numerous occasions. It was left to Jackeen to secure his heifers by constant fence-mending and extreme vigilance by himself and his wife all day and all night from early springtime onwards. Jackeen's pure-bred Friesian heifers, eight in number, were separated from the remainder of the mixed herd for breeding purposes and were truly the apples of their proprietor's eye. He walked among them morning and evening after the herd had been milked. He noted their sprightliness and playfulness and allowed that they were a prime lot well worth the time invested in them.

When the scrub bull could no longer contain himself he became increasingly agitated. Normally this agitation might not appear until the late autumn when he would have expended all his energies. This particular form of agitation, however, was different. It was, if you'll forgive the pun, born out of mounting frustration. He was a young bull and had already accounted for all of his master's cows and heifers.

Jackeen redoubled his labours at the fences and would look apprehensively through the well-stitched thorn hedge at the restless fornicator who rarely took his eyes off the forbidden fruit in the next field. Jackeen decided to change his charges to more distant pastures at the earliest opportunity. On the other hand Mickey Martin cared not a whit for the state of his fences or the sexual ardour of his scrub. When Jackeen spotted him one evening on his way to town he shouted after him that he should move the scrub to another field.

'You get your Friesians to stop teasing him,' Mickey called back before disappearing through a gap in another pasture. Meanwhile Jackeen fretted and fumed as he awaited the arrival of the department inseminator, an industrious young man already working round the clock in order to fulfil his many commissions. Jackeen's nights were sleepless. He would rise several times from his bed as would his wife. From their upstairs window their eyes swept the moon-lit fields but the bull was nowhere to be seen. Occasionally they would hear him bellow and there came a time when Jackeen would hear bellowing in his imagination until black rings began to appear under his eyes.

So jaded had he and his wife become from their sapping vigils that they went straight to bed after the evening milking and rarely visited the cavorting Friesians who taunted their mesmerised admirer with swishing tails and fancy steps. Then of a sudden when he could endure the anguish no longer the scrub found a gap in the hedge. It was only a small gap but by the time he had forced his way through it was considerably larger, certainly large enough for the pure-bred Friesians, no longer mindful of their vaunted pedigrees, to pay return visits to the paddock of their less exalted pursuer. In record time Mickey's tireless impregnator accommodated each and every one of the eight heifers. Amazingly he showed no loss of taspy after his endeavours but he did, according to a boastful Mickey, have a long and sound sleep for himself, in case he might be called into action again.

In the spring of the following year the cows calved. One of the five bull calves presented to the world by the pedigreed Friesians stood out above the others. Although spindly and knock-kneed at birth as we have said he assumed his true pose and carriage after a few days.

Eventually Christmas began to advertise its proximity. The streets of the nearby town took on a carnival atmosphere and indulgent parents made haste to book their personal Santa Clauses in advance of the great feast day. There was an air of excitement abroad and a heart-warming type of burgeoning goodwill which only Christmas can generate. Then came the great Christmas cattle fair, an annual event which drew cattle of all ages and breeds from far and wide. The great square in the nearby town was the traditional venue and although the square boasted two churches, one Catholic and the other Protestant, it was conceded by reverent and irreverent alike that no other place had the capacity to accommodate the large numbers of livestock and their owners.

Jackeen and his wife Maryanne were plain to be seen. Maryanne's presence was imperative if the eight weanlings they offered for sale were to be prevented from straying. Jackeen and Maryanne carried light hazel sticks more for intimidation than physical punishment. Brandishing was sufficient, for the most part, although from time to time the more adventurous had to be rounded up and returned to the preserved area outside the main entrance to the Catholic church. It was here that all the generations of Coynes as far back as anybody could remember were known to have traditional standing rights for their stock. With Christmas only a week away, and money scarce or so the farmers maintained, the Coynes were anxious to dispose of their weanlings before the fair ended and darkness fell. Their Christmas shopping would follow.

They had arrived at their small domain outside the church at seven o'clock and, as the early-morning hours lightened, the jobbers were afforded better conditions to inspect what was on offer. There had been several tentative approaches from first light. None was satisfactory although there was a farmland saying about an owner being better advised to accept the morning price. Jackeen, however, suspected that the adage was originally invented by the jobbers. It would be true to say that farmers always suspected jobbers in the first place and would bide their time until the market settled and the vendors had consulted each other about prices.

Maryanne was already well versed in such matters having been tuned in to the agricultural programmes on radio and television for weeks before. It was she who put an asking price on the eight weanlings consisting of five bull calves and three heifers. As expected the buyers wanted only the special bull calf who was a far more attractive specimen of his species than his brothers or sisters.

'Pity they hadn't the pure drop in them,' Jackeen declared angrily to his wife on more than one occasion when he went to count them. 'I promise you I wouldn't be selling but with their father a scrub what can I do?'

'We'll do fine,' Maryanne assured him. 'They're good-looking weanlings all. They'll make my price. You'll see now.'

Sure enough as the morning hastened towards noon the offers began to improve until Maryanne's reserve was nearly reached. The square, by this time, was chock-a-block with cattle young and old. Calves bawled for their milk and as the shouting of jobbers and cattle-tenders intermingled with the bawling and bellowing of hungry cattle there was a situation akin to pandemonium in the great square. Then and only then did Maryanne notice the absence of Blueboy, the pet name with which they had christened the cherished bull calf. They searched high and low but there was no trace of their pride and joy. Jackeen later admitted that he had been reluctant to offer him for sale in the first place. Opinions among local experts had been divided as to whether he would pass the bull test when his time came. Some voted nay and some voted yea. Between the jigs and the reels Jackeen decided to sell. He would reseed the Friesian heifers the following spring and he would make sure that the inseminator got to them before Mickey's scrub.

In desperation Jackeen engaged some local youngsters to search for the calf. All they brought back were conflicting reports. One had seen the weanling crossing the river and another had spotted him disappearing into a lane-way. When the lane-way was searched there was no trace of the missing calf.

It was then that Maryanne decided to invoke the aid of St Francis of Assisi. Rosary beads in hand she entered the adjacent church where she quickly located a plaster statue of the Franciscan founder and, head bent in supplication, she prayed for the recovery of the missing weanling. Normally she would spend an hour and sometimes longer on her knees but her husband would be waiting. As she was about to leave the church she was surprised to see a large crowd gathered in the vicinity of the crib. Some were tittering and smiling. Others wore serious expressions. Despite her hurry she allowed her natural curiosity to get the better of her. She forced her way through the gathering and wondered what the attraction might be. Another moving statue perhaps or maybe one of the plaster occupants of the crib was bleeding! She knelt at the crib railing and closed her eyes the better to concentrate on her prayers and also to convey the impression to the watchers all around that she had no interest in anything bar her own supplications.

After the third Hail Mary she opened her eyes and could scarcely believe what she saw before her. There lay Blueboy with a contented look on his face, his mouth stuffed with high-grade straw. He had taken up his position between the life-sized cow and donkey where he knew he would be safe.

Earlier his nostrils had been assailed by the odour of freshly disturbed straw. Compared to the graveolence all around him this was truly a heaven-sent fragrance which had to be investigated. He made his way into the church, empty save for the presence of a few elderly people who would hardly have noticed had a lion appeared in front of the main altar. Blueboy was reassured by the presence of the other animals and had no trouble in making his way into the crib where he attempted to satisfy his hunger. The first person to notice something out of the ordinary was an old man, a regular visitor to the crib from the moment the parish clerk had erected and populated it.

'I declare to God,' he said with a smile on his wrinkled face, 'if it isn't a sacred calf.' His words carried to the ears of two old ladies nearby who had waited all their lives for some manifestation of recognition from the spiritual world.

'A sacred calf.' They echoed the words with awe and reverence and when Maryanne blinked her eyes in disbelief as the old ladies whispered into her ear from either side of her she nodded good-humouredly. She hurried into the square to tell her husband the good news. He threw his arms around her in delight and lifted her high in the air. Did I say earlier on that they were a young couple and very much in love! Maybe not. I should have and I'm sorry I didn't but it's out now and we'll all be the better for it.

Jackeen recovered his calf and brought him back into the fold.

'I say to you,' he said to his wife with a twinkle in his eye, 'that a calf which is lost and then found must be kept.'

So it was that Jackeen disposed of the remaining calves at a fair price and so too did he hand over the money to his wife for she would surely make better use of it than he. That night as they lay in bed they spoke of the day's events and recalled the recovery of the sacred calf with much laughter.

'We will never part with him,' Jackeen promised Maryanne, 'for as sure as that's a wind in the curtains it was a message from above we received this day.'

'St Francis had a hand in it,' Maryanne reminded him. 'We'll say a prayer to him now in thanksgiving.'

'He'll make a powerful bull,' Jackeen whispered when the prayer was finished.

Jackeen's prophesy came true. Two years later the sacred calf was presented for inspection at Abbeyfeale cattle fair. The inspector from the Department of Agriculture declared that in all his days he had never come across a more promising bull.

'His grandfather was a latchiko,' the inspector recalled, meaning that the parent in question was sometimes remiss in his obligations towards consenting heifers and often turned his back on what more industrious bulls might regard as golden opportunities.

'His father now was a different kettle of fish,' the inspector went on, 'and could not be kept away from members of the bovine species regardless of age. Luckily for the future of the cow population of this country the bull I have just passed is the image of his father in this respect.'

Christmas came with some gentle flurries of snow and if the nights were cold itself Maryanne was able to announce to her doting husband that the cow population wasn't the only outfit that could expect an increase in the following year. On hearing the news Jackeen leaped from his bed and with a series of delighted whoops danced around the room until he was totally exhausted. In the years ahead the rescued bull would account for countless cows and heifers and like all great bulls he treated young and old with equal tenderness and affection so that he had many calls upon his extravagant nature. I might well have called this tale 'The Sacred Bull' but because of the season that's in it I think we should call it 'The Sacred Calf'.

Two Gentlemen of the Law

Forty years ago our public house was raided by two elderly members of the garda síochána, two gentlemen if ever there were gentlemen as you shall see if you proceed to the finish. For the benefit of those in other lands a member of the garda síochána is simply a member of the police force.

The exact time was the night before Christmas Eve and a stormy night it was with a stiff sleet-laden easterly gale confining many of the town's drinking fraternity to their homes. Not so the intrepid folk of the town's hinterland. They braved the elements and drank their fill. They would not drink again until St Stephen's night or the night of the wren as they called it.

The only creatures to be seen out of doors were tomcats for, as everybody knows, your common tomcat cannot survive without regular sexual excursions into the night. I have lost count of the times I have encountered exhausted tomcats returning to their bases even on the sacred occasion of Christmas night. A creature with nine lives has surely nine sexual drives or so people say.

There were also two members of the garda abroad or so it was rumoured but it was believed that they were not engaged in public house duties. This could be deduced, by experienced observers, from their gait and mien and general attitude. They strolled round the streets rather than policed them so the proprietors of public houses could not be blamed if they presumed they were in for an easy ride on the occasion.

In our own premises there were a half-score of hardened public house denizens whose love of liquor far exceeded their fear of storms. It wasn't that they drank excessively. Rather did they lower a few pints to cure what ailed them and help them get over the sleeplessness which affects so may souls on stormy nights. They were called regulars and at that time every public house in the town had its quota. Uncharitable members of the community would accuse them of being drunkards and ne'er-do-wells but the more charitable would say that they were merely anxious for drink.

That time there were roughly seventy public houses in the town. Now there are only forty. You could say that time caught up with the vanished thirty. Let us proceed, however, with our tale of Christmas benignity and let it serve as a reminder that kindnesses are remembered when insults are forgotten – that charity and chivalry are cherished when boors and begrudgers are benighted.

In those days I had a man working for me on a part-time basis. When he finished milking his employer's cows he came to me to tap barrels, to box bottles and to keep an eye on the back door among other things. You might say that keeping an eye on the back door was his chief duty. It was an onerous chore calling for vast experience in the ways of the world. When the prescribed number of knocks were knuckled on the back door he would admit the knocker or knockers. The door was a stout one and no one could look out unless one knelt or lay down to look underneath. Neither could anybody see in and no self-respecting policeman would stoop to peep when, by merely announcing his presence, admission would be automatic by virtue of the authority invested in him by the state.

But, the dear reader will ask, suppose a guard knuckled the secret knock after hours what would be our man's reaction? There would be no reaction for the good reason that no self-respecting member of the garda síochána would stoop to such a ruse. All guards liked to knock imperiously on the door and intone the time-honoured caution: 'Guards on public-house duty!'

How then would my doorman respond to this official knock? My man, whose name was Jimmy Jay, would first kneel and then rest his head sideways on the ground where he could look out under the door to make sure that it wasn't a local prankster assuming the role of guardian of the peace. If the knocker wore grey shoes or brown shoes, suede shoes or white shoes or wellingtons he was admitted by Jimmy Jay. Members of the garda síochána wore only black shoes or black boots while on duty. There was another, equally important, guideline in the identification process – guards on duty had no folds on their trousers. All punters, therefore, with folds on their trousers were seen to be above suspicion and were granted immediate entry. This, let me state at this important juncture, is how our story came about. Let me put it another way. If there were no folds no story would unfold and we would be without material for our yuletide tale.

I don't have to tell my readers that this is a true story. The men who were present in the public house that night will bear witness to its veracity.

Now let us adjourn to the outside world, to wit the windy streets of my native town where our limbs of the law were sauntering along the main streets and the little streets, the big square and the small square and the limited suburbs where nothing ever happened. Seemingly casual and somewhat lackadaisical on their patrol it has to be said that nothing could be further from the truth for the good reason that our pair of custodians missed little. Not a blind was drawn or raised nor a solitary curtain opened without their committing it to memory. The number of strangers were counted, their mannerisms and physical features noted with care and every shadow was pierced by the experienced eyes of our alert duo.

The names of our patrollers were Mike and Jerry. The pair rarely troubled the town's public houses except when called upon to do so by the proprietors of the public houses in question when the latter might become apprehensive in the face of blackguardism. Others who sometimes got in touch with the guards were mothers of large families whose husbands were recklessly squandering their wages on liquor and allowing their children to starve. Other informants might be the occasional publican who would be acting out of jealousy or just plain, ordinary malice. In such instances the members of the force had no option but to investigate and issue summonses where necessary. Rarely did they prosecute the wretch who so profligately spent his wages. Instead they quite rightly prosecuted the publican and administered several well-aimed kicks to the posteriors of the aforementioned wretches. These kicks worked wonders but today it is against the law.

Anyway our jolly policemen, and jolly they were unless provoked, encountered a drunken wretch on the street. He claimed that he had been refused drink here on these very premises because of his politics. The truth is that he was refused drink because he was abusing his wife and family when under the influence. The limbs of the law, however, had no choice but to investigate the goings-on behind our closed doors. They would do so without fear or favour. They had spent the greater part of the day papering and painting some rooms in Mike's house. Mike was expecting American visitors in the spring, cousins of his wife, and who better to help him than his colleague and long-term friend.

The pair proceeded to our back door where Jimmy Jay sat in an out-house awaiting knockers. Jimmy was slightly deaf. He heard the guard's knock all right but he didn't hear them announce themselves. He went through the customary motions and knelt down before looking underneath the door from the accustomed angle. Jimmy looked for the usual tell-tale signs, the chief of these being trousers without folds. Seeing trousers with folds he opened the door and admitted the waiting guards who stepped briskly into the back-yard with a view to entering the back kitchen where our customers were happily seated, engaged in soft conversation as they discussed the events of the previous days, national and local. Tones were hushed and no voice carried. In fact, it could be said that the exterior of a busy public house after hours when guards are about is quieter than a grave-yard at night.

'What's the meaning of this?' Jimmy asked as he drew himself to his full height of five feet, two inches.

The two civic guards were greatly taken aback and quite rightly, believing that it was they who should have been posing such a question and not Jimmy Jay.

'Explain yourself,' said Mike.

'Yes,' said Jerry, 'explain yourself.'

After they had spoken they pushed their caps back on their foreheads and spread their large feet as they awaited an explanation.

'Bad form,' said Jimmy, with all the righteousness he could muster.

'Dang it man,' said Jerry, 'we're only doing our job.'

'Doing your job,' said Jimmy truculently, 'with no trousers on!'

The pair looked downwards to reassure themselves that they had trousers on. They looked upwards into a much-improved starry sky, a Christmas sky, before looking downwards again to confirm that their trousers were indeed on. Whiskey can play strange pranks even on policemen so they felt their trousers to be sure.

'We have trousers on,' they said in unison.

'Yes,' said Jimmy Jay, 'but not guards' trousers and that's not very sporting.'

'Not very sporting!' the minions of the law echoed incredulously.

'When I looked out under the door,' Jimmy Jay informed them, 'I did not see trousers without folds so I admitted you in good faith, thinking you were ordinary folk like myself but what do I find, only two guards!'

Mike and Jerry explained that they had been engaged in some interior decorating all day and forgot to change into their on-duty trousers. They were most contrite and assured Jimmy that they would never involve themselves in such duplicity.

Did I say earlier that they had drunk the best part of a bottle of whiskey between them during their extra-curricular activities? The bottle had been a gift from Mike's wife. She stayed in the house until the painting and the wall-papering were completed, measuring out drops of the precious whiskey every time they seemed to flag or lose concentration.

'We're truly sorry Jimmy,' said Mike, 'because this not our style at all.'

'Yes,' said Jerry, 'truly sorry. It was bad form on our part and it is not our style at all as Mike says.'

'I'm glad to hear you say that,' said Jimmy Jay, 'it restores my faith in that wonderful body of men known as the garda síochána but I have to say that if tonight's visit was intentional then it was unsporting.'

'It was most unsporting,' said Mike who nudged Jerry with an elbow and was nudged back in return.

'Unsporting it was without doubt,' Jerry agreed, 'but we are now prepared to withdraw and let the matter rest.'

So grateful was Jimmy Jay that he invited the pair to have a pint. He was permitted such extravagances in the rarest of circumstances only. The guards declined on the grounds that they were a danger to shipping already.

'I'll tell you something now Jimmy,' said Mike, 'and it is this. I will never again raid a public house without a guards' trousers on me.'

'Me too,' said Jerry as they hurried home to don their lawful trousers.

THE GREAT WILLIAM STREET SHOWDOWN OF 1964

One of the neighbours wrote a song about it in the air of 'The Great American Railway'. The exact words escape me just now but they went something like this:

'Twas the year of sixty-four
Those outlaws bold fell in their gore
He shot them down with his forty-four
In the famous William Street showdown.
The Kid stood his ground quite unafraid
Saying 'Undertaker where's your spade?'
Come take these boys to yonder glade
From the famous William Street Showdown.

I remember that far-off morning as though it were yesterday. The crows had taken leave of the street's tall chimneys and sashayed westwards shortly after the peals of the nine o'clock bell announced the arrival of a watery sun.

'That sun sure don't look too good,' the crows seemed to caw to each other but then they were gone and the street assumed an eerie silence. It was a silence of a kind that the street had never experienced before and old folk who were abroad at the time would say later that it boded no good.

'Well cut my legs off and call me Shorty,' said one old-timer, 'if there ain't a showdown o' some kind this mawnin'.'

'You reckon?' said his wife.

'I reckon,' came the studied response.

New Year's Eve would fall on the following day and the William Streeters, no strangers to strong liquor, would celebrate and hold hands and sing 'Auld Lang Syne' and other sentimental songs until they could sing no more.

At approximately nine-thirty my four-year-old son Conor, resplendent in his new cowboy suit, appeared on the street. He pushed back his stetson and took stock of his bailiwick.

Jim Carroll addressed his employer Stuart Stack who owned the Arcade next door: 'It's the William Street Kid,' he said in awe and hurriedly hung up the remainder of the coarse brushes before skedaddling indoors to safety.

'Howdy Kid,' said Stuart. He knew the Kid well and was sure he wouldn't shoot a neighbour. Then a dog barked from a nearby doorway and the Kid went for his gun.

'It's just a dawg,' Stuart spoke mollifyingly.

The William Street Kid returned the gun to its holster and went back indoors for his porridge.

Time passed. So did some overhead clouds and so did a mild drizzle and the watery sun reappeared but the sense of foreboding and the feeling of tension had intensified. A cat appeared, an indication that the neighbourhood dogs smelled trouble and decided to spend the morning in bed. Then it happened out of the blue.

A few elderly stragglers made their way homewards from nine o'clock Mass and out from the bowels of the post office, in full regalia, stepped Mick the Post. A rotund, dark-jowled individual in his late fifties, he did not escape the attention of the William Street Kid. Mick the Post stood for a while on the pavement, sniffing the wind for rain, a common practice at the time. When he was satisfied that no rain was likely he tightened the strap of his bag and moved down the street.

Mick the Post, however, wasn't all that he seemed to be. To the elderly Mass folk he was their neighbourhood postman with nothing in his head but the safe delivery of his letters, especially the registered ones. The William Street Kid wasn't so easily duped. He recognised the hardened features of Black Bill the rustler under the official post office cap. The Kid's hands hovered over his guns, a steely look in his blue eyes, his legs apart, his body hunched forward. Black Bill saw the Kid almost at once. He stood stock-still, his jowl set as he wetted his trigger fingers from his rapidly drying gums. He loosened his bag straps and allowed the post-bag to fall to the pavement. He did not go for his guns at once. His hand movements were fidgety. His body leaned from one side to the other. His facial muscles flickered and then he sang out that terrifying command that had petrified sheriffs and posses alike: 'Go for your gun!'

The Kid smiled wryly but made no move. Jim Carroll and his boss Stuart Stack held their coarse brushes close to their chests. The elderly slipped into the neighbourhood shops and waited for the trouble to blow over.

'Dang you, you mangy hound dog,' Black Bill was at it again, 'I won't tell you no more. Go for your gun!'

Still the Kid made no move.

'Go for yours,' he commanded in a tone free of emotion. Black Bill hesitated. The terror of a hundred cowtowns, with forty notches on his gun-handle, drew like lightning. One minute his hands were empty and the next they were filled with blazing guns. Fast as he was he wasn't as fast as the Kid. His move was faster than lightning. He didn't draw two guns. He drew one. He didn't shoot twelve times like Black Bill. He shot once. Black Bill clutched his breast. A despairing cry escaped his throat. The cry was made up of a gurgle, a groan and a grunt. He staggered up and he staggered down. He staggered hither and he staggered thither and then he fell to the ground on top of his saddle-bags.

'He's deader,' said Jim Carroll, 'than an Egyptian mummy.'

The William Street Kid relieved Jim and his boss of their coarse brushes. They surrendered them meekly. They promised never to use them again.

Later, well out into the day, there was a New Year spirit abroad. The four principals, the Kid, Jim Carroll, Stuart Stack and Mick the Post, sat in the snug of these here licensed premises where they partook of some festive drinks. Mick the Post looked alive and well considering that he had been plugged only a few hours before. Then the snug door opened and Berkie Browne, the butcher, burst in.

'I need a posse fast,' he explained. The four comrades stood to attention after they had bolted their drinks.

'You guys promise to uphold the law?' Berkie Browne posed the question asked of many a brave cowboy before.

'We shorely do sheriff,' Jim Carroll spoke on behalf of his deputies. So the posse, led by their sheriff, headed south across the mesquite for Jet Carroll's pub where they made camp for the night.

Shortly afterwards the William Street Kid returned home. He hung up his guns and allowed himself to be tucked in.

'Where's yore podners?' I asked.

'My podners is a singin' round Jet's campfire,' he answered drowsily as he gently spurred his mount towards the horizon, beyond which lay the river of dreams and the Land of Nod where all small boys must go sooner or later.

THE WORD OF A WRENBOY

He lived in a lane-way close to our street. To say he was spare would be unfair to him. He was sparer than spare and he would be dapperer than dapper as well if only he had a decent suit. Despite this one could see that he was made to be dapper but was denied by circumstance. When I first knew him he was roughly seventy years of age although some said he was nearer to eighty. He survived on a modest subvention from the state and on the occasional gifts from friends and neighbours. His full name was Walter Aloysius Rogan but he was known locally as the Wrenboy Rogan.

All his life he had been an unpaid errand boy. Well maybe he wasn't altogether unpaid because everybody in the street gave him something for Christmas, a few shillings or even a pound, often a drink or a meal if it was going and he chanced to be in the vicinity. It was on the day of the wren or St Stephen's Day that he came into his own.

The traditional bands of wrenboys from the countryside within a radius of ten miles would appear sooner or later and march round the streets and squares, visiting pubs and soliciting from all those they chanced to meet. With the money gathered each group would host a wren dance before January blew itself out.

The Wrenboy Rogan did not belong to any group of wrenboys nor did he wear the traditional dress of the wrenboys nor did he proceed outwards into the countryside, for fear of getting wet. When it rained or hailed or snowed he withdrew to the nearest tavern and beat gently on the toy tambourine which was really no more than a travesty of the great b*odhrán*s or goatskin drums which authentic wrenboys always carried

The traditional wrenboys suffered the presence of the Wrenboy Rogan when it became apparent to them many years before that it was not his intent to traduce themselves or their venerated drums. Sooner or later before the day ended the toy tambourine would disappear. Generally it would be left behind in a pub but there had been times when neighbourhood blackguards would purloin it so that they might tease its owner when he emerged from a pub after the rain or the sleet had ceased.

When the Wrenboy Rogan demanded the return of his property all he received was abuse. Too drunk to apprehend the thief and too old to give chase after those who mocked him he would be obliged to sit on a windowsill from where he would recount the besmirched family ancestries and pauperised circumstance of his persecutors-in-chief. The Wrenboy Rogan had a tongue harsher than driving hail and a genuine penchant for exposing the most sensitive areas of his enemies' family cupboards. Some of his more blistering assessments had found a deserved place in the local top twenty of outstanding personal smears. When left alone he was a mild enough soul, well liked and even respected despite his obvious flaws. The problem lay in his merciless accuracy in the realms of revilement. He made enemies, enemies without the wit or vocal skills to reprimand him in kind. This left the enemies with no choice but to retaliate physically which they often did.

'It is truly an astonishing fact that professional boxers of my acquaintance,' Dr Matt Coumer confided to his friend Sergeant Ruttle, 'have assured me that there is no way a boxer could survive the Wrenboy Rogan beatings without being punch-drunk or even dead.' They were seated at either side of the Wrenboy's bed in Trallock General Hospital on wrenboys' night. Earlier the Wrenboy had gone a taunt too far with the result that his victim, a disgraced amateur boxer, had given the Wrenboy the worst beating to which he had ever been subjected.

The amateur boxer had snatched the Wrenboy's toy tambourine from the hands of a less militant mischief-maker and danced on it. He then folded his arms and asked the Wrenboy what he proposed to do about it. Incapacitated by drink as he was the Wrenboy nevertheless rose to his feet and assumed a fighting pose.

'In a sober state,' Bill Ruttle was to say later, 'my money would be on the Wrenboy in spite of his years.' The sergeant had seen his fancy in several brawls but with a mixture of skill and sheer courage the Wrenboy had always come out on top. With drink inside him he looked and behaved like a boxing clown.

As he lay on the bed he winced whenever he was obliged to change his position. Despite his scarred face the Wrenboy was not in the least repulsive and, according to the sergeant, was never short of a girlfriend.

'He has a way with dogs, with children and with certain local damsels.'

'Excuse me,' the doctor cut across him, 'it goes beyond local damsels. My own wife says he's the most likeable rogue in town.'

'And so does mine,' Bill threw back. The friends sat together marvelling at the constitution of the veteran on the bed. Matt took the Wrenboy's wrist in his and shook his head.

'Bad?' Bill asked concernedly

'There are worse walking the streets,' the doctor informed the sergeant, 'but this man's problem is his age and, of course, his drinking. What happens now?'

'What happens now,' the sergeant responded, 'is that he'll follow the usual pattern. That is to say he'll depart this place some time tomorrow or after or as soon as his head clears. Then he'll lie up for a day or two. If you were to take up your position near his abode you could see the usual soft-hearted carers arriving in turns with cloth-covered trays and soup tureens and occasionally your favourite dessert and my favourite scones. He won't starve and that's for sure. He'll recuperate and put a little fat on that skeletal frame of his and then as he's been doing for years he'll call to the presbytery and ask if our beloved parish priest, the Right Reverend Canon Cornelius Coodle, is available. The housekeeper will look him up and down and ask him if he's hungry but he'll inform her in his own charming way that he is hungry not for food of the body but rather is he hungry for food of the soul. She will lead him without a word to the sitting-room and gently knock upon the door.

'"Who is it?" a drowsy voice will ask.

'"It is Mister Rogan to see you canon," Mrs Hanlon will call back.

'"Come!" the voice from within will call and so once more comes round the annual confrontation between the Wrenboy Rogan and Canon Cornelius Coodle.'

When Dr Coumer and Sergeant Ruttle left the district hospital they hit upon the idea that a visit to their favourite hostelry might not be amiss. So it was that they found themselves in the back room at Crutley's. After four pints of stout apiece they decided upon a few turns round the town square after which they gravitated naturally to the humble and deserted abode of the Wrenboy Rogan. They were surprised to see the open door and to hear the flurry of female feet as three unidentified women seized the opportunity, in the Wrenboy's absence, to turn his dwelling-place inside out. All that could be seen from the lane-way outside were the forms of frantic females as they changed bedclothes, washed ware, cleaned the fireplace and performed the countless other chores which can transform a house.

'Let's move,' Bill cautioned, 'before they find something for us to do.' The friends resumed their stroll. As they were about to pass by the grave-yard Matt suddenly stopped as though inspired by the nearness of the parish's faithful departed.

'We both know,' Matt looked absently at the Celtic Crosses and lesser monuments, 'that the Wrenboy is headed for this very spot if he breaks out again.'

'Well I don't know,' Bill spoke hesitantly, 'but I'll take your word for it if you say so.'

'It's odds on,' the doctor assured him, 'there will be a coma and then the heart will fail and that will be that.'

'And if he doesn't break out?'

'If he doesn't break out he could enjoy a few more years, that is if life can really be enjoyed without booze. Still, it would be my opinion that he could have a few worthwhile years without the drink. It's just a matter of putting his mind to it.'

'You really think he'll fall by the wayside again?' the sergeant asked.

'It's his choice,' was all Matt would contribute by way of answer.

A surge of loneliness unexpectedly overcame the sergeant. He recalled a night when he was new to the division and bit off more than he could chew. He was put to the pin of his collar to defend himself against three blackguards who had assaulted him when the town was asleep. Apparently they had become incensed at the sight of the uniform. Then the one calamity that he feared most overcame him when he accidentally slipped and fell to the ground. It was at that precise moment that the Wrenboy Rogan appeared. With flailing boots and fists he shocked the blackguards with the fury of his assault. Add to this the blood-curdling whoops that surely belonged to some inhuman creature from the grave-yard nearby.

It was just the opening the sergeant needed so desperately. Between them the lawman and his deputy apprehended the blackguards and left them with painful posteriors for many a day afterwards. A bond developed between the two men. Chapter by chapter over the years the Wrenboy unfolded the sorry saga of his life from the awful day in his early twenties when his wife ran away with another man. He had come to the town where he now resided from the east of the country. He had been a roustabout with a circus but had lost his job for repeated drunkenness.

'I've been proceeding backwards all my life,' he told Bill, 'and that's the story of my life.

'If any man can get him to go off the juice, you're that man.' Matt's waters flowed freely against the graveyard wall. 'He respects you more than any man in town. If you were to ask him to give you his word that he would abstain from the drink for good he might just do it.' Matt tied his flies and looked up at the sickle moon. 'Do you notice a preponderance of sickle moons lately,' he asked, 'or is it my imagination?'

'Too much drink,' his friend replied.

'You mean too little drink,' Matt countered.

'What brings you friend?' Canon Coodle asked as the Wrenboy stood abashed with bent head and trembling hands. It occurred to the canon that he had been asking the very same question since his first annual meeting with the parish's most distinguished drunkard.

'I've come to take the pledge canon,' the Wrenboy opened. It was exactly what the canon expected because every year since his appointment to the parish the Wrenboy had arrived unfailingly a few days after the beginning of the new year and announced that he wished to take the pledge. Each year he seemed to be more forlorn and more emaciated.

'If the pledge is what you want,' the canon said resignedly, 'the pledge it shall be.'

Immediately the Wrenboy went on his knees and made the sign of the cross. Neither was strictly required but the canon felt that they added dignity to the occasion and should not be discouraged.

'For how long this time?' the canon asked, the resignation still unmistakable in his voice.

'For life,' came the terse reply.

'For life!' the canon wanted to make sure he heard right.

'For life!' from the Wrenboy.

'Now,' said the canon planting his long legs apart and folding his arms to show that he was not taking the request lightly, 'you have been coming here for as long as I can remember and on each occasion you have taken the pledge for life. My sources tell me that far from taking the pledge for life all you seem to be able to manage is a week or two and on occasion you broke all records by going off it for a month when you had pneumonia.'

'It's different this time,' the Wrenboy Rogan assured his parish priest. 'This time I mean it.'

The Wrenboy allowed his hand to gingerly touch his badly scared face. He placed his index finger on the most recent acquisition to the many eloquent disfigurations which covered his countenance from ear to ear.

'I can't take any more of these,' he told the canon, 'so you see it has to be for life this time.'

'Maybe you're being too hard on yourself.' The canon placed a wooden crucifix in the applicant's hands. 'Nobody would think any the worse of you if you tried it for six months or a year or, better still, until the first day of Trallock Races. That would give your stomach a chance to settle and your mental outlook could only improve as well. It's just a little over eight months away and you would also have the satisfaction that you kept your bond with your saviour and with yourself.'

'No canon,' the Wrenboy was adamant, 'it has to be for life.'

'You're the boss,' Canon Coodle told him.

'All you have to do now is promise that you will never touch another drink for the remainder of your natural life.'

The canon was beginning to enjoy himself. He particularly savoured the determined features and the grim mouth, the closed eyes and the head bent in supplication as the tears of remorse began to flow and the torrent of aspirations as the hands tightened on the crucifix.

'I promise,' the Wrenboy sobbed, 'never to touch another drink for the remainder of my natural life.'

'With the help of God now you'll be able to change your ways,' the canon helped him to his feet, 'a bit of resolve is all you need.'

'Would you hear my confession canon while you're at it? I'd like to be in the state of grace starting out.'

Donning his stole the canon indicated a chair near the canonical armchair and turned his head towards the penitent. He listened without change of expression and, as always with the Wrenboy, the canon felt reassured and in some ways consoled by the humility and the innate goodness of the misfit beside him.

'There but for the grace of God', the canon told himself after he had dispensed forgiveness and imposed a simple penance. Canon Coodle accompanied the shrivelled Wrenboy to the presbytery entrance where they shook hands and wished each other well.

The days after Christmas stretched themselves imperceptibly and old people would say to each other 'there is a cock's step after coming into the days'. The saying was a relic from the Gaelic and the more scholars dwelt on it the more valid it seemed to be. The strutting cock had a very high, and therefore a very short, step. It would be several days before the stretch in the afternoons became noticeable.

In the estuary the first salmon began to show themselves before moving upriver and the lapwings, birds of the five names as they were called locally, began to break up into smaller flocks preparatory to mating. The names were lapwing, green plover, crested plover, peewit and pilibeen. The last were two Gaelic names resembling the cries of the bird in question depending on how skilled the human interpretation might be. Showers of hail became more common and there were flurries of snow but by and large it was a moderate winter. Snowdrops brightened the sheltered areas and there were signs that the more adventurous of the daffodils would bloom in the weeks ahead. All in all there were ample signs that spring was just around the corner.

Then on the fourth day of the new season, thirty-two days after he had taken the pledge for life, Walter Aloysius Rogan went back on the booze. Word spread quickly and those who always said so said, 'I knew it would happen any day now.' He had managed to save a sizeable part of his dole money and, because he had been well fed and well looked after during his sojourn in the world of sobriety, he made an all-out assault on liquor for three days which saw him stretched on the third night under the blind eye of Trallock Bridge in a state of semi-consciousness. Nobody ever found out how he got there. None could recall having seen him in the vicinity of the bridge and the Wrenboy himself had no recollection whatsoever. When he was discovered by two salmon poachers they firmly believed that he was dead but when they dragged him to high ground they heard the moans which told them that he was still in the land of the living.

When the Wrenboy opened his eyes in a bed in Trallock District Hospital the first face he saw was that of Canon Cornelius Coodle.

'The last time I saw you I gave you the pledge,' the canon told him, 'and just now I've anointed you. What have you to say for yourself at all you unfortunate creature?'

'Drink, canon,' the Wrenboy replied before he closed his eyes to sleep as he had never slept before.

The Wrenboy spent several days recuperating. Not once did he speak of the events which very nearly led to his demise under the blind eye of the bridge where at least two errant drunkards had died from exposure within living memory. For hours at a time he had padded round the hospital in a pair of new bedroom slippers bought for him by the epic poet Mental Nossery. They were the first bedroom slippers he ever owned. When he believed that his full health had returned to him he made his plans. After counting his remaining money he came to the conclusion that he had sufficient for a comprehensive two-day booze. The Wrenboy counted his resources in drinks. His dole money for instance, after a few minor items such as food and electricity were deducted, amounted to six half-whiskeys and eleven pints of stout with the price of a box or two of matches left over.

On the day of his departure from Trallock District Hospital he was visited by Sergeant Bill Ruttle who asked for a personal favour.

'I won't put a tooth in it,' Bill Ruttle opened, 'I have come here to see you for one reason only and that is to ask you for a personal favour.'

'I'll do anything for you,' the Wrenboy promised.

'Will you go off the drink for me?' Bill asked.

'That's a different story.' The Wrenboy's face grew serious.

'Will you or won't you go off the drink for me?'

'I could try,' from the Wrenboy.

'That's not good enough,' the sergeant told him.

'What's gotten into you?' the Wrenboy asked while he studied his friend's face.

'Nothing's gotten into me,' the sergeant looked out the widow into the bleak afternoon beyond.

'You really want me to go off the drink on a permanent basis?'

'What I really want,' the sergeant turned on him, 'is to see you hold on to your life for a few more years.'

'I'll take the pledge,' the Wrenboy volunteered.

'No you won't,' Bill Ruttle injected a new inflexibility into his tone. 'I am asking you to give me your word as a gentleman that you will never put an intoxicating drink to your lips again.'

'I am not a gentleman,' came the evasive reply.

'Then,' said Bill, 'I'm asking you on the word of a man.'

'I'm not much of a man,' came the equally evasive reply.

'I'm beginning to see that,' the sergeant observed angrily.

A silence followed. It was that kind of silence where the wrong word could bring negotiations to an immediate end.

'All right,' Bill was now using a more reasonable tone, 'I'm asking you on the word of a wrenboy.'

There would be no evasion this time and Bill knew it. The sounds from the nearby corridors and wards became more pronounced as the silence between the two men became more pronounced. The Wrenboy sat on the side of the bed on which he had been lying and covered his face with his hands. He felt like saying to his friend that what was being asked was grossly unfair, that it was totally impossible, that it was not in his capacity or character to make such a promise, that he just didn't have the will-power. Instead he said nothing at all. He just sat there looking at Bill's beefy side-face. Then he rose and took his friend's hand. As he shook it he spoke: 'On the world of a wrenboy,' he said.

No other words passed between them at that time but Bill Ruttle said many years later as he and Matt Coumer looked down at the coffin of Walter Aloysius Rogan that a wrenboy's word was his bond.

A CHRISTMAS SURPRISE

Masterman sipped his whiskey elegantly knowing that he was being watched by the tall grey-haired lady who had just entered the hotel's plush bar. He noticed her earlier in the foyer and, from her easy air of proprietorship, guessed that she was a member of the staff.

More than likely she was a supervisor of some sort. It wouldn't surprise him if she turned out to be the manageress. He guessed she would be in her mid-fifties. While she continued to take stock of him he produced a spotless white handkerchief from the breast pocket of his second-best suit. He did not blow his nose. He never did so publicly. Rather did he remove some non-existent specks from the sleeves of his coat.

She was moving about now, outside the counter, but at the far end of the bar. The barmaid followed her to the outside and rang the Waterford glass time-up bell which she carried in her hand. The older woman left the bar, stately as a sailing ship and erect as any mast.

Masterman noted the trim figure and especially the way her buttocks flickered tantalisingly as she passed by. She favoured him with the barest of nods as though nods were at a premium at that time. Then she paused briefly and with a hint of a smile informed him in low tones that he was to ignore the bell and stay where he was until she returned. He nodded eagerly and looked at his watch. In a mere ten minutes it would be Christmas Day, the twenty-eighth such day he had spent in a world which, he felt, still owed him something substantial for his years of sexual frustration and general all-round suffering.

He might have married but on the two occasions where matters had taken a turn towards permanence he had withdrawn from the relationships. His sister had married and was coming home for Christmas. The reason he found himself in the hotel on Christmas Eve was due to the fact that his in-laws, notably his brother-in-law, a despicable wretch perverted and mean, were spending Christmas in the family home where he himself had spent the previous twenty-seven Christmases. The hotel he had chosen attracted him for two reasons. Firstly it was at the opposite end of the country to his family home and secondly the rates were more than reasonable for the Christmas period. His in-laws would be departing the family home on the day after St Stephen's Day and this would give him the opportunity to spend a day with his parents.

His thoughts returned to the hotel manageress who, he had by now deduced, she undoubtedly must be. He looked at his watch. Half-past twelve. Over a half-hour had passed since she intimated that she would be returning. No sign of her. Customers had been vacating the bar on a regular basis in the interim, wishing each other the compliments of the season. None had over-looked him as they exited. All had extended to him Christmas greetings and he had dutifully responded.

At last the bar was emptied and he turned his thoughts for a second time to the manageress, sophisticated and mature without doubt and immaculately preserved to boot, he imagined she would have a lot to offer if the mood caught her but, of course, she could have asked him to stay for any number of reasons.

He had heard from other commercials that women of her ilk and age were at the top of the scale, skilled, practised, discreet and totally abandoned once they had committed themselves.

Masterman recalled similar females he had encountered in his travels. He had been singularly unsuccessful in engaging the attention of a solitary one. In fact he had found them gruff and even surly when they discovered what was on his mind. Why then, he asked himself, should this particular one ask him to remain behind until she returned?

He looked at his watch a second time and then he drifted into a deep sleep induced unexpectedly by the hundreds of miles he had travelled that day and by the countless whiskeys he had drunk.

In his sleep he dreamed of far-off days when youth held little care. He dreamed of the same dark-haired nymph who led him countless merry dances through radiant summer scenes and when he woke up several hours later he found himself looking into cold grey eyes set in beautiful, if rather severe, features.

He closed his eyes temporarily to make sure that the visage overlooking him was not part of the dream sequence he had just experienced. When he reopened his eyes the over-hanging face was still there. The rich red lips which were the outstanding feature of the face opened and from there issued forth a soft vocal chain of apology. She had meant to return but had fallen asleep herself explaining that she had spent seventeen hours on her feet throughout Christmas Eve. Would he forgive her and join her for breakfast in the dining-room? She took him gently by the hand lest he refuse and led him into a corner where a smart young waitress with a beaming smile awaited their instructions.

Full Irish for two and no frills. As they waited he observed that her lips were impeccably lip-sticked but that she wore no other make-up. There was about her a crispness and a freshness which he had never before encountered in a female. It was as if she had spent the preceding hours at nothing else but immersing herself in fragrant waters, drying herself and re-immersing herself until her full vigour had been restored.

The lights of the dining-room shone brightly for it was still dark outside but she shone brighter albeit in a different way.

'I had the night porter keep an eye on you,' she confided, 'can you guess how long you've been sleeping?'

He shook his head for it was not in his power to produce a spoken reply. He was, as he was to confide afterwards to a fellow-commercial, in a trance. 'I felt,' he had said at the time, 'like one of those romantic Gaelic poets who has been discovered in the wilderness by a beautiful goddess in the dead of night.'

The woman who sat opposite him at the table was now in full vocal spate, had been widowed some ten years before, heart attack, no children, lived presently with her sister and doting husband and three young children, four, six and eight, the younger, girls, the oldest a boy. Dream kids all, fun-loving and sweet.

When breakfast arrived she ceased talking for a moment in order to pour the scalding tea. As he wolfed down his food she proceeded with her life's tale. Now in her early fifties she had never considered remarrying. She had found happiness with her sister and her family. She had resumed her hotel career a few short weeks after her husband's death and this had been a blessing in that she worked herself into total exhaustion every day and night so that sleep presented no problem and she didn't have time for self-pity.

Promotion followed and she was now the hotel's manageress. As she spoke she reminded him sometimes of a nun, sometimes of a schoolmistress, sometimes of a madame and occasionally of a sergeant-major. There was no denying one important factor however. She was still a beautifully preserved woman.

'You must have noticed that I spent more time than I should watching you in the bar last night,' she told him coyly. Before he could answer she explained that she had good reason. She went on to tell him that she would not go into it there and then.

'All will be revealed,' she assured him, 'and I promise you will be pleased and fulfilled.'

It was the language that baffled Masterman. It had religious undertones when it shouldn't. Then he reminded himself of commercial tales about prim, prudish women who exceeded themselves when the chips were down, unbelievable tales but authentic as any tale could be and verified by the fathers of commercial rooms up and down the country ever since sales representatives forgathered to exchange business experiences and gripping yarns of sweet romance.

'Now,' she said with finality as she looked at her watch, 'it's twenty minutes to eight and,' here she paused briefly, 'at ten minutes to the hour we will leave here and hasten to the church which happens to be just around the corner.'

Before he could utter a single word she placed a finger firmly on his lips and cautioned him to silence. 'Speak not,' she whispered fervently as she looked into his rather bloodshot eyes. 'Speak not,' she begged, 'or my dream will fade.'

Masterman submitted himself once more to the trance world he had occupied earlier. Dutifully he followed her and found himself shortly afterwards seated in the very front pew of the church ablaze with light and reverently hymnal all around.

Masterman, if he was asked by a colleague, would admit that he hadn't seen the inside of a church since his sister's wedding ten years before.

When Mass was over they returned to the hotel and in the foyer she faced him with a strange revelation.

'I'm asking you to do something for me now,' she said, 'and afterwards there won't be a single word to anybody. It will be our secret.'

Masterman nodded eagerly and did not object when she took him by the hand and led him upstairs to the door-way of his very own bedroom.

Masterman's astonishment did not show on his face. It would never do, he told himself, to behave as if such a thing had never happened before. She handed him the key which she had earlier collected at reception. It was she who led the way into the room where, immediately, he endeavoured to place his trembling hands around her.

'Patience,' she admonished. He dropped his hands to his sides.

'Now,' she spoke curtly, 'take off your coat and your shirt and I'll be back in a minute.' So saying she lifted the key from the bed where he had flung it, and vacated the room.

Masterman sat baffled on the side of the bed which he hoped to utilise to its fullest before the morning took its course. Without further reflection he jumped to his feet. First things first, he told himself. He would do as she had told him. Off would come coat and shirt and he would await further instructions. When the door opened after a gentle preliminary knock she entered bearing a large plastic bag. From it she withdrew a tasselled, crimson Santa Claus hat and an equally crimson, outsized Santa Claus coat.

'Now,' she said with her sergeant-major voice, 'get these on you and we'll head for my sister's.'

A Christmas Disappearance

When I was younger and more observant I spent some of my spare time studying the corner across the street from this very room where I presently write. I also studied the denizens of the area and when my room window was partly open I would often catch fragments of conversation.

The corner had one resident boy by the name of Johnny Muller. Passers-by would sometimes stop and endeavour to begin conversations with him. He never responded even when asked for the location of a bank or the post office.

If he was in talkative mood he might sometimes acknowledge the weather assessments of an old lady who passed down every morning and up every evening.

''Tis soft,' she might say.

'Soft enough,' he might reply.

Once she asked him if the weather would hold.

'Could,' he replied.

Lay people do not understand the function of a corner boy. He is not obliged to respond to questions or make observations. His function is to be there, to maintain his corner no matter what. Johnny Muller took his job seriously and this is the reason why he never smiled.

From my vantage point at the upstairs window I occasionally examined his face. There were no wrinkles and no blemishes. There were no repulsive aspects and no scars. I could never deduce whether he was grey-haired or bald because of the peaked cap which he always wore. I suppose the fairest thing to say would be that it was a good enough face as faces go. It certainly wasn't distinguished but neither was it forgettable. Some said that it was a face without character but there would be no way of confirming this until he was put to the test. As a rule when put to the test corner boys vanish from the scene or surrender their attention to distant vistas unseen by the layman's eye.

It took me several years to discover that Johnny Muller's face was incomplete as indeed are the faces of most corner boys. In Johnny's case it was clear that none of the great emotions had ever tampered with it. It seemed to me that it was awaiting alteration. His facial disposition was drab. His throat clearances and coughs were run-of-the-mill as were his rare utterances. Only his sneezes had colour. Unfailingly they were highly explosive and when they erupted in close continuity they shook him to his very foundations. Otherwise there was hardly anything to him but we should be forewarned that things change just when it seems that they will never change.

Johnny Muller was a resolute corner boy. He spent that part of his life which he didn't spend in bed, at his corner. When he first took over, after the previous incumbent had expired in the wake of a one-sided contest with a carelessly discarded banana skin, he foolishly believed that he would have little to do save pass the time and be mindful of his protectorate. It wasn't long before he learned that his responsibilities were legion.

Dogs had to be chastised and moved on. Querimonious and uppity passers-by had to be studiously ignored. Patrolling civic guards who stopped to rest up a while had to be hummed and hawed upon their constitutional way. There were other duties too numerous to mention.

When he arrived at his chosen corner at nine o'clock each morning he would first look up the street and then look down. He would then address his attention to the adjoining street and, satisfying himself that all was as it should be, would thrust his hands deep into his trousers' pockets and submit himself to a comprehensive bout of scratching. He would withdraw his hands after a while and draw upon the lobes of his ears, the point of his chin and the end of his nose. He would rub his shoulder blades and his behind against the wall at his rear. Finally he would scratch his ankles and his heels with their corresponding ankles and heels. Then and only then would he relax and enter into a period of meditation. He would be roused after a half-hour or so by the chiming of the parish clock.

One day he was about to return once more to his reflections when he beheld, out of the corner of his eye, a most uncommonly attractive creature coming his way. As she passed by a wonderful fragrance assailed his senses. Johnny noticed the elegant figure, the glamorous eyelashes and the beautiful blonde hair which fell gracefully over her slender shoulders.

'No chicken,' he whispered to himself as he roused himself totally to concentrate the better upon this enchanting apparition. 'But then,' he concluded as he finished his initial survey, 'no old maid either.'

By his reckoning she would be a young sixty. By my mother's, I discovered later, she would be nearer to eighty than seventy.

When the visitor turned on her heel and retraced her steps Johnny Muller gave her the nod of friendly salutation and also the nod of absolute approval. An almost imperceptible smile appeared on her angelic features. From the look on Johnny's face it was clear that he was smitten. He was overcome by an unfamiliar giddiness. It was the kind of giddiness that overwhelms characters of Johnny Muller's ilk once in a lifetime. He had, up until this time, been fond of saying to himself, 'I wouldn't give tuppence for a woman, any kind of woman,' when an attractive member of the opposite sex passed his corner.

Suddenly she had stopped and was looking straight into his eyes. A sparkling smile had now spread itself across her heavily made-up face. She had noticed him before, not once but several times and always from a distance. She was certain that he had not seen her. He would have reacted if he had. Now that it was Christmas she would make the most of her chance.

'What do you do here all day?' she asked gently. It was the way she said it that hastened the melting process which had already begun in the underworked furnace of his heart.

Normally he would never answer when a strange female addressed him but now his reply was warm and instant.

'I keeps an eye on things,' he told her.

A puzzled frown appeared for a moment on her shining visage.

Johnny was quick to notice that perplexity added to her allure.

'You sort of watch over things?' she suggested.

Johnny nodded eagerly and then, to give substance to his role, his features assumed a deadly seriousness as he looked up and down and hither and thither as he scanned the faces of passers-by in search of evildoers. Satisfying himself that his bailiwick was secure, he favoured her with a smile of unconditional reassurance.

'Do you watch over me?' Her voice quavered as though she would burst into tears.

'You above all,' Johnny found himself saying.

'Me above all!' she repeated the words as though they were the last line of a prayer. Johnny nodded reassuringly as they sought to solve the mysteries in each other's eyes. Her next move was to take him by the hand. He followed without a word until they reached the entrance to a clothier's called The Man's Shop.

After they had entered, some female onlookers, my mother among them, commented on the incident. The conclusions they drew were interesting. Johnny Muller always had an untouched look about him. It was certain that he had never been touched by a woman's hand, at least not since his infancy when he submitted himself to his mother's ministrations.

'That woman's search is over,' my mother spoke with assurance. 'She always knew what she wanted and she's found it at last.'

When the happy pair emerged from The Man's Shop there were gasps from the onlookers. Gone were the shabby clothes, the greasy cap and the worn shoes. Resplendent in his new outfit Johnny Muller took his fiancée's hand and led her across the road where he bade good-bye to his corner of forty years.

What the onlookers would remember most was Johnny's face. It was the complete product at last. For her part she radiated happiness. Her new partner was a far cry from the shop-soiled assortment she had put through her hands over a lifetime.

Neither of the happy pair was seen again in the locality but the locals evinced no surprise.

'It's that kind of town,' my mother would announce modestly whenever Christmas came round and the subject of the disappearance was drawn down.

Oh! Oh! Antonio – You Left Us All Alonio!

Older readers will remember a man by the name of Antonio Feckawlo and if not, maybe their fathers will. They should remember Hanratty's circus as well for that was his home since he departed Brindisi. Antonio's demise occurred a few days before Christmas and that is why he is especially remembered at this time. Those who have a soft spot for Casanovas and waxed moustachios will toast his memory this Christmas and for many a Christmas to come, all going well. Antonio Feckawlo was a circus knife-thrower, roustabout and fribbling fracturer of a hundred female hearts.

Only last summer in a well-known hostelry in Ballybunion I encountered an elderly lady who happens to be a native of Limerick city. She recalled with ease her first sighting of the amorous Italian whose uncle Giuseppi Feckawlo was a Vatican monsignor and confidante of several popes or so they said. If you were to see Antonio's features in the light of a setting sun against a backdrop made up of the cliffs of Doon overlooking the Ladies' Strand in Ballybunion you would notice that the rakishness and the sinister scars had gone and that they had been replaced by features of great aristocratic charm.

Antonio, however, was far from being a man of piety and the Limerick woman who had first seen him some eighty years before (she is now ninety-three) was quite carried away at the time by his good looks. In fact she swooned with the many other females present as he flung knife after knife at the voluptuous body of Gina Moldoni his sometime companion of an out-house palliasse. Her real name was Gert O'Day. Antonio, a knife-thrower of the first water, never drew blood from a target. He drew blood, however, from several masculine noses and was responsible for the discoloration of many an eye. He also had a powerful voice and he was irresistible when he went on his knees and sang in broken tones to the memory of his lost love.

Then one night not long before Christmas the circus was performing in Tubbernamuckerry. The tent was full and the crowd responsive. All the acts had been cheered to an echo. After Gina Moldoni had fed the lions with their rations of minced donkey-meat she was returning to the main tent when she heard strange noises coming from the monkey house. She looked in and there was Antonio in the arms of the female slack wire walker and the pair scandalising the innocent baboons.

She was greatly taken aback to put it mildly. She had always known that he was a practitioner in the unchaste art of seduction but it was the first time she had caught him red-handed. She decided to do nothing just then. All she did was to fling the bucket and what was left of the minced donkey-meat at her rival before cursing the pair roundly and vowing that she would have her revenge on Antonio Feckawlo. The opportunity presented itself shortly afterwards. Just before the knife-throwing act which was one of the highlights of the programme Gina Moldoni decided that the time had come to put manners on her erring partner.

To a roll of drums Antonio stepped forward and threw the first of his twelve knives at Gina. It embedded itself in the wooden frame a mere two inches from her left ear. There was rapturous applause. The second knife embedded itself a solitary inch from Gina's other ear. Again, there was a tumultuous cheer. The third knife landed two inches above the crown of her head and the fourth and fifth, in quick succession, implanted themselves at either side of her shapely throat. Now there were no cheers. Instead there were gasps. Antonio turned to acknowledge the gasps. He had experienced yells and hoots, sustained handclaps and cheers but gasps never!

As he bent to acknowledge this unprecedented tribute Gina Moldoni withdrew the knife at the left-hand side of her throat and stepped forward, to the astonishment of the onlookers. Antonio was so absorbed in the crowd's reaction that he presumed the silence to be another aspect of audience participation. Gina raised the knife and aimed for the right heel of her unsuspecting partner. The deadly missile missed its target but what it did not miss was the extended left buttock of the knife-thrower. It embedded itself firmly in the solid flesh and even when Antonio leaped forward from the pain and shock, the knife remained rooted where it had lodged.

Gina Moldoni, in the middle of the consternation, made good her escape. As she exited through a side flap in the canvas she was met by the trick cyclist who had already tied her luggage to the carrier. He bore her on the bar of the bike to a place far from the hills and vales of Tubbernamuckerry.

Rumour had it that the pair fled the country and ended up their days as itinerant evangelists in South Carolina.

After Gina's departure a score of females erupted from ringside seats. Between them they managed to extract the foot-long weapon from the great lover's Brindisian bum. He would sustain other wounds before he was drowned while attempting to evade his enemies as he crossed the Feale River near Listowel while that august waterway was in full flood.

'He never deserved to drown,' said a cuckolded north Kerryman, 'not while there was rope in plenty to hang the hoor.'

This was not a nice thing to say but it should not be taken too seriously since they are greatly given to hyperbole in north Kerry.

'When he died,' said the elderly lady I encountered in Ballybunion, 'the city of Limerick gave itself over to mourning.'

Apparently, its female population was inconsolable while many of its male population regretted that he had not been sexually incapacitated long before his demise.

There was no funeral because there was no body. Some said that it had been eaten by sharks halfway through the Atlantic. Others, pathological liars as well, maintained that his body had been de-boned before being chopped up and minced for the three elderly lions who made up most of the menagerie of Hanratty's circus. It was widely rumoured at the time that they consumed each other after they had polished off the baboons.

One of my late informants also informed me that Antonio Feckawlo always behaved like a gentleman until a member of the opposite sex appeared on the scene. He could not and would not stay clear of females, attached or unattached, and they, for their part, would not stay clear of him. In another age, a film would be made about him and his exploits. Like all great lovers, he was deeply misunderstood by his detractors but not by those he loved.

Let us hope that he is with his sainted uncle Giuseppi in the high halls of heaven for, all else aside, he was a lover of the old school and so, let us toast him.

LAST CHRISTMAS EVE OF THE TWENTIETH CENTURY

I wish I had the rind I left behind
And the hag I wouldn't kiss.

I heard sentiments like these, or in some way resembling these, from a very old man on a Christmas Eve night halfway through the final century of the last millennium. He wasn't bemoaning his lot and, as I recalled at the time, he wasn't a natural grouser. What he was really trying to say was that he did not know when he was well off and that I should benefit from his experience and always appreciate the time that was in it in order that I might never think of the rind I might have left behind or the hag I wouldn't kiss.

I was twenty years old at the time and awaiting my friends in an ancient public house popular with the young folk of the community. It was a good premises to be in on Christmas Eve. The proprietor approved of song and he approved of things like gallantry and decency and if he frequently took a drop too much he would always remind his critics that it was his own money he was drinking and his own liver he was besieging.

Time passed and, sure enough, my friends arrived, all at the same time and all fairly full of Christmas love and Christmas cheer and Christmas beer.

I passed on the old man's words. My friends understood and we made up a modest sum which we offered him. He accepted it the way a highly successful forward accepts an expected pass in front of an open goal. I am happy to be able to report that the contribution made his night. The young men, Tom and Moss and Danny, were the proprietors of open hearts and of pockets that always emptied quickly. They were good men as men go and would not waste a single minute bemoaning the past.

These friends are still to the good as the end of the last millennium approached. They are grey now and a little wrinkled as well as being a bit battered but they are never down and they are deeply appreciative of what's left to them. That, my friends, is the only way to be at Christmas.

On that far-off Christmas Eve we sang many a song and downed many a glass and if we didn't how would publicans prosper and bring up their families and how would breweries hold on to their workers and how would the women at home hear the gossip that can only be heard in public houses. Times have changed and often 'tis the women that bring home the gossip now and that is as it should be.

Our financial reserves would be low after our revels but who cared! We could always dress up as wrenboys on St Stephen's Day and partially banish the emptiness from our pockets.

On our last Christmas Eve of the twentieth century we had mustered enough wisdom over the years to know that Christmas with the wrong jock in the saddle can be a bucking bronco. We don't have the youth for speed nor the endurance for lengthy boozes at our age but we are blessed with the acquired wisdom that every age is a good age if you give it half a chance and that our perceived enemies are not really enemies at all but delusions fashioned by prejudice and mental instability. Our real enemies are ourselves.

But back to my friends on that Christmas Eve fifty years ago. On St Stephen's night we would be meeting our girlfriends and after a brief sojourn in the same public house we would proceed to the Astor Ballroom at the top of the town where Darkie Devine and his Devon Dance Band would be playing from nine o'clock in the night until three o'clock in the morning. We would be made welcome to these far-off Terpsichorean revels by the simple expedient of forking out the sum of three shillings apiece and for this, as Byron put it, there would be:

No sleep till morn when youth and pleasure meet
To chase the glowing hours with flying feet.

As I sit here writing I am very much aware that the theme for another is being hatched all over this long-suffering, much-abused sphere. It simply says, 'no more domination for me if you please. Do not order me about ever again. Do not murder or main me or starve me or indoctrinate me as you've been doing for so long. There has to be a better way.'

Today I celebrate my seventy-first Christmas Eve aboard this topsy-turvy planet we have christened Earth. It's been a good barque to me although my late mother used to say that I would never really take off until I was banned.

In spite of hiccoughs, assorted misfortunes, minor catastrophes and misunderstandings I'm still aboard. I was marooned a good few times all right and I fell overboard several times but was always hauled back aboard by my fellow-mariners when all seemed lost.

Christmas Eve always arrives at the town of Listowel like Aurora herself. Aurora stuns the intellectuals with her brightness but she is loved by poets and balladeers who serenade her drunk and sober. Aurora lights up the streets and squares and alley-ways in this little town. She opens tightly closed purses and softens the hardest of hearts. She brings tears too but they are tears of joy and they are the prelude to love and laughter.

Two thousand years is a mighty long time but the memory of the man whose birthday we celebrate is dearer and more cherished than ever.

On the cross he forgave the thief by his side and said to him, 'This day you will be with me in paradise.' To me those are the most important words ever uttered because in them is hope of salvation for every man.

Of human lines there are many that I cherish too and with the new millennium Tennyson comes to mind with the most appropriate quote of all:

Ring out false pride in place and blood,
The civic slander and the spite;
Ring in the love of truth and right,
Ring in the common love of good.

Ring out old shapes of foul disease;
Ring out the narrowing lust of gold;
Ring out the thousand wars of old,
Ring in the thousand years of peace.

Ring in the valiant man and free,
The larger heart, the kindlier hand;
Ring out the darkness of the land;
Ring in the Christ that is to be.

A happy Christmas now and the grace of God to all my readers and to all those near and dear to them and to all travellers whoever or wherever they may be and please change those of evil intent to good.